The Reckoning

A Secrets of Redemption Novel

Other books by Michele Pariza Wacek
https://MPWNovels.com/books

Secrets of Redemption series:
It Began With a Lie (Book 1)
This Happened to Jessica (Book 2)
The Evil That Was Done (Book 3)
The Summoning (Book 4)
The Reckoning (Book 5)
The Girl Who Wasn't There (Book 6)
The Room at the Top of the Stairs (Book 7)
The Search (Book 8)
The Secret Diary of Helen Blackstone (novella)

Charlie Kingsley Mystery series:
A Grave Error (prequel novella)
The Murder Before Christmas (Book 1)
Ice Cold Murder (Book 2)
Murder Next Door (Book 3)
Murder Among Friends (Book 4)
The Murder of Sleepy Hollow (Book 5)
Red Hot Murder (Book 6)
A Cornucopia of Murder (Book 7)
A Wedding to Murder For (novella)
Loch Ness Murder (novella)

Standalone books:
Today I'll See Her (novella)
The Taking
The Third Nanny
Mirror Image
The Stolen Twin

The Reckoning

A Secrets of Redemption Novel

by Michele Pariza Wacek

The Reckoning Copyright © 2020
by Michele Pariza Wacek.
All rights reserved. Printed in the United States of America. No part of this book may be reproduced or transmitted in any manner or by any means, electronically or mechanically, including photocopying, recording, retrieval system, without prior written permission from the author, except in the case of brief quotations embodied in a review. For more information, contact Michele Pariza Wacek, PO Box 10430 Prescott, AZ 86304.
info@LoveBasedPublishing.com.

ISBN 978-1-945363-22-1

Library of Congress Control Number: 2020950831

For my family, for always believing in me.

Chapter 1

I found Jonathan standing by the window in the kitchen. The silvery light of the full moon shone on his broad, naked chest and tight jeans, making him look like a statue of a Greek god. As always, my heart melted at the sight of him.

Our affair had been ongoing for six weeks, and it was still as intense and hot as it when it first began. We saw each other as much as we could. It was like we were newlyweds, although that word always made me cringe when it crossed my mind.

I wasn't proud of what I was doing. But I also couldn't stop.

Jonathan didn't like to talk about his marriage either, but one night, he did bring it up. "I knew almost immediately it was a mistake."

We were lying in bed together, my head tucked into his shoulder as he trailed his fingers gently across my naked back, sending delicious shivers down my spine. The windows were open, and a cool breeze rustled the curtains.

"We were dating, but it was pretty casual. Mostly, we were friends. Really good friends, but friends," he said. "We certainly weren't in love."

"Then why would you marry her?"

He sighed. "She was desperate. She was graduating and couldn't find a job anywhere. She was terrified to go home, sure that if she did, she'd never leave. Her father is an abusive tyrant. It had taken all her courage to leave the first time, but if she couldn't figure out how to support herself, she would have to go back.

"I couldn't stand seeing her like that. I also didn't think I would ever fall in love. After all, I do have my own trust issues," he quietly laughed. "So, I thought, why not marry her? I could bring her back to Redemption, where I already knew I had a job, a good job, waiting for me. I could support us both, and she wouldn't have to go back home to that bastard.

"She started crying when I asked her. She wanted me to promise to keep her safe—to never put her in a position where she would have to go home. And I did." He sighed a sad, discouraged sigh.

"I don't understand. What does that mean?"

"It means I can't just divorce her," he said. "I can't break that promise."

I lifted my head, propping it up with my arm to look at him. He gave me a crooked smile. "I realize how strange that sounds, seeing as I've already broken my marriage vows," he said.

"You think?"

"Well, like I said, we're friends. We don't have much of a marriage. We never have."

"Are you saying she's okay with this?"

He put his arm under his head. "I wouldn't go that far. But she's ... accepted it. Just as long as we stay married and she and the kids are supported and taken care of. At least, for right now, that's the way it has to be."

I didn't tell him that Felicity had come into Aunt May's one afternoon for ice cream for the kids. She sat in my section, Darrel clamoring on the seat across from her while she propped Tina in her lap. I wouldn't have known who she was, but Claire pulled me aside as I was about to approach her table. "That's Jonathan's wife," she hissed in my ear. "Let me take her order."

I hung back and watched as Claire breezed up, her cheerful "Felicity, it's so nice to see you. And look how big Darrel has grown!" echoing in my ears.

At the time, nothing seemed amiss. Felicity seemed happy to chat with Claire. I told myself her coming in was coincidence. After all, why wouldn't a mom bring her kids in for ice cream on such a hot afternoon?

As the kids ate, I studied her out of the corner of my eye, taking extra time to clear tables and refill coffee. She was pretty in a waif-like way—very thin and tiny with straight, blonde hair—right out of the seventies. Her eyes were pale blue, and her features were pixie-like. No wonder Jonathan wanted to take care of her ... she looked like a fragile, porcelain doll.

His son was adorable, the spitting image of his father, and his daughter was awfully cute, as well. Theirs was a truly beautiful family.

What the hell was I thinking?

Despite the guilt, I couldn't pull my eyes away. It was like the urge to pick at a scab even though it hurt. There I was, milling about the dining area, watching Jonathan's family eat their ice cream while enjoying a lovely family day.

It wasn't until Felicity was leaving, sliding out of the booth with Tina's carrier in hand, that she turned to look directly at me.

The hate in her eyes was so intense, I almost dropped the plates I was busing.

But, just as fast, she turned away, calling Darrel to wait for her and not get so far ahead, leaving me trembling next to a partially bused table.

Jonathan could tell himself their marriage was based on friendship instead of love all he wanted. I was fairly certain that Felicity had a different perspective.

"Did you hear it, too?" Jonathan asked.

He had spied me hovering by the doorway. "I didn't mean to scare you."

I went to him, tucking myself under his shoulder as he wrapped his arm around me. His distinct scent of maleness was always so comforting. "You didn't scare me," I said. "I just wasn't sure what was taking you so long."

He moved the curtain a fraction of an inch. "I was sure I heard something."

"Out there?"

He grimaced. "It was probably just the creaking of the house, but sometimes, it's hard to tell if it's coming from inside or out. I wanted to be sure."

"And are you?"

He didn't answer right away, instead continuing to peer out the window. "I'm not seeing anything."

"That's a good thing, right?"

He didn't respond, just hugged me. "I wish you weren't here all alone," he said. He didn't continue, but I knew he was thinking it.

I wish I could stay here with you.

Ever since the night of the séance, things had been quiet ... at least on the Alan front. There had been no other signs of him being in Redemption, or even that he was alive. I hadn't had another dream.

On the surface, it appeared it had worked.

Yet, I knew Jonathan wasn't convinced. He rarely said anything about it, probably because he didn't want to worry me, but I could tell he was keeping an eye on me—regularly searching the house and grounds, stopping by the diner when I was working, even just calling in the middle of the day to make sure everything was okay.

On one hand, it was nice to feel so watched over and protected. It made me feel loved and cared for at a level I wasn't sure I had ever felt.

On the other hand, it made me uneasy.

Was there something I had missed? Something I wasn't seeing?

Beware. It's coming.

The cryptic message I had seen in the mirror the night of the séance. At first, I thought it referred to Alan, but as time passed and there was no sign of him, I started to wonder if maybe it was referring to something else.

Or maybe I hadn't really seen it at all.

Jonathan's back had been to the mirror that night, so he couldn't help. I didn't even bring it up with him, because I didn't want to worry him any more than he already was.

The person I wanted to talk to about it was Claire. I felt like she would know what had happened that night. It was all such a blur to me, and every day, the events seemed to get fuzzier and more indistinct.

I felt like a conversation with my friend would really help me get clear. But ever since that night, Claire had been withdrawn and distant. I'd tried a few times to get her to open up. I'd invited her for a drink or a meal, but she was always busy or had too many things on her plate.

At first I thought it was me, but one day, Lou came into Aunt May's waving cheerfully at me and calling out how we all needed to get together again soon before asking if Claire could wait on her. That's when I overheard her asking Claire what was going on ... why she didn't have time to see her anymore. Claire had answered with the same vague, nebulous non-answers she had been giving me.

Something was up with Claire.

Jonathan sighed as ran his hand down my back, making my spine tingle again. "I have to go," he whispered.

"I know."

He dipped his head to nuzzle my neck. "I don't want to."

"I know."

He nibbled on the delicate skin behind my ear as I stretched my neck out, before pushing me gently away. "I mean it. I have to go."

"I know."

He stared at me for a moment, his eyes dark with desire. "You're going to be the death of me, Charlie."

I smiled my most innocent smile. "I don't know what you're talking about."

He stepped away, raking his hands through his hair. "I'm going, I'm going. But call me if anything happens."

A murmur of unease whispered through me. "Why do you think anything is going to happen?"

He headed to the living room where his shirt was pooled on the floor. "I don't. I didn't see anything outside."

I followed him to stand in the doorway. "What exactly made you look?"

He sighed as he started buttoning his shirt. "I don't want to scare you ..."

"Bit too late for that."

He didn't look at me, focusing instead on his shirt.

"Jonathan."

"I thought I heard something, okay?" he said, his voice exasperated. "But I was wrong. Where are my keys?"

"Why are you so upset?"

He pushed his hands through his hair again. "Why do you think? I don't like leaving you. Especially since we don't really know. Where are my keys?"

I watched him search the living room, swearing under his breath. I knew this was hard on him; it was hard on everyone. And there were no easy answers.

I spied his keys under the hallway table and went over to scoop them up for him. "Look," I said, as I handed them to him. "I'm fine. You searched the house earlier, right?"

He closed his eyes briefly. "Yes."

"All the doors are locked. You know this because you went through the house. I'll lock the front door behind you. I'll be fine. And the reality of the situation is that Alan died in the car crash, and we are making ourselves crazy over nothing."

He took a deep breath. "You're right. I'm overreacting. Probably because I ... well, never mind." He leaned over and gave me a gentle kiss. "Lock your door." He waggled his finger in my face.

I saluted him. "Aye aye, sir."

He stepped outside and I shut the door behind him, immediately turning the deadbolt. I knew he would stand there on the porch until he heard the click of the lock sliding into place.

I turned and saw Midnight lightly leap onto the couch. While he didn't seem to be bothered by Jonathan, he mostly kept out of sight until Jonathan left. He locked his green eyes onto mine and meowed.

"Yeah, it's time to go to bed," I said, yawning. I had a kitchen to clean, as I had been a little distracted after making Jonathan dinner. Plus, I had the early shift at Aunt May's in the morning. I had dropped back to part-time while I worked on getting the tea business going. In fact, I reminded myself to make sure I dropped off Nancy's tea order after work, and decided I'd better put it out now, so I didn't forget.

I headed up the stairs, my mind ticking off the normal to-dos I had to accomplish for the next day.

Still, I found myself glancing over my shoulder.

Wondering if I was truly was alone.

Or, if there was someone out there, in the shadows, watching me, just waiting for me to let down my guard.

I quickly pushed that thought out of my head. I was fine. It was exactly like I told Jonathan. Alan was dead. I was safe and building a brand-new life in my new home.

The worst was behind me.

The Reckoning

Chapter 2

"Can we talk?"

Claire and I were in the staff room getting ready for our shifts. Claire was digging around in her purse, carefully avoiding my eyes. "What do you need?"

"Not here," I said. "After work."

She pulled out a compact mirror and flipped it open. "I can't."

I leaned against my locker. "Then when?"

She clicked the compact closed, barely using it. "I don't know right now. I'll have to check my schedule."

"Claire, are you mad at me?" I asked. "Did I do something wrong?"

She didn't respond, instead shoving her compact back in her purse and hanging it in her locker. She didn't look well. There were dark, baggy circles under her eyes and her hair seemed frizzier and more out of control than usual, falling out of her normally tightly contained ponytail.

"I thought we were friends," I said. "Was I wrong?"

She paused, but still didn't look at me, instead staring into her locker. "We are," she said. "I just ..."

"There you two are," Fred said. Even though it was early, there were already a few beads of sweat on his forehead and his white cook hat was askew on his head. "C'mon, let's get out there. We've already got a crowd lined up."

"Coming," Claire said, slamming her locker door and following Fred out without even a glance in my direction. Whatever she was going to say was lost. I wanted to bang my head against the locker in frustration.

Fred was right about being busy. For most of the morning and through lunchtime, it was all I could do to make sure my customers were fed and happy. There was no time to try and corner Claire to see if I could recapture the moment.

The lunch rush was just about over, and I was standing behind the counter taking a quick break and drinking a Diet Coke when Jonathan walked in.

"Slacking off, I see," he said with a grin, although the look in his eyes said a lot more.

I smiled back, pressing the cold beverage against my face to try and make my blush a little less obvious. "Can't a girl catch a break? I've only been back here for a minute."

"She has," Chester, one of the regulars, confirmed. He was eating a toasted ham and cheese at the lunch counter. His bald head gleamed under the light.

"See," I said. "I'm going to need a foot massage after a day like today."

"Hopefully, your boyfriend is up to the task," Jonathan said with a wicked gleam.

"If he's not, I might have to replace him," I said, turning away and pretending to wipe down the back counter as a distraction from my need to catch my breath. "Are you eating here or taking out?" I asked over my shoulder.

"Taking out. It should be ready. It's for all of us."

That meant I was looking for a big order. I moved to the kitchen and found it. Behind me, I could hear Chester and Jonathan chatting, but I was far enough away to not make out specific words.

I was bringing the order out when I heard a booming voice.

"Is there a Charlie working here?"

Startled, I almost dropped it, but quickly recovered. "I'm Charlie," I said. "Can I help you?"

A huge guy was standing next to Jonathan. He had flaming long red hair and a beard to match. He wore a black Megadeth tee shirt that was stretched tight over a beer belly. His face was pockmarked with old acne scars.

Jonathan's entire demeanor had changed. When he first walked in, he was relaxed and flirtatious. Now, he had adjusted to more of a combat stance, legs spread, arms loose at his side. His body was tense and his eyes watchful as he eyed the huge red-haired man.

"You're Charlie?" he asked, his voice still booming.

"I am," I said, coming a few steps closer. I could see heads turning toward us and was hoping I could get him to lower his voice.

"Hey Red," Chester said. "What do you want with my favorite waitress?"

Red didn't answer, his eyes fixed on me. He pointed a thick finger at me. "Someone has been asking about you."

I could feel the blood drain from my face. At the same time, there was a loud crash, making me jump.

Claire was standing there, surrounded by a pile of shattered plates and now-inedible food. Her face was as white as a sheet, probably like mine.

"Sorry," she muttered, surveying the wreckage. "Oh God, I'm so sorry." She knelt down, her hands trembling, to gather up the worst of it as the busboy hurried over with a broom.

I wanted to go help her, but I couldn't move. I felt like I was rooted in my spot, held like a bug pinned under glass, by Red and his thick, pointy finger.

I swallowed. "Who?"

Red shrugged, his massive shoulders shifting under his tee shirt like boulders. "Some guy. Definitely an out-of-towner."

"What did he say?"

"He kept asking if anyone knew of a Charlotte who had recently moved to town." His eyes narrowed as his gaze turned calculating. "Charlie is short for Charlotte, right?"

I couldn't answer. It felt like my tongue had stuck to the roof of my mouth. Sweat beads dotted my forehead as both hot and cold flashes surged through me at the same time. My body was still frozen in place. I couldn't move, not even as my glass slipped through my numb fingers and crashed onto the floor.

From a far-away distance, I could hear voices talking to me, but they sounded like they were at the end of a tunnel, and I couldn't make out a word they were saying.

I could only think of one thing.

Alan.

He's alive.

And he found me.

"Charlie," Chester was standing up, waving a hand in front of me. "Are you okay?"

I shook my head, trying to clear it. "Yeah, sorry. It's been awhile since I heard that name is all." I looked down to see the damage. Soda and ice were everywhere; my socks were even stained brown. At least the red plastic glass hadn't broken.

Chester didn't look convinced. "Are you sure?"

"Yes, it's just ..." What could I say that would make my reaction seem normal? My head was spinning, and I was lightheaded. *My ex is alive, and he's here.*

"I don't know who would be looking for me," I said. "My friends and family know where I am, so this doesn't make much sense. It's just kind of creepy." Another thought struck me then, and I gave Red a hard look. "Speaking of creepy, how did you know where to find me? I have no idea who you are."

"Oh, that's Red," Chester said. "He owns The Lone Man Standing bar. He knows everyone."

"Yeah, but I've never been to The Lone Man Standing," I said, still staring at Red. Was he actually a private investigator?

Red seemed amused by my reaction. "Darling, everyone knows who you are. Did you forget about that nice write-up in the *Redemption Times?*"

Oh God. I *had* forgotten about that. After I bought Helen's house, otherwise known as the Witch House, the *Redemption Times* did an article about me. Red was right; everyone would know who I was and would be able to point Alan in my direction. I wanted to wring that reporter's neck.

"So, I guess you told him then," I said, feeling defeated. I wondered if there was enough time for me to go home and pack, at least the essentials, before getting out of town.

Red laughed, an out-and-out belly laugh. "Darling, you're one of us. You're family now. Besides, none of us know anyone named 'Charlotte.'" He winked at me and turned to head out of the diner.

Chester still had a concerned look on his face. "You sure you're okay?"

"Yes. It was just a bit of a shock," I said, grabbing a rag and bending down to mop up the spilled soda. What a mess. I considered getting a mop.

Someone bent down next to me. "I've got this," Claire said. She was holding the mop. "If you need a minute ..."

Before I could respond, Jonathan's voice floated down. "Hey, I forgot to order the sodas. Can I get two Cokes and one Diet?"

"Sure," I said automatically, straightening up to fill the order. When I turned back, Jonathan had left cash on the counter. "Keep the change," he said, scooping up the bags and grabbing one of the sodas. "Oh," he said, his voice innocent. "Would it be possible to help me carry the other sodas?"

I glanced at Claire, whose lips were pressed tight together. "Sure," I said. "I have a break coming. Chester, do you need anything before I go?"

Chester waved his hand. "Naw, I'm fine. You probably need a walk in the sun after that."

"Thanks," I said, picking up the sodas and following Jonathan out.

The day was hot and humid. "A typical August day in Wisconsin," I'd been reliably informed by the locals. The sun beat down overhead, and the air was thick and damp. The sweat immediately started trickling down my back and between my breasts.

"We have to check this out," Jonathan said. His muscles were tight and taunt, and his eyes were hard.

"It's too dangerous," I said. "If it is Alan. I should just leave ..."

"No," Jonathan said, his voice so loud it made me jump. He saw that and forced himself to soften his tone. "We fight. We don't run."

"But ..."

"No 'buts,'" Jonathan said, shaking his head. "This is your home now. You have a house. A job. A business that's just taking off. You're not leaving because of this sick bastard."

That was all true. But it also meant I had everything to lose.

"Besides, do you really think I would let anything happen to you?" Jonathan's voice was low but fierce. I glanced sideways at him. His face was set, his jaw tense.

I wasn't sure what to think. On one hand, I felt a rush of warmth, of safety, of being cared for.

On the other hand, I was uncomfortable with it. It wasn't my place. Jonathan shouldn't be focused on protecting me. He had a wife, a family.

This wasn't healthy. I needed to say something, to stop it before it went too far.

Even if that wasn't what I wanted.

Before I could find the words, Jonathan started talking again, his voice back to normal. "You know, it might not be him."

I gave him a look. "Are you serious? He called me 'Charlotte.'"

"Everyone in New York knows you as 'Charlotte,'" Jonathan said. "Are you so sure it's not someone else?"

"Well, no one else would be skulking around at a bar asking about me," I said. "They would have just phoned my sister. And she would have told them how to get ahold of me."

"Maybe it was someone who wasn't close to your sister," he said. "Or who is on the outs with your sister. Did you think about that?"

I hadn't. Although it was true that Annabelle didn't have many friends. She had a lot of acquaintances. There were a lot of people who were willing to socialize with her because of our family reputation and money, but not a lot of people who genuinely liked her.

"Or," Jonathan continued. "maybe someone wants to surprise you."

I looked at him in disbelief. "What?"

He shrugged. "What if it's an old boyfriend who heard that Alan had died and wants to rekindle the flame? Is that so out of the question?" He grinned as he asked, but it was clearly a little forced.

I nudged him. "Jealous?"

He laughed. "Absolutely."

I smiled back, but inside I was pondering what he said. Was it possible it was one of my exes? It was true I tended to be the one to do the breaking up, but still. I couldn't really picture any of them showing up in Redemption to win me back.

"Regardless," he said. "Rather than assume it's Alan, we should actually find out."

"How do you propose we do that?"

"Go to The Lone Man Standing," he said. "We'll hang out. Have a drink. See if he shows up, and if he doesn't, we can ask around and get a description. Then we'll know." He studied me for a moment. "I don't suppose you have a picture of Alan?"

I gave him a look. "Seriously?"

He grinned. "I had mixed feelings about asking. On one hand, it would help us a lot if you did. But ..."

"Don't worry. No photos," I said.

We had arrived at the Grant Street Auto, where Jonathan worked. "I can't stay much longer," I said. "But I don't know if it's a good idea we show up at the bar by ourselves. I mean, won't it look like a date?"

"Good point. I'll ask Jesse to come," he said. "We might need backup."

I was trying to get my head around me going to a bar with Jesse and Jonathan and how that would look when Jonathan took the sodas from me. "Here, I've got it. Go on back. I'll call you after work."

I rubbed my hands against my jeans. "See you," I said, turning away quickly before one of his coworkers could see us together. Not that it mattered. Even I could see that we were the worst-kept secret in town.

The Reckoning

Chapter 3

"What took you so long?" Claire hissed in my ear as soon as I opened the door to Aunt May's. The cool air-conditioning flowed over me, a welcome relief from the oppressive heat.

"I just walked to Grant's Auto and back," I said. "What is your problem?"

She glared at me. "We have to talk," she said under her breath. "Kitchen. Now."

After weeks of ignoring me, this was how she was going to act? What was going on with her? "I need to check on my customers ..." I started to say, but she interrupted me.

"They're fine," she said. "I've got them covered. And Liz just got here, so she can handle it."

"Okay," I said. "But I need a sec."

Without waiting for her to answer, I headed for the waitress station where we kept the sodas. I quickly filled a glass with ice and Diet Coke, fanning myself as I waited for it to pour. Man, it was hot. And being back there in the kitchen with how irritated Claire seemed, it was bound to get even hotter. I definitely needed a cold drink in hand.

I pushed open the door to the kitchen. Waves of steam along with the scents of fried onions and beef hit me square in the face. Fred was standing by the grill muttering to himself, sweat glistening on his face.

Claire was off to the side, pacing back and forth. As soon as she saw me, she grabbed my arm and yanked me closer, jostling the soda in my glass. "What did Jonathan say to you?" Her cheeks were red and blotchy, but whether from the heat of the kitchen or because of how upset she was, I couldn't tell.

"Claire, what is going on with you?"

"Just answer."

"He wants to check it out," I said.

"How?"

"We're going to The Lone Man Standing tonight," I said, dislodging my arm from where she was clutching it. "Have a drink, ask questions, and see if we can get a description."

Claire's eyes widened. "Oh no. You can't do that. You already look like a couple of lovebirds. You can't go to a bar together."

"I know that," I snapped. "I'm not stupid. He's asking Jesse to come, too."

Claire's mouth dropped open. "Jesse? He's asking *Jesse*? That's it. I'm coming, too."

I stared at her in amazement. "What do you have against Jesse being there?"

"Because it can't be you, Jesse, and Jonathan. Especially in that place. It needs to look like a group of friends."

"Oh, so what, you're going to come and that's going to make it better? Two girls and two guys? That just looks like a double date!"

As soon as I said it, I knew I had hit a nerve, even though that hadn't been my intention. Claire reared back like I had slapped her. She stared at me, her eyes shocked and horrified.

And then I got it. "You're sleeping with him, aren't you?"

She pressed one hand against her forehead and squeezed her eyes shut. "I never meant to," she said. "It just ... happened."

"Is that what's been going on with you? You're feeling guilty because of the affair?"

Claire sighed, but it was a reluctant one, as if it were being pulled out of her against her will. "It's not just that."

"Then what else? And when did it start?"

She opened an eye to look at me. "The night of the séance."

Of course, it did. I wanted to smack myself for being so dense. I had seen the way the two of them were looking at each other. How could I have missed the obvious?

Although, to be fair, I had been a little distracted.

"You should have said something," I said. "It's not like I wouldn't have understood."

She pressed her lips together and shook her head. "It's not just that. Although, yes, it's not something I'm proud of."

"Does Doug know?"

"I don't think so. He's pretty focused on work. He's been putting in extra hours, trying for a promotion. But I need to have a conversation with him. It's time."

"I take it Lou doesn't know either."

She shook her head again. "Trust me, neither one of us want to have *that* conversation."

That certainly explained why Claire had been ignoring Lou.

"But, it's more than just that," she said, leaning closer to me. "It was also what I saw."

"What you saw? What are you talking about?"

"The night of the séance. I saw ..." she bit her lip as Fred yelled out. "Are you two about done? We could use some help out here."

"In a sec," Claire shouted back, before turning back to me. "It's too long to tell you here. After work. We'll talk. Before we go to The Lone Man Standing."

"I'm going to hold you to that," I said as we went back out to the dining area.

***

"I need a shower," Claire said, plucking her once-white tee shirt, which was now stained with sweat and grease, away from her chest. We were both standing by our lockers collecting our belongings.

"So do I. And a meal, too. I never did get to eat," I said.

"I didn't either," Claire said. "Actually, that reminds me. I ordered us some food. It's probably boxed up for us. Let me go grab it."

She disappeared, reappearing a moment later holding two boxes. "When are we meeting them?" she asked, handing me one.

"Couple of hours."

She huffed a sigh and ran her hand through her damp hair. "Not a lot of time."

"Then why don't you tell me now what you saw, and then we can both go home and get cleaned up?"

She frowned, glancing at the open door. "You're right. Here. Let's sit down and eat. No one will question it."

I wondered why anyone would question anything and why she was making such a big deal about it, but did as she wanted, squeezing into the bench in the corner, my back against my locker as I huddled next to her.

"So, what's going on?" I said, opening my box and picking up my turkey-and-provolone sandwich.

Claire opened her box and took a French fry out, but she didn't eat it. "Remember when I told you about seeing a girl in that room?"

My entire body tensed. Suddenly, I wasn't hungry. I put the sandwich back and rubbed my hands against my jeans. I hadn't dreamed about the Holly Hobby girl for weeks now, since before the séance, and hoped that meant I was done with her. "Is that who you saw the night of the séance?"

She barely nodded.

"So, what happened? What did you see?"

She chewed on her lip, the fry continuing to dangle from her fingers. "I saw ... it was like a vision. There's a group of people. They're all wearing old-fashioned clothes, like muslin dresses and bib overalls. And they're all standing out in this ... field, I guess. There are trees all around and what looks like crops. There's also a small building. It's grey and weathered and looks like it's about to fall over.

"All the people are angry. They're holding things like pitchforks and shouting."

She paused, as if trying to reorder her thoughts. I didn't interrupt. I was too busy trying to get my head around what she was describing. "They're *really* angry," she said finally.

"Why?"

She shrugged. "I don't know. They're just ... mad."

Her voice had gotten higher and younger somehow. The lines in her face seemed to have relaxed as well. It was like she had regressed, become a child again.

"Then what happened?"

"There's a pile of wood. And the townspeople keep adding to the pile. It's getting bigger and bigger. And," she licked her lips. "There's a girl there. Tied up by the pile."

My eyes widened. "A girl? The same girl?"

Claire slowly nodded.

I almost didn't want to ask, but I couldn't not know. "What happened to her?"

Claire swallowed. "One of the townspeople is holding a torch. He walks over to the pile of wood and throws it on there."

"She was burned?"

Claire closed her eyes and turned away. "I didn't see it. I heard screaming and then the dream ended."

"You mean the vision."

Claire opened her eyes and looked at me directly in the eyes. "I mean the dream."

"Wait, I'm not following."

She blew the air out of her lungs and dropped the fry she had been holding, wiping her hands on her jeans. "I don't even know if I can explain this. It's going to sound so weird."

I gave a short bark of laughter. "Weirder than any of this?"

She smiled, but there was no humor in it. "You'll see. There's something that happens here in Redemption to the kids. Well, not all the kids. You have to be born here, and it's always at a certain age—I think around five or six. There's a dream we all have. Actually, it's more of a nightmare."

"You all have the same dream? Like something that happens at night while you're sleeping?"

"Yes."

"But that can't be. How can everyone have the same one?"

"Believe it or not, there are actually lots of anecdotes about people having the same dream. It's not as uncommon as you might think. There's even a psychiatric disorder where you can share hallucinations, which I know aren't the same as dreams, but it's possible."

"But a whole town?"

She cocked her head. "Charlie, you're focusing on the wrong thing. That's actually not the strangest part. The strangest part is we all forget."

I felt like my brain was going to explode. I pressed my hands to my temple as if to keep my head in one piece. "How is that, when you're telling me about it right now?"

"That's the thing. It's like when it happens, the adult will say, 'Oh my kid had the dream,' and for that brief moment, we'll all remember. 'Oh, yeah. There's that shared dream again.' And then, in the next moment ... the memory just disintegrates."

She gave me a sad smile. "I told you it didn't make sense."

"So, you ... forgot this dream?"

She nodded. "Until that night in the closet. I realized the girl in it was the girl who was tied to the stake. But this time," she leaned closer to me and whispered. "This time, I didn't forget."

Her face was so close, I could see a light dusting of freckles across her nose that I had never noticed before. Her eyes were wide and intense, almost scaring me.

"What do you think it means?" I asked.

"That's the problem. I don't *know*." Her voice was plaintive, almost like the wail of a child's.

"So, let me get this straight," I said, mostly because I felt like I needed to ground the conversation somehow ... to bring it back to reality, if that were even possible. I could feel myself wanting to freak out, but I knew that would be the worst response. Whatever was going on, I had to keep my head on straight. "As children, you all have a dream where you see a young girl get burned alive. And then, you all forget. But you saw your dream play out the night of the séance. But that time, you didn't forget. Is that right?"

She sat back. "That's it."

I rubbed my forehead. "This is so bizarre."

"You're telling me."

"So, why didn't you say something sooner?"

She gave me a look. "Oh, because I was real excited to have you question whether you even believe me, like you're doing now?"

"I do believe you, I'm just ... I need a moment to get my head around it."

She smirked. "Actually, you're the easiest. It's Lou and Jesse and Jonathan. I don't know what they would do if I said something. Remember, no one remembers. At first, I was so freaked out about it, I didn't want to talk about it. To anyone. And then, I wasn't sure what would happen. Except for you, of course," she laughed a bit. "I figured you would react pretty much the way you have."

"I'm glad I didn't let you down," I said drily. "But seriously. This is all so weird. This town. What you saw. How I ended up here. I don't know what to make of all of it."

"Not to mention if Alan is here or not. Speaking of which," Claire glanced at the clock. "We should get going. We don't have much time before we're supposed to meet them."

"Oh. You're right." I packed up my food, hoping my appetite would return after I took my shower, but paused. "I thought you said having the séance would protect me from Alan."

Claire wasn't looking at me, focusing instead on packing up her own food. "Yes, that's true."

"So, how do you explain it if he's here?"

Claire shrugged as she stood up. "Redemption takes care of its own. Just because it doesn't look the way we think it will doesn't mean it's not happening."

I rolled my eyes. "Good non-answer."

She laughed. "Look, you're fine. Right? And you got a warning. We're going to go check it out. Trust me." She blew me a kiss as she left the room.

The Reckoning

Chapter 4

"What a dive," Claire muttered under her breath as we entered The Lone Man Standing.

"You haven't been here either?" I asked, my voice low. We were walking behind Jonathan and Jesse, who were also having a quiet conversation.

She shook her head. "Never."

I glanced around. "I can see why."

The bar was dark, which was probably a good thing, as what I could see was run down and seedy. The wood floors were scuffed and stained, the tables had words and pictures carved into them, and some of the bar stools and chairs were broken. Two rough-looking guys wearing black leather jackets and chains paused their pool playing to stare at us. One had a cigarette hanging out of his mouth. A cloud of smoke hung around the bar, and under the typical underlying bar odors of alcohol and sweat, there was a definite dampness—a hint of mold and mildew. My shoes stuck to the floor with every step.

"Let's sit here," Jesse said, gesturing to one of the worn-down tables. I gingerly sat down in a cracked chair, hoping it would bear my weight. It seemed to, at least for the moment.

"I'll get us some drinks," he said. "What do you want?"

"Hmmm. This doesn't strike me as an establishment that would be known for its wine," Claire said.

"Maybe a cocktail?" I asked.

Jonathan raised an eyebrow. "It depends. Do you trust them to do a better job cleaning the glassware than the rest of the bar?"

"Maybe a beer," I said. "In the can." I had never been a big beer fan, but I could choke one down.

"Any preference?"

"Whatever you like," I said.

"I'll do the same," Claire said.

The two men went up to get our drinks as Claire looked around. "God, this place gives me the creeps," she said, shivering and rubbing her hands over her bare arms. "Anyone look familiar?"

I scanned the bar. Along with the two playing pool, there was another couple of guys sitting at the bar, beers in front of them, and another older man sitting by himself near the dartboard pounding shot after shot. As I watched, a heavily made-up waitress with a big mane of black hair brought him a beer. He was in the shadows, so I couldn't see his face, but he looked tired and worn. The phrase "rode hard and put away wet" came to mind.

"Nothing yet," I said. Which didn't really surprise me. The Alan I knew would never set foot in a bar in like this. Not to mention it made no sense for him to pick this place to start his search. It was starting to feel more like a wild goose chase.

Claire frowned. "I guess it would be too much to ask to have it happen immediately so we can get out of here."

"Probably," I said.

"Here you go," Jonathan said, placing a can of Old Milwaukee in front of me. I cautiously took a sip, trying not to make a face at the taste. Jonathan laughed.

"Did you guys find anything out?" Claire asked.

Jesse took a swig of beer before shaking his head. "We just ordered the drinks. I didn't think peppering everyone with questions the moment we walked in would be the smartest way to get them to open up."

"I suppose not," Claire muttered, shivering again.

Jesse eyed her. "Are you cold?"

"It's not that. This place is giving me the heebie-jeebies."

Jesse raised an eyebrow. "The 'heebie-jeebies'?"

"It is kind of creepy," I said. "Don't you think so?"

Jesse glanced around. "Well, it certainly could use some repair work and a good cleaning, if that's what you mean."

Claire hunched into herself. "More like a good fumigation," she said. "On top of everything else, it's probably crawling with cockroaches."

I was about to gamely try another sip of my beer but decided to leave well enough alone.

"They probably aren't crawling over the beer cans," Jesse said, his eyes crinkling with laughter as he watched me push the beer aside. "So you're safe." He winked. I rolled my eyes.

"Do you see anyone familiar?" Jonathan asked.

"No. Claire already asked me, but no, I'm not seeing anyone."

Jonathan frowned. "Maybe we need to talk to Red."

"Let's try the waitress first," Jesse said, waving her over before holding up his beer and pointing to it.

"Is that smart to get a second beer so quickly?" Claire asked.

"How else are we going to talk to her?" he countered. "Besides, there's no law that says we have to finish it."

The waitress came over and put a second can of Old Milwaukee in front of Jesse, who flashed her an especially sexy grin. "What's your name?"

"Rosie," she said. Her face was hard beneath the layers of makeup, reminding me of the other guy in the corner. She had lines around her eyes and mouth and a hollowness to her cheeks.

"Thank you, Rosie," he said.

She gave him a look and his grin turned sheepish. Clearly, she had Jesse's number. "Can I get the rest of you anything?" she asked, turning toward us.

Jonathan nudged me under the table, and I cleared my throat. "Well ..."

She nodded at my beer. "Want another?"

"Actually, I was wondering about some information," I said, feeling incredibly stupid and awkward. I was starting to feel like I was in a bad thriller movie.

She gave me a strange look. "What kind of information?"

"Um, well your boss, Red, he came to see me today ..."

"Red?" She glanced over at him, her expression incredulous. "Him? Are you sure you have the right guy, sweetie?"

"Yeah, I'm, uh, Charlie. I bought Helen Blackstone's house ..."

Her expression cleared. "Oh, you bought the Witch House."

"I guess I did, yes," I said, looking around the table and wishing someone would help. No luck—they all seemed happy I was taking the lead. "And I guess someone was in here asking about me?"

"Rosie?" Red bellowed from the bar. "I don't pay you to chat."

"I have to get back to work," she said, starting to turn away.

"I'll have another beer," I called out desperately.

She glanced knowingly back at me before heading to the bar.

Jesse raised an eyebrow. "See?"

"Fine," I said. "I have no idea what I'm going to do with two beers."

"Someone will drink them," Jesse said. "Or you can pour them down the sink. Either way works. Also, depending on what she tells you, you probably want to leave a nice tip."

I was starting to wish I had brought more cash with me. Maybe Jonathan would lend me some.

Rosie came back with my beer. "Yes, he was in here the other day," she said, her voice low.

"Can you describe him?"

Rosie puckered her face. "He sure didn't look like the type of guy who would be hanging out in a place like this." She gave us all a pointed look. "He had dark hair, a mustache, and a beard. Well, not much of a beard. It was like he was just starting out or something. It was really pretty pathetic."

A mustache? Beard? Dark hair? Didn't sound like Alan at all. On the other hand, he might have purposefully disguised himself.

Rosie glanced nervously at Red. "No one said anything to him, if that's what you were wondering. But look, you need to talk to Red if you have any more questions."

"Why?"

Rosie licked her lips. "Let's just say he's had an eye on your house for a while."

My eyes widened. "My house?"

"Rosie," Red yelled.

"I'm helping a customer," she yelled back. "I've got to go," she said to me.

"What is she talking about?" I asked as Rosie went back to the bar, screeching something about panties being in a wad.

Jesse shook his head. "I have no idea."

"You think he wanted to buy the Witch House?" Jonathan asked. "But why?"

Claire shivered. "Maybe he likes to collect weird, creepy places."

"But my house isn't like this at all," I said.

"Not now," Claire said. "You cleaned it up, remember? When you first bought it, it was pretty much a disaster."

"Only because Helen couldn't keep up with it."

"I'm not trying to criticize Helen," Claire said. "I get that she had a valid reason for not being able to clean. You only had to look at her hands to see it. Red doesn't have that excuse, though." She glanced in Red's general direction, a disapproving frown on her face.

"So, cleanliness aside," I said. "Why would he possibly want to buy Helen's house? And why wouldn't he just ask Helen to sell it to him?"

"Maybe he did, and Helen refused," Claire said.

"But, why?"

Claire spread her hands out. "Look at this place. Can you blame her?"

"Yeah, do you really think she saw it?" I asked. "How would she know?"

"She knew," Claire said darkly.

"Well, all of that aside," I said. "If he was upset I bought the house, why would he warn me that was someone was looking for me? Wouldn't it make more sense to just let me be found?"

"Good point," Jesse said, tipping his beer toward me. "Maybe you should ask him."

"Maybe I should," I said. This whole exercise was starting to irritate me. Why couldn't I just be left alone to live my life? Why did things like this keep happening?

"Maybe you shouldn't," Jonathan said, watching my face.
"Why not?"
"Well, do you really think it's such a good idea?"
"Was coming here a good idea?" I asked. "Look, we want answers, right? Maybe it's time to get some." With that, I got up from the table and marched over to the bar.

Red was polishing a glass with a rag that was almost as dirty as his black Judas Priest tee shirt. He eyed me as I approached. "Can I help you?"

I smiled sweetly. "I was wondering if you could tell me more about this guy who was asking about me?"

Red shrugged. "Not much to tell. He was clearly an outsider."

"What did he look like?"

"Dark hair. Mustache. Something resembling a goatee on his chin. Pretty pathetic if you ask me."

Did I hear him right? Rosie had used those exact words. The sense of wrongness I had felt from the moment I walked in went on high alert. Did this guy even exist? Was this all a setup?

But why would Red make him up?

And how would he know I would even take the bait?

"Did he say why he was looking for me?"

Red shrugged again. "Not our business."

"If it wasn't your business, why would you find me to tell me about it?"

Red made a show of putting the glass away, making me glad I resisted the temptation to order a cocktail. "I told you," he said. "We take care of our own here in Redemption."

"But you don't even know me," I said. "I've only been here a few months."

Red started washing a shot glass. "You're still one of us now."

He was lying. I could tell by his body language.

But about what?

"I heard you had an interest in my house," I said casually.

My shot hit the mark. His entire body went rigid. "Clearly, I need to have a talk to my employees about the word 'working,'" he said.

Oh crap. I hadn't meant to get Rosie in trouble. "It wasn't an employee," I said.

He glared at me from under thick red eyebrows. "Then who was it?"

"Someone from the diner," I said. "You were hardly discreet. Everyone heard you. A couple customers mentioned something after you left."

This wasn't true, but Red seemed to buy it, which made me breathe a little easier. I certainly didn't want anything to happen to Rosie. "So what if I was interested in the Witch House," he said. "That doesn't mean anything."

I shrugged. "I didn't say it did. I'm just curious is all. I was under the impression most people in this town weren't interested in living in a haunted house, which is why she was so happy when I was."

"I'm not most people," he said. "Now, unless you're going to order a drink, I have to get back to work."

He was dismissing me. I gave him a slight nod before heading back to the table.

All of three of them were watching me, Jonathan with a slightly worried expression on his face. "What happened?" he demanded as soon as I sat down.

"Not much," I said. "He basically gave me the same description Rosie gave us."

"Is that what Alan looked like?" Jesse asked.

"Not at all. Alan was very preppy. Clean shaven. With light-brown hair."

"He could have been disguising himself," Jonathan mused.

"He could have," I said. "But there's something that doesn't feel right ..."

Claire looked at me sharply. "What?"

"I don't know exactly. I just get the feeling he's lying about something," I said.

"Why would he lie about that?" Jonathan asked.

"I don't know," I said. "But both him and Rosie used the word 'pathetic' to describe this guy's goatee. How common is that?"

"Maybe it *was* pathetic," Jesse said.

"Maybe," I said, glancing back at Red, who was busy pouring a shot. "But there's something about it that bothers me."

"Just one thing?" Jonathan grumbled. "Everything about this bothers me."

Maybe this was my shot. I gave Claire a pointed look before I continued. I had wanted to ask Jonathan and Jesse about the dream thing ever since Claire told me, and I had been trying to figure out how I could work it into the conversation. "Especially since I thought this wasn't supposed to be an issue," I said.

Claire gave me a dirty look.

"What do you mean?" Jesse asked, finishing one of the beers and picking up the second.

"Well, I thought since we asked Redemption to help, Alan wouldn't be able to show up here, even if he was alive. So why is this happening now?"

Jesse shrugged. "We can't always predict *how* Redemption is going to do something. We just have to trust it's happening."

I laughed, but it was more of a short bark. "It's hard to trust when someone I don't even know tells me someone is looking for me."

"You said it yourself," Jesse said. "Maybe it's not even Alan."

I kicked Claire under the table. She frowned at me.

"Or maybe it's something else," I said.

Jonathan studied me. "What are you trying to say, Charlie?"

"Oh nothing," I said, glaring at Claire. She glared back.

Jonathan glanced between us. "What is going on?"

"Ask her," I said, pointing.

Claire sighed. "I didn't want to bring this up, but do you remember the dream we all had as kids?"

"Dream?" Jesse asked. Jonathan looked confused.

"Yeah, THE dream. The one about the girl in olden times."

"Oh," Jesse said. "Yeah, the dream. I don't think I ever had it. Did you, Jonathan?"

Jonathan shook his head. "I don't dream."

Claire was staring at Jesse. "Yes, I know you had the dream, because Lou told me you both had it the same night."

Jesse shook his head, tipping his beer back. "I think you're remembering wrong, but now that you say it, yeah ... I think Lou did wake me up one night with that dream. Woke us all up. Screaming bloody murder." He shook his head. "Anyway, what about it?"

I looked at Claire, who had a distinctly uncomfortable expression on her face. "It was just something I saw the night of the séance."

Jesse looked surprised. "I didn't realize you saw anything that night."

"Yeah, it was ... well, like a vision, almost."

"Where did you see it?"

"In the closet. It was open, and ... well ..." She swallowed, reached for her beer, then changed her mind and put her hand down.

"What did you see?" Jonathan asked.

"Something that took place a long time ago. Everyone was wearing old-fashioned clothes. There was a girl tied to a stake in front of a pile of wood. Then, the townspeople threw a lit torch on the wood."

Both Jesse and Jonathan looked stunned. "You saw that? In Charlie's closet?" Jesse asked.

"Yeah." She turned to face Jesse, her face pleading. "Don't you remember? It's the dream. I saw the dream."

"Sounds like a nightmare," Jonathan said, looking shook up. He reached for his beer, his hand shaking.

Jesse's face looked almost ashen. "Even if it was the dream, what would that have to do with anything? With Charlie or Alan? Charlie's only been here for a few months."

Claire shook her head. "I don't know. That's the problem. I keep thinking there's something else going on. Something ..." her voice dropped to almost a whisper. "Something deeper ... darker. I feel like we might have unleashed something that night—something we never should have."

The three of us stared at Claire. I licked my dry lips, feeling both hot and cold. "Are you saying we shouldn't have done it?"

Claire chewed on her lip. "I don't know what I'm saying," she said. "It's not like I don't want you here, safe and protected. But ... I think something went wrong. It wasn't like before, when we were kids. Something else happened that night, and I don't think it was good."

Jesse shifted uncomfortably in his chair. "I don't know, Claire ..."

"What could we have done differently?" Jonathan asked. His face had gone pale as well in the dim light of the bar. "We did it exactly like we did when we were kids."

"No, we didn't," Claire said.

"What was different?"

Claire leaned forward. "The room," she hissed. "I knew the moment Lou suggested it, it was a mistake. We never should have done it in that room."

"Johnny!"

The guy drinking shots in the corner next to the dart table was staggering toward us, weaving drunkenly between tables. "I thought that was you," he said, looking at Jonathan. "I didn't think you came here."

Jonathan's lips thinned. "Frank," he spat. "I should have known."

Frank? Jonathan's abusive stepfather? I looked around the table, seeing the horror on Claire's face and disgust on Jesse's. Yep, it was definitely *that* Frank.

"Let me buy you and your friends a drink." Frank could barely get the words out. He tried to signal Red but ended up knocking over a chair.

"You're drunk," Jonathan snapped. "Go home and sleep it off."

Frank huffed, his expression turning pouty. "But Johnny, I never see you anymore. You never call, you never ..."

"Because I'm not interested in having a relationship with you," Jonathan hissed. "And don't call me 'Johnny.' That's not my name."

"Oh, what, you're too good for me, *Jonathan?*" the old man asked, his voice suddenly full of venom. "After all the years I took care of you after that whore of a mother left me, left both of us ..."

Jonathan shot out of his chair so fast it tipped over. "Do NOT talk about my mother, you sick son of a bitch." His hands were clenched into fists, and for a moment, I thought he was going to punch him. Jesse's eyes widened, and I saw his muscles tense. He was ready to jump in if need be.

"Frank, it's time to go home now." Just like that, Red had appeared, grasping Frank by the shoulder and the arm. "Do you want me to call you a cab, or can you walk?"

"But Red," Frank whined. "This here is my boy. Don't you think we deserve a celebratory drink?" His voice stumbled on "celebratory."

"Sure, Frank," Red said, starting to escort Frank out. "We'll do that tomorrow. I'll break out the champagne."

"But Red."

Frank's voice faded out as Red propelled him to the door.

Jonathan stood for a minute longer, breathing hard. A vein was pulsing in his neck.

"Hey," Jesse said, leaning over to straighten his chair. "Have a seat, man. It's over."

Jonathan didn't move for a moment, his eyes still fixed on Red shoving Frank out the door over Frank's loud objections.

"Jonathan," Jesse said again, his voice louder.

"Hey," I said quietly, leaning over to touch his hand. "It's over. Shall we sit?"

That seemed to break through whatever trance he was in. He glanced down at me briefly, his eyes cloudy with confusion. He took one last moment to scan the room before finally sitting back down.

"You okay?" Jesse asked.

Jonathan picked up his beer and took a long drink. "I haven't seen Frank in years," he said, as he put the beer down. "Since high school, really."

"It doesn't look like he's improved with age," Claire said.

That brought a faint smile to Jonathan's lips. "No, doesn't seem that way." He sighed before dragging his hand through his hair. "Sorry, guys. I guess ... well, just seeing him brought up all sorts of bad memories."

"Don't worry about it," Jesse said. "He's bad news. It's written all over him."

"Sorry about that. You folks okay?"

Red was standing by our table, his beefy arms folded in front of him. I hadn't seen him come back in.

"We're fine," Jonathan said stiffly.

"Frank don't mean anything," Red said. "Just an old drunk. But let me know if he bothers you."

"We will," Jesse said. "Thanks."

"Need anything else?"

"No, I think we're good," Jesse said.

I thought he was going to leave, but he just stood there. "Lot of history in this place," he said.

"That's true," Jesse said. "This bar has been here a long time."

Red squinted as he looked at Jesse. "Did you know this building was here before it happened?"

I opened my mouth to ask what had happened, but Jonathan kicked me under the table, and I snapped my lips shut.

"Yep, this building has been here well over a hundred years."

"A hundred years?" I asked incredulously. "They had bars back then?"

Red smiled a rather nasty smile. "What, you think people didn't drink in the 1800s? But this wasn't a bar in 1887. It was actually a house. It was slowly added onto over the years." He waved his hand toward the back. "That's why the floors are uneven, and things don't always look like they fit together. My father was the one who gutted the inside and turned it into a bar. It would have been easier to just tear it down and start over, but he refused. Said it would be a shame to lose the history."

I wondered why he was telling us all of this. I took a quick peek at everyone else at the table, and they seemed equally perplexed.

"Lot of history," he said again. "I do whatever I can to keep that history alive, too."

Was this some sort of message to me? That I should make sure to take good care of the house I just bought? "I agree," I said. "It's important to do whatever we can to keep history alive."

Red didn't immediately answer. Instead, he just kept staring at me, his eyes the color of old pennies.

"I didn't realize this bar had so much history," Jonathan said, shifting next to me and redirecting Red's attention. "Charlie tells me you were interested in the Witch House? Makes sense now."

Red moved his gaze to Jonathan. "The Witch House is also full of history. More than you know."

"Ghosts, too," Jesse said, clearly trying to lighten the mood. "Got any ghosts here in the bar, Red?"

Red looked at Jesse. "Never make fun of ghosts," he said. "Ghosts have power. And if you're not careful, you'll find yourself on the wrong side of it."

Jesse's eyes went wide. "Uh," he stammered.

Claire put a hand on his arm. "Thanks, Red," she said, standing up. "You know, I just realized how late it is. We better go."

"Yeah," Jesse agreed, pushing his chair back as we all stood up. "It is pretty late."

Red nodded as he watched us collect our things. "Thanks for stopping in. Come back and see us again." Despite the friendliness of the words, the hard look in his eyes made me think he really meant the exact opposite.

"Thanks again for coming to Aunt May's," I offered as I moved away from the table. "And if anyone else comes looking for me, feel free to let me know."

"Will do," he said without moving. I followed Jesse and Claire out the door, Jonathan walking beside me, his hand resting lightly on the center of my back.

Jesse pushed the door open and a cool breeze wafted in, so fresh and clean after the griminess of the bar. I glanced behind me one last time before stepping out into the parking lot.

Red remained standing by the table, hands still folded across his chest, watching us go. His face was an unreadable mask.

I shivered as I ducked through the door, glad to get as far away as possible from that cold, flat gaze.

Chapter 5

"What was that about?" Jesse asked.

After leaving The Lone Man Standing, we all met on the street in front of my house. We leaned against our cars, letting the cool night air cleanse us of the muck and ickiness of the bar. The moon was full, casting a silvery light over us.

"I have no idea," I said. "But it was definitely one of the weirdest nights of my life."

"What I want to know is why Red went out of his way to find you in the first place," Jonathan said, slapping at a mosquito at his neck.

"Right? Why tell me someone is looking for me and then be so vague on the details?" I added.

"Not only that, but it seemed like he didn't even want us there," Jonathan said. "Why find you to tell you someone was looking for you if he didn't want you coming to the bar for more information?"

Claire shivered. "Because he's evil."

We all stared at her. Her skin looked grey in the moonlight. "That's kind of a strong word," Jesse said.

"That place was *definitely* evil," she said flatly. "Every part of it, even the smell. Anyone who chooses to own and work in a place that tainted has to be tainted himself."

"I don't know about evil, but it does have a reputation," Jonathan said. "Drugs and gangs. Even some prostitution."

"Drugs, yes. Prostitution, sure. But gangs? In Redemption? I've never believed that," Jesse said.

"I don't know. After being there, I can see how it would attract gangs," Jonathan said.

"I agree about something being off with the place and with Red," I said, brushing a mosquito off my arm. "Nothing about tonight makes sense. I'm starting to wonder if there was even someone out there looking for me at all, or if it was all some kind of ruse."

"You think?" Jesse asked, slapping both of his arms. "He knew your first name was Charlotte."

"Charlie is a common nickname for Charlotte. It could have been a lucky guess," I said.

"But it would be pretty random for him to say someone was looking for you, considering everything with Alan," Jonathan said.

"Again, it could have been a lucky guess," I said. "Look at my history. I showed up here a few months ago because I got lost, and I ended up buying a house and living here. No matter what the circumstances, it hardly looks like a planned move. So, saying some guy was looking for me is hardly a stretch."

"So you don't think someone is actually looking for you?" Claire asked.

"No, " I said. "It's mostly just a feeling. Both Rosie and Red used practically the same words to describe the guy. Wouldn't they have picked up on different details if it were real? And I just can't picture Alan in that place or growing a mustache and goatee."

"But if no one was looking for you, why would Red come find you?" Jesse asked.

"THAT'S the question," I said. "Why the ruse in the first place?"

"Unless," Jonathan frowned. "Hey, what if this *is* about your house? What if he's trying to drive you out, so he can buy it from you?"

"How would what happened tonight scare Charlie away?" Jesse asked.

"Maybe that wasn't the point," Jonathan said. "Maybe he was just trying to gather intel about Charlie. What better way than to make up a story about someone asking about her and see how she handles it?"

"Right. And then if I show up asking questions, he knows there's maybe something there," I said. "So he's got something to use against me."

Jonathan stared at me. "We played right into his hands," he said. "How could we be such idiots?"

"Well, he's going to find out the joke is on him," Jesse said. "Alan is dead. So there's not much he can use to scare you."

"I wouldn't be too sure," Claire said. "There's something going on. And right now, it feels like we're two steps behind."

We all stared at each other. In the silence, the buzzing of the mosquitos was even more pronounced. Claire slapped her neck.

"We don't have to stand here getting eaten alive," I said. "Let's go in."

"No, I really better go," Claire said. "It's pretty late."

"Yeah, I better go too," Jesse said.

"I'll leave in a minute as well, but could I use your bathroom first?" Jonathan asked.

"Of course," I said, shaking my keys in my hand. "Thanks for coming out tonight."

"Anytime," Jesse said. "Happy to help."

"Hopefully, it was a help," Claire said. "See you tomorrow." She flashed me a quick smile, making it feel like old times again.

I headed up to the house, Jonathan behind me, as Claire and Jesse took off, their headlights dancing on the streets as they both made U-turns. "Are you staying awhile?" I asked Jonathan, as we mounted the porch stairs.

He shook his head. "No, I have to go." His voice was regretful. "But, since I'm here, I want to do a quick search."

Midnight was waiting for us on the porch, his tail swishing impatiently. "I thought you'd be hunting," I said to him. He stared back, his green eyes slowly blinking.

"He *is* 'hunting,'" Jonathan said. "He's making sure that food dish in the kitchen doesn't escape."

I laughed as I unlocked the door. Midnight darted through the moment I opened it, disappearing into the kitchen.

"Do you really think this is still necessary?" I called out as Jonathan went through each room, turning the lights on. "Especially if tonight was just an elaborate hoax?"

"It's even more important if it is a hoax," Jonathan said, his voice muffled as he searched the rooms on the other side of the house. "There's something about all of this that is making me very uneasy. I think we need to be even more careful, not less."

"Okay," I said, heading to the kitchen to boil water for tea. I needed something to chase away the taste of that beer.

I was pouring the water into a cup when Jonathan appeared in the doorway. "All clear?" I asked.

He nodded. "But, make sure you …"

"Lock the door after you," I finished. "Yes sir. Do you want a cup of tea?"

"No, I really need to go. Walk me out?"

I put the kettle down and dried my hands on a towel before following Jonathan back outside and onto the porch where he took me in his arms and kissed me.

"I wish I could stay," he whispered.

"I do too," I whispered back. "Are you absolutely sure you can't?"

"I am." He let go of me and took a step back. The moonlight slashed across his face, making his expression even more grim. "I really don't like you being here alone."

"I know, but you checked everything out," I said. "And I'll lock the door behind me."

"Do it now while I wait," he said.

"Okay, dad," I said, rolling my eyes as I stepped back. He didn't smile back.

"Any trouble, page me. I don't care what time it is."

"I promise," I said as I backed into the house. I locked the door and then moved to the window, pulling back the curtain so I could wave at him.

He waved back, blowing me a kiss, before turning to walk to his car.

I was about to turn away as well so I could get my tea, but instead, I found myself fixated on him as he walked. He seemed so alone, so vulnerable out there. If someone was waiting and watching in the shadows, he would be exposed, maybe even unable to protect himself if that person moved too quickly …

Stop it! With an effort, I pushed those thoughts away. No one was hiding out there, and nothing was out to get us. Everything was fine.

Still, I couldn't tear myself away from the window until I saw Jonathan safely get into his car and drive away. On one hand, I was relieved to see him go.

On the other, I was suddenly aware of how alone I was, too.

Okay, I really had to get myself under control, or I was never going to sleep. I dropped the curtain and headed back to the kitchen, determined to keep my thoughts positive. I was safe and protected. There was nothing for me to worry about.

The kitchen was warm and comforting, the cozy scent of my lavender tea filling the air. Such a contrast from The Lone Man Standing.

Still, I still couldn't quite shake the feeling that I was being watched.

***

"Hold still," Annabelle ordered. She was leaning over me, a makeup brush in her hand. "You want to look your best, don't you?"

"My best for what?" I asked.

"Why, your wedding," Annabelle exclaimed, brushing on the eyeshadow. Her hands shook. "I told you to hold still!"

"Married? I'm not getting married."

"Silly, of course you are." Annabelle laughed, but there was something forced and brittle about it. "Now, sit still so I can finish. He's waiting."

Fear began to bubble up inside me. "Who's 'he'?"

"Your fiancé. Who else?" She bit down on her lip as she focused on brushing more makeup on my face. A drop of blood bloomed on her mouth.

"I don't have a fiancé."

"Of course you do." Annabelle glanced behind her, her movements jerky and nervous. "Stop saying such nonsense. You'll make him mad."

I could barely breathe. A lump of fear lodged in the back of my throat, choking me. "Who?? And why would he get mad? It's the truth."

"Charlotte, stop this." Annabelle's voice was loud. "You're being ridiculous. Now, see how beautiful you are?" She spun me around so I could see myself in the cracked, warped mirror. My hair was a tangled mess below a rotting and decayed veil, and my makeup was a garishly hideous disaster.

Annabelle leaned closer so I could see her face in mirror next to mine. "I have been waiting so long for this day. You'll finally have a husband who will take good care of you, and I can stop worrying."

"You don't need to worry," I said, through lips that resembled a bloody gash across my face. "I can take care of myself."

"Oh, really? Like when you sleep with a married man?" She "tsked" me. "That's not responsible at all."

"It isn't like that," I said.

"It's exactly like that," Annabelle corrected me. "No, what you need is a good, strong man who will keep you in line. One who isn't afraid to correct you when you get out of hand."

"*Correct* me?" I asked, incredulous. "Annabelle, I'm your sister. You should be on my side."

"I am on your side," Annabelle said. "I raised you. I know what you need to be safe. And right now, what you need is …" she spun my chair around so she could lean over and look me directly in my eyes. "… to not make him mad. Do you understand?" Her voice grew more urgent. "You are making him very, very angry right now. And I am begging you to stop."

From somewhere outside the room, I heard a thump. Annabelle's eyes widened. "Oh. That's him. We've run out of time. Remember, whatever you do, don't make him mad."

I awoke with a jerk. The sheets and I were soaked with sweat, and my heart thudded in my ears.

Another wedding dream.

Had I heard something? Is that why I woke up?

I strained to listen, but all I could hear was the harsh sound of my breathing and the pounding of my heart.

I pulled the drenched sheets away from my body and stood up. The light outside was beginning to turn grey and the birds were singing in the trees. Maybe that was all I had heard. Maybe it had nothing to do with that feeling of being watched last night, that someone was out there lurking in the shadows, watching, waiting ...

Behind me, I heard a thump. I let out a strangled scream as I spun around, my heart pounding so hard, I was sure it was going to burst through my chest.

But it was only Midnight, waiting for me by the door with an expectant look.

Of course. It was time for breakfast.

I pulled on a robe and opened the door to head to the kitchen, Midnight padding softly beside me.

The kitchen was filled with soft grey light, so I didn't bother to turn on the lights as I set about getting Midnight his breakfast and heating water for tea. Outside, the grass was heavy with dew. A robin hopped through the lawn searching for worms while a couple of rabbits munched on the leaves and plants in my garden.

My mind turned to the garden. Maybe there was enough time to do a little work in it before I had to get ready for work. Gardening—feeling the rich earth in my fingers—always grounded me. That was probably exactly what I needed to shift my mood after that horrid dream.

But, as I stared out the window watching the world slowly wake up, the uneasiness crept back in. I could almost feel myself being watched.

Which was silly. It was early in the morning. Even if someone had been out there the night before, he surely wouldn't still be there now, at this time.

Regardless, I couldn't shake the feeling. My garden would hold no peace for me.

Sighing, I prepared a cup of tea and then wandered through the house. As I passed through the family room, I noticed the blinking light on my answering machine.

Hadn't I checked it yesterday? I thought back over my day and realized I hadn't. I had been so rushed after work to get ready to go to The Lone Man Standing, and I was too tired when I got home.

I pushed "play." The first message was from Nancy, asking me when I was going to bring her tea. Crap. I had forgotten to do that, too. I made a mental note to swing by before work.

The second was from a woman named Pat who had apparently been a customer of Helen's and had heard from Nancy I was starting the tea business up again. She wanted to buy some tea.

It was too early to call her back, but that didn't mean I couldn't look through my files to see what I could do.

I went to my upstairs office to find Pat's file as well as see if any of Helen's leftover herbs and flowers would work for her tea while I cultivated fresh ingredients.

Helen had left me quite a number of glass jars filled with various dried plants. She had retrofitted the closet with rows and rows of metal shelves, and they were all crammed with jars. While everything was carefully labeled, as far as I could tell, there was no rhyme or reason to her organization. I had been meaning to go through the jars and put them in a better order, maybe alphabetically to start, which would also give me a better idea of what I had to work with.

It seemed as good a time as ever to do it.

It was a dusty job. I took all the jars out, cleaned them off, and examined them before replacing them in a more organized fashion. I lost track of time as I worked, studying the different ingredients, smelling them, and getting to know them. Then, I located a small glass jar tucked in a corner, far back on the shelf.

I reached in to pull it out, wondering if it had fallen off at some point and Helen had just forgotten about it when I saw the label.

Hemlock.

Stupidly, I stared at the jar. Hemlock? Wasn't that a poison? I seemed to recall someone famous dying from it. Was it Aristotle? Socrates?

I got up to find my plant identification reference book, flipping through the pages to locate the entry.

Hemlock. Grows like a weed in nearly every state in the U.S. in addition to Canada. Very toxic. No antidote.

I studied the jar, feeling a faint sense of foreboding tickling the back of my neck.

Why did Helen have an incredibly toxic poison in her tea closet?

I turned it over in my hands, examining it. I knew I should get rid of it. Throw it away immediately. There was no reason to have it. What if it accidentally got mixed into a tea I made for someone? That would be horrible.

The smart thing to do would be to toss it in the garbage right then and there, being careful to bury it underneath the other trash so no one would accidently find it. It's not like I would ever want to poison anyone. I would never have a use for it.

Right?

Instead, despite the logical voice of my mind, I shoved it back in the corner of the closet. *It wasn't going anywhere,* I reasoned. *I could always get rid of it later.*

Besides, how much harm could it do hidden in the corner of the closet? It was clearly labeled. Plus, the jar was much smaller than the others. There was no way I'd accidentally mix it up with something else.

I wanted to do more research. After all, Helen had it for a reason. Maybe there was some sort of health benefit. Maybe in a very small dose, it could do some good. There were poisons out there like that. A tiny dose could actually be a good thing in certain cases.

In the meantime, I went back to my cleaning and organizing. I didn't have a lot of time before I had to get ready for work, and I wanted to make sure everything was put back and in order before I left.

The Reckoning

Chapter 6

"Charlie!" Nancy poked her head out of the kitchen and gave me a big smile and a warm wave. "Give me a moment. I'll be right with you."

The little log cabin hotel was as charming as I remembered it with its warm polished wood, colorful rugs, and cozy furnishings. The air smelled like coffee and fresh baked zucchini muffins, and I could see a few guests finishing up their breakfast in the side room. My stomach rumbled. Normally, I wasn't much of a breakfast eater, but being there reminded me of how good Nancy's baking was. Also, now that I thought about it, I realized I had only eaten about half my dinner before leaving for The Lone Man Standing.

As soon as the thought occurred, Nancy appeared from the kitchen, a muffin wrapped in a napkin in one hand. She limped toward me. "I'm so glad you were able to stop by."

I held up the little brown paper bag full of tea. "I'm so sorry I didn't drop it off yesterday."

Nancy waved her hand. "Nonsense. I know how busy you are with the new house and working at Aunt May's. I'm just glad you're getting things started again. Did Pat call you?"

"She did. I'm working on her order, as well."

"Good to hear." Nancy handed me a muffin. "Here, I brought you one for the road."

"Oh, you didn't have to do that," I said as I accepted it. Even through the napkin, I could feel how warm it still was.

"Of course I did." Nancy winked at me. "I couldn't have you stop by during breakfast without giving you a muffin."

"Well, thank you," I said, watching Nancy wince as she rubbed her leg. "What's going on?"

Nancy sighed. "Just my arthritis acting up. It's in my knee. It was particularly bad this morning."

"I don't remember it being that bad when I stayed here."

"It comes and goes. It always gets worse when the seasons change, or when a storm is coming."

A storm is coming. Beware.

I pushed away the thought and glanced out the window. The sun peeked out from behind a white fluffy cloud in a bright, blue sky. "It sure doesn't look like there's a storm coming."

Nancy grimaced. "Oh, there's one coming alright. My knee never lies. Probably won't happen until tonight. So, what do I owe you?"

"You already paid," I held up the muffin.

Nancy waved her hand. "Oh, pish posh. I need to give you actual money. How much?"

"Try it first. I want to make sure what I did is what you remember. If it is, then you can pay. Sound like a deal?"

"A little too good of a deal, but okay," Nancy said. "I'll let you know."

I waved goodbye and headed out the door. A gentle breeze carrying the scents of pine trees and cut grass greeted me as I stepped outside. I paused to look around and breathe in the cool, humid air.

Nancy's knee was probably wrong this time. It didn't look at all like it was going to storm.

As beautiful as the day was, something prickled at the back of my neck, making my hair stand on end.

It felt like I was being watched. Again.

I whirled around, but no one was there.

I was alone except for a few cars in the parking lot and a dark sedan parked on the street.

Everything is fine, I told myself as I started to make my way to my car in the parking lot. *I'm safe and protected. I'm not being followed or watched.*

Or am I?

I paused halfway to the parking lot and turned to stare at the sedan in the street. Why would someone park that car in the street when there was a perfectly good parking lot?

Maybe the driver wasn't going to the hotel, I reasoned. *Maybe he had business elsewhere.*

Except, where? The hotel was located off the main block, which was where all the businesses were located, and there were certainly much closer places the driver could have parked.

Maybe he wanted to walk, I told myself. There was no crime in parking far away. Maybe he was trying to be healthier and exercise more.

Maybe.

I studied the car, trying to remember if it was there when I arrived. I didn't think so. No, I was pretty sure it wasn't. I would have passed it as I pulled in. I was sure I would have remembered it.

I wondered if I should walk over and check it out. Just to make sure it was empty. Maybe even write the license plate number down.

Just to be sure.

But what if it wasn't empty? What if there WAS someone still inside, hiding in the front where I couldn't see him? What if he was waiting for me to get closer to the car so he could leap out and grab me?

I spun around on my heel and headed to my car, my hands trembling as I pulled out my keys. *I'm being silly,* I told myself. There was no one in that car. There was no one following me.

Still, my hands shook so hard, I dropped the keys twice before I made it to the car. I fumbled a third time with them before I was finally able to unlock the door, nearly diving inside.

I sat there for a moment, breathing hard, trying to slow down my heart rate before turning on the ignition. I kept staring at the parked car, trying to see if there was any movement inside.

It appeared empty. Just a car parked on the side of the road. No big deal.

I wondered if I was losing my mind.

I was still holding the muffin Nancy had given me, and miracle of miracle, it was still in one piece. Even though my stomach was churning unpleasantly, I forced myself to eat it.

Not only would some nourishment make me feel better and help keep my energy up through my shift, but it gave me an excuse to sit there and collect my thoughts, which had shifted to the dream I'd had that morning.

It was only a dream, I told myself. It did not mean that Alan was alive. It did not mean I was being followed or watched or anything else. It had nothing to do with that car parked on the street.

There were more than enough strange things going on in Redemption. I hardly needed to invent a stalker. What I really needed to do was calm down and be observant. Just keep an eye on things. No need to panic. Just be watchful and aware.

I popped the last bite of the muffin in my mouth, already feeling much better, and started the car. I slowly drove out of the parking lot, and even though I tried to keep my eyes focused on the road, they kept darting back to the parked car, as if by their own volition.

Nothing moved. It looked empty.

I turned onto the street and drove to work.

***

"What did you mean yesterday when you said you thought we unleashed something with that séance?" I quietly asked Claire. We were standing behind the counter during a lull—that short window of time between breakfast and lunch.

She gave me a sharp look. "Why?"

"Because I feel like I'm being watched."

Claire's hand trembled slightly, and she put her coffee cup down. She didn't look well. Her face was drawn and pale, and she had rings of dark purple under her eyes. I wondered if she had slept at all. Since she had been at Aunt May's, she had been drinking coffee nonstop, which wasn't like her at all. "Who do you think is watching you?"

"I don't know." I glanced around the diner, but everyone seemed to be enjoying their food and not in need of anything. "I did have this dreadful dream last night about Alan, but I'm still not convinced he is hanging around The Lone Man Standing."

Claire looked longingly at her coffee cup but didn't pick it up. "What kind of dream?"

"A creepy getting-married dream." I shivered. "At least, I'm assuming it was him. I never actually saw him in it."

"Do you think someone is following you?"

"I'm not sure." I gave her a quick summary of the car parked in front of the Redemption Hotel. Her face turned grim as she listened.

"What do you think it means?" I asked, trying not to become alarmed at her expression. "Should I be worried?"

She shook her head. "Honestly, Charlie, I don't know what's going on. Everything is such ..." She sighed and ran her hands through her hair. "I just have a terrible feeling that something awful is about to happen, and there's nothing I can do to stop it."

My stomach clenched and my chest felt tight. Too tight. I couldn't breathe. "What do you think I should do?"

She looked up a me, her eyes haunted. "I have no idea."

"Charlie! How's my favorite waitress?" Chester was striding through the diner, heading to his usual spot at the counter, a big grin on his face. I gave him a tight smile in return, automatically reaching for the pot of coffee and a cup.

"Hanging in there," I said. "Want the usual?"

"You read my mind," he said, plopping onto the stool and picking up his coffee. I wrote down "toasted ham and cheese with fries" and slipped the ticket to the kitchen.

"Do you have any idea who might be looking for you?" Chester asked as he slurped his coffee.

I froze, my hand still on the ticket. "Why do you think someone is looking for me?" I asked, trying to keep my voice normal.

"You know, what Red was talking about yesterday," he answered.

I spun around, unable to believe I had completely forgotten that Chester had been there. He wasn't paying any attention to me, but instead was gazing around the diner.

"No, I'm not sure what Red was talking about," I said, making sure to keep my voice casual. "What do you know about Red, anyway?"

He frowned. "He's a strange one."

I could feel my heartbeat quicken. "Strange how?"

"He gets obsessed with things and just can't let go. Like how that bar has been around since 1887. Or how Helen wouldn't sell the Witch House to him." Chester rolled his eyes. "I just got sick of his rantings and quit going." He paused and took a second look at me. "Hey, you own the Witch House now. Did he try to buy it from you yet?"

"Not yet." My heart was pounding so loud, I was sure Chester could hear it. *Was* this whole thing nothing more than a big ruse to scare me, so Red could buy my house? While I would of course be relieved if Alan wasn't really alive and skulking around Redemption, was this alternative scenario any better? Having a flesh-and-blood person stalking me and making up stories to get me out of my home? Not only that, but I had no idea how far he would go.

"Just wait," Chester said darkly. "That's another of his obsessions—collecting things from around 1887 and 1888. You know, when all the adults disappeared? You heard the story, right?"

"Yep," I answered, topping off his coffee.

"Have no idea why," Chester grumbled. "It was a hundred years ago, for goodness sake."

"Do you think Red is violent?"

Chester's fuzzy eyebrows went straight up his forehead. "Why would you ask that?"

Inwardly, I cursed myself. I probably could have been a little more subtle. "Just what you say about him wanting to buy my house. Do you think he'd do anything, well, violent to get me to sell?"

"Nah. He would never do that," Chester said, dismissing it. "Although," he continued, eyebrows furrowing. "There was that unpleasantness a while back."

Alarm bells started going off in my head. "What 'unpleasantness'?"

"Let me think." He pursed his lips, frowning slightly. Behind me, I heard the bright "ding" signaling an order was up.

"I'll be right back," I said, hoping it was Chester's order. My delivering it would give me an excuse to stand there a few more minutes. It was.

Chester brightened when he saw the food, immediately reaching for the ketchup I placed on the table. "Now I remember. Some guy came in making a big stink. Claimed Red's family stole that bar because he was the one who owned it."

"Was it true?"

Chester shrugged. "Haven't a clue. Records back then weren't what they are today. Add to that all the adults disappearing, and who knows who owned what."

"So, what happened?"

"Nothing." Chester picked up his sandwich and took a big bite.

"Nothing?"

Chester shook his head and swallowed. "Well, this guy claimed he had proof or something, and was threatening to take Red to court. And then, he just disappeared."

The alarm bells turned into a roar inside my head. "Disappeared?"

"Yeah. I don't know if he just left or what. One day he was here making all sorts of commotion, and the next, he vanished." Chester put his sandwich down as his expression turned contemplative. "Now that you mention it, I always did think Red had something to do with it."

"What do you think he did?"

"Nothing illegal," Chester said hastily, no doubt concerned by the expression on my face. "Well, maybe barely illegal. That place certainly skirts a fine line. I was just thinking he threatened him or something. Not that he would actually do anything, mind you."

"Charlie." Fred was gesturing to me from the kitchen. I held up a finger.

"So, do you think I should be worried about him or not?"

"I don't think so. You're not trying to take his bar away. And nothing happened to Helen." But still, his face looked troubled.

I headed off to the kitchen where Fred glared at me through a cloud of steam. "A little help back here, if you have a moment?"

"Right," I said, moving briskly. But inside, I kept turning Chester's words over and over in my head.

Someone wanted Red's bar. He supposedly had proof. He disappeared.

Red had made a point of finding me and telling me a story that would lure me to his bar.

What did it all mean?

And, more importantly, should I be worried?

Chapter 7

I could hear the phone ringing the moment I walked into the house. I kicked the door shut behind me and hurried to the kitchen, my arms juggling two grocery bags full of food.

"I'm coming," I muttered, propping the bags onto the counter so I could reach for the phone. "Don't hang up on me now."

"It's me," Jonathan said.

"Oh, I was going to call you," I said, tucking the receiver between my ear and shoulder so I could start unpacking the bags. "I have a steak and a bottle of red wine with your name on it. When did you think you could get here?"

"That's why I'm calling," he said, his tone regretful. "I can't tonight."

"Oh," I said, trying not to sound too disappointed. "Is there a problem?"

"No problem. There's some event at Darrel's school, and I promised Felicity I would go."

"Oh, of course you have to do that," I said, already feeling the loneliness of the night stretching out in front of me. "I'll save it for another evening."

He heaved a sigh. "I know, it's not that. I just really hate leaving you all alone right now."

"I'll be fine," I said, trying to sound more optimistic than I felt. I was definitely feeling out of sorts after everything that had happened earlier—Chester's story, the sedan on the street. I told myself I was being silly. The sedan was probably my imagination running wild after that creepy dream, and the chances of Red doing something tonight were pretty much nonexistent. As much as I wanted to tell Jonathan about all of it over a nice dinner, there was really no immediate need to. It could wait.

Of course, I also wanted to see him just to see him.

"If anything happens at all, page me," Jonathan said.

"I will."

"I mean it. Even if it turns out to be nothing, call me anyway. I don't mind making sure."

"I promise. But I'm sure nothing will happen."

He heaved a deep sigh. "I'm sure you're right. I'll call you tomorrow."

I hung up and finished putting away the groceries as I thought about what I wanted for dinner. Maybe something simple, like grilled chicken and a salad.

I was so engrossed in my thoughts, I almost stepped on Midnight. He let out a loud meow, swishing his tail and giving me a dirty look.

"Midnight, what are you doing in here? Didn't I let you out this morning?"

The cat fixed his jade-green eyes on mine, like he was trying to tell me something.

I thought back to the morning. Yes, I remembered trying to balance opening the door with holding my purse, keys, and tea for Nancy as Midnight darted beneath my legs, almost knocking me over.

So, if I *had* let him out, how had he gotten back in?

An uneasy sense of foreboding crept up my spine. Had I left a window open? Or had he come in just now as I opened the door? It's possible I hadn't noticed, being so focused on getting the phone.

I wandered over to the front door, just to check, and felt my heart stop in my chest.

It was wide open.

How did that happen? I remembered kicking it shut with my foot.

Or did I? Maybe I hadn't kicked it hard enough.

I went over to take a closer look. Outside, the wind was starting to pick up, and the sky was turning that mustard grey as deep purple clouds crawled across it. Nancy was right ... a storm appeared to be brewing.

A storm is coming. Beware.

I shivered and stepped out onto the porch to look around. The street was empty. No cars, no people. Totally normal.

I stepped back in and closed and locked the door firmly. The chance of someone coming by and seeing the open door, then sneaking in during the few minutes I was on the phone and putting groceries away was basically nonexistent.

Right?

The hair on the back of my neck bristled. I turned to look around the living room. It appeared the same as always. I walked around the downstairs, peering in closets and corners before going upstairs and doing the same.

The house was empty. It was just me and Midnight.

Still, a part of me itched to call Jonathan. Just have him swing over and do a quick search ...

No, I didn't need to do that. I checked the place myself. No one was hiding in my home.

I headed back to the kitchen to make myself a cup of tea and start dinner, even though I had lost my appetite. I needed to eat. That was probably why I was feeling so anxious.

Despite my inner pep talk, it still took me a long time to even begin to relax.

***

"How could you?" Annabelle hissed as she glared at me, pacing back and forth in the small, bare room we were in. "How could you do this to us?"

"Do what?" I asked. "What's happening?"

Annabelle clutched at her hair, which was up in a very messy and greasy bun. "Why couldn't you just go along? Why did you have to make him angry?"

"Make who angry?"

Annabelle didn't answer, just muttered to herself as she pulled at her hair and continued her nervous pacing. She wore a pale-pink taffeta dress that was stained and torn.

A pale-pink taffeta dress.

A bridesmaid's dress.

From a distance, I heard a thumping sound.

"What's going on?" I asked warily.

"You never think about anyone but yourself," Annabelle moaned. "And now you've ruined us all."

Another thump.

"Annabelle, what is going on?" I demanded.

"If you just followed the rules, none of this would have happened."

Thump. It was getting closer. And louder.

"Annabelle," I snapped. "What is happening?"

Thump.

Annabelle whirled around. "What do you think?" she shrieked. "You were supposed to get married. You were supposed to do the right thing. The smart thing. And now ..." her voice broke, and she sank to the floor, curling up into a tiny ball. "You've doomed us all."

Thump.

It was right outside the door. The noise was so loud, the door shuddered and shook in its frame. I jumped back, trying to get as far away as possible.

"Who is on the other side of the door?"

Annabelle turned to me. Her makeup was smeared down her face and clumps of oily hair had fallen out of her head. "Does it matter?" she asked, her voice barely audible, a whisper through lips colored blood red. "He's going to kill us all, now. And it's your fault."

Crash.

I woke with a scream.

Someone was in the house.

I leaped out of bed, pressing my back against the wall, trying to look everywhere at once. Was someone in the room with me? The shapes of the bureau and dresser mocked me. Was someone hiding in the shadows?

What about the bathroom? I tried peering out of the open door, but I couldn't see much other than the countertop, the side of the toilet, and the shower. Was there someone there? Hiding behind the shower curtain or behind the door? I couldn't tell, and I was too terrified to move any closer.

Desperately, I tried to quiet my panicked breathing so I could better listen. But all I could hear was my heart pounding, the blood rushing in my ears, and the rain falling outside.

Wait a minute. Rain?

A bolt of lightning lit the room, revealing no one. Then, a boom of thunder.

Was that the thumping and crashing I had heard in my dream? Thunder?

The windows were open, and the wind blew the curtains around, sending in sprays of water. It had been nice and cool the night before, which is why I opened the windows. But now, the rain was coming in.

I rubbed my chest, trying to slow my heart rate before partly closing the windows. One was stuck, and I had to yank it hard before I got it to move. The floor was a little damp, but not too bad. I glanced at the bathroom door, my heart still fluttering anxiously in my chest like a trapped bird, but it appeared empty. I grabbed a towel to mop up the floor.

Feeling a little foolish, I sat on the edge of the bed, still trying to collect myself. Maybe a cup of tea would help me relax so I could go back to sleep.

I looked at the closed door to the bedroom. Did I really want to go down the stairs? Was I absolutely convinced the house was empty?

Of course it was. It must have been thunder I heard.

Right?

The longer I sat there, the more uneasy I felt. Could I really be sure the house was empty? I kept remembering the open front door. Was I absolutely *sure* no one had snuck in?

God, I wanted to call Jonathan. He wouldn't mind. In fact, he would probably insist.

I gazed longingly at the phone. If I called and there was no one in the house, I would feel silly.

But if there was someone inside ...

Of course, in that scenario, who I really ought to call was the cops. But then I would feel even more stupid if there was no one.

Maybe I should just get my act together and go down and check out the house myself.

I was just about to get up to do that when I heard it.

A creak.

Downstairs.

Like from a footstep on the floorboards.

I froze. At that moment, lightning flashed and thunder boomed, making me jump.

I snatched up the phone and dialed Jonathan's pager number. I no longer cared how stupid I would feel if there wasn't anyone to be found. There was no way I was going downstairs until I knew for sure no one was there.

I punched in the first four numbers of my address. That was our agreed-upon code if I needed him to come over.

Dropping the phone back in the cradle, I pressed myself against the wall close to one of the open windows, so I could hear the engine of his car when he arrived. My eyes refused to leave the bedroom door. Jonathan would come soon. He was probably throwing his clothes on and grabbing his keys at that very moment.

In ten minutes or less, he would be running up the porch.

I only had to wait ten minutes.

Every one felt like an eternity.

I stared at the door, sweat trickling down my back, straining my ears for any other sounds, like a footstep. Or the clicking of the doorknob twisting ...

Enough of that. If I kept it up, I'd likely hyperventilate and lose my mind. What I really needed to do was think. I was trapped in my bedroom, and there may or may not be someone in the house. Jonathan was on his way.

I needed a weapon.

But, what? I looked wildly around my room, but all I saw were clothes, jewelry, and books. I supposed I could throw a hardcover book at someone. I picked up the Sidney Sheldon book I was reading and felt the weight. Not very substantial. I longed for a knife. Or even a bat. Either would work.

My eyes fell onto the lamp next to my bed. It was made of brass and had a heavy base. Without taking my eyes off the door, I reached out to unplug it, then wrapped the cord around it and removed the lampshade.

If I held it upside down, it was sort of like a bat. It could work. Not the best weapon, but it would do in a pinch.

I already felt much better holding the lamp. Not nearly as vulnerable as before. Plus, Jonathan would arrive any minute. Maybe he was making the turn down my street even as I thought it.

Any minute.

Any minute.

While it was likely only a few minutes later, it seemed like another eternity passed before I saw the flash of headlights in the yard and heard the roar of a car.

The relief that rushed through me was so intense, my knees buckled, and I sagged against the wall.

In just a few more minutes, everything would be fine.

I heard the engine cut off and the slam of the car door. He was probably running up the steps now, key turning in the lock, coming into the house, and any minute, he would call my name.

Bang. Thud.

Silence.

Every nerve in my body fired at once, jolting me into an upright position.

What just happened? Did Jonathan trip?

I strained my ears, waiting to hear something, anything. Jonathan calling for me. His feet running up the stairs, laughing about how clumsy he was.

I heard nothing.

The silence was deafening.

Sweat dripped down my body, soaking the thin tee shirt I slept in. Now what?

Maybe I'd better call the cops.

I reached out a trembling hand to pick up the phone.

No dial tone.

I nearly dropped the receiver as I reached over to frantically click the button, trying to get it to work.

The phone was dead.

Panic was welling up inside me like a trapped animal, clawing at my chest, my throat. It was all I could do to keep myself from screaming.

Who was in the house?

I was going to have to go downstairs. There was no way I was going to stay cowering in my room like a terrified mouse, waiting for whoever was there to come up and find me.

Besides, I had to find out what happened to Jonathan.

It took every ounce of my energy to peel myself from the wall and creep across the floor. My knees were like Jello. I wasn't even sure they would hold me up.

I grasped the doorknob and turned it, half expecting it to be stuck or blocked somehow, but it turned easily in my sweaty palm.

I opened the door, convinced there would be someone there, some dark shape, maybe even grinning at me, but there was no one. The hallway was empty. Everything was quiet, almost like the house itself was holding its breath.

I had no choice. I was going to have to walk down that long hallway in order to reach the stairs.

Slowly, I took a step outside the room, and then another. My slow creep down the hall that seemed to stretch and grow like something out of a fun house felt like forever.

I didn't think I was ever going to reach the end.

Finally, I found myself at the top of the steps.

I peered down, trying to see something ... anything. All was dark and quiet.

I was going to have to go down.

Carefully, I eased down each step, clutching my lamp and pausing to look around, but nothing happened. I kept straining my ears to hear something, but there was nothing other than my gasping breath and pounding heart. The lamp was slick with sweat and slid in my grip. I wondered if I would even be able to use to it should the time come.

I desperately wanted to call out for Jonathan, wanting so badly to hear his voice, to know he was okay, but I knew I had to keep my mouth shut. Maybe it was just a burglar, and Jonathan had surprised him. Maybe he had decided to make a run for it, and Jonathan was out chasing him. Or maybe Jonathan tripped and fell and hit his head, which is why he was so quiet. Once I got downstairs and turned on the light, I would find him in the center of the living room, perfectly fine, and we would laugh and laugh and laugh.

The living room light clicked on, causing me to scream and drop the lamp. The sound of thunder crashed across the living room.

"Hello, Charlotte."

It was Alan.

The Reckoning

Chapter 8

He had positioned one of the kitchen chairs against the front window and was seated there watching me. His face was thinner than I remembered, his hair darker and longer, but no mustache or goatee. He wore a black tee shirt and black jeans and had his legs crossed, his ankle on his knee. He looked relaxed and in total control.

"Come sit," he said, waving his hand invitingly.

I didn't move. "You're supposed to be dead," I said, my voice hoarse.

He laughed. "The reports of my death are greatly exaggerated," he said. "As you can see, I'm very much alive. Come and sit down, Charlotte. We have a lot to talk about."

"I'm not interested in talking to you," I said, trying to sound stronger and more intimidating than I felt. "I think you should leave."

He sighed. "Don't be like that, Charlotte." He held up his other hand, which is when I saw it.

He was holding a gun.

All my blood seemed to drain from my body. My knees shook, and I was afraid I would topple over. I tried to lick my lips, but my mouth was dry and parched.

"Sit down, Charlotte," he said. His voice was still calm, but his eyes had changed. All the humanity had drained from them, transforming them into shark eyes—flat, cold, and hard.

I swallowed hard, willing myself to move. My legs felt weak and wobbly, and I didn't even have my pathetic weapon anymore as it was now lying on the ground. Not that I thought it really would have done any good, anyhow. Yet not having it made me feel even more naked and vulnerable.

It was all I could do to make my way to the couch. I was sure my knees were going to buckle, and I would fall to the ground, helpless to whatever Alan wanted to do. It wasn't until after I had collapsed on the couch that I saw Jonathan.

He was lying in a crumpled heap on the floor at Alan's feet, not moving. I gasped and started to go to him, but Alan made a loud "tsking" sound, waving the gun at me.

"None of that," he said. "You and I need to talk. Your lover has nothing to do with this."

"What did you do to him?" I couldn't tear my gaze away from Jonathan, desperately trying to pick up on any sign of life. What if he was dead? What if he was dead, and I was the one who killed him, because I had called him? I started to hyperventilate again. How could I have been so stupid? I should have called the police while I had the chance.

Alan shrugged. "I defended myself. What do you think?"

I thought I could detect a slight movement of Jonathan's chest, and relief flooded over me. I closed my eyes briefly. "He needs to go to the hospital."

"He needs no such thing," Alan said. "He's fine right where he is."

I finally focused my gaze completely on Alan. "What do you want? Why are you here?"

"What do you mean, why am I here?" He seemed genuinely perplexed. "You're my fiancé. I'm here to bring you home."

"This *is* my home," I said. "And I'm not your fiancé. We broke up, remember?"

"No, we didn't," he said. "I never agreed to that."

"I don't care what you agreed to," I said, my fear turning to anger despite the small voice inside me warning me to not let my emotions get the better of me. "I don't want to marry you anymore."

"You just have cold feet," he said. "It's common. Once we're married, you'll realize how foolish you're being."

I ground my teeth. "It is *not* cold feet," I said. "I ran away from New York to get away from you."

"And I forgive you for that," he said.

He was insufferable. And delusional. My anger was growing so fast I could barely see, but I knew I had to stay in control. He would win if I didn't keep myself together. "How did you even find me?" I asked abruptly, trying to give myself time and space to get ahold of myself.

"Your sister."

My eyes widened. "Annabelle told you?" So much for trying to calm down. My blood pressure was immediately through the roof.

He laughed softly. "Not exactly."

He was enjoying this. Enjoying how upset I was. I tried to will myself to relax. "How exactly?"

"She told me she wired you money, although she wouldn't say where. But the paperwork was on her desk, just lying out there in the open. I didn't even have to search for it." He shook his head, his smile like that of a father patronizing a dimwitted child. "She had written the city and state right there."

"Then why didn't you just come find me?" I asked. "Why did you pretend to be dead?"

"Isn't it obvious? I knew you were going to disappear the moment you got your car back. You had your sister fooled. She thought you were coming home. But I knew. And if you left Redemption, it was going to be a lot more difficult to trace where you went. I figured you would be smarter in the future and not call her to wire you money. Of course, she probably wouldn't send you any again, anyhow. But still. It would take a lot more time and money to find you a second time. So, what could I do to keep you from running? Have you think I was dead."

"But there was a body in your car," I said. "Who was it?"

He shrugged again. "Some homeless guy I picked up. He looked enough like me to pass. I offered him money and drugs if he was willing to go for a drive with me."

"You *killed* someone?" I asked aghast.

He waved his hand. "He was a druggie. He would have been dead within the year, and probably in a lot more painful way than what I did. It was quick and painless."

"Being burnt alive in a car is hardly quick and painless."

"He was dead before the car went over," Alan said. "I knocked him out. He didn't see it coming. Then I put a bag over his head. Fast and simple. Once he was dead, it was easy to position him in the driver's seat and send the car over the ledge."

I was horrified. This was the man I wanted to marry and spend the rest of my life with, to have a family with. And there he was, talking about killing a man as if it were no more difficult than squashing a bug.

"How could you do that?" The question was out of my mouth before I could consider the wisdom of challenging him.

"I needed a body," he explained, even though that wasn't what I'd meant. "Otherwise, there would always be questions about my death. I needed to make sure there were no loose ends, so you would feel safe. Then, you wouldn't disappear."

His voice was calm and even, like he was merely recapping his day. Only his eyes betrayed the monster inside him.

In that moment, I knew I would not be leaving the house alive with him. What would be the point? Eventually, he would kill me anyway, and it would likely be a long, slow, painful process. At least if he killed me then and there, it would be fast.

It was either him or me. No other choice.

"Still, it was quite a gamble," I said, my voice just as clear and even as Alan's. I was surprised at how calm I was after making such a decision. Instead of dissolving into a mess, I sat up straighter and folded my hands, which had stopped shaking, onto my lap. It was almost like we were having a friendly, if not slightly dull, conversation. "I could have left Redemption. There were no guarantees I would stay."

"No," he agreed. "But I figured odds were you would either stay here or go back to New York. So I waited to see what you would do." His eyes narrowed and he frowned at me disapprovingly. "I had no idea what a whore you would turn out to be."

"How do you know what I've been doing?" I asked. "Have you been watching me? Like some sort of Peeping Tom?"

His eyes narrowed slightly. A vein jumped in his forehead. "I have every right to watch my fiancé," he said, his tone not betraying the fact that my barb had hit home. "And yes, I have been watching you and your whorish acts for a few weeks now. I even knew you'd call *him* to come rescue you, which is exactly what I wanted, so I could deal with both of you. Frankly, Charlotte, I'm quite disappointed in your behavior."

"Is that so?" I asked, sounding bored even as my fingers dug painfully into my palms. How could I have done this to Jonathan? I should have called the police. "Unfortunately for you, I really don't care."

"Oh, you will," Alan said as a slow, evil smile spread across his face. "You most definitely will."

"Why is that?" I asked. "Because you're going to hurt me? Torture me?"

His smile turned pained. "Charlotte, I never *want* to hurt you. Don't you understand how you make me do it? These decisions you make—you leave me no choice. First, you run off and disappear, completely embarrassing me, and then you sleep with this ..." Alan kicked Jonathan with his foot, causing Jonathan's body to jerk. It was all I could do to not show my distress. "This bastard, and you don't understand how that makes you a whore? You're still my fiancé! You've turned into a cheater and a whore. What I'm doing now is for your own good."

"I'll say it one more time, real slow so you understand," I said, leaning forward slightly. "I am NOT your fiancé. We are NOT engaged. And besides," I sat back and gave him a sweet smile. "I'd rather be his whore than your wife."

Alan got very still. The vein began pulsing in his forehead again as his hands began clenching and unclenching. For a moment, I faltered. I was sure I had pushed him too far ... that he was going to raise the gun and shoot me. He closed his eyes and took several deep breaths in and out before opening them again. He smiled at me, an empty smile that made my skin crawl. "You little bitch," he said. "I changed my mind. I'm going to enjoy disciplining you now."

A slight movement caught my eye. Jonathan stirred slightly. Was he awake? Oh, dear Lord, let him be okay.

I didn't want to look away, but I also didn't want Alan to notice, so I forced myself to make eye contact with him. "I'm not going anywhere with you," I said.

Alan's smile widened. "Oh, but you will. Did you forget this?" He held up the gun.

"I have not," I said. "But that changes nothing."

Alan raised his eyebrows. "It changes nothing? I find that hard to believe."

I shrugged. "Quite honestly, I don't care what you believe or don't believe. I'm not going with you."

Alan cocked his head and studied me for a moment. Then he slowly raised the gun and pointed it at me.

I flinched even though I tried not to. He smiled slightly. "Not so brave, eh?"

"Bravery has nothing to do with it," I said, and met his gaze. "I'm still not going with you."

He stared at me for a moment, then nodded. "I think you might even mean that," he said. "And I almost admire your courage. But I wonder if you'll still be so brave if I do this?" He tilted his hand, pointing the gun at Jonathan.

I sucked in my breath. "Leave him alone. He has nothing to do with this."

"Oh, I disagree. I think the man screwing my fiancé has very much to do with this."

"This is between me and you," I said. "Not him."

"Does that mean you'll come with me?"

Jonathan's eyes fluttered, one eye opening a crack and peering at me before closing again. *He's alive.* I swallowed hard, trying to hide my joy. "Only if you promise not to kill him."

Alan's lips stretched into a triumphant smile, although his eyes remained cold and flat as stones. "Great. I'm glad we got that settled. Now come over here and give your fiancé a kiss."

I didn't move. "I'd rather you come here."

His smiled dimmed and he shook the gun. "Remember your promise."

"*Our* promise," I corrected. "And if you shoot him, I'm not going anywhere with you."

He paused for a moment, frowning slightly before his expression cleared. "All right, Charlotte. I'll do that for you. But first, I have to do one thing." He shifted forward slightly and raised his gun hand over his head.

Realizing what he was going to do, I screamed, "Jonathan, watch out!" as Alan slammed his hand down toward Jonathan's head.

At the last second, Jonathan rolled, running into Alan's legs. Alan was already off balance and in an awkward position leaning over the way he was, so the collision caused him to tumble out of the chair, the gun going off with a loud "bang."

Someone screamed, I think it was me, and then everything got very confusing. Jonathan sprang to his feet and punched Alan before going for the gun, and Alan tried to wrestle Jonathan to the ground. There was a lot of grappling and fighting, and with both on the floor again and Alan on top, it looked like he had the upper hand.

Without thinking, I grabbed a heavy vase from one of the end tables and swung it at Alan's head. Alan saw it coming and ducked, but it glanced off his shoulder, jarring the gun from his hand.

Jonathan made a grab for the gun at the same time Alan did. Both men fought for it, grunting and gasping ...

Bang.

My hands flew up to my mouth, my eyes wide with horror, as I saw the dark-red blood spread across Jonathan's chest. "Jonathan, oh my God ..."

Alan slumped over, and Jonathan pushed him off. "I'm okay," he said, scrambling to his feet and reaching for me, his hands slick with blood. "I'm okay. I'm okay."

I felt his arms circle around me as I clutched at him, burying my face into his shoulder as I let go and the tears fell. He held me, rocking me slightly and stroking my hair as I sobbed, whispering into my ear how everything was going to be okay.

As I slowly got myself under control, it began to occur to me that while both of us were alive and Alan would never be a problem again, I now had a different problem.

A much, much worse one.

I sat back. Jonathan's shirt was stained with tears and blood. I was covered with blood. Even more blood was pooling on the floor.

And Alan's dead body lay sprawled in the middle of it.

I raised my eyes to Jonathan's, as the same realization dawned on him.

"What have we done?"

Chapter 9

"We have to call the police," I said. "Except the phone doesn't work. He did something to it."

Jonathan was shaking his head. "I don't think we should call the police."

"Why not? It was self-defense. He was in my home. He had a gun. I'll just say I struggled with him and it went off. It was an accident."

Jonathan's face was ashen beneath streaks of blood. I could see swelling on his temple where a lump was starting to form. "It's my gun."

I blinked. "What? You have a gun?"

"I wasn't going to come in here unarmed," he said. "I didn't know what I would find."

"But ..." I gave my head a quick shake, trying to process this new information. "Alan didn't have one? He wanted to make me come with him. How did he think that was going to happen if he didn't have a gun?"

"I don't know why he didn't have one, or what he was thinking," Jonathan said. "Maybe he couldn't get one. He's supposed to be dead, right? So it's not like he could use his ID."

I stared at Alan, watching the blood congeal under his body. His eyes were still open and staring. I shivered. "Well, maybe I can say you gave me your gun," I said, trying to think of a story. "We can just say we're friends. We hang out together sometimes. People see us at the Tipsy Cow. And you knew I was feeling nervous out here by myself, so you lent me your gun to make me feel safer."

Jonathan was shaking his head. "Charlie, that's not going to work. If the cops investigate, Felicity will tell them I wasn't home ... that I got a towing call. And if the cops pull the phone records, they'll see you called me."

"But ..."

Jonathan reached over and took my hands. His hands were burning hot against my ice-cold skin. "Charlie, don't you get it? We have a golden opportunity here."

"I don't understand."

Jonathan squeezed my hands tightly. An odd light shone in his eyes. "Everyone thinks Alan is dead, right?"

"Right," I said slowly.

"So, no one is going to be looking for him. All we have to do is get rid of the body and make sure it's never found. No one is ever going to know the difference."

I stared at Alan. His dead, lifeless eyes seemed to stare back at me. Blood was streaked across his forehead, in his brown hair. I could smell it, thick, heavy, and metallic. My stomach twisted and I wondered if I was going to be sick. "I don't know, Jonathan. That doesn't seem ... right."

"Right? He murdered a man, Charlie! He was going to kill me, and who knows what he was going to do to you. He deserves to be dead for real. That's all that happened here. All we have to do is get rid of the body and clean up."

"How?" I asked, feeling so heavy, I could barely move.

"I'll do it," he said immediately. "You don't have to worry about it. Just help me get him into the car."

"How are you going to do it?"

"I'll bury him," Jonathan said. "I'll get some lye. My brother-in-law has some. And I'll take him out into the middle of nowhere and bury him there. The lye will keep him from smelling, so the animals won't dig him out. Plus, it will dissolve the skin and organs faster."

My eyes widened in horror, and Jonathan squeezed my hands again. "I didn't mean to be so graphic," he said apologetically. "It won't happen that fast. I'll put the lye on him and cover him with dirt. No one will be the wiser."

Something was bothering me about the conversation, something other than the obvious fact that we should be calling the cops instead of discussing how to get rid of the body, but I couldn't figure out what. Whatever it was buzzed around in my head along with everything else that had happened, and I couldn't focus on anything. "I don't know," I said. "What if you get caught?"

"I won't get caught," he said. "Look, it's the middle of the night. It's still dark outside. And raining. No one is going to be out at this time of night. The ground will be nice and wet, easy for me to dig. Will you help me?"

I stared into Jonathan's eyes. He looked so confident, so sure of himself. I, on the other hand, felt so lost and confused and completely overwhelmed by my emotions. This really wasn't a good idea. I knew it wasn't. I knew I should insist on calling the cops. That was the right thing to do. The *smart* thing to do.

Instead, I found myself agreeing. "Okay," I said.

Jonathan's eyes lit up, and he leaned over to give me a quick kiss. "You made the right choice," he said. "We'll get this all cleaned up tonight, and then we'll never have to talk about it ever again. You know that wouldn't be the case if we brought the cops in."

"You're right," I said, but the uneasiness persisted.

Jonathan got to his feet, feeling in his jeans for his keys. "Open up the garage, and I'll move the car in." Without waiting for a reply, he disappeared out the front door.

I obeyed, my body moving mechanically as I went to the garage, opened it, and watched Jonathan back in. The wet car gleamed in the weak light of the garage. I could hear a steady "drip drip" of the rainwater as it trickled onto the floor.

Jonathan told me to shut the garage, which I did, and began muttering to himself as he searched through the overflowing junk Helen had left behind—dirty tools, blocks of wood, a rusted gasoline can. After a few moments, he located a shovel and a tarp, neither of which I had any idea I had. He tossed the shovel into the back seat and led me back into the house with tarp in hand.

The living room was a mess. Blood seemed to have pooled everywhere. The smell made me gag, and my stomach heaved.

Jonathan rubbed the middle of my back. "Do you need a moment?"

I fought with my stomach, willing the contents to stay down. The sooner we got Alan out, the sooner I could put the entire nightmare behind me. "I'm okay."

"Breathe out of your mouth," he advised.

I nodded, not trusting myself to speak.

He turned back to the disaster, still holding the tarp as he seemed to weigh his options. I wasn't sure what good the tarp would do ... wrapping Alan in it would drench it in blood anyhow, so what was the point?

Jonathan appeared to come to the same conclusion as he tucked it under his arm. "You're going to have to clean all the floors," he said apologetically. "Even in the kitchen. I don't see any other way."

"It's fine," I said. Although it wasn't. None of it was fine. But I was too dazed to protest.

"Help me line the trunk," he said, gesturing for me to follow. I obediently did.

Back in the garage, he popped the trunk and we silently lined the inside with the tarp. Leaving it open, he went back into the house, and I followed numbly, feeling completely surreal. *I must be in some weird dream,* I decided. None of this could possibly be real. Any minute, I would wake up and find myself in bed, the sun shining through the window, and my relief would be so overwhelming, I would probably start giggling uncontrollably ...

Jonathan was back in the living room, grabbing Alan's shoulders and chest. "Get his feet," he said.

I reached down mechanically and picked up his legs as we half-dragged, half-carried him out of the house. He was awkward and heavier than I thought he really ought to be.

"Gives new meaning to the words 'dead weight,'" Jonathan huffed. I eyed him, wondering if it was a joke, but his expression was serious. I didn't answer. It was all I could do to keep myself focused on the task at hand without slipping on the blood dripping onto the floor or losing my grip. Not to mention I had to keep breathing through my mouth to avoid being overwhelmed by the smell. And I absolutely refused to let myself process that I was carrying the dead body of my ex-fiancé—a man I once thought I was going to spend the rest of my life with—a man I had let touch me and make love to me. If I let myself go there, I knew I might start screaming and never stop.

We wrestled him through the door into the garage. I could already see the blood staining the cement step and floor and wondered if bleach would get it out. After another tussle, we were able to shove him into Jonathan's car, folding his arms and legs inside. Jonathan slammed the trunk down before leaning over to kiss me.

"It's all going to be fine," he whispered.

"I know," I whispered back, even though I knew it was a lie. Nothing was going to be fine. Not ever again.

Jonathan got into the driver's seat, and I opened the garage door. I watched him pull the car out into the rain and dark, watched the water drum down on the car, watched him pull out into the street, his headlights slowly fading away.

Lightning flickered through the night, followed by the answering rumble of thunder.

A storm is coming. Beware.

We had killed a man.

Not just a man, but Alan. Alan. We had killed Alan, my ex fiancé.

Yes, he deserved it. Yes, it was an accident.

But we had still killed him.

And now we were covering up his murder.

What had we done?

The Reckoning

Chapter 10

The smell of blood hit me square in the face the moment I came back into the house, and I could no longer control my queasiness. I rushed to the bathroom, slipping twice on the pools of blood, and just barely made it.

I threw open the toilet seat as I dropped to my knees. Even after I emptied my stomach contents, I couldn't stop heaving. At some point, the tears started to flow, and I ended up lying on my side, curled up around the toilet, bawling.

I had no idea how long I laid there, gasping and choking on my own tears and vomit, but eventually, I got myself under enough control to pull myself to my feet.

I turned on the water and studied myself in the mirror. I was deathly pale; my hair was a tangled mess; and I was covered in a mess of tears, blood, vomit, sweat, and snot.

A shower would make it right. A super-hot one so I could scrub and scrub and scrub every inch of myself, although I wasn't sure I would ever feel clean again. Maybe I needed to burn my clothes while I was at it.

But no, it didn't make sense to take a shower yet. What made sense was cleaning the house. What if Claire came over? Or, God forbid, a neighbor?

Clean the house first. Clean myself second.

I did take a few minutes to wash up in the sink, lathering up my face, neck, and arms. It didn't help—I still felt dirty. Looking around the bathroom, I realized my feet were covered with blood, and I was tracking it everywhere in the house, so I did a quick wash of them and the floor, telling myself I would do a better job later cleaning the bathroom.

I made my way back to the kitchen, avoiding the blood, and filled up a bucket of hot water and soap. I found a sponge and a pair of gloves and got to work.

I was in a state of shock. I didn't dare think about whose blood I was cleaning up. *(Alan's blood. This is Alan's blood. Alan is dead. Jonathan is burying his body at this very moment.)* Every time my thoughts went there, I shut them down.

I couldn't afford to have another meltdown. I had to focus on cleaning.

It was a long, slow process. I had to keep changing the water as when the water got too red, I couldn't bear to keep using it, even with the gloves. And even after I went through the house with soap and water, it still felt filthy and disgusting, so I'd fill the bucket again with hot water and bleach and keep scrubbing. I even washed the beautiful wood floors in the living room with bleach. Then, I went through the house a third time with just hot water, rinsing everything.

My knees were red and achy, my arms felt like they were about to fall off, and my eyes were burning from the bleach before I finally decided I was done. The house was as clean as it was going to be, at least for the moment. I might be scrubbing it all again the next day, but at that point, I was done.

I stood up, exhausted, my legs trembling, dumped out the last of the water in the bucket, stripped off my gloves and clothes, and threw them into the washer set on "hot" before heading to the shower where I scrubbed myself raw.

The sun was starting to peek over the horizon when I emerged from the bedroom dressed in a clean pair of jean shorts and an oversized tee shirt, my wet hair pulled back in a ponytail. I was shaky, numb, and so very tired. I wanted nothing more than to crawl into bed and sleep for the next week, but Jonathan would be back soon, and despite my knotted-up stomach, we both needed to eat.

The downstairs still smelled strongly of bleach, which was better than blood and despair, but still irritatingly sharp. I opened all the windows and welcomed in the fresh, clean scent of the rain-soaked earth. I breathed deeply, wanting to cleanse myself of the entire night. A couple of robins were hopping on the lawn, most likely looking for their breakfast, while other birds merrily chirped away. Everything seemed so fresh and innocent.

I wished with all my heart I could wind the clock back to that moment when I was huddled in my room, wondering if there was someone in the house, so rather than calling Jonathan, I could call the cops, instead.

Just that one little decision. A tiny one, really. If I could just do that one thing differently, everything would change.

Instead, because of it, not one of us who had stood in that living room would ever be the same again.

I left the window and went to bring the chair Alan had moved back to the kitchen. As I adjusted it, I noticed the chef knife lying on the middle of the butcher block kitchen table.

I let go of the chair and leaped backward with a yelp. It might as well have been a snake curled up in the middle of the table.

But unlike a snake, the knife didn't move. It simply glinted dully in the early morning light.

Why was it there? Had I put it there the night before?

No. I was sure I had put it back in the knife block after I washed it.

Alan must have put it there. But why?

Maybe that was his weapon, a little voice whispered inside me. *Maybe he planned on using the knife to get what he wanted.*

I swallowed hard, pressing my hand against my chest, the flutterings of fear beating there as I considered what could have been.

It doesn't matter, I reminded myself. *Alan is dead.*

I took a few steps forward and gingerly picked up the knife before hurrying to the sink to wash it in hot, soapy water. I thought about Alan's reaction when he found the gun on Jonathan. He must have thought he hit the jackpot.

He never would have dreamed it would be his doom.

After a good scrubbing, I dried it and put it back, thinking of how it might be a while before I could bring myself to use it again.

I also discovered why my phone was dead. Alan had taken the kitchen phone off the hook. I replaced it, scrubbing the phone receiver with the wet washcloth first.

I wondered how long it would take for me to stop incessantly cleaning.

I still wasn't hungry, but I turned my attention back to breakfast. Making breakfast was a normal thing to do. Maybe if I made breakfast, I would start to feel normal. I went to the refrigerator, considering eggs or maybe even an omelet, but the next thing I knew, I was pulling out the ingredients for a breakfast casserole—eggs, milk, bacon, cheese, onion, and mushroom with a biscuit base.

I stirred and chopped and grated and seasoned. The kitchen began to fill with the warm, comforting scents of bacon and onions. Completing the familiar tasks worked its magic, soothing me, and making me feel like everything just might be alright.

Jonathan was right. No one knew Alan was alive. I suspected no one had seen him, and if anyone did, it was nothing noteworthy. I didn't even think he had been to The Lone Man Standing. Sure, his hair was darker, but he didn't have the mustache and goatee.

He could have shaved it off, a little voice inside me said. I nicked myself with the knife. I automatically stuck my finger in my mouth to suck on it, but the moment I tasted blood, I started gagging uncontrollably. Quickly, I washed it off in the sink and hunted up a Band-Aid.

Why would he bother shaving it off? I argued with the little voice. *What would it matter if I had seen his disguise?*

No, the logical conclusion was he had never been to The Lone Man Standing, which is precisely what I had always thought. That also meant that Jonathan was right. No one knew about Alan. No one would miss him. Everyone thought he was dead anyway. All we did was finish the job.

I popped the casserole into the oven and brewed a pot of coffee. I was going to need all the caffeine I could get. I had a shift at Aunt May's that afternoon.

I was on my second cup when I heard the front door open. "It's me," Jonathan called out. I ran to greet him.

He was soaking wet and covered in mud. He looked exhausted, but somehow triumphant. "It's done," he said simply, before looking around the living room. "Perfect," he said. "It's like nothing ever happened."

I bit my lip. Oh, how I wished nothing had happened. "Anyone see you?"

He shook his head. "Everything went smoothly. Would you mind if I jumped in the shower?" He held up a pair of jeans and a shirt. "Luckily, I keep a spare set of clothes in the car."

"Of course," I said. "Give me your clothes and I'll wash them."

He quickly stripped in the entryway, and I took each item as he removed it. It was so clinical, so mechanical. For a moment, I thought of all the other times he had stripped his clothes off in that very room, both of us too desperate to make it up the stairs and into the bedroom.

Now, there was nothing. No charge, no spark. Sadly, I wondered if it would ever return.

He headed up to the shower and I to the washing machine.

By the time he came down dressed in clean jeans and a work shirt, his hair damp from the shower, the casserole was done, the table was set, and the coffee was ready.

"You read my mind," he said, accepting the cup I handed him. He took a long drink. "It smells wonderful. I'm starving."

"I thought you might be," I said. "Dig in. It's all ready for you."

We both sat down at the table. I let him serve himself first. My stomach still felt twisted in a knot, and as much as I knew I needed to eat, I wasn't sure if I was going to be able to.

"Did you clean with bleach?" he asked, forking up a big bite.

I nodded as I scooped some casserole onto my own plate.

"Good," he said. "I was going to tell you to use bleach, but I forgot."

I picked up my fork, but I didn't eat. "Why?"

"It destroys the blood evidence," he said. "Even if the cops wanted to test in here, it won't matter. They won't find anything."

My mouth dropped open as I stared at him, and I suddenly knew what had been bothering me. "How do you know that?"

He took a big bite. "What do you mean?" he asked, talking around a mouthful of egg.

"That. How do you know that bleach destroys blood evidence? Or about lye destroying bodies?"

"Oh." He flushed a little. "Back when my mother went missing, I did a bunch of research on how crime is investigated. I wanted to see if there was a way I could prove Frank, my stepdad, had something to do with her death. It became sort of a hobby of mine."

"Oh." What he said made sense. I knew how much he had wanted to blame Frank for his mother's death. But still, something nagged at me, and I couldn't quite put my finger on what it was.

Jonathan looked pointedly at my plate. "You need to eat," he said. "It's important we act as normally as possible."

Obediently, I picked up my fork and ate a bite. The casserole was as warm and comforting as it smelled, but it still tasted like sand in my mouth.

"Today will be the worst," he said. "But it will get better. I promise."

How can you be sure? I wanted to ask, but was afraid of the answer.

"I'll come by after we both get off work today. Maybe we can have some dinner together, and talk about things." He reached over and stroked my hand. His fingers were so warm, especially compared to mine that felt like ice. "It's going to be okay. I know it was a shock ..."

"We killed a man," I said bluntly. "We killed my fiancé."

Jonathan's face went still. "Ex," he said.

"Yes, my ex," I said, dropping my fork to bury my face in my hands. I squeezed my eyes tightly closed as I pressed my fingers to my temple. I could feel a headache starting.

"Do you ... do you still love him?" Jonathan's voice was tentative.

I was so surprised, I dropped my hands. "What? No! That's not what this is about. We *killed* someone. Yes, I was afraid of him. Yes, I left him. Yes, I never wanted to see him again, but none of that changes the fact that we killed a man. And not just any man, but one who, at one point, I was going to marry."

Jonathan's face softened. "I know this is difficult for you," he said. "I'm here for you. If you need to talk. But remember, he was a bad man. An evil man. He came to us, remember? It was self-defense."

"I know that," I said. "And self-defense is legal. We have the legal right to defend ourselves. So why are we covering it up? Why are we hiding it? It all just feels so wrong."

"Okay, so let's say we do it your way," Jonathan said, putting his fork down. "We call the cops now and get them involved. We already covered it up. How do we explain that? We *look* guilty. Now everything is tainted. But let's say we had called the cops before we cleaned everything up. Do you really think it would have been as simple as what you're saying? That we could have answered a few questions and gone on our way? Of course not. Chances are it would have dragged on forever. Do you really want your life upended for however long because of a police investigation? Do you really want to pay thousands of dollars in legal fees to defend yourself?"

I scowled at my plate of food. "No."

"Of course not. And just because what we did was legal and right and moral, just because we know it was an accident, that we weren't trying to kill him, but were just defending ourselves because he wanted to kill us, just because we know the truth doesn't mean the courts will rule in our favor. The courts make mistakes all the time. Do you really want to take the chance of both of us ending up in prison?"

"No."

"And, even if it does work out for us, even if the courts get it right and we're found innocent, or maybe we're never even tried at all, what about the court of public opinion? What are people going to say? What is the newspaper going to print? That's stuff we have to live with forever."

What Jonathan said made sense. We *were* defending ourselves. We knew the truth. Why put ourselves through the expense and stress of a trial?

All that said, why did I still feel like we made the wrong choice?

"Doesn't it bother you?" I asked, watching Jonathan resume eating. How could he eat like nothing was wrong? He just buried a man, a man he killed. Why wasn't he more upset?

"Of course it does," he said. "But we did the right thing."

My mouth twisted in a sardonic smile. "Was it?"

Jonathan looked surprised. "Of course. Why would you question that? What other choice did we have?"

"Because the choice we made resulted in a man being dead and us hiding the body," I said, my voice rising. "Jonathan, what have we done? *What have we done?*"

An expression flashed across Jonathan's face—something I couldn't immediately identify. It twisted Jonathan's features into something I didn't recognize. Something dark and disturbing. Something that didn't seem quite human.

But then it was gone, so fast I wondered if I had imagined it. *I must have,* I told myself. A shadow went across the sun is all. That was it. The Jonathan I knew and was falling in love with was here, had always been here, sitting next to me. His face was grim but resolved, his eyes narrow, but firm and unyielding.

"What we had to."

Chapter 11

Jonathan was right. It did get better.

The first day was nightmarish. I was exhausted, both physically and emotionally, and was still having trouble wrapping my head around what had happened. Things like that didn't happen to normal people in normal lives. How did it just happen to me?

Somehow, I made it through that day. The next day was a little better, and the day after that a little better yet.

It had been nearly two weeks, and I was finally feeling like things were going back to normal. I no longer felt like obsessively cleaning my house every day, and I found it easier to be a part of normal human interactions. I could joke, laugh, gossip, and waitress successfully.

Yes, everything was normal.

Except for the nightmares.

I could no longer sleep through the night. At some point, I would be jolted awake from a deep sleep, convinced I had heard a noise and that someone was in the house.

No matter what I told myself, I couldn't relax until I had armed myself with a baseball bat and heavy-duty flashlight and prowled through the house. Most of those times, Midnight padded along beside me. I always felt safer when he did, not because he was big enough to be much of a threat, but because I knew he didn't like people. So I figured chances were high there was no one in the house if he was accompanying me.

Still, I did occasionally find myself toying with the idea of getting a dog. But every time I did, Midnight would suddenly appear at my side with a reproachful look in his jade-green eyes.

Hopefully, the bat would be enough to eventually make me feel secure.

Jonathan was doing his best to help, staying with me far into the night. He was sweet and attentive, worrying about the growing circles under my eyes. Many nights, he would stay until I fell asleep in his arms before tiptoeing out the door.

It didn't matter, though. Eventually, the nightmare would come, in which I relived that awful night. Except in the dreams, Alan wasn't the one who was shot. It was always either me or Jonathan.

And every time the gun would go off in the dream, I would awaken, panicky and hyperventilating, sure what had really woken me was a noise in the house.

Hopefully, over time, the nightmares would fade away as well, but for the time being, they were a part of the healing process that I just had to get through.

My job at Aunt May's was a godsend, along with my garden and tea business. They were welcome distractions, getting me out of the house and spending time with people and living, growing things.

They kept me grounded. They kept me sane.

They were my lifeline to that perfect, normal world.

I could almost convince myself that everything was going to be fine, and now that Alan was truly gone, I could firmly close that chapter of my life forever.

Then, Red walked into the diner again.

I didn't immediately see him, as it was in the middle of our lunch rush and I was consumed with getting people served and fed as quickly as possible. It wasn't until I went to refill two sodas that I saw him standing behind the counter, his arms folded across his massive chest and dark eyes watching me.

"Have you been helped?" I asked, purposefully concentrating harder than I needed to on the sodas.

"I was in the neighborhood. Just wanted to see how you're doing," Red said. This time, he had an Iron Maiden tee shirt on. The grinning skull seemed to be leering at me, like it knew what I did. I quickly averted my eyes.

"I'm good," I said, flashing him a wide smile. "Busy, but good."

I hoped he would take the hint and leave, but he didn't move. "Glad to hear that. Hey, I was wondering if you ever heard from that guy who was looking for you."

My hand jerked, and I spilled half the soda down my arm. I swore under my breath as I put both glasses on the counter so I could wipe up the mess. I really just wanted out of the conversation. "Nope. Never did find anything out."

"Hmm," he said, watching me mop my arm with a rag. Luckily, the two men sitting at the counter were too busy talking to each other to notice either me or the conversation. "That's odd. He really seemed keen on finding you."

I picked up the drinks. "Well, what can I say? Maybe he was looking for a different Charlotte. I can't be the only one in Redemption."

"No, but you're probably the only one who came from New York," he called after me.

My steps faltered, and I nearly spilled the drinks a second time, but I tightened my grip, took a deep breath, and turned back to him. "I don't know what to tell you, but I have no idea who, if anyone, was looking for me. Now, if you'll excuse me," I nodded to the full restaurant. "I have customers to help."

"Of course," Red said as he nodded back, although his eyes gleamed with a strange sort of glee. "I won't keep you. And who knows? Maybe you'll discover the man's identity when you least expect it."

I half-nodded as I hurried away to deliver the sodas to the two women who were looking at me expectantly. Apologizing for the delay, I covertly watched Red stride out the door. What was he talking about? Did he know something about Alan after all?

For the rest of my shift, I kept turning the conversation over and over in my mind. Did he know something more? If he didn't, why would he bother coming in at all?

I was desperate to talk to Jonathan.

As soon as my shift was over, I made a beeline for the door. My plan was to drive to the body shop and grab a few minutes with Jonathan to see when we could meet. As I reached for the doorknob, Claire called out to me.

"Charlie, got a minute?"

"Gotta run," I said. "There's something I have to do. Talk tomorrow?"

Claire gave me a questioning look. "Sure. That's fine. Tomorrow then."

The words were barely out of her mouth before I was out the door, waving at her.

Jonathan was talking to an elderly woman with a white cap of tight curls and thick, horn-rimmed glasses that made her look rather owlish when I pulled up. He saw me and nodded. I impatiently hung back, listening to him explain how regular oil changes were an important part of a car's maintenance, and if you skipped them, you could have problems down the road, exactly like those she was having.

She seemed completely perplexed, saying she had been getting them all along. "No ma'am," Jonathan explained. "When they check your oil when you get gas, they don't change it. They're just checking the level."

"Oh, for heaven's sake. George was always in charge of that, bless his soul," she said.

I forced myself to take deep breaths, telling myself a few more minutes wouldn't make any difference.

She still didn't seem completely clear on the specifics, but finally, it seemed to sink in, and she agreed to leaving her car overnight. "I'll get someone to drive you home," Jonathan said, escorting her by the elbow to the door. "And I'll call you tomorrow as soon as we're finished."

"You're such a dear," the old lady said, patting his cheek. "Okay, I'll let you help this young lady. You're in good hands," she called out to me.

"Yes ma'am," I called back as Jonathan helped her out.

He came toward me quickly. "Everything okay?"

I shook my head. "I don't know. But we have to talk. Are you coming over?"

He glanced at his watch. "I won't be able to until later. What is it? What's going on?"

I looked around uneasily, making sure we were alone in the little office. I quickly told him about Red and what he had said.

Jonathan's face grew pale. "What do you think he meant?"

"I don't know," I said. "I mean, he couldn't have seen Alan. Alan didn't have a mustache or goatee that night."

Jonathan frowned. "Unless he shaved them off."

"Why would he do that? That makes no sense. And like I said before, The Lone Man Standing is not a bar Alan would go to."

"Yeah, but he must know *something*," Jonathan said. "Or why would he come find you again at all?"

"I don't know," I said, before another thought struck me. "You weren't anywhere near the bar that night, were you?"

Jonathan shook his head firmly. "No. Of course not."

"So you don't think anyone saw you."

"No. Of course not. That's what I said before." Jonathan scanned the room behind him. "Look, I have to go. I'll try to come by later. But if not, tomorrow for sure."

"Later," I said.

He started to leave, but turned back to me. "It's going to be okay, Charlie. You'll see. It's going to be fine."

I swallowed hard, forcing a smile on my lips. "I hope you're right."

* * *

There were voices downstairs.

I could hear them. Rattling around. Talking. Making a racket.

Talking?

I pulled my robe on and opened the bedroom door. The house was lit with a silvery grey light, like that from a full moon.

I hurried down the stairs straining my ears to make out the conversation. The two voices seemed to be arguing. Why would anyone break into a house and then argue?

"I kept saying she needed to leave," a girlish voice said. "I told you. But you wouldn't back me up. And now look what happened."

If not her, it still would have happened another way. You know this. You know what year it is.

There was a wildness to the other voice—something not quite human. It was familiar somehow, but I couldn't place it.

"You don't know that," the girlish voice insisted.

I do. And you do, too.

I turned the corner and was standing in the kitchen lit by the ghostly light of the moon. The Holly Hobby girl sat in a chair facing the cat on the table.

Ah. There you are. The black cat swished its tail. *We were waiting for you.*

"Do you see now?" The Holly Hobby girl asked, her voice bitter. "Now, do you see why you should have listened to me?"

"Is this about Alan?" I asked.

The girl rolled her eyes. "Alan is the least of your worries."

"What do you mean?"

"Well, he's already dead, for one," she said, like it should be obvious. "What you need to worry about is what's coming next."

A bolt of lightning flashed through the kitchen. The electricity seared up my arm, giving me a jolt. Thunder boomed, making me jump a second time. "What's coming next?"

The cat fixed its dark-green eyes on me. *It won't help you to know.*

"But it will get worse," the girl continued ominously, picking at a thread in her stained dress." Much worse. You chose the hard way."

"What does that mean?"

There were things put into place a long time ago, a hundred years ago, to be exact, that are coming to a head. No matter what you did or didn't do, there is a reckoning coming. No matter what you did, it was going to be difficult. Unfortunately, the path you chose made it the most difficult for you.

"I don't understand."

You will.

"What can I do to fix it? There must be something."

The Holly Hobby girl let out a laugh that resembled a bark. "Yeah. You could have left when I told you to."

"I mean now," I snapped. "And you're a fine one to talk. Showing up at our séance and scaring Claire the way you did."

The Holly Hobby girl turned even more white. "Oh no," she whispered to the cat. "It really *is* too late."

The cat swished its tail. *You knew it was going to happen. Why are you so surprised?*

She hung her head. "I wanted to be wrong."

I looked back and forth between the girl and the cat. "What are you talking about? Wasn't it you at the séance?"

The girl shook her head, still staring down. "It wasn't me."

"Then who was it?"

She slowly lifted her face, her eyes huge and terrified. "I hope to God you never find out."

Not that it matters. The cat started to clean itself. *If you know or don't know. The reckoning is coming. Nothing you can do now will stop it.*

"Then what's the point?"

The cat jerked its head up to stare at me. *The point is, you still have choices. You still have a role to play. Now, you can make it easier or more difficult for good to prevail. You need to make the right choice. Or ...*

The cat made a shrugging motion.

From a distance, I could hear the rumble of thunder. Beads of sweat dripped down my forehead as my stomach twisted into knots. "Or what?" My voice was barely above a whisper.

Or evil will win.

I opened my eyes.

The darkness was just beginning to lighten to the grey of predawn. Outside, the birds happily chirped, welcoming the sun with their songs of joy. Midnight, who was sleeping on the pillow next to me, stirred and gazed at me with his dark-green eyes.

The beginning of a brand-new day, full of promise and possibility. Yet my dream lingered like a thin layer of tar on my skin that wouldn't come off no matter how hard I scrubbed.

Or evil will win.

I had no idea what any of it meant. I wanted to tell myself it was just my subconscious processing what happened. I had done some research, and it wasn't uncommon to have vivid nightmares for weeks, months, or even years after a trauma.

Somehow, I could feel that wasn't what was going on.

I had a terrible, sinking suspicion that things were going to get worse. I was on a path that was only going to get darker and more twisted the longer I stayed on it.

But that wasn't the worst part.

The worst part was I had no idea how to get off.

The reckoning is coming.

Midnight stood up and nuzzled me, meowing loudly. Breakfast time. It didn't matter what else was happening in the world, the cat still needed to be fed.

"Okay, okay," I grumbled, swinging my feet out of bed. I really wasn't that annoyed. Feeding the cat breakfast was a welcome distraction, as was my cup of tea.

As we headed down the stairs and into the kitchen, my thoughts kept jumping between my dream and my most recent conversation with Jonathan.

He wasn't able to come over, so he called me instead. "I think Red knows something."

"What could he know?" I asked. "You said he didn't see you that night."

"He didn't," Jonathan said. "He couldn't have. There's no way."

"Are you sure?"

"Yes," Jonathan said, but he didn't sound as confident as he had earlier. "I'm sure."

I didn't like how the story seemed to be changing. He was definitely less sure now that he hadn't been seen. Still, it didn't seem like the right time to press the issue. "So, if he didn't see you, then what could he possibly know?"

"I don't know. Maybe Alan really did go to The Lone Man Standing."

"Like I said, I seriously doubt that."

"Would you bet your life on it?" Jonathan asked.

"My life? What are you talking about?"

"Charlie, think," Jonathan said. "What if Red *did* meet Alan at some point, either at The Lone Man Standing or somewhere else? Red could be lying about where they met, but they did actually meet. And now, Alan has gone missing. Maybe Red is now putting two and two together."

I gasped. "You really think Red knows?"

"I don't know," Jonathan said. "But it's a possibility."

"You said you were taking care of the body so no one would find it."

"And I did. No one is going to find it," Jonathan said quickly. "But that doesn't mean Red couldn't still make things difficult for us."

My stomach was queasy. I pressed my hand against it, trying to settle it down. Maybe some tea would help. I stretched out the phone cord so I could get the water boiling. "Maybe it's not so dire," I said. "Maybe he's just trying to get into our heads. Remember what Chester said about the guy who tried to get the bar away from him? Maybe all that's going on is Red wants to scare me, so I sell my house to him."

"Possibly," Jonathan said, although his tone sounded like he doubted it. "But I think we better check it out."

"How are we supposed to do that?"

"We can go back to The Lone Man Standing and ask him more questions."

"Like what? 'Was the guy you talked to named Alan? What did he tell you? Or are you just trying to scare me into selling you my home?'"

"Well, we have to do something," Jonathan said.

"I don't think we have to do anything right now," I countered. The more Jonathan talked, the more uncomfortable I was getting. I did not want him anywhere near Red. That felt like an extremely bad idea. "I think we need to wait and see. We don't know enough to do anything. And the last thing we want to do is make Red think we have something to hide."

"I don't know," Jonathan said. "That doesn't feel right, either. Look, I have to go. We can talk about it more later. Love you."

He hung up, leaving me staring at the receiver in disbelief.

He said he loved me.

A married man, who made it clear he wasn't going to leave his wife, just said he loved me.

What was I supposed to do with that? I felt both hot and cold, giddy and depressed.

How did everything get so complicated?

The tea kettle whistle jerked me out of my jumbled thoughts. Midnight paused to give me a dirty look before resuming his breakfast. I prepared a cup of tea, still not sure what I felt about any of what was happening.

What did the girl in my dream mean when she said it was going to "get worse"? Did Red actually know something? Had he seen something?

Or had we overlooked something else?

I wracked my brain, but other than Alan's body turning up—which it shouldn't, as Jonathan had assured me he had not only buried it deeply, but also used lye to speed up the decay process—I couldn't imagine what Red could possibly know.

Surely, Red was fishing. Trying to get us to incriminate ourselves in some way, so he could use it to force me to sell my home.

It had to be that. Nothing else made any sense.

But no matter how much my logical brain continuously insisted there was nothing that could tie us to Alan, I couldn't shake the uneasy feeling that there was something I had missed.

And whatever that something was would ruin everything.

Chapter 12

"What can I get you?"

I stood with my pencil poised above my order pad and blew a piece of hair out of my face.

The man was seated by himself at a booth. He had thick glasses, short brown hair, and the thin, flabby build of someone who never worked out yet was still able to maintain his weight.

He pushed his glasses up on his nose and ordered a chef salad and Diet Coke. I scribbled it down and turned to go.

"You're Charlie, right?" His voice was slightly nasal, as if he had allergies or chronic stuffy nose.

I turned back with a smile. "I am. Is there something I can help you with?" I wondered if he was a potential tea customer. I might be able to help him with that nasal drip.

He didn't smile back. "I'm Tad Clark, and I work for the *Redemption Times*."

My smile faded. The journalist who had called me for an interview when I first bought my house. The same one who wrote the article that helped Red track me down. "Is there something I can help you with?" I repeated.

"I just have a few questions. Is now a good time?"

I glanced around. "Not particularly. I'm working, as you can see."

"Well, on your break then. Do you have one coming up?"

I put my hand on my hip. I didn't really like where this was going. "What is this about?"

He adjusted his glasses again. "I'd rather ask you when you have a few minutes and aren't rushed. When is your break? I can come back."

I waved the order slip. "Does this mean you don't want your lunch?"

"No, I still want it. If you can't spare a few minutes before I'm done, I'm happy to come back."

I narrowed my eyes. "Are you looking for an interview for an article you're writing?"

He held his hands up. "I just have a few questions is all. We can talk off the record if you'd like."

I mumbled something as I warily backed away from him, unsure of exactly how to answer in that moment. I put the order in to the kitchen and went to get his Diet Coke. Claire joined me at the ice bin as I shoved ice into his glass.

"What does *he* want?" she asked, her voice low.

I glanced at her. "You know who he is?"

"Of course I do," she said scowling. "I went to school with the little weasel."

"He's got some questions for me."

Claire's eyebrows went up. "What kind of questions?"

I shrugged as I picked up the soda gun. "Beats me. He wants to talk to me while I'm on break."

She bit her lip as her eyes flicked over to him. "I don't like it," she said darkly. "There's something going on …" her voice trailed off and she shook her head.

I gave her a sharp look. "What?"

She shook her head again. "Now isn't the time. We'll talk later." She grabbed the coffee pot and headed toward one of her customers, who was waving at her and holding up her cup. "Coming, Mrs. Polak," she called out, a big smile on her face.

I brought over Tad's Diet Coke, dropped it off without a word, and headed to my other tables. I wondered what I should do. Should I try and rearrange my break to talk to him while he was eating? Should I make him come back later in the day? Or should I just tell him I wasn't interested?

I wished I could talk it over with Jonathan. But I didn't think calling him while we were both at work was a smart move.

We hadn't had a chance to talk much since he said "love you" on the phone. I could feel the blood rushing to my cheeks as I thought about it. I also wasn't sure what to do about it. Should I say something? Or no?

Why did everything have to be so confusing? Didn't I have enough going on without worrying about this new development in our relationship, too?

I brought Tad his salad when it was up, still no closer to a decision, although I was feeling edgier and edgier.

Why was he at Aunt May's?

Did it have anything to do with Red?

What if someone had seen Jonathan after all?

I finally made up my mind. I needed answers. Besides, I knew if I told Jonathan he had stopped in without knowing why, Jonathan would have a cow.

I told Fred I was taking my break.

"Do you want your food?" he asked.

I shook my head. "Bag it. I'll take it home with me."

He eyed me from under his white cook hat. "You better eat it," he said. "You look like you're wasting away."

I rubbed my hands against my loose jeans. It was true. I hadn't had much of an appetite for weeks. First, because I was way too much in lust with Jonathan to feel like eating, and then Alan and, well.

Food was the last thing on my mind.

"Promise," I said as I hurried out into the dining room.

Tad was just finishing up when I slid into the booth across from him. "You've got five minutes," I said. "Talk. And, to be clear, this *is* off the record."

He adjusted his glasses and took another bite of salad. "Are you sure you want to do this here?" he asked around the mouthful of lettuce.

My anxiety went up a notch. "What are you talking about?"

"Well, it's just ..." he swallowed, then made a big show of pulling out his notebook. "Perhaps this is something you'd rather your coworkers didn't overhear?"

What did this guy know? "I could hardly say, since I don't know what this is about. What would you suggest?" I asked, my tone acidic.

He patted his mouth with the napkin, his movements almost prissy, then pulled out his wallet. "What are the damages?"

Claire was right. This guy really was something. I pulled out my order pad, tallied it up, and gave it to him. He studied it, then handed some bills to me. "Keep the change," he smirked.

I stuffed the bills into my apron pocket. "Thanks. Now what?"

He gestured with his head. "Walk with me."

It appeared I didn't have much choice, so I followed him out of the diner. "You know, you're making this seem like a much bigger deal than if you had just asked me your questions in the diner," I said, once we were out on the sidewalk.

"Just tell them I wanted to protect my sources and keep the conversation private," he said.

I rolled my eyes. The *Redemption Times* protecting its sources? Give me a break. "So, what is it? I don't have a lot of time."

He started slowly walking up the street. I fell into step beside him, trying not to gag over the strong whiff of the aftershave he clearly bathed in. In the diner, the smell of food must have covered it up. "The police found an abandoned car a few blocks from your home," he said.

Good lord. All this because of an abandoned car? "Wasn't mine," I said. "Is that it?" I turned to go back to the diner.

He kept his slow plodding. "It was a rental," he continued.

"Okay," I said. "Still don't know anything about it."

"From New York."

My feet tangled up with each other, and I almost tripped.

"Careful," Tad said, reaching out a hand to stop my fall. I ignored it and righted myself.

Oh God. Alan's car. I hadn't even thought of it.

This must have been what the dream was warning me about. I wanted to kick myself. How could I have been so stupid? Of course he would have had a car. How else would he have gotten to Wisconsin?

But why a rental, I wondered? Wouldn't it have made more sense to buy another car than rent something? He could have purchased something used for cash. A rental car would have paperwork. "I still can't help you," I said, although my mouth was so dry, it felt like my tongue was stuck to the roof of my mouth.

"No?" Tad seemed surprised. "You're from New York, right?"

"New York is a big place," I said drily. "Lots of people are from New York."

"That may be. But we don't get a lot of New Yorkers here."

"I don't know what to tell you. I don't know anything about a car."

Tad paused, his head down as he studied the cracks in the sidewalk. "You don't think it's a little weird that a rental car from New York is abandoned just a few blocks away from the house of Redemption's newest resident, who is also from New York?"

I shrugged. "What can I say? As everyone who grew up here tells me, Redemption has its own ideas about who lives here and who doesn't. How would I have any clue?"

"Hmm ..." Tad said, eying me from behind his thick glasses.

We passed a mother pushing a stroller and holding the hand of a toddler who was jumping around like she was part grasshopper. The mother looked harried and exhausted, her blonde hair dull and lifeless, like it had been a while since she had taken a shower.

I waited until we had passed them before continuing. "What I don't understand is why you're even talking to me. You said it was a rental car, right?"

"Yes."

"Then why don't you check with the rental company as to whose it is?"

"Well, that's the problem," Tad said. "The man who rented the car doesn't appear to exist."

I felt a lump in my throat, as if my heart had leaped from my chest and lodged itself there, beating painfully. "What do you mean?"

"According to the rental company's records, the man's name was Jerome Davis. But the real Jerome Davis had his wallet stolen, and that's what someone used to reserve the car."

Of course. Why would you bother buying a car when you could rent one with a stolen credit card and just never return it?

It was ingenious, actually. I silently gnashed my teeth together. Trust Alan to think of everything.

"Have you seen anyone hanging out around your home?" Tad asked. His tone was neutral, but the sideways glance he threw me was calculating.

"Why would you think this has anything to do with me?" I asked. "I keep telling you, I don't know anything about a rental car. And I don't even understand why this is worth investigating. Is crime really so low in this town that you're spending your time checking out abandoned cars?"

He didn't take the bait. "You didn't answer the question."

"No," I said, trying not to sound as frustrated and defensive as I felt. "I haven't noticed anyone hanging around. But you said the car was parked on a different street. Have you tried asking those residents?"

Tad reached into his pocket and pulled out a pack of gum. He offered me a piece, but I declined. "No one really saw much," he said, unwrapping the gum and popping it in his mouth. It was Wrigley spearmint, and the smell hit me in the face. "One older woman swears she saw a guy she didn't recognize 'skulking around.' Her words. But she can't connect him with the car."

"Was she able to describe him?" I asked, and then mentally kicked myself. I didn't want to sound too interested.

"White, in his thirties. Brown hair. She thought he had a mustache, but wasn't sure."

My stomach hit the sidewalk. Had a mustached Alan been slithering around Redemption all this time? What if he really had been to The Lone Man Standing after all? I thought I was going to be sick.

Tad gave me that sly sideways glance again. "Sound like anyone you know?"

"I keep telling you, I don't know anything about an abandoned car." I glanced at my watch. "I gotta get back to work."

Tad's expression was nonplussed. "Okay. Thanks for taking the time to talk to me. You may want to keep your eyes and ears open, just to be safe. And, if you do see anyone hanging around you don't know, I'd appreciate a call."

"Is this something you think we should be worried about? Do you think this guy is dangerous?"

Tad shrugged. "I have no idea. We don't know who he is. But it certainly seems a little fishy to rent a car under a false identity. Wouldn't you say?"

I had no answer. Instead, I gave him a slight wave and hurried back to the restaurant.

My stomach was roiling, and I desperately wanted to talk to Jonathan, but I also knew Tad was watching and I needed to act normally.

I pulled open the door to Aunt May's. Claire looked up from a table as I entered. She raised her eyebrow in question, but I gave her a quick shake of my head. *Not now.*

She went back to taking an order, and I hurried to the kitchen to let Fred know I was back.

The rest of the afternoon was a little too busy for me to get away to talk to Jonathan or to even get a quick moment with Claire. It was only when I was getting ready to leave that she pulled me aside.

"So, what's going on? You looked as white as a sheet when you came back in. What did he say to you?" Claire's face was redder than normal, and wisps of hair stuck to the sweat against her forehead. She didn't look well.

"Apparently, there is an abandoned rental car from New York that's parked a few streets over from my house," I said.

Claire's face drained of color. "Is it Alan?"

I shrugged. "Your guess is as good as mine. The car was rented using a stolen identity and credit card."

"Oh my God." Claire pressed her hands to her mouth. "I bet it's Alan. Have you seen him?"

"No, not like before," I said. "I haven't seen anyone who looks like him in public like I did before." Which was true. I hadn't seen him out in public at all.

Claire, who still looked shocked, didn't notice my verbal gymnastics. "It's got to be him. Charlie, you must be careful."

"I am," I said. "Jonathan checks the house regularly, and I'm always locking the doors and windows."

She didn't look convinced. "First The Lone Man Standing and now this? This is really not good." She paused, biting her lower lip as if she were struggling to decide whether to say something to me. "Charlie, I really don't have a good feeling about this. I've been feeling like something has been off for some time."

"What have you been feeling?"

"I just ..." she pressed her fingers against her temple. "Okay, look. You know I like Jonathan. I grew up with him, and he's a friend. And," she lowered her voice. "Lord knows I'm not in any position to discuss anyone's sexual choices. But, Charlie. You're playing with fire here. I told you how there's always been a streak of darkness inside him. He's always held it in check before. But, now? I feel like something has shifted. The darkness isn't as contained as it once was. Charlie, I'm worried about you."

"Don't be," I said. "Everything is fine. He hasn't shown anything like that to me." This wasn't completely true, but how could I even begin to explain my uneasiness without telling her everything?

Her expression was skeptical. "Just ... be careful, Charlie. Especially now that we know Alan is around here somewhere."

"Truly, I'm very careful," I said, trying not to show how uncomfortable I was with the conversation. All I wanted to do was get out of there and go home to wait for Jonathan, so I could tell him what happened. "I'll be even more vigilant. Promise. I have to go; I'm running a little late."

I had taken just a few steps before she called out to me. "You'd tell me if anything had happened. Right? You're keeping me in the loop?"

I turned back to her, plastering a smile on my face. "Of course. You'd be the first to know."

Chapter 13

Jonathan's face was ashen. "How could we have missed the car?"

I moved my food around my plate with my fork. "I don't know."

After leaving Claire, I had come home and cooked a big meal—baked ziti with salad and garlic bread. I wanted something with a lot of calories. Also, as I promised Fred, I did eat half my club sandwich and most of the fries he had packed up for me. The leftovers were in the fridge. At the moment, I was wishing I hadn't eaten so much as the food was churning unpleasantly in my stomach.

Jonathan pushed his plate aside and picked up his wine. "So, a rental car," he repeated.

"That he rented using someone else's identity and credit card," I said.

"So how did they find it? The rental company?"

"No, I think the neighbors called it in, because it was abandoned. It must have been sitting out there for a couple of weeks now."

He swallowed his wine. "Did anyone see him?"

This was the part I was dreading. "There was an older woman who I guess saw some guy."

"Was it Alan?"

"I don't know. She described someone with brown hair and maybe a mustache."

Jonathan slammed a hand on the table, making me jump. "I knew it! He *was* at The Lone Man Standing."

"We don't know that," I said quickly. "It doesn't sound like she was sure. And she didn't say anything about the goatee."

Jonathan was shaking his head. "It doesn't matter. He was at The Lone Man Standing. I knew it. Red *did* see him."

"Even if Red did see him, so what?" I raised my voice, trying to penetrate the fog of anger Jonathan seemed to be lost in. "He can't prove anything. He doesn't know what we did."

"He suspects," Jonathan said darkly. "And clearly, he said something to Tad, or Tad wouldn't have gone sniffing around you."

"Tad had called me before, and I wouldn't talk to him," I reminded Jonathan. "He might still have a bug up his butt about that. Red may not have said anything to him at all."

"I'm trying to remember if those two were friends when we were kids," Jonathan said. "I have to ask Lou. She remembers that sort of stuff."

"You know, it could have been the other way around, too," I said.

Jonathan cocked his head. "What do you mean?"

"Maybe Red found out about the car some other way, and that's why he came into the restaurant the other day. It might not have anything to do with Alan showing up at the bar or Red saying anything to Tad. We may be assuming things that just aren't right."

"I still think we need to talk to Red," Jonathan said. "Find out what he knows."

"How? What would we say to him? Again, I think that would be a huge mistake."

In one quick move, Jonathan got up from his chair, scooped up his wine glass and headed to the kitchen to refill it. "We have to do something."

"Not doing anything is doing something," I argued. "We could make things worse. What if we tip our hand? And then Red knows something is up? Then he really will start digging around. We really don't want that."

Jonathan filled his glass to the brim and took a long swallow. "We don't know that he's not already doing that."

"Yeah, but he still doesn't know anything," I said. "We don't want to make him think he's on the right path."

Jonathan paused and studied his wine glass. "You may be right," he said finally. I breathed a sigh of relief. "At least for now, we'll wait and see."

"This all could blow over really quickly," I said. "What's happened? A rental car has been recovered. That's it. That's hardly a major crime. What do they have to go on? There's still no link between that car and Alan, and everyone still thinks Alan is dead."

"That's true. Unless they can somehow tie Alan to that stolen identity," Jonathan said.

"I think that would be tough. Everyone thinks Alan is dead, so how would that even work? But if that somehow happens, we'll cross that bridge when we get to it. Even if they did connect Alan with the stolen identity, and even if they then took another step to talk to me about it, there's still nothing to connect me and Alan here in Redemption."

"I still don't like it," Jonathan grumbled.

Then why did we hide his body in the first place, I wanted to shout. *If we had just called the cops that night, there would be no issue right now.*

But there was no point in saying that. It would just cause an argument. And there was nothing either of us could do to change it.

There was no going back.

"Just as long as they never find Alan's body, I don't see how anyone can prove anything," I said. "Even if they somehow figure out Alan was in Redemption, that doesn't mean anything. He could have left another way. He stole one car, so what's to stop him from stealing another?"

"All right, all right. You've convinced me," Jonathan said. "We'll wait and see. Even if it kills me." The last sentence was more of a mutter, and he picked up his glass to take another long drink.

I watched him in silence. He seemed agitated, his fingers drumming on the counter, his eyes darting around the kitchen.

What was going on with him?

"You ARE sure no one will stumble upon the body, right?"

Jonathan's entire body tensed up. He made a motion like he was going to slam the wine glass against the counter, but at the last moment, seemed to realize how delicate it was and gentled the motion. "Why do you keep asking me that?" He asked through gritted teeth.

"Because you're acting really peculiar," I said. "If it's as you say, and you hid the body where no one will find it and no one saw you, then why are you so upset?"

He stared at his hand, clenching and unclenching his fist. "I'm as sure as I can be," he finally said. "Everything seemed to go perfectly smoothly. But the more things like this that crop up, the more I start to worry. Did I miss anything? Is there something I overlooked? Should I go back and check? Should I leave everything alone? I'm just not sure."

He looked so lost and forlorn, it broke my heart. I could picture him as a child, hurt and confused over things he couldn't control. I stood up and went to him, wrapping him in my arms. He smelled of harsh soap and motor oil along with his natural male essence.

"It's going to be okay," I said. "We just have to hold strong. If we can do that, it's all going to work out."

Jonathan sighed and leaned into me. "I hope you're right."

"I *am* right. We just can't panic. That's when mistakes are made. We just have to stay calm, cool, and collected. We can do that. Right?"

He didn't immediately answer. I could feel the tension in his broad shoulders.

I gave him a little squeeze, trying to ignore the flutter of fear in my stomach. "Right?"

"Right," he replied, but he didn't sound convinced.

The flutter grew more incessant, like a moth beating itself to death on a streetlamp. Something was off. I could feel the tension inside him, the stress building up. And if he couldn't handle it, if the pressure became too much ... if he broke and did something stupid ...

No. I had to make sure that didn't happen.

"What's wrong?" I asked.

He shook his head and swallowed some wine. "I told you. I'm just worried I missed something."

"Why? Did something happen to make you worried?"

I had assumed he would tell me it was because of Red and Tad, but he stayed quiet, swirling the wine in his glass. I tried to tamp down my own alarm.

"I had a dream," he said finally.

I blinked in surprise. "A dream?"

"Yeah. It was ... really creepy. Spooky. Basically, that it wasn't over, and the worst was yet to come. Except that's not the word that was used. It was something else ... something biblical ..."

"The reckoning is coming."

The words were out of my mouth before I could judge the wisdom of saying them.

Jonathan swiveled his head to stare at me. "Yeah, that's it. 'The reckoning is coming.'"

I tried to swallow, but my mouth was dry. Sweat dripped down my spine. "I had a dream like that, too."

His eyes widened. "You did? How is that possible?"

I shook my head. "I don't know. But yes. That was my dream, as well. Things are going to get worse, because the reckoning is coming."

His expression turned to horror. "Oh my God, does that mean something *was* missed? I better go out there to check ..." he glanced at the window and swore under his breath. "No, it's too dark. Maybe tomorrow ..."

I pressed my fingers against his lips. "No. That's not what it means. Part of my dream was about Alan being the least of our worries. Whatever is coming, it's not about what you did or didn't do with Alan."

There was almost a wildness in his eyes. "Then why is Red hanging around the way he is? Why is he acting like he knows something? And the car ..."

I firmly shook my head, shushing him. "Jonathan, we have to keep it together. What happened with Alan is in the past. No one knows anything. No one can prove anything. Look, if someone could, wouldn't the police be here by now? Asking us questions? Have the police contacted you?"

Jonathan slowly shook his head, the madness starting to dim.

"And Red. I mean, think about it. If he really knew something, something that could tie us to Alan, why would he come into the diner saying cryptic things? Why wouldn't he just come straight out and do whatever he's hinting about? Whether it's blackmail or whatever. It makes far more sense he doesn't know anything and is trying to goad us into a mistake."

"Maybe you're right." He sighed heavily. "What you say makes total sense, but then I start to wonder, maybe I did miss something. Maybe he does know more and is just toying with us."

"Even if he is toying with us, eventually he's going to have to show his hand," I said quickly. My stomach was twisting in ever-tighter knots the more I listened to him. He radiated tension and stress. I couldn't let him snap. I just couldn't.

He smiled at me, a sad smile, before kissing my temple. "I hope you're right." He tossed the last of his drink into his mouth before checking his watch. "It's late. I better go. See you tomorrow?"

I nodded as I watched him gather his keys and prepare to leave. I tried not to read into it—after all, he did say "love you" the other day.

Still, I couldn't help thinking it was the first time he had come over that we didn't end up in bed. Well, other than the night Alan showed up, but that really didn't count.

I tried to tell myself it didn't mean anything. Or maybe all it meant was our relationship was maturing.

But no matter how much I tried, I still felt hollow and incomplete as I listened to the click of the door closing.

Chapter 14

"It's just like old times," Lou said, looking around the table and beaming at us. Even in the dim light of the Tipsy Cow, I thought she looked exhausted. "I wasn't sure if we would ever get together again."

Claire gave her a strained smile. "Yeah, things have been hectic."

Lou's smile turned brittle. "They must have. I've never had so much trouble getting a hold of you before."

I stared down into my rum and Diet Coke. I had ordered it mostly because I felt like I should have at least one drink, seeing as I was in a bar. But now that I had it, my stomach felt way too queasy to drink it. I wondered if I should just order a club soda with lime.

In contrast, Jonathan had nearly finished his beer and was scanning the restaurant for a waitress for a refill. I was worried about him. He was drinking way too much, and he hadn't made eye contact with me at all since he'd joined us for drinks.

I really hoped he hadn't done anything stupid.

Claire seemed to be struggling with her response to Lou. "I know I haven't been that responsive, and I'm sorry about that." She looked pale and tired as well, with dark puffy circles under her eyes. Man, did we all look awful. Was that just a coincidence?

"So, what *has* been going on?" Lou asked, her voice as sharp as her smile.

Bill laid a hand on Lou's. "Now, now, Lou," he said. "This may not be the best time." I couldn't help but notice how healthy and, well, happy Bill looked. His skin had that ruddy tone that sometimes appears after a day in the sun, and he looked rested and refreshed. It was especially noticeable compared to how awful Lou looked. Maybe their daughter was waking up at night, and Bill was making Lou get up with her. If that was the case, Bill should really take a turn, so Lou could get a couple of good nights of sleep.

Lou shrugged Bill off. "If not now, then when?" Her smile was still plastered on her face, but it was as cold and hard as her expression. Clearly, she was angry, and no amount of polite conversation was going to cut it.

Claire looked like she was physically in pain. I wondered what her affair with Jesse was costing her. And I wondered if it was worth it.

She opened her mouth, then closed it.

"Lou," Jesse began. He looked almost as uncomfortable as Claire.

"Not now, Jesse," Lou snapped. "I want to hear from Claire."

Claire looked trapped. "It's nothing, Lou," she started, but I interrupted her.

"The séance didn't work," I said.

Everyone at the table jerked their head toward me, their expressions startled. That is, except for Jonathan, who looked horrified.

"Charlie," Jonathan began, but I shook my head. I had to do something. I couldn't let Claire sit and twist in discomfort.

"What do you mean?" Lou asked. "What happened? Has Alan contacted you?"

I took a deep breath. I had to be careful. I was walking a fine line. "Claire didn't want to say anything because of me." Claire's eyes darted toward me, but she kept her mouth shut. "She saw something that night in the closet."

Lou's eyes were wide. "What did she see?"

I waved my hand. "I'll let her tell you. And just so you know, she didn't want to tell me, either, but then Red came into the diner."

Bill looked confused. "Red?"

"He owns The Lone Man Standing," I said. "And he said someone was hanging around the bar and asking about me."

Lou's mouth dropped open. "Oh my God. Is Alan here?"

I leaned forward. "I don't know, but Tad Clark, you know, from the *Redemption Times*? He stopped in the other day to tell me they found an abandoned rental car from New York here."

"What?" Jesse yelped. "Are you saying he's been here all along?"

I shrugged. "I don't know."

"Was he the one who rented the car?" Bill asked.

"We don't know. It was rented using a stolen identity."

"Oh my God," Lou said again. "And what about Alan? Did he contact you?"

"Look, I think Alan is dead," I said. "Personally, I think Red was lying about seeing Alan. He gave some half-assed description that sounded nothing like Alan. But," I leaned forward, making eye contact with everyone at the table. " I do think something is going on here. It may have all started with Alan, but that's not where it's ending. And it all began the night of the séance." I deliberately dropped my voice. "I think we opened something up."

Lou gasped. "What? Like what?"

I sat back and nodded my head toward Claire. "It's better coming from Claire."

Claire shot me a look that was part amused, part grateful, and part annoyed as Lou turned to her. "What is Charlie talking about?" Lou asked. "And how come you didn't tell me?"

"I should have, but it was too hard to talk about," Claire said.

"You told Charlie," Lou said.

"Only because she's more at risk," Claire said. "And, trust me, I didn't want to tell her, either. I didn't say anything for weeks."

"So what happened?" Lou's voice had softened and her body posture, so rigid and uncompromising earlier, had begun to relax. Hopefully, that meant her anger toward Claire was fading, as well.

Claire shot me another exasperated look. "It's about the dream."

Lou looked at her blankly.

"*The* dream," Claire said again. "The one we all had when we were kids."

"Oh," Bill said, turning to Lou. "Didn't Jillian have a bad dream like that a few years ago?"

"Yeah, I think there was something," Lou said vaguely. "Apparently, all the kids in her class had it, too. The teacher probably told them a scary story or something."

"You had it, too," Claire said. "Don't you remember? It took place long ago. People were wearing old-fashioned clothes, and they tied that girl up to a stake."

Lou looked confused. "That wasn't me," she said. "You must be mixing me up with Jesse. He had that dream when we were kids."

"No, I didn't," Jesse said. "It was you. Don't you remember?"

"There's nothing wrong with my memory," Lou snapped. "You're the one who doesn't remember. You never remember anything."

Claire extended her hand toward them. "You both had it," she said gently. "You've just both forgotten it."

"That's impossible," Lou said, glowering into her drink. "I don't forget anything."

What was going on with Lou? Why was she so upset? First at Claire, which at least made sense if she thought Claire was ignoring her. But why was she so mad at her brother?

"There's nothing to be ashamed of," Claire said gently. "It's happened to all of us."

Bill cleared his throat. "So what does this dream have to do with 'opening something up?'" He made air quotes.

"That night of the séance? I saw her," Claire answered.

"Her?"

"The girl in our dreams. The one who gets tied to the stake."

"Okay, but I still don't get the connection," Bill said. "Seeing that girl in your dream opened something up how?"

Claire looked around the table, her mouth opening and closing, before shrinking into herself. "It was just a feeling I had," she mumbled. "A really strong feeling that something shifted in that moment. It's like there was a boulder blocking an opening. But what we did that night pushed the boulder aside. And whatever was inside could then get out."

Everyone was silent for a moment.

"Look," I said. Everyone jumped, like they had forgotten I was there. "I know I'm the outsider here. But you guys kept telling me the story about how the town decides who stays and who goes. I don't know ... it feels like something has changed. Red is starting to become a real pain. He's been to the diner twice now, saying such cryptic things. And apparently, he had wanted to buy the Witch House from Helen, but she refused to sell to him."

"Did he ask you to buy it?" Bill asked.

"Not yet. But he's up to something. And then there's Tad Clark. Why is the reporter of a newspaper so interested in me? Did Red put him up to something? And why is this all happening now?"

"Maybe Red is trying to drive you away," Bill said. "I wouldn't put it past him. As for Tad, he was always a little snot-nosed tattletale. Even when we were kids. Remember when he told on you, Jonathan, for putting that firecracker in the boy's bathroom?"

"Yeah, he got me suspended for two days. I almost got expelled," Jonathan grumbled. "I still don't even know how he found out. No one was with me other than Jesse."

"Yeah, and you'd think he would have tattled on me, too, if he had seen us," Jesse said. "I have no idea why you were the only one to take the fall, but thank God you did. I would probably still be grounded, if my dad knew I had anything to do with that."

"Fat lot of good it did you," Lou said darkly into her drink.

"He was the ultimate hall monitor," Jesse said, pointedly ignoring his sister. "Always had to be poking around in things that didn't concern him. I don't know if I would worry too much about him, Charlie."

"The point I'm trying to make is that I think we need to make things right," I said. "Maybe Tad is just being a little weasel, and maybe Red is just trying to buy my house. But why is this all happening *now*? Is it related to what happened the night of the séance? And if it is, is there any way we can reverse it? Roll the boulder back over the opening, so to speak."

"Since we don't know how we rolled it away in the first place, I'm not sure what we can do to put it back," Jesse said.

"And, even if we did put it back," Claire added darkly, "It doesn't mean whatever we set free would be trapped again."

The reckoning is coming.

I shifted uneasily in my booth. It felt like a cold draft had blown across the back of my neck, as if something had touched me ... something with long, icy fingers trailing across my skin ...

"I need another drink," Jonathan said, interrupting my thoughts. He gestured to the waitress who was taking an order at another booth. "Another round?" He glanced around the table.

"Absolutely," Jesse said at the same time as Bill said, "You read my mind."

"I'd like a club soda with lime," I called to waitress. Jonathan raised his eyebrow at me. I shrugged. "My stomach is feeling a little queasy."

"I'll have the same," Lou said.

Everyone stared at her, and she looked around self-consciously. "What? I can't have club soda?"

"Not without vodka," Jesse said. "What's wrong? Aren't you feeling well?"

"Like you would care," she snapped.

"I do care," Jesse said, his voice rising slightly. "Why do you think I've stayed in Redemption this long?"

"Don't do me any favors," Lou said, and went back to glowering into her drink.

Everyone shifted uncomfortably. Bill nudged Lou slightly. "I think you should tell them."

Lou shook her head, muttering something under her breath.

"Tell us what?" Claire asked, alarmed. "Lou, is everything okay?"

Lou glared at her husband. "Everything is fine. I'm healthy. The baby is healthy. We're all healthy."

Jesse stared at her as Claire's eyes got round. "Baby?"

"Yes, I'm pregnant," she said.

Everyone erupted into congratulations. Bill beamed, and Lou tried to smile.

"Were you trying?" I asked.

"It was a happy accident," Bill said, putting his arm around Lou. Lou shrugged him off.

"No, we weren't trying," she said. "One is enough. More than enough. Jillian is already a handful, and the idea of no sleep and bottles and diapers all while dealing with Jillian ..." she huffed out a big sigh. Bill's face fell.

"I bet Jillian is looking forward to being a big sister," Claire said.

Lou cracked a tiny smile. "She is."

"Maybe you can channel some of her energy into helping you with the baby."

"Maybe," Lou said, but her face was thoughtful.

I looked at Jesse. "And I bet you're excited to be an uncle again."

Jesse opened his mouth to respond, but before he could, Lou interrupted. "No. He doesn't care at all about being an uncle."

Bill gasped. "Lou, that's enough."

"Lou, you know that's not true," Jesse protested. "I love spending time with Jillian."

"Then why are you leaving?" Lou cried out, tears in her eyes. "Why would you do that?"

Jesse was leaving? Had Claire known? I immediately tried to catch Claire's eye, but she had lowered her face, hiding her expression.

"Lou, we've been over this," Jesse said, dropping his face to his hand.

Bill reached to put a hand on Lou's arm. "Lou, maybe this isn't the best time to discuss it."

Lou slapped him away. "No. It's the perfect time to talk about it. He won't tell me why when we're in private. Maybe he'll finally share with his friends." She sat back defiantly, crossing her arms over her chest.

Bill closed his eyes. "Lou ..."

"Lou, all my life, you've known I've wanted to be an actor," Jesse said. "This isn't a secret."

"But you *are* acting," she said. "You're in community theater ..."

"That's not the same," he said before leaning across the table and taking her hand. "Look. I tried. I really did. I don't want to leave you or mom or Jillian or anyone. But I have dreams, too. And I'm getting older. If I want a shot, I need to take it now."

"But, it's so hard to be an actor," Lou said, tears sparkling on her lashes. Her makeup was smeared around her eyes. "What if you don't make it?"

'Then at least I'll know I tried," Jesse said. "I couldn't live with myself if I never even tried."

Lou turned away, hiding her face, as Jesse sat back. The waitress arrived and started handing out drinks.

"I'll still visit," Jesse continued. "I'll be back for Christmas and Thanksgiving, and when my new little nephew or niece makes his or her appearance. And I'm not leaving until after your Labor Day party."

"I don't even know if I'll have it this year," Lou said, dabbing at her eyes. "I'm not really in a partying mood."

"Oh, come on," Claire said. "You can't not have a party. How will we know fall has officially arrived?"

Lou grumbled an answer. Claire glanced at me.

"Every year, Lou and Bill host the best Labor Day party in Redemption," she said.

"Not to mention the only," Bill said drily.

Claire brushed him off. "Everyone who's anyone wants an invite."

I raised my eyebrows. "Oh. I hope that means I'll get one."

Claire winked at me. "I'll get my people on it."

"I really don't know about a party," Lou said. "I've got a terrible case of morning sickness, I'm already exhausted, and my feet hurt."

Bill squeezed her hand. "It's going to be an awesome party," he said. "I've already got some people lined up to help."

Lou eyed him. "You've asked people to help?"

"Of course. You need to rest. Don't worry about a thing."

A couple of tears escaped Lou's eyes, streaking down her face. "Pregnancy hormones," she gasped as she grabbed a napkin and tried to cover her face.

Bill looked at her with such love that it made my own eyes tear up. I glanced at Jonathan, who was paying more attention to his drink.

Until, well, the night Alan showed up, Jonathan had looked at me like that, too. But I wondered what it would feel like to be married to a man who did. To have it all out in the open instead of skulking around in the shadows.

Jonathan raised his drink to his lips. His face was ragged, his eyes so haunted.

I was struck by a wave of guilt. What price had he paid to fall in love with me?

What had I done?

And then, like an echo in my head, I heard it again.

The reckoning is coming.

The Reckoning

Chapter 15

I was clearing a table at Aunt May's when I saw the newspaper article.

I was already in a foul mood. I hadn't slept well at all, tossing and turning as I kept reliving what happened at the bar.

I got up as soon as it was light out, drank a cup of tea, fed Midnight, got dressed, and headed to Aunt May's for an early start to my shift. The idea of eating made me queasy. I promised myself I would have a good lunch.

The newspaper was folded over, so all I could see was part of the headline below the partially filled-out crossword puzzle, but I immediately knew what it was.

Mystery Surrounds Abandoned Rental Car.

My heart clenched in my chest, and I was instantly grateful I had skipped breakfast.

Trying to be as nonchalant as I could, I flipped over the newspaper so I could read the full article as I slowly continued clearing the table.

Police are requesting any information about an abandoned rental car found on Elm Drive.

Janice Anderson, who lives on Elm Drive, started the investigation by notifying the authorities about the car.

"I first noticed it on my walks," she said. "Every morning, I take Wilson for his walk, and that's when I saw it. After a week, I realized it never moved. I asked all my neighbors if it was one of theirs, and when they all said 'no,' I thought I'd better call it in."

While abandoned cars are not that unusual, abandoned rental cars are less common, especially when the person who rented the car used a stolen identity.

The name used to rent the car was Jerome Davis, but he had reported his wallet stolen around the time the car had been rented.

None of the local hospitals have reported treating any John Does in the past month.

If you have any knowledge of the driver or vehicle, please contact the police department.

"Hey, Charlie."

I jumped, knocking over a glass half-full of soda. The dark liquid spread over the table like a pool of blood. Glenn, the dishwasher, was staring at me. He was a thin, pimply faced kid who was about to start his senior year in high school.

"Sorry," I said, quickly mopping up the spill. I plucked the newspaper up before it could get wet and tucked it into my pocket. "You startled me."

Glenn nodded toward the kitchen. "Your order is up. Fred has been banging that bell for a few minutes now." He moved toward the table, holding the grey bucket. "I can take care of this."

I flashed him a quick smile. "Thanks."

He ducked his head, a faint blush staining his cheeks. I hurried to the kitchen and an irked Fred. "What are you doing out there? Taking a nap?" he grumbled.

"Didn't sleep well," I said. "I'll grab some coffee. That should take care of it."

He humphed. "Maybe you should get something to eat instead."

I started to tell him I was fine, but then I thought about it. Maybe Fred was right. Maybe a decent meal was exactly what I needed.

"Can you make me a tuna melt?" I asked.

He shot me a look. "Are you kidding? With fries, I assume."

I grinned. "I wouldn't have it any other way."

Even though my stomach still felt queasy, I was determined. A decent meal might make all the difference.

It was a few hours later before there was enough of a pause in customers for me to take my break. Fred had my meal ready and waiting for me in the kitchen, so I took it back to the break room to eat.

Claire was standing by her locker, fussing with her hair. "Oh, I didn't know you were working today," I said, picking up a fry. The food smelled better than I had expected, and my stomach grumbled hungrily.

Claire half-turned toward me. "I wasn't supposed to. I'm subbing for Liz. She has to take her daughter to the doctor today."

Claire looked awful. She was even more pale than the night before, and she had massive black circles under her eyes. It looked like she had tried to cover them with concealer, but the effect made it even worse. "How are you feeling?"

She glanced at me and forced a smile. "I'm fine."

I picked up my sandwich. "You sure?"

"Yeah. Well, I didn't sleep all that great. But that's nothing new." She slammed her locker shut.

I glanced at the door, making sure we were alone. "Did you know Jesse was leaving?" I asked, my voice low.

Claire paused, her head down, her back to me. She was breathing hard. I suddenly realized how thin she was—how the bones of her spine protruded from her thin tee shirt. Maybe I wasn't the only one Fred should be badgering to eat.

"I'm thinking about going with him," she said, her voice equally low.

I nearly dropped my sandwich. "What?"

She looked at me, her expression haunted. "It's crazy, right?"

I wasn't sure what to say. "Is it what you want?"

She dropped her gaze, hiding her face from me. "It's what I have always dreamed about. It was always my plan."

Which wasn't really an answer. "Yeah, but that was when you were in high school," I said carefully. "You weren't married then. Things have changed."

"I know," she said softly. There were lines on her face, around her eyes. I wondered if this decision was what was keeping her up at night.

"Have you talked to Doug yet?"

She shook her head sadly.

I sighed. "Oh, Claire."

"I know I have to tell him," she said. "I'm just waiting for the right time."

"I get that it's difficult, but don't you think it would be better to do it sooner than later?" I was trying to be as gentle as possible, but clearly, Claire was making herself sick. The sooner she came clean to Doug, the better.

She grimaced, hunching her shoulders as if I had physically hurt her. "It's not that simple," she said. "You don't know what it's like. I don't want to hurt him. He's a good man. He's just ..." she paused, seeming to struggle for words. "He's not right for me," she said at last. "He never was."

There was so much I wanted to say. Even though I understood—God, how I understood making a mistake and feeling trapped—she still made a decision that she needed to take responsibility for. I certainly wasn't judging her for what she was doing, as I was in no position to do that ... but it was obvious to anyone with eyes that she was tearing herself apart.

She had to stop lying. To herself, to Doug, to everyone, and come clean, letting the chips fall where they may. This weird people-pleasing thing she was doing, where she was trying to make everyone happy, was probably killing her.

But I didn't say any of that. It wasn't the time, and I wasn't sure if I was the right messenger. "What does Jesse say?" I asked instead. After all, this had to be just as obvious to Jesse as it was to me. Maybe he could talk some sense into her.

Claire made a big production out of finding a tissue and fiddling with it near her face, which she kept hidden from me. She mumbled something I couldn't hear.

"What?"

"We haven't talked about it," she said again, louder.

"You haven't talked about your conversation with Doug?"

She shook her head, her narrow shoulders trembling. "We haven't talked about me going with him," she said.

I stared at her, sure I hadn't heard her correctly. "Wait, you didn't just say you and Jesse haven't talked about you leaving with him, right?"

She scrubbed at her face with the tissue. "I have to get in there," she said. "I'm going to be late."

"But Claire," I said, reaching out to pluck at her arm as she went by. "This is important. Did Jesse tell you he wanted you to go with him?"

She avoided looking at me. "There are some things that don't need to be said," she said stiffly. "I know how he feels."

"Not in this case," I said. "Look, I'm not saying he doesn't care about you. That's obvious. It's written all over his face when he looks at you. But he kind of has to tell you he wants you to go with him before you blow your marriage up over this."

She squished her face up, and I saw the tears leaking from her eyes. I immediately felt horrible. "Oh, Claire. I'm sorry. I didn't mean to ..."

"It's fine," she said, brushing me off and snatching her arm away. "I have to go. We can talk about this later."

I watched her hurry down the hallway, her hands fluttering around her head as she no doubt tried to make herself as presentable as possible.

A part of me felt bad about our conversation. The timing had been rotten with her about to start her shift.

And yet ... I couldn't explain it, but I had a really bad feeling she was about to make a huge mistake, and that mistake was going to have bigger repercussions than any of us knew.

I quickly finished my lunch, making sure I ate every bite. I couldn't afford to get sick with everything that was happening around me, not to mention needing to keep my strength up. I made a mental note to start eating more regular meals. Then, I went out to hopefully grab a few quiet minutes with Claire and continue our conversation.

Unfortunately, that never happened as we were pretty busy the rest of my shift. The few times that I could have chatted with her, she was busy doing something else.

I even stayed a few minutes late, but she wasn't having any of it, telling me she had to leave immediately.

I didn't push her. She had to figure things out herself.

Still, I wished we could talk. Not just about what she was going to do about Jesse and her marriage, but also to get her take on the newspaper article. Even though Claire didn't know what really happened to Alan, and I would have to be careful when I spoke to her, I still thought she would be a better sounding board than Jonathan.

Jonathan was starting to worry me. Maybe it would be better if he didn't see the article. I didn't want him getting any more upset than he already was.

As I headed to my car, I saw Maude trundling toward me, pushing her ever-present shopping cart, its wheels making a "clickety clack" noise on the sidewalk cracks. "Hey, Maude," I called out.

Maude appeared to be too busy talking to herself to hear me, which was more common than not. I stood to the side of the sidewalk to let her pass, marveling at the amount of colorful clothes she was wearing. How she could stand the heat was beyond me.

She had almost passed me when her head snapped up. Her eyes fixated on mine. "I'm sorry about the cat," she said.

I blinked. "What cat?"

Her eyes looked directly into mine. They were a pretty, dark-emerald green. Her gaze was clear and focused, lacking even a trace of the madness that so often accompanied her like a dark cloud.

"The black cat," she said.

My mouth fell open. "What? What are you talking about?"

Maude turned away from me, continuing to plod past me. I ran back a few steps to face her. "What cat? What are you talking about?"

Maude shook her head, continuing to mutter. Her eyes were cloudy again, almost like a film was covering the irises. Whatever that moment was had vanished. I would get no more.

My unease growing, I hurried to my car. I had to get home as quickly as possible. Luckily, it was less than ten-minute drive, but that ten minutes felt like a lifetime.

As I pulled into my driveway, I saw a black furry mound on my porch stoop and felt the tightness in my chest relax. Midnight was waiting for me. Maude was confused, but it was all okay. Midnight was there, and spending the evening with the uncomplicated affection of my cat was the exact medicine I needed after the day I'd had.

I parked the car and got out, calling out happily to Midnight as I approached. But the closer I got, the more I started to sense that something was wrong. There was something off about what I was seeing. It was like Midnight had contorted his body in a very strange way. In fact, there was something unnatural and ...

I gasped, my hands flying up to my face as I dropped my purse.

Oh no. Not Midnight.

I ran up to the porch, trying not to scream, the tears already blinding me. No, no, no.

I fell to my knees next to the dead cat. His throat had been slashed, and blood had stained his black fur. I could smell the metallic scent of it, and for a moment, my vision swam, and I was kneeling in front of Alan as the blood pooled out of him, soaking my clothes, my skin ...

I pressed the heels of my palm against my eyes. *No, no, no. This isn't happening again. Stop it.*

I didn't want to look. I didn't want to see my cat like that. But I knew I had to, so when I felt like I had gotten myself under control, I slowly peeled my hands away, swiping the tears away from my face to focus on the terrible scene in front of me.

It wasn't Midnight.

I blinked a few times and leaned forward to take a closer look. While the poor little cat's face was stiff and contorted, there was a white patch of fur under its chin that not even the dried blood could completely cover up.

Clearly not Midnight.

The rush of relief made me sag, despite the touch of guilt about being so relieved.

Maude was wrong. It wasn't Midnight after all.

Except ... didn't she say, "sorry about THE cat"?

The feeling of uneasiness was back, and it was bigger. Prickles of fear made my skin stand up with goosebumps.

How did Maude know?

Could she do something like this?

If it wasn't her, then who?

And what did it mean?

And where WAS Midnight?

I glanced around the yard, but it was empty. No sign of my cat or of who could have done such a terrible thing.

I looked back down at the cat and saw the body was lying on a newspaper. There appeared to be something written across it, except the cat's body was hiding the words.

With trembling hands, I picked up the bottom of the newspaper and shook it, so the body would slide across. I gasped as I read them.

Go home.

I dropped the paper as if it had burned me and backed away so quickly, I almost fell off the porch.

The words appeared to have been written in the cat's blood.

Who would do something like that?

And why?

A cloud passed across the sun, plunging the yard into darkness. I shivered, folding my arms across my chest. My stomach heaved, threatening vomit, but I managed to keep everything down.

Suddenly, the thought—*was whoever did this still here?*

My head snapped around as I tried to look everywhere at once. Was someone standing in the shadows of a tree, watching me in my panic? Just waiting for the moment when I was most vulnerable to attack?

My skin crawled, sure there were eyes studying me. I wanted to scream. I wanted to get into my car and drive as far away as possible.

Meow.

My head jerked toward the sound. Midnight was trotting toward me, tail straight up in the air. As soon as he was close enough, he leaped into my arms and started to purr.

It took me by surprise. Midnight had never allowed me to pick him up before. But in that moment, it was exactly what I needed.

He was warm and soft and heavy and *alive*. Oh, so wonderfully alive. His aliveness grounded and reassured me. I squeezed him tighter, burying my face in his fur. A few hairs tickled my nose as I breathed in the wonderful cat smell.

He's alive. He's alive. He's alive.

Finally, my heartbeat and breathing calmed down enough to allow me to think clearly. I needed to get into the house and to a phone. I had to call the police and Jonathan.

Still holding Midnight, who was being very patient with me clutching him as tightly as I was, I reached down to scoop up my purse and keys and made my way into the house.

The Reckoning

Chapter 16

Jonathan was the first to arrive.

I watched him drive up from the living room window, holding a hot cup of tea almost as tightly as I had held Midnight.

He pulled over on the side of the road and leapt out of the car, hurrying up the walkway at a dead run. I found myself wondering if that's what he did the night I paged him because Alan was in the house.

He raced up the steps and stopped in his tracks when he saw the cat. I watched as he pressed his lips together and squeezed his hands into fists, his chest heaving.

I went over to the front door and opened it.

"Want to come in?"

Jonathan kept staring at the cat. "Who could have done this?" His voice was low, almost as if he was talking to himself. "It's got to be Red. I just never thought he would have it in him to kill an animal."

"Hopefully, that's what the cops can figure out."

He ran one hand roughly through his hair. I could see the tension on his face. "You called them already?"

"Yes, they should be here within the hour," I said. "Do you want to come in and wait for them?"

Jonathan looked up, an odd expression on his face. "Maybe that wasn't such a good idea," he said.

I frowned. "What are you talking about? You told me to call the police."

"Yes, but ..." he gestured toward the cat. "Didn't you see the newspaper?"

"Yes. I already told you. It says, 'Go home.'"

He shook his head. "No, the article."

"What are you talking about?"

He gestured again. "Look again at the article."

I didn't want to look. I already knew I'd have nightmares. But I could tell from the set expression on Jonathan's face that he wasn't going to take "no" for an answer. I shuffled a couple of steps forward and peered down.

The blood had stained the newspaper, so it was hard to make out individual words, but I was able to decipher some of the headline.

Mystery ... Abandoned Rental Car.

My stomach twisted sickeningly and dropped to the floor. I met Jonathan's eyes and saw the same horror reflected in them.

"Maybe it doesn't mean anything," I said. "Maybe it's a coincidence."

Jonathan's eyes bored into mine. "You really believe that?"

I looked away, focusing instead on the green evergreen trees gently swaying on the side of the property. "I don't know what to think," I said at last. "But even if it was intentional, it still doesn't mean whoever did this knows anything."

Jonathan's mouth worked and his hands balled into fists. "I don't like it," he said. "I don't like anything about this."

I folded my arms across my chest. "You think I do?"

That seemed to sink in. He looked up, his expression full of anguish. "Oh, God. Babe, I'm so sorry." He took two steps toward me and I was in his arms, feeling his warmth and inhaling his masculinity. I shuddered, trying not to cry, knowing if I started, I would never stop. "You have no idea how much it tears me up inside having to leave you here alone and unprotected. I will do everything I can to make this stop."

Something stirred inside me uneasily when he said that, but before I could analyze it, he was letting go of me and the moment passed. "Let's get inside," he said. "We don't need to be out here when the cops come. Although," he shot me a hopeful look. "There's probably no way you can cancel it."

I gave him a look. "Seriously? Don't you think that would be *more* suspicious?"

His shoulders sagged. "No, I guess you're right."

It took another ten minutes before we heard the knock at the door. I was in the kitchen making Jonathan a cup of tea, even though it was clear that he really wanted a stiffer kind of drink. I made a comment about keeping a clear head, and he agreed to the tea.

I heard Jonathan open the door and greet the cop. Carrying both cups of tea, I went out to join them.

The cop was crouched down examining the cat, but he stood when he saw me, holding out his hand and introducing himself as Officer Murphy. Officer Murphy was an older, grizzled-looking cop with grey hair, a slight paunch, and a calm and thoughtful demeanor. "Sorry we had to meet under such circumstances," he said. His voice was low and gravely, and he smelled of cigarettes and old coffee.

"Not a problem," I said, although I couldn't help but wonder how often people meet a police officer other than under difficult circumstances. "Would you like something to drink? Tea or coffee?"

"No, ma'am. If I have any more coffee, I might float away." He smiled slightly as he said it, before shifting back to examine the cat again. "Do you want to tell me what happened?"

I swallowed, steeling myself to explain the details again. Jonathan caught my eye and smiled encouragingly. It struck me then how strange it was to have Jonathan there. What must Officer Murphy think, to find a married man alone with a single woman? But if he was bothered by it, he hid it well.

Haltingly, bolstered by many sips of rapidly cooling tea, I relayed the story of coming home and finding the cat. Officer Murphy nodded as he took notes in a small notebook he had removed from his breast pocket.

"So, you have a black cat?" he asked.

"Midnight," I said.

"Where is Midnight now?"

"In the house. Safe," I said.

He nodded, studying the cat. "You may want to keep Midnight inside for a while."

I swallowed hard again and nodded. Midnight may not like being stuck inside, but he'd have to get used to it.

"Who else knows you have a black cat?"

The question took me by surprise. "I, ah ..." I looked helplessly at Jonathan. "I have no idea."

Officer Murphy glanced up at me, one grey eyebrow raised. "You have no idea?"

"I inherited Midnight," I explained. "He's Helen's cat. Well," I amended. "I don't know if he's really anyone's cat. He kind of comes and goes as he pleases. But Helen was taking care of him, and when she sold me the house, I took over. So, I don't know who else knows about him. I haven't really talked about him, I don't think."

Officer Murphy nodded and straightened up. I could hear the creek of his knees. "Is this how you found it? Did you touch anything or move anything?"

"It's basically how I found it. I picked up the newspaper by the back to move the cat so I could see the words." It was hard to talk past the huge lump in my throat.

"So, the body was covering the words?"

I nodded.

"What about you?" He eyed Jonathan.

"I didn't touch anything," Jonathan said.

Officer Murphy nodded. "Okay. Let me bag this up. Then, can we talk inside for a few minutes?" Despite the phrasing, it wasn't exactly a question.

My mouth was so dry, I could barely answer, but I was able to nod. "Of course."

I backed into the house, followed by Jonathan. Not sure what to do, I headed into the kitchen. Maybe I would make more tea for everyone. That would be better than searching every nook and cranny for any drops of blood I had somehow missed despite my obsessive cleanings.

"Don't be nervous," Jonathan said in a low voice. "Murphy is a good guy."

My hand shook as I filled the tea kettle. "You know him?"

"Everyone knows Murphy."

I put the tea kettle on the stove. "Do you think he thinks it's ... weird that you're here?"

"I told him you and I were friends, and I was just here to give some moral support."

I shot Jonathan a look. "Friends? You think he bought it?"

Jonathan shrugged. "Does it matter?"

I supposed it didn't, at least not when it came to investigating a dead cat on my porch. But I didn't like the way the lies were all starting to pile up around me. Would there come a time when they outnumbered the truths? And, if that happened, would I cease to know the difference between the two?

"Definitely push him toward Red," Jonathan said.

"We don't know it's Red."

"Of course we do," Jonathan hissed, coming closer to me. "Who else would it be?"

Jonathan had a point. But then the image of Maude watching me with her dark, emerald-green eyes (not completely unlike Midnight's eyes, now that I thought about it) resurfaced in my mind.

I'm sorry about the cat.

"Maude knew."

Jonathan stared at me like I had lost my mind. "Maude? Who's Maude? You don't mean Maude, Maude."

"Yes, her. I saw her on my way home. She said, 'I'm sorry about the cat.'"

Jonathan sighed as he tugged at his hair again. "You know Maude is crazy, right?"

"Maude is doing the best she can. And yes, I know she's not in her right mind, but I don't know that we can dismiss her like that."

"Okay, okay. You're right. Maybe you misheard her or something."

I put the tea pot down with a clatter on the counter and turned to face him. "I did NOT mishear her. When I asked her what cat, she answered, 'The black cat.'"

Jonathan was silent as I went back to my tea preparations. "Okay, look. I'm not going to pretend I understand what that was about. But Maude is harmless. She would never hurt a cat."

"How did she know?"

"Maybe she saw something. Maybe she even witnessed it."

I turned back to him. "You think so? But I've never seen her out here before."

Jonathan shrugged. "Maude gets around. You'd be surprised where she wanders on her daily trek."

The tea kettle started to whistle. I took it off the stove to fill the tea pot. "I hadn't considered that. What an awful thing for her to see. Poor Maude."

Jonathan started to reply, but a firm knock at the door stopped him. "I'll get it," he said.

I nervously wiped my hands on my jeans before picking up the tea pot and cups to bring to the table. The kitchen is clean, I reminded myself as my eyes darted around it one last time.

Jonathan came back into the kitchen, followed by Officer Murphy, who had taken his hat off, revealing a mostly bald head with a few wisps of grey.

"I thought you might like some tea," I said, trying not to sound as anxious as I felt.

Officer Murphy nodded. "Thank you, ma'am. That will hit the spot."

I joined them at the table, fussing with the tea as I poured it. "Do you want cream or sugar?"

"No, this is fine," he said, picking up the cup and taking a sip. "Wow, I've never tasted anything like this. What kind is it?"

"It's my own blend," I said. "Lavender mostly, with some lemon and rose petals, plus a few other things."

"It's really good," he said, taking another sip. "My wife would love it."

"Well, you can buy her a bag, if you'd like," I said, half-jokingly.

He raised his eyebrow. "You're selling tea?"

"Yeah, it's a little side gig," I said. "But don't feel like you actually have to buy any. I was just kidding."

"We'll talk more," he said, putting the cup down and fishing out a little notebook and pencil. "Okay, so do you have any idea who would do something like this?"

I eyed Jonathan, who gave me a tiny nod. "I think it might be Red."

Officer Murphy started to scribble. "Last name?"

"I don't know his last name, but he's the owner of The Lone Man Standing."

Officer Murphy glanced at me. "And why would you think he's behind this?"

I took a deep breath. "He's been coming into Aunt May's during my shifts and saying things."

"What kind of things?"

"That someone has been looking for me."

"Who?"

I realized how cold I was. I pulled my tea closer to me, wanting to draw in the heat. "I don't know. He didn't say who. Just some guy from New York."

Officer Murphy stopped writing. "Do you think it has anything to do with that abandoned rental car?"

"Maybe. I don't know. I have no idea who, if anyone, was asking for me."

Officer Murphy grunted and made a few notes. "Do you know anything about that abandoned rental car?"

"No sir."

"How do you know Red?"

"I don't. I mean, he came into the diner to tell me about some guy asking questions about me in his bar."

"And that's it?"

I clutched my mug tightly. I wanted to take a drink, but I was afraid my hands would shake so much, I would spill it all over. I desperately wanted to look at Jonathan but was afraid of what Officer Murphy would see. Despite his calm, grandfatherly ways, I had a feeling he was a sharp observer. "He came back one more time. To check to see if whoever it was had found me."

"Why would he be so interested? Especially since it sounds like he doesn't know you."

I licked my dry lips. "I think he wants to buy my house."

Officer Murphy went back to writing. "And how do you know that?"

"He told me he tried to buy it from Helen."

"When did he tell you this?"

"When we went to the bar."

"You went to the bar? When was this?"

"After the first time he came in. We wanted to ask him some questions, so we went that night."

"Who's 'we'?"

"Claire, Jesse, Jonathan, and myself."

Officer Murphy asked for last names, and Jonathan jumped in to tell him, before chiming in on what he saw that night. "I think he's trying to chase Charlie away," he finished.

"Maybe," Officer Murphy said, making a little noncommittal sound. "We'll check it out. Anything or anyone else?"

I shook my head.

"Made any enemies?"

"I haven't been here long enough to make any enemies," I said, with a squeaky laugh.

Officer Murphy smiled. "Of course not. What about any ex boyfriends or bad breakups?"

"No. I mean, I was engaged, but he died." I felt like I was stuttering. My tongue seemed to swell to three times its normal size.

Officer Murphy looked contrite. "Oh, I'm so sorry."

"Don't be. I mean," I waved my head, feeling more and more like a fool. "We had broken up, and he got in a car accident. I mean, it's sad, but ..." I was babbling. I forced myself to shut my mouth.

"Ah. Well, that's too bad. However, I guess we can safely cross him off the list of people who would be asking about you."

I smiled, but it felt stretched too thin and overly taunt. I gritted my teeth to keep myself from saying anything more.

Officer Murphy fished around in his pocket and pulled out a card. "If you think of anything else, please call. Anytime."

I reached over to pick it up. It had both the police station number and a pager. "I will."

"So, what's going to happen to Red?" Jonathan asked.

Officer Murphy sighed deeply as he tucked his notebook and pencil into his pocket. "At this point, probably not much."

I stared at him. "What?"

He held his hand out. "We'll look for evidence on the newspaper and body. And, of course, I'll go talk to him. But, unless we can uncover some hard evidence, it's going to be nearly impossible to prove."

"But he killed a cat," I said.

"Allegedly. If there's no proof, there's not a lot we can do."

"But ..." I was flummoxed. How could there be nothing the cops could do? "What about the 'Go home' on the newspaper? Isn't that a threat?"

"It is, but if we can't prove he had anything to do with the cat, we're not going to be able to prove he left that message."

"What if there was a witness?" The words were out of my mouth before I could decide whether it was a good idea.

Officer Murphy's eyebrows went up as he patted his pocket with the notebook. "Witness?"

"Yes, Maude." Now that I had started it, I might as well go all in. "You know, the homeless woman? As I was leaving the diner today, I saw her. She told me she was sorry about the cat."

Officer Murphy was busy writing. "Sorry about your cat?"

"No. THE cat. She said 'THE,' not 'your.' And when I asked her what cat, she said, 'The black cat.'"

Officer Murphy paused to stare at me. "Then what?"

"I asked her for more details, but she was ... lost again, I guess you would say. I was really uneasy and rushed home. Anyway, what if she saw what happened? What if she's a witness?"

"I'll talk to her," Officer Murphy said. "It certainly seems like she saw something. Anything else?"

I shook my head. Officer Murphy finished writing and replaced his notebook in his pocket. "I'll be in touch," he said, standing up and reaching out a hand to shake mine. "And I'll also be in touch about that tea." He winked at me.

I thanked him and walked him to the door. "Remember to keep your cat inside," he said as he stepped out, putting his hat on his head. "And you might want to be extra cautious, as well. Lock your doors and windows, and keep an eye out for any strange cars or people around your house or in your neighborhood."

The sun was starting to set, filling the yard with long, twisted shadows. The temperature had dropped as well, and I folded my arms across my chest for warmth. "Should I be worried?"

"Cautious, not worried," he said. "More likely than not, this was kids playing a really sick joke. Maybe they found a dead cat and decided to mess with you. I would definitely be cautious and observant. Call me if you see anything you don't think looks right. But chances are, this is the end of it."

I really hoped he was right.

When I returned to the kitchen, Jonathan was pulling a beer out of the fridge. "What the hell are our taxes paying for?" he fumed, digging in the drawers for the bottle opener. "I can't believe he's not going to do anything."

"He didn't say he wasn't going to do anything," I said, keeping my voice as calm as possible, hoping that would calm him down in turn. "He said he was going to investigate."

"And then what?" He shook his head violently. "Nothing is going to happen. You can tell he already thinks he isn't going to find anything."

"He didn't say that exactly," I protested, although it was sort of what he said. "And besides, he told me when he was leaving it was probably just kids playing a sick joke."

Jonathan shot me a look. "You don't really believe that, do you?"

I had no answer. I silently watched him as he took a drink.

"I can't stand it," he said. "Leaving you here. Alone. After seeing what was done to that cat. Who does that? Someone twisted, that's who. And that person's out there, and the cops are no help."

"I'll be careful," I said. "I'll keep the doors and the windows locked at all times."

"That didn't stop Alan from breaking in," he said darkly.

I winced. He saw my face and immediately, his expression softened. "I'm sorry, babe. I'm not trying to worry you. I just don't like this. I *really* don't like this."

"Alan may have snuck in earlier," I said, my voice low. "I had left the door open when I first came home." I left out the part where I had been talking to Jonathan on the phone at the time. "I checked the house, but it's possible I missed something."

"Seems unlikely he was inside for that long," Jonathan said. "But it's possible. Still." He frowned as he looked around the house. "It's not like this house is Fort Knox."

"I'll call a locksmith," I said. "Have them put in a deadbolt. Maybe change the locks, as well. It's possible someone has a key from when Helen was here."

"That would help," Jonathan said, but he continued to frown.

"I'll call tomorrow," I said.

He drummed his fingers on the counter. "I still don't like you here alone. Even with new locks."

"Let's start with that," I said. "Maybe we can also look into some sort of alarm system."

Jonathan drained the rest of the beer. "Okay, you do that," he said. "And I'll see what I can do."

I was instantly on edge. "What do you mean?"

"Well, I think I need to go to the source," he said, dropping the bottle in the recycle bin.

Oh no. "What does that mean?"

"I think it's time to have a little chat with Red," he said, fishing out his keys.

Every cell in my body screamed what a bad idea that was. "Jonathan, no. We talked about this, remember? We agreed it was a bad idea to talk to Red."

"It was a bad idea to talk to Red before," he corrected. "But now, we have a cat to discuss."

"I really don't think that's a good idea," I said. "We should just leave this to the police."

"Do you mean the same police who told you it was kids playing a prank?

Does that sound like he's taking it seriously?"

"You don't know he won't investigate. He's probably just trying to make me feel better as he looks into it."

"And do you really think he's going to find something with an attitude like that?" Jonathan shook his head. "Charlie, we have to take matters into our own hands, here. We have no choice."

"At least let's wait and see what Officer Murphy comes up with," I said, feeling desperate. "Maybe he's right and it IS just kids."

Jonathan came over to me, drawing me into his arms and kissing my temple. "Charlie, I am NOT going to let anything happen to you. We have no idea how long it's going to take Officer Murphy to get around to investigating. In the meantime, your safety is my priority. We need to put this behind us so we can get on with our lives. It will be fine. I'm not going to reveal anything. I'm just going to ask a few questions, that's all. That way, even if he is behind it, he'll probably think twice before doing anything else."

"Why don't I come with you?"

Jonathan was already shaking his head. "I think it's better if you stay here. It's safer. I'm already worried enough about you."

"Then at least call Jesse," I said. "Don't go there alone. That will be worse. Especially if Frank is there."

He sighed. "Okay, if it will make you feel better, I'll call Jesse." He kissed me again, squeezing my arms. "Don't worry. I'll be very discreet. Even if Frank is there. I promise I won't let him get to me."

"But if something happens to you ..."

He put a finger in front of my lips. "Hey. Nothing is going to happen to me. I'll be fine. All I'm going to do is get to the bottom of this and stop this harassment. That's it. Okay?"

"Okay," I said, but I didn't believe it.

He hugged me. "I have to go, but I'll check in later. And don't forget to lock your doors."

"And you don't forget to call Jesse," I said.

He smiled, blew me a kiss, and left.

I automatically went to the door and locked it, then watched him head to his car. There was a determined air about him that was completely different than the worry and tension of the past few weeks. It was the walk of a man who had made a decision and was at peace with it.

In a different place and time, maybe I would have felt reassured watching him, knowing he had everything under control.

Instead, I was filled with a dark sense of foreboding.

The Reckoning

Chapter 17

I called Claire.

As the darkness started to fall, nestling the house in a pillow of darkness, all I could think about was the dead cat.

Go home.

The idea that maybe there was someone out there, watching me, someone sadistic enough to kill a cat, ate at me. Added to my worry about what Jonathan was doing, I was a complete wreck.

At first, Claire was hesitant when she realized it was me. But once I told her about finding a dead cat on my doorstep, her hesitation disappeared. "I'll be over in a half hour," she said.

I hung up, already feeling a little better. Even though I knew it would be tricky talking to her without revealing too much, I felt like I had to take the chance. If I didn't tell someone, if I didn't relieve the pressure in my chest, I thought I might explode.

While I waited for her to arrive, I heated up some soup and forced myself to eat it, along with some cheese and crackers. My stomach grumbled and threatened to revolt, but after I got a few bites down, it started to settle. Not eating right wasn't good for me. I was sure it was adding to my general anxiety.

I had just finished making another cup of tea when Claire arrived.

"That really smells good," she said.

"Want me to make you a cup? Or I have wine."

"Tea is good. Let's do that."

I went back to the kitchen to start preparations while she sat down at the table. "So, you actually found a dead cat on your porch? Tell me from the beginning."

I pulled a clean mug out of the cupboard for Claire and started to talk. I told her everything, from running into Maude to Jonathan leaving in frustration.

By the time I was done, the tea was in front of her and I was at the table clutching my own mug, trying to soak up every ounce of warmth into my oh-so-cold body.

"This is terrifying," Claire exclaimed when I took a breath. "And why aren't the cops taking it more seriously?"

"I don't think Officer Murphy thinks they're going to find anything," I said.

"Yes, but still. And how did someone know you had a black cat? That doesn't sound like kids to me. Were you being watched?"

The taste of tea on my tongue turned bitter. I forced myself to swallow. I had been trying not to think about that. "I don't think anyone was watching me, but I don't know. Midnight has been hanging around here for a while. It's possible they knew because they've seen him before."

"I suppose, but it's not like Helen had a lot of visitors." Claire sipped her tea. "This is really good. You definitely have to sell this."

I smiled, my first real smile since I'd left work. "Officer Murphy thinks so, too."

Claire raised an eyebrow. "Officer Murphy? Nice. See, you're getting clients left and right. You'll be quitting Aunt May's in no time."

"Well, let's not get ahead of ourselves," I said. I wasn't sure if I was ready to start my own business. There was still so much I didn't know. Having a steady job felt safer.

"You really think it was Red?" Claire asked.

I shrugged. "Jonathan sure does."

Her eyes narrowed. "But what about you?"

"Who else could it be?"

Claire gave me an odd look. "Alan."

I gulped, spilling my tea. "What? Alan?" I reached for a napkin to mop up the table. "Why would you think of him?"

Her expression shifted so it was tinged with suspicion. "Isn't it obvious? The car."

Oh crap. The car. An abandoned rental car from New York. Of course it would seem obvious that it was Alan. I wanted to whack myself on the head. How could I have been so careless?

"It's not really Alan's style to kill a cat," I said. "He's more likely to show up and demand I return home with him."

Claire's eyes were round. "Charlie, are you listening to yourself? If he's alive, he's already killed a man. What would stop him from killing a cat?"

I was silent. She was right.

Claire's expression softened as she reached over to grasp my hand. "Look, maybe it's not that," she said, and I realized she was misunderstanding what she saw on my face. "Maybe it's not Alan after all."

I looked at her in surprise. "What?"

"Hear me out," she said. "I've been thinking about this. It's weird that you haven't seen Alan anywhere, nor does there appear to be any proof he's staying anywhere. On the other hand, who else could this be? Unless," she paused dramatically. "It's someone Alan sent."

I was having trouble breathing. "Like who?"

"A private investigator, maybe. Or," she said, warming up to the thought. "Maybe it's a criminal."

My eyes widened. "A criminal?"

"Why else would the person have rented a car under a fake name? It would explain a lot, like why he was hanging around The Lone Man Standing. A criminal would definitely feel at home there." She let out a short laugh. "And it would also explain why the description didn't sound like Alan."

I couldn't answer. All I could do was stare at her, my mouth hanging open.

Was it possible? Had Alan hired some sort of thug to come and torment me?

And maybe that thug didn't even realize Alan was dead.

This was just getting worse and worse.

Claire saw my face, and her eyes widened. "Oh Charlie. I didn't mean to scare you. I thought that would make you feel better."

"It's okay," I managed. "It's just ... I didn't even think about Alan having a partner in all of this. But yeah, it would explain pretty much everything. But, oh God, Claire." I buried my face in my hands. "I don't even know what this guy looks like. How am I supposed to protect myself?"

"Hey, hey, it's going to be okay," Claire said, reaching out to grasp my hand. "Now you know it's a possibility, which is the first step in coming up with a plan. Maybe the place to start is to tell Officer Murphy all about Alan and whatnot, and then he can keep an eye out, as well."

I wasn't entirely sure if it was a good or bad idea, but I nodded, mumbling "tomorrow" into my palms. Then I groaned as another thought struck me.

"Jonathan. Do you think I should tell him?" I lifted my hands away to look at Claire.

She gave me a confused look. "Well, yeah. Eventually."

"I mean now. He might be going to The Lone Man Standing to talk to Red. Although Jesse should be with him."

She cocked her head to study me. "Do you think it matters?"

"Well, it's just ... he's upset and wants to protect me," I said. "I don't want him going off on Red because he thinks Red is lying when there's another possible explanation."

Claire was quiet for a moment. "Can you get a hold of him?"

"Yeah, I have his pager." I got up and went to the phone, punching in the code we had if I just wanted him to call.

Claire silently watched me as she sipped her tea. "Can I ask you something?"

"Sure," I said, distractedly. I stayed by the phone, watching it closely, willing it to ring.

"Are you afraid of Jonathan?"

I snapped my head around. "What?"

At that moment, the phone rang, and I scooped it up.

"What's going on?" Jonathan demanded. "Are you safe?"

"I'm fine," I said quickly. "Claire is with me."

"So, what's going on?" He sounded guarded.

"What if Alan hired someone?"

"What?"

"The abandoned car," I said quickly. "Claire thought maybe Alan hired someone to spy on me. Either a private investigator, which is probably not likely because whoever rented the car used a fake identity, or some sort of criminal. And if that person doesn't know Alan is dead, he still could be here in Redemption watching me and trying to scare me."

Jonathan was quiet for a moment. In the background, I could hear the sound of a car backfiring. "So, you're thinking this person Alan hired may be the one who did that to the cat? Instead of Red?"

"Yes, that's what I'm saying."

Loud voices sounded in the background. "Charlie, I've got to go. We'll talk later."

"Jonathan, are you hearing what I'm saying?"

"Yes, I heard you. I have to go."

"Say hi to Jesse," I said.

"What? Oh, sure. Talk soon."

He hung up before I could ask him if Jesse was actually there. I put the phone in the cradle. "More tea?" I asked brightly.

"Sure," Claire said, watching me carefully. "So, are you?"

I didn't look at her, instead focusing on refilling the kettle. "Am I what?"

"Afraid of Jonathan."

I still didn't look at her. "Why would you ask that?"

"Because of how you're acting," she said. "You're acting like you're afraid of him."

I put the kettle on the stove and sighed. "It's not that I'm afraid of him," I said, my voice low. "I'm just worried. He's wound so tight, and he's so concerned about me. He hates leaving me here on my own, and when that cat appeared ..." My voice trailed off, and I busied myself pulling the tea leaves out of the cupboard.

"Charlie."

I jumped. Claire had gotten up silently and moved closer to me without my realizing she had left the table. "You have to watch yourself with him."

"I know. I am. But it's not me I'm worried about. I just don't want him to do something tonight that he regrets."

As soon as the words left my mouth, I realized how true they were. What if Jonathan said something he shouldn't? Or, even worse, what if he ended up doing something?

"Maybe I should go," I said.

"To The Lone Man Standing?" Claire started to shake her head. "I think that's a really bad idea."

"Why?"

"Well, you don't know who killed that cat for one," she said. "Do you really want to put yourself in danger? If, God forbid, that were to happen, how do you think Jonathan would react then?"

Good point. "That's true."

"And how do you think it would look to show up at The Lone Man Standing looking for Jonathan? How do you think Jonathan is going to react if it seems like you're chasing him down?"

Another good point. "Yeah, that's true, too."

"Jonathan is an adult. He's going to have to get himself under control. You can't be the one chasing him down. Besides, Jesse is with him, right? So, what's the worst that could happen?"

I could think of all sorts of things—they were popping into my brain like popcorn. But Claire was right. Me running into The Lone Man Standing looking for Jonathan could easily backfire, and if Jonathan was hellbent on talking to Red, which I knew he was, he would just find another time to go there. And next time, he might not bring Jesse.

Hopefully, Jesse really was there.

I brought the tea pot over. "I just feel so helpless. I wish there was something I could do."

"Well, staying safe is a good first step," she said, watching me pour the tea. "Which includes keeping yourself safe from Jonathan."

"Jonathan would never hurt me," I said. "At least not physically."

She gave me an unreadable look. "I hope you're right."

"Changing the subject," I said. "Do you want to talk about Jesse? We don't have to," I said, as I could see Claire's expression start to close down. "I'm really grateful you came over tonight. I needed someone to talk to. So, I'll respect whatever you want to do."

Claire picked up her cup, but only held it. "I appreciate that. I know I have to talk to Jesse. And Doug. And I'm dreading the conversations. I also don't want to leave Redemption, but every time I think about living without Jesse, it feels like my heart stops beating." She sighed and rubbed her forehead. "I don't want to be in this situation. I really don't. I want everything to go back to the way it was."

I leaned forward to rest my forearms against the counter. "Is there any way Jesse would change his mind?"

"I doubt it. He seems pretty determined. And the more Lou pushes ..." She gazed up at the ceiling in exasperation. "If Lou hadn't been acting as insane as she's been, Jesse probably would have stayed until after the baby was born. But she's like a woman possessed. I'm sure it's the pregnancy hormones, and I know she didn't want another child."

My eyes widened. "She didn't? I mean, I know she didn't seem that happy about it, but I just thought she was having a bad moment."

Claire shook her head. "No. To be honest, she never wanted children at all. Not even when we were younger. It was always Bill. Bill would love nothing better than to have four, five kids, maybe even more. Even though Lou didn't want kids, I think she resigned herself to having a couple. After all, that's what you do, right? You grow up, get married, have a couple of children, and then retire. But Jillian was enough for her. More than enough. She didn't want anymore, even though Bill did."

"Was Bill pushing her?"

"Not exactly. I think he kept hoping she would change her mind. So, when she got pregnant accidentally, he was over-the-moon excited. Lou, on the other hand, immediately became depressed."

"And now, she finds out her beloved brother is leaving at the same time she's pregnant." I let out a deep sigh. "I guess I can see why she's so crazy right now."

"Yeah, but unfortunately, all she's doing is making her worst nightmare come true. She's pushing Jesse away, pushing me away. Bill is a saint, but eventually, she might succeed in pushing him away, as well. And then she really will be alone." Claire's expression darkened as she stared into her cup, but then she glanced up at the clock. "Oh, my. It's later than I thought. I have to go. I have to open tomorrow. Except," she paused as she gave me a hard look. "Are you sure you're going to be fine?"

"Yes," I said, and I meant it. "I'll lock the door behind you, and tomorrow, I'll call about getting the locks changed and new deadbolts."

"I can sleep over if you'd like," she said, although she didn't sound enthused about the prospect. I didn't blame her. She was going to end up having to get up awfully early if she had to open and she slept here. "I'll just call Doug ..."

"No, I'll be fine." I said firmly. "Look, whoever left the cat clearly meant to scare me. If someone wanted to hurt me, why leave a warning like that? I suspect whoever it was wants me to stew for a while, and then leave." At least, that was my hope. My words sounded more confident than I felt.

"If you're sure," Claire said.

"I'm sure." I picked up her keys and bundled her out the door.

I walked out with her, standing on the porch step. The air felt muggy and heavy, like a storm was coming.

Claire started down the driveway, but paused halfway down and turned to me. "Charlie, be careful."

Her face was in the shadow, so I couldn't see her expression, but her voice was odd, causing a shiver to run down my spine. I hugged myself and said, "Of course, mom," trying to lighten the mood.

"I mean it," she said. A breeze rustled by, blowing her hair back at the same moment the moon came out from behind the clouds and shined its silvery light on her face. In that moment, she didn't look like Claire at all. She reminded me of one of those statues of saints or angels, their expressions filled with a noble grief.

"Are you sensing something?" The question popped out of my mouth without even realizing I was going to ask it.

"I'm not sure," she said. "I just ... I don't have a good feeling about this. About any of this. And especially about Jonathan. Something isn't right with him. I don't know what it is, but there's something ... some darkness brewing inside him. Please be careful, Charlie. I don't know where any of this headed, but wherever it is, I don't think it's good."

The reckoning is coming.

The air pressed itself around me, suffocating me. I was having trouble breathing.

I thought about Jonathan, about how he seemed to be hanging on by a thread. The night we killed Alan, I had been amazed at how he had held it together. But now, he seemed to be unraveling more and more every day.

What would happen if he completely fell apart?

"I'll be careful," I said quietly. "I promise."

She studied me for another minute, cocking her head before giving me a tiny nod and turning to leave.

I watched her go, trying not to think about all the places someone could hide on my property and watch without my knowing. I could almost feel eyes on me, my skin itching and crawling with that sensation, before I practically fled into the house.

The Reckoning

Chapter 18

"Look at what you've done," Annabelle wailed.

She was hunched over on a wooden bench missing a leg. Behind her was a counter messy with smeared makeup, combs with broken teeth, and clumps of hair. Above that was a cracked mirror.

Annabelle was wearing rags that had at one point been a bridesmaid's dress, but was now reduced to a mess of filthy and torn material.

"What did I do?"

Outside was a thump, so loud it rattled the furniture. Annabelle flinched. "You could have just married him, but no. You had to reject him. And now look at what you've put into motion."

Another thump outside, accompanied by an odd dragging noise. The sweet smell of decay filled the air. "He was abusive, Annabelle. You know this. You saw what he did to me."

Thump. Screech.

"Maybe you should have thought about that before you got engaged," Annabelle said bitterly. "Did you ever think about that? You were in such a hurry to get married. You dove into a relationship without taking the time to see if he was someone you even wanted to spend the rest of your life with."

My eyes widened. "You wanted me to get married," I said. "I thought it was what *you* wanted."

Thump. Screech.

"Oh yeah, this is exactly what I wanted," Annabelle snapped. "I wanted you to be happy. I always told you that was all I ever wanted. Yes, I wanted you to get married and have kids, but my God. Was it so hard to find someone who would treat you well? Instead of falling for a guy who nearly killed you?"

I wanted to defend myself. I wanted to tell her she wasn't being fair.

But the truth was, she was right. I had been in a rush, wanting my 'life' to start. I didn't want to wait for the perfect man. I wanted the fairy tale right then.

So, I settled. For the first man who offered it to me.

Yes, sure, I tried to tell myself I was in love. But, if I was being brutally honest, I knew I wasn't. I just thought whatever we had would be enough.

How could I have been so wrong?

Guilt rose up inside me, nearly choking me, almost drowning out the smell of death and decay that was getting stronger by the minute. The first night I met Alan flashed through my mind. It was at a party. I hadn't wanted to go. I had a headache, and all I wanted to do was curl up on the couch with a movie and a cup of tea.

But Trudi had been incessant. "Come," she said. There's going to be a lot of eligible guys there. It's time you moved on from Chuck. You need to get back out there."

So, I got dressed and went, even though no part of me wanted to.

Afterward, I had thought Trudi was my guardian angel. But maybe she was more like a devil tempting me to my own demise.

If I had never met Alan, if we had never dated, would any of this be happening?

Thump. Screech.

Whatever was making that sound was getting closer. Annabelle tried to squeeze into a smaller ball, trying to disappear.

"Always remember," Annabelle hissed. "Whatever happens, however this ends up, however many people end up dying, this is all because of you. You're the one with blood on your hands."

Whatever was outside crashed against the door. Splinters flew off as the old wood groaned under the weight. Clouds of dust filled the air.

"What other people?" I asked. "No one has died except for Alan, who probably deserved it."

Annabelle's lips stretched into a hideous grin. They turned black, and she seemed to have way too many teeth in her mouth. "Just you wait," she said. "The death count has only just begun."

Before I could question her further, the door flew open with a bang, and Alan stood on the other side. He was covered with blood and insects, and one leg dragged behind him. The smell of decay was so strong, it made me cough.

He smiled, showing rows and rows of rotten teeth. "I hope I'm not late. I got here as quickly as I could." His tongue was black.

"You're dead," I said.

His grin widened. "Are you sure? Maybe your boyfriend didn't do such a good job."

A black cat wove its way through Alan's legs, purring. I could see the long bloody slit around its neck. "It was you! You left the cat?"

"Alas, no, I can't take credit for that. But maybe I helped inspire the one who did."

"Who was it?" I demanded.

"All in good time," he said. "Right now, you have bigger worries. Much bigger worries." He stepped closer to me, his leg practically coming off. A couple of squirming maggots fell on the ground with a plop. "Wake up. The reckoning is coming."

I awoke with a jolt. Outside was the low rumble of thunder in the distance. Was it raining again, or was it just threatening? Was that what woke me?

Wake up. The reckoning is coming.

No, it had to be the thunder. It couldn't be Alan's corpse, or whatever that was. It was just a nasty, terrible dream.

Alan is dead. He can't hurt you anymore.

I stared at the ceiling, chanting the words over and over, feeling my breathing start to relax and calm down. *It's just my subconscious healing,* I reminded myself. It wasn't uncommon to have horrible dreams for months or even years while the brain fully processed a trauma.

I lay there for a while, trying to decide if I would be able to fall back asleep, but every time my eyes closed and I started to drift off, I would see Alan's grinning, decomposed face leering at me.

You have much bigger worries.

Finally, I gave up and decided to make myself a cup of tea. I slid out of bed, careful not to disturb Midnight, who picked his head up anyway and watched me. He stood up and stretched before hopping off the bed and padding toward the bedroom door.

I didn't bother turning on any lights. I felt my way down the stairs, one hand lightly touching the wall to help give me my bearing.

I was about to step into the kitchen when I froze, my heart beating erratically.

There was someone there.

I could see the dark shape standing against the window.

Before I could stop myself, I gasped, then clapped my hands across my mouth to not make a sound. All I could think about was Alan's dead, decaying body, lurching toward me from my dream.

Are you sure? Maybe your boyfriend didn't do such a good job after all.

No! Alan was dead. He was dead! He wasn't standing in my kitchen in the dark, covered with writhing insects, smelling of death and blood, just waiting for me to come downstairs so he could grab me and drag me back to his open grave ...

The blood was pounding in my ears so loudly, I couldn't hear anything. The shape hadn't moved. I wondered if I could make it to the phone, or if it would be safer to run back upstairs to a phone up there, but that would mean being trapped upstairs ...

The dark shadow moved, and I tried to keep myself from screaming. "Charlie, it's me," Jonathan's voice floated toward me in the darkness.

I nearly collapsed in relief. "Jonathan. Oh my God, are you trying to kill me? What are you doing down here in the dark? Why didn't you say something sooner?"

"I didn't realize you were there. I'm sorry." His voice sounded odd.

"Well, why are you standing there in the dark?" I asked again, moving toward the light switch.

"No!" His voice stopped me. "Keep it off."

I stood in the doorway, my hand still hovering in the air. Something was off. I could feel it. My skin was practically crawling with it, like I just stepped on a bed of maggots. "Jonathan, what's going on? You're scaring me."

"I couldn't decide if I should wake you or not. I'm sorry."

"What is going on?"

There was a strange smell in the room, thick and metallic, and somehow familiar. It was mixed with something else—something dank and wet and earthy. My stomach twisted, and I wanted to retch.

The death count has only just begun.

"I didn't mean for it to happen," he said. "You have to believe me. I didn't mean to do it. It was an accident."

"Do *what*?"

"Kill her."

Thunder rumbled from somewhere in the distance. I couldn't have heard him right.

"Did you say, *'kill her'*?"

"I didn't mean for it to happen. You have to believe me. It was an accident."

"Jonathan, are you telling me you killed someone tonight?" My knees were shaking so badly, I didn't think they could hold me up, and I wildly flung my arms out to grab something, anything, to steady me, to ground me in this swirling, dark nightmare. The back of my hand hit a chair and I lunged for it, holding on for dear life.

Whatever happens, however this ends up, however many people end up dying, this is all because of you. You're the one with blood on your hands.

"It wasn't my fault," he said. "She knew."

"She knew? What did she know?"

"Alan. She knew about Alan."

My whole world tilted sideways. Claire. Oh my God, he killed Claire. My stomach heaved, and I was sure I was going to be sick. "Who knew?" I could barely push the words out of my mouth. "Jonathan, who did you kill?"

Jonathan took a couple steps toward me, close enough so I could make out his features, even in the dark. His eyes were wild, and his face was smeared with something. Blood? Tears?

"Charlie, I had no choice. I didn't want to, but I had to do something. I wasn't trying to kill her. It just happened."

"Who. Did. You. Kill?" If he didn't answer, I thought I would start to scream and never stop.

"Rosie."

For a moment, I could only stare at him, unable to compute the words that came out of his mouth. I was so certain he was going to say "Claire" that at first, I thought I had heard him wrong. "Rosie? Who the hell is Rosie?"

"The waitress at The Lone Man Standing."

Now my knees did buckle, even while hanging onto the back of the chair. Jonathan swooped forward and caught me, guiding me gently to sit at the table. "I can make you some tea," he said.

"You can't make tea," I said, but Jonathan was already moving to the kitchen, bustling around, filling the tea kettle.

"We've both had quite a shock," he said, pulling tea out of the drawer. "I'll make tea and we can talk."

"Jonathan, what ..." I started to say, but he shook his head firmly.

"Tea first, then talk."

I fell silent, watching him prepare the tea. The kitchen was already lighter than when I first walked in, the night outside melting into dawn. It must be later, or earlier, depending on how you looked at it, than I thought.

He deposited a mug in front of me, then pulled a chair closer to me. His hands were cracked with patches of something dark. Was it blood? I didn't think so.

He clutched his mug but didn't drink it, almost like he was trying to suck the warmth out of it instead. "Drink," he said.

I wanted answers, not tea, but I obediently picked up the mug and took a sip. It was really sweet; he must have added sugar.

"For shock," he said, picking up his own cup like a toast. "I have it, too." He took a long drink.

"I guess you want to know what happened," he said finally.

"Please," I said. The tea was helping. I could feel my blood pressure start to lower, but it wasn't doing anything about the feeling of dread that was growing inside me.

"I went to The Lone Man Standing," Jonathan began. He was already calmer, more in control of himself, more like the Jonathan I remembered. "I couldn't talk to Red right away because it was busy, so I ordered a beer and sat at the table. Frank was there, but he was getting drunk at a table in the back with a couple of other losers, so he never even noticed me. Anyway, I was sitting at that table when you called."

"You and Jesse," I said. "Right?"

He looked abashed. "Jesse wasn't there."

"What? You told me he was."

"I know, I know," he said, rubbing his eyes. "Look, I did call him, but I couldn't reach him. So I just went on my own."

I couldn't decide if I wanted to hit him or howl in frustration. Maybe both. Or maybe I just wanted a good cry. "Why did you tell me he was there?"

"Because I didn't want to get into it with you right then," he said. "The reason why it was busy was because there was a big group in there, and they were leaving as we were on the phone. I wanted my chance to talk to him."

"So, what happened then?"

Jonathan slammed his hand on the table, making me jump. "Nothing. I'm sure that bastard is lying."

"But he might not be lying. Alan could have sent someone …"

"We both know he didn't," Jonathan said, glaring at me. "Although I'm glad Claire thinks that. Otherwise, that car could be trouble for us. No, it was Red. I'm sure of it. Even though he refused to admit it."

"Why do you think he's lying?"

"Because he had this smug expression on his face the whole time. 'A dead cat, you say. Sounds like someone wants Charlie to go home.'"

"Well, that *was* the message," I said.

Jonathan shook his head in frustration. "You don't understand. I didn't tell him about the words on the newspaper. I just told him there was a dead cat left on your doorstep. He knew those exact words. Why would he say, 'Go home,' and not 'Leave,' or 'Move,' or something else?"

"It could be coincidence."

"Please." Jonathan rolled his eyes.

"Maybe we should call Officer Murphy," I said.

"No," Jonathan said quickly. "We can't. Not now."

"You don't think Red is going to tell Officer Murphy you were there tonight?" I asked incredulously.

Jonathan paused. "You're right. We should get ahead of this. Show we have nothing to hide. Let's talk to him tomorrow."

None of this was sitting right with me. I was feeling more and more uneasy at how calculating Jonathan was being. "What about Rosie?"

"I'm getting to that," he took another long swallow of tea. "I was so pissed when I left the bar. I knew he was lying, but I couldn't prove any of it. Do you know he actually said, 'Maybe it would be safer if Charlie left. Have you considered that?' It was a threat! Plain and simple. He was threatening you. But there was nothing I could do. So I sat in my car and fumed, trying to figure out what I could do to keep you safe.

"Then I remembered where I was. I could ask the town to help."

Oh no. I pressed my hand against my stomach, willing myself to keep the contents down. "What did you do?"

"Well, first I had to get the candles. Which was fine, because I didn't want to leave my car in the parking lot anyhow, so I was going to have to drive somewhere. I had to sneak into my house. Luckily, everyone was asleep. Then I drove back, but I parked on a side street a few blocks away and hiked over there.

"I found my way back to the same area where we did it as kids. I arranged the candles, lit them, and ..." His voice trailed off.

I closed my eyes. "And, what?"

"I asked Redemption for help with Red. But I also, well ... it's hard to explain. I just started talking, and everything I had been worried about—if I had hidden Alan's body well enough, if I should check, if there was anything else I should do—came out.

"Then I heard a noise behind me. The sound of a branch snapping. I turned around and there was Rosie, staring at me. Her eyes were wide and, even in the dark, I could see how terrified she was."

He started talking faster and faster, his words tumbling out of him as if it would somehow cleanse him of his sin to speak them. "She tried to get away, but I couldn't let her. You get that, right? I couldn't let that happen. So, I ran after her. I didn't want to hurt her. I was just going to try and talk to her, try and explain, try and do something, but then she started to scream, but I couldn't let her do that either, so I ... I shoved her. She slammed her head against a tree and just crumbled to the ground. I knew she was dead. The way her legs and arms were all twisted up, no one alive would have fallen like that."

My lips were completely numb. "Then what?"

"Well, I couldn't leave her like that, so I picked her up and carried her to a spot that was near the road, but without buildings or houses around, and I went back to get my car."

"She's in your car now?" I should have been horrified, but at that point, I felt like I was beyond horror.

He shook his head. "No, I took her to the same spot I buried Alan. And you know what? Totally undisturbed. I guess I was worried for nothing." He laughed a little. "Anyway, I buried her and used the lye, just like with Alan."

"What about the car?"

He frowned. "I moved it. It's back behind a shed. I did that before I buried her. I'm going to need your help. I think we should dump it further away, and maybe take off the license plate, as well."

My brain was foggy and slow, feeling almost like I was drunk. I was having a lot of trouble getting my head around everything he had told me. "You got all of that done tonight?"

"Yeah, it was kind of amazing," he said. "Everything just sort of ... fell into place."

Fell into place. I couldn't believe what I was hearing. "Jonathan, a woman is dead. How could anything have fallen into place?"

His mouth twisted up. "I know, and I feel terrible about it. I didn't mean to kill her. But what was I supposed to do?" He spread his hands out. "I couldn't have her going to the police or telling Red. I had no choice."

"We should have called the cops after Alan. If we had done that, then none of this would be happening."

"Yeah, things could also be a lot worse for us," he said sharply. Then he continued, softening his voice. "Look, there's no sense playing the 'What If?' game. We made our decision, and now we have to live with it. No, I'm not happy about Rosie, but it was an accident. A terrible accident. Now we have to pick up the pieces and move on."

I stared at Jonathan, watching his lips move as he spoke, feeling more and more disconnected from my body. Who was this man sitting at my table, so calmly talking about a murder being a terrible accident? Had I really loved him once?

Claire's voice floated through my head. *Be careful.*

I should have listened.

"Jonathan, I think we should turn ourselves in." My voice sounded rusty, like I hadn't used it for years, and it felt like it took all my energy to push the words out. "It's gone too far. I think we need to go to the police and confess and ..."

"No! Charlie, what are you talking about? It's not like it's going to bring either of them back. Why would we do that to ourselves? We're talking life in prison."

I swallowed hard. I didn't want to go to prison either, but this was getting so out of control. "But we can't keep killing people ..."

"And we won't," he assured me hastily. "Alan, we had no choice. It was self-defense. He would have killed you if we hadn't killed him first."

"I know, and if we explain ..."

"We can't explain," he interrupted. "Not anymore. The time for explaining was after it happened. How can we explain hiding the body? Living in silence for so long? No, we have to keep quiet now."

"But Rosie ..."

"Was a terrible accident," he said. "Accidents happen."

"Are there going to be any more accidents?" I asked, my voice bitter.

Jonathan stared at me in surprise. "Charlie, how can you think that?" He reached over to take my hands. I wanted to pull away. I didn't want him touching me, but I didn't stop him. His fingers were dry and warm. I could feel the grittiness of the dirt. I thought they would feel different, inhuman, but they felt just like Jonathan. "I'm not a killer. I'm trying to protect us, protect you. There's not going to be anyone else."

"How can I know that when there shouldn't have been a Rosie?"

"Because now I know," he said simply. "Look, I was so worried after Alan. I was sure I made a mistake. But now I know. I didn't make a mistake. All is fine. We just have to be calm and cool. I agree it was stupid for me to go into the woods the way I did, but now there's no need for me to do it anymore. And if no one else knows, there's nothing else that needs covering up."

"Promise?" I raised my gaze to stare into his eyes. "Promise me there will be no more killing?"

"I promise," he said. "Do you think I *wanted* to do this? I will happily promise you that."

His eyes were warm and full of love. *This is Jonathan,* I told myself. Jonathan. The man who had been trying to protect me and keep me safe since he showed up at Aunt May's parking lot, reassuring me about my broken car. He put himself in danger on more than one occasion for me. He got up in the middle of the night and rushed over here when Alan was threatening me. He defended me from Alan. He cleaned up the mess for me and kept me out of jail.

Was it so much to keep quiet about this? After all, it's not like he would be in this situation if it wasn't for me. Plus, Jonathan was right—nothing we did now would bring Rosie back.

All we could do was to go forward … to love each other and live the best lives we could.

"Okay," I said. Something shifted inside me at that moment, and I knew.

There was no turning back.

His eyes brightened, and he leaned over to kiss me. "I love you, Charlie," he whispered against my mouth. There would have been a time hearing him say that would have thrilled me. But my emotions must have been too wrung out, too exhausted, because it left me empty.

"I love you, too," I said. In a way, it was true. I had most definitely fallen in love with the Jonathan before everything happened.

I wasn't so sure about *this* Jonathan. But I also knew it didn't matter.

We were together. We would always be together.

"I have to take a shower," he said. "Do you mind washing my clothes again?"

"Not at all," I said. "Just leave them outside the bathroom. There's clean clothes in the closet for you, as well."

He kissed me again. "You're the best. What would I do without you?"

"Hopefully, you'll never have to find out."

He let go of me, finished his tea in one long gulp, then got up from the table. I listened to his footsteps on the stairs and down the hall. After a few moments, I heard the water turn on.

My stomach heaved and I lunged out of the chair, knocking it over in my haste, then running down the hall. I barely made it to the toilet in the downstairs bathroom before throwing everything up.

The Reckoning

Chapter 19

My shift at Aunt May's finally ended, and I immediately punched out and headed to my locker.

It was getting more and more difficult for me to show up to work. I was constantly exhausted, constantly nauseous. I was throwing up a lot more, which wasn't like me at all.

Needless to say, being on my feet all day and smelling food wasn't helping.

But, at least for the moment, the tea business had stalled, and I wasn't that interested in applying for a new job, so I was just dealing with it.

Actually, that was the real reason. Deep down, I felt like maybe I should suffer. I had caused everything that had happened. If I wasn't going to jail, then maybe I should suffer in other ways.

Other than scrubbing the shower like a fiend and washing Jonathan's clothes, there wasn't much to clean up after Rosie. Well, other than moving her car. Which was difficult. Jonathan drove it and I followed behind in mine. Twice, I had to pull over on the side of the road to vomit. By the time I reached the Milwaukee airport, which was where we were leaving it in long-term parking, I was a wrung-out emotional wreck. Jonathan took one look at my face and told me to get in the passenger seat. Our drive back was quiet. I closed my eyes and pretended to sleep, although my stomach was churning.

I grabbed my stuff out of my locker, making sure I avoided Claire. I had been careful to not talk to her for more than a few minutes since Rosie. She had wanted to talk about what happened at The Lone Man Standing with Jonathan, but all I said was that Red hadn't said much. I also told her that Officer Murphy had called with an update, which wasn't an update. Basically, the investigation was stalled. There was no evidence on the cat or the newspaper, and Red had denied everything. As for Maude, that was a dead end as well. He didn't tell me what she said, but it didn't sound like it was anything useful or even coherent.

In a way, it felt like I was stuck in some sort of holding pattern. Like someone had hit a giant pause button, and while time was continuing to go forward and I was moving through the motions of living each day, nothing felt real. Instead, it felt like I was waiting, holding my breath, for the other shoe to drop.

And I had a terrible feeling that I wasn't going to like it when it happened.

I went out the back door to the diner, even though that meant I had to walk around to get to my car. The day was hot and muggy, so damp it felt like I was breathing water, yet I preferred that to going through the restaurant and maybe getting stopped by someone.

I turned the corner and stopped dead. There was someone wearing a Black Sabbath tee shirt leaning against my car smoking a cigarette, bright-red hair gleaming in the sun.

Red.

For a second, I thought about turning around and heading back into the restaurant, but I could tell he saw me. Still, I hesitated. Even though the sun was out and there were people occasionally walking and driving by, there was no one else in the parking lot.

No one to hear me scream.

Enough of that. Did I really think he was going to attack me in broad daylight in downtown Redemption with potential witnesses all around us? What did I think he was going to do to me?

Still, he clearly knew what kind of car I drove. As creepy as that was, I couldn't allow my fears to run away from me. There was probably a perfectly legitimate explanation for how he knew. Maybe, now that I thought about it, it was because I still had New York license plates on the car.

On top of that, if I ran away from him now, did I think it would be the last of him? I had no doubt he would track me down another time so he could have his say, and it might be an even worse time and place. I might as well get it over with.

I squared my shoulders and walked over to him.

He watched me approach, a faint smirk on his face. My hand itched and I wanted nothing better than to slap it off.

"Red," I said by way of greeting. "Wasn't expecting to see you here today."

"Charlie," he said, taking the cigarette out of his mouth and dipping his chin slightly. "I was hoping to catch you after your shift."

I cocked my head and studied him. "And how did you know when my shift ended? Red, are you stalking me?" I kept my voice light and teasing while inside, my stomach twisted painfully. What was with this guy?

He held his hands up, palms up. "Not me. I don't need your boyfriend coming after me."

"I don't have a boyfriend," I said.

His lips curled in a sneer. "Oh, I think you do. But I confess ... I did call Aunt May's and asked when you would be getting off."

I ground my teeth. Ugh, Fred. It must have been him. Both Claire and Sue would have said something to me, and I certainly didn't take that call. Why would he tell a stranger my work hours? And why didn't he warn me?

Still, maybe it was better this way. Just get it over with.

"Well, I don't have a lot of time. What do you need?" I dangled my keys, shaking them so they sounded a merry jingle.

"I was just wondering if you've seen Rosie?"

My heart stopped. It took everything I had to not let my expression change. "Rosie? I'm afraid I don't know a Rosie."

"She was my waitress," he said, his eyes boring into mine. "She waited on you the night you came in."

I desperately wanted to back up or drop my gaze, anything to keep him from reading the truth from inside my soul, but a part of me knew that would be the biggest mistake I could make. Instead, I forced myself to hold my ground. "Oh, yeah. Right. I remember her. Why do you think I would have seen her?"

"Because she's missing."

I widened my eyes. "Missing? Well, that's a shame. Have you talked to the police?"

Red put his cigarette between his lips and deeply inhaled before blowing out a smoke ring. "I have."

"Well, then, I'm sure all is in good hands. If you'll excuse me," I made a move toward my car.

Red took a small step sideways, blocking my progress. "The thing is, it's very strange that she went missing the night after your boyfriend came to visit me."

My stomach tied itself in knots as the blood roared in my ears. It was so loud, I was sure he must hear it, too. "I don't know what to tell you," I said. "I'm not a detective, and I didn't know Rachel at all."

"Rosie," he corrected, his eyes narrowing. "Her name was Rosie."

"I still didn't know her," I said. "In fact, I'm not really sure why you're here at all. I don't know what I can do to help."

He stepped toward me, drawing himself to his full height. I could feel myself choking, my breath strangled in my throat. I was suddenly very aware of how alone we were, even in the hot sun standing in the middle of a parking lot. I should have listened to my instincts and gone back inside. "Here's the thing, Charlie. I think you can."

"Are you threatening me?" He reeked of cigarette smoke, sweat, and cheap whisky. I wondered if he had done a couple of shots before coming to see me. His black tee shirt was stained with sweat, and the faded skeleton on the shirt seemed to be jeering at me, as if it knew my secrets.

He gave me a twisted smile. "Not at all. But, I just think it's very ... *odd* that the waitress who has been with me the longest up and disappeared without saying a word to anyone the day after your boyfriend came in all hot and bothered about a dead cat on your stoop."

"Are you accusing me of something?"

"Not you. Your boyfriend."

"I don't know who you're talking about. I don't have a boyfriend."

"You know damn well who I'm talking about," Red snarled through gritted teeth. "Jonathan Decker."

"Oh, Jonathan," I said. "Jonathan is a friend of mine. He was just being neighborly, helping me out. I have no control over what he does and doesn't do. If you think he had something to do with your waitress disappearing, then maybe you should take it up with him."

Red dropped his cigarette to the concrete and ground it out with a booted heel and a little more force than I thought necessary. "Maybe I'll do that. Have a nice day, Charlie. I hope nothing bad happens to your cat."

"Charlie?"

I turned and saw Claire standing at the corner of the parking lot. "Everything okay?" she called out. I was so relieved to see her, I could have kissed her.

"Everything is fine."

"You forgot this," she said, holding up a Styrofoam package. I was about to call out that I didn't know what she was talking about, but then I thought better of it and jogged over to meet her.

"Why is he here?" she asked in a low voice once I caught up to her, her eyes never leaving Red.

"Is he gone?

"Yeah, he's leaving. What did he want?"

"I guess his waitress is missing. Rosie, I think her name is."

Her eyes shifted to focus on me. "Why would he think you know anything about that?"

I shook my head. "I have no idea. I think it's because of the dead cat that was left for me."

"What? Why would that dead cat have anything to do with Rosie missing?"

"I have no idea. But the cops interviewed him. Maybe Rosie overhead something? Didn't want to work with him anymore? Who knows?" I gestured to the container. "What's that?"

"Oh, this? It's a turkey, bacon, and provolone sandwich." She thrust it at me. "Fred made it for you and was fussing that you left so fast, he couldn't give it to you. I'm starting to think he's in love with you."

I took the container, not sure if I should be grateful or concerned. The last thing I needed was any other complications. "How did you know I was out here?"

She grimaced. "Gut feeling. That, and Fred was also fussing because he didn't have a chance to tell you some man had called to find out when you were off of work."

"Well, if he was fussing about it, why on earth would he tell Red in the first place?" I asked crossly.

Claire shook her head. "I don't know. I don't think he was thinking. I got the sense Red called when Fred was in the middle of a million things and answered without really thinking it through. By the time he figured it out, you were already gone."

I huffed a sigh. "Well, regardless of that, I'm glad you came out when you did."

"I am too." She gave me a quick hug. "I have to get back inside, but I'll watch to make sure you get to your car safely."

"You don't have to do that," I said, but I was secretly relieved she offered. I was still feeling shaky and unsteady after the encounter. Red wouldn't follow me to my house. Would he? Maybe I would drive around first, just to be sure. Although, the more I thought about, I realized how silly that was. Red didn't have to follow me anywhere. He knew where I lived.

I would just have to be extra careful. Thank God I had the locks changed a few days before and new deadbolts put in on all the doors. I had also bought pepper spray and a baseball bat. Although, I realized as I got in the car and turned the key, the pepper spray was at home. One canister in the kitchen and another in my bedroom. After today's encounter, I think I needed another to carry with me in my purse.

As I pulled out of the parking lot, I found myself wondering if all of that would be enough.

Chapter 20

I called Jonathan the moment I got home. "Has Red been to see you yet?"

"No, why?"

"He was waiting for me by my car after work," I said. "I think he might be visiting you soon."

Jonathan swore under his breath. "Are you home?"

"Yes."

"Okay, as soon as I can get off work, I'll be there. I have something else I want to tell you, anyway."

He hung up before I could ask any more questions, leaving me with a sick feeling in my stomach.

I wasn't sure I could take any more bad news.

I made myself a cup of tea to settle my nerves and decided to focus my energy on making dinner. I ended up making meatloaf, mashed potatoes, gravy, biscuits, chocolate chip cookies, and a salad. Everything from scratch. Once I started cooking, I couldn't stop.

I hoped Jonathan was hungry as there was no way I could eat all of it.

I was taking the cookies out of the oven when Jonathan walked in. "Wow, it smells amazing," he said, snagging a biscuit that was cooling on the rack and giving me a kiss. It was such a domestic moment, it brought tears to my eyes, and I quickly busied myself checking the potatoes.

This is crazy messed up, I told myself. *Get a hold of yourself.*

"What happened with Red?" he asked, picking up the corkscrew that lay next to the bottle of red wine and starting to open it. "Tell me everything."

I went through the whole story as he poured two glasses of wine and started sipping his.

"Bastard," he muttered when I was finished. "We gotta watch out for him."

"Clearly, he suspects something," I said. "Whether or not he knows something or is just fishing, I don't know."

"He's fishing," Jonathan said darkly, selecting another biscuit.

I was silent for a second as I focused on transferring the gravy to a bowl. "You're sure about that? That he didn't see anything?"

"Of course I am. There's no way." Jonathan came up behind me and wrapped his arms around my middle. "He didn't see anything. And there's no way they'll ever find Rosie's body. So, the worst that will happen is they'll trace Rosie's car to her, and they'll assume she's just gone. It's not a crime for an adult to disappear. There's no reason for anyone to dig much deeper than that."

"I'm sure you're right," I said, gently disengaging myself so I could get the food ready to serve. "But you should be prepared if Red comes to talk to you. He's definitely suspicious that Rosie disappeared the night you were there."

Jonathan picked up the salad and the platter of biscuits. "Well, as far as he knows, I was long gone by the time she left work. Remember, I left while the bar was still open. My car wasn't in the parking lot. Although ..." he paused as he picked up the butter and salad dressing.

I didn't like the way that sounded. "Although what?"

He shot me a sheepish look. "I'm not going to say anything to Red," he said. "But if he does bring in the cops or escalates it somehow, I may need to tell them where I went."

Oh no. I didn't like at all where this was going. I focused all my attention on the meatloaf, even though the smell of it was making me ill. "What are you saying?"

"I'm not asking you to lie," he said, although that was precisely what he was asking. I could see where this was going a mile away. "After all, I *did* come here that night. All I would need you to do is confirm I was here. That's all."

That's all. Just one more lie on top of all the other lies chipping away at my soul.

What's one more when I've already told so many? And all of those lies were so much worse than this one?

"Charlie?" Jonathan's voice floated toward me. "Did you hear me?"

What options did I have? I was already an accomplice in both murders. I was already in over my head, practically drowning in the muck and sewage of the lies.

And if I didn't agree to this one, then what? Was I going to let everything come crashing down because I refused to compromise about a few hours?

I wasn't sure what my problem was. It really ought to have been an easy "yes." So, why was I hesitating?

I straightened my shoulders and turned to face Jonathan with a smile. "Of course you can count on me. I was just distracted with the food." I held up the meatloaf with a flourish.

Jonathan's face relaxed, and he smiled back. "Looks wonderful, babe."

Still smiling, I brought it to the table. "Let's eat."

"So, you know," he said as he sat down in front of me. "The chances of me using you as an alibi are slim. I'm not looking to make our relationship public. I don't want to do that to Felicity. But, in case it comes down to it, I wanted you to know."

My smile became brittle. More lies. And the worst part was I had no one to blame but myself. I was the one who jumped into this nest of lies with my eyes wide open. I deserved everything I got.

"I get it," I said, wanting to change the subject. The last thing I wanted to do was talk about Felicity. Speaking of lies, I had no idea what he was telling her to explain why he simply didn't come home some nights, and at that moment, I didn't want to know. "So, didn't you say you had news?"

"Oh, of course," Jonathan said, shaking himself like he couldn't believe he had forgotten. "Frank called me."

I blinked. "What?"

"Yeah." Jonathan started scooping mashed potatoes on his plate. "I couldn't believe it either."

I put a biscuit and some salad on my plate. "What did he want?"

"Well, it was hard to understand as he was pretty emotional. I think he was drunk, too." Jonathan shook his head in disgust.

"Drunk?" I glanced at the clock. "When did he call you?"

"This afternoon, at work. But Frank never let a little thing like time of day get in the way of him and his whisky. Anyway, I guess he had gone in for some tests and the doctor called him. The results aren't good."

"What's wrong with him?"

"I think he said he has cancer," Jonathan said, taking a huge bite of meatloaf. "This is really good, by the way," he said to me around a mouthful.

"Thanks," I said. "Aren't you ... upset about it?"

Jonathan looked at me in surprise. "Why would I be upset? That son of a bitch beat me, beat my mother, and I'm sure he killed her even though no one could prove it. The beatings only stopped when I got big enough to hit back. The world would be a better place without him."

While I couldn't really blame him for thinking that, I still felt a wave of grief wash over me as I watched him eat. Suddenly, all I could see was the boy he must have been, all dark hair and eyes, with such an earnest, desperate-to-please expression. I wondered what would have happened if his mother hadn't married Frank, thereby subjecting her boy to such abuse. Maybe she would even still be here, a part of his life.

Maybe he wouldn't have been vulnerable to getting sucked into the mess I had dragged both of us into.

"Hey," Jonathan said, his expression shocked as I dabbed at my eyes. "Why are you upset?"

"I'm just ..." I paused, wondering how to put the words to what I was feeling and if it would even make sense if I did. "It makes me sad to think about your childhood and all you had to endure."

He reached over to squeeze my shoulder. "None of that," he said softly. "I'm fine. Maybe even stronger because of it. In fact ..." He broke off, shaking his head.

"In fact, what?"

He smiled slightly. "Nothing. Not important. It just goes to show that karma is real. It took a few years, but Frank is finally getting his."

A part of me wanted to push it, to ask Jonathan what he had been about to say. I knew he was hiding something. Was it something I should be concerned about?

Or would it turn out to be something I really didn't want to know?

I smiled and changed the topic to something else. Even though I might regret it later, in that moment, I didn't want any more unpleasant surprises.

***

"This isn't good," the Holly Hobby girl moaned. "This is worse than I ever thought it would be."

We were sitting across from each other at the little table in the backyard. Except it didn't look like the backyard, because the sky was a strange, reddish-orange color.

"What do you mean?" I asked.

"What he did ... what happened that night ...." She buried her face in her hands.

"What happened what night?"

She muttered something in response that I couldn't understand. She looked dreadful, way too thin, her cheeks gaunt, the skin grey. Her clothes were in tatters and her hair was coming out in clumps. She seemed to be just wasting away.

"What did you say?"

"We're doomed," she said. "We're all doomed."

The orange light seemed to darken, becoming more intense ... as if we were sitting in hell. My skin crawled. All I wanted to do was run into the house, lock the door, and get as far away from the orange light as possible. Except, when I turned to the house, I thought I could hear something. It sounded like the crying of a child.

You still have the power to stop it.

The black cat leaped onto the middle of the table and sat down, tail curled around its feet.

"Stop what?"

"We're not going to get anywhere if you keep ignoring the truth," the girl snapped. "You know what."

The crying seemed to get louder. I glanced at the house, wondering if I should investigate.

It won't be easy. But it's possible.

"It's too late," the girl said. "She can't stop it now. The blood sacrifice changed everything."

Shivers went down my spine. "What blood sacrifice? What are you talking about?" Even though I knew. Deep down, I knew.

The cat stared into my eyes. *Rosie.*

"She shouldn't have been there," the girl said. "I didn't think *she* would call her. But *she* did. And now we will all pay the price."

The cries seemed to change, become higher pitched. Almost like a scream.

Pay no attention to that.

"But ..."

It's a distraction. If you truly want to stop this, you must be strong. You must be focused. It's going to be the hardest thing you'll ever do. There will be consequences. But you CAN stop this.

I couldn't think. The orange and red sky seemed to press down on me. The cries—the screams—distracted me. I couldn't concentrate. "I don't understand," I said. "What am I stopping? It's over, right? Alan is dead. Rosie is dead too, but that was an accident. It's not going to happen again."

The cat and the girl looked at each other. Something seemed to pass between them.

"What?" I demanded.

It's not too late.

"You're delusional," the girl said disgustedly. "*She's* already won."

She certainly will if you give up.

"I don't know what you're talking about," I said, looking between the two bewilderedly. I was so confused. "Who is she? What am I supposed to be doing?"

"It doesn't matter," the girl said darkly. "The reckoning is coming. It's almost here."

We're out of time. We'll try and come back. But, whatever you do, don't pay attention to the crying.

I opened my eyes.

The bedroom was dark. Midnight was sleeping next to me. Jonathan had left hours ago.

For a moment, I wondered if I would see an orange and red sky if I peeked outside. But no, the room was too dark. It was the middle of the night. I was safe. All was well.

But was it?

What were my dreams trying to tell me? What was the message?

What was going to keep happening?

What was I supposed to stop?

I had a terrible feeling I knew exactly what the answer was, even though I kept telling myself it couldn't possibly be true.

No, I had to quit thinking those thoughts. I was just freaked out over the dream.

Everything was fine. Jonathan had assured me no more accidents would happen. Our lives would go back to normal. It would take some time to process everything that happened, but it would go back to normal.

I had no reason not to believe him. Why would he want to keep killing people? He wasn't a killer. He was just trying to protect me.

Right?

The Reckoning

Chapter 21

"Can I get you something to drink?" The words were out of my mouth before I recognized the man sitting in the booth.

He smiled at me and pushed his glasses up on his nose. "Hi, Charlie."

"Tad," I said, nodding my head. Inwardly, I groaned. This was the last thing I needed. "Would you like something to drink?"

"Diet Coke," he said. I quickly turned away before he could say anything more.

Things were just starting to calm down. Red hadn't been back to see me, nor had he approached Jonathan. At least, I assumed Jonathan would have told me if he had. Jonathan gave no indication of any type of run-in. In fact, he had been calmer, less concerned, almost happy.

Maybe things were finally going back to normal.

The only real issue was me. I was still having trouble sleeping, and even when I finally would drift off, I would be plagued by nightmares I couldn't quite remember when I awoke, other than that they seemed to be filled with fire and blood.

I was also having trouble keeping food down, throwing up practically every morning. It was awful. The only things that helped settle my stomach were tea and small amounts of dry toast.

This morning, however, nothing seemed to help. It was almost lunch time, and I was still horribly nauseous, on top of being exhausted after tossing and turning all night.

"Do you know what you want?" I asked, depositing the soda in front of Tad. I had debated handing him off to Claire, who would have taken over, but I was hesitant to show weakness. Better to look like I had nothing to hide.

"That chef salad was pretty tasty. I'll have that again," he said, his nasally tone even more pronounced. I wondered if his allergies were bothering him. I hurried away to avoid conversation.

It wasn't until I went to check on him after I brought his salad that he finally said something. I was just beginning to relax, thinking maybe he just had a hankering for a chef salad, and it was nothing more ominous than that when he said, "I was wondering if you could help me with something?"

"What?" I was hoping it was around my recommendation for dessert, but alas, that wasn't where he was going.

"Were you aware that a waitress at The Lone Man Standing disappeared?"

I stilled, my hand over my order pad. "I'm not sure how I can help you."

He smiled an empty smile and adjusted his glasses. "You could answer the question."

"Yes, I had heard that, but I don't see how that helps you."

"I didn't ask that. Just if you had heard."

I glanced over my shoulder. "I have to get back to work."

"Why are you so nervous?"

"I'm not nervous," I said, tucking my order pad back in my apron. "I just have to work."

"It's a simple question."

"And I answered it." I started to walk away, but Tad called after me. "So, you're saying you don't know anything about it?"

I turned back around, telling myself to stay cool, to not take the bait. "Of course I don't," I said. "I don't know her at all. She waited on me once."

"So you did know her."

"I met her," I corrected. "She served me a couple of drinks. Just like a lot of other people in Redemption. Perhaps you should be talking to them."

"You don't think it's strange? How she disappeared after meeting you?"

I put my hand on my hip and gave him a long, level stare. "You're still here," I said. "And I've met you." With that, I turned and headed back to the kitchen. I could feel myself shaking, but I willed myself to stay strong. I couldn't show weakness.

I broke down the moment I pushed past the doors, my knees trembling as I leaned against the metal counter.

Fred regarded me with alarm. "Charlie, are you okay?"

I waved him off. "I just need to sit down a moment. I haven't been sleeping well."

"You ought to eat something, too."

I forced a smile even though my stomach turned over at the thought of food. "Good idea." I fished out a few packages of saltines from the small bins we served with cups of soup.

Fred frowned. "That's not a meal."

"I know," I said quickly. "It's just a snack."

I tore open the packages as I headed back to the break room. Maybe Fred was right. Nothing else was helping.

I sank down on the bench as I nibbled on the crackers. I wanted some tea as well, but I didn't want the little store-bought bags that we served at Aunt May's. I wanted *my* tea. Maybe I needed to start bringing some with me. Then, I'd only need hot water. It probably wouldn't have mattered anyhow, as I didn't want to go back in the dining room either, where the waitress station and drinks were located.

How did Tad know so much? Was someone feeding him information? Was he friends with Red?

"Hey," Claire stuck her head in the doorway, her face worried. "Are you okay? Fred said you were back here."

"My stomach is upset. And I haven't been sleeping well," I said.

"Want some tea? Or ginger ale?"

"Ginger ale would be fantastic. Thank you."

She disappeared, and I closed my eyes, willing myself to relax. *Regardless of who was talking to Tad, he didn't really know anything*, I told myself. If he had, he would have asked me to walk with him again to push me with more questions. Instead, he just threw out some random, basic ones. I just had to get my head on straight.

Claire reappeared with the ginger ale, and I took it with a sigh. "You're a godsend."

"Happy to help." She fidgeted for a moment, still standing by the doorway. "What was Tad saying to you?"

I sipped the soda, shaking my head. "Nothing. He was asking me about Rosie."

"Rosie?" Claire cocked her head.

"The waitress who disappeared. Remember? She worked at The Lone Man Standing."

"Why was he asking you about that?"

"I have no idea." I tore open the second package of crackers. They were definitely helping. I was even starting to feel hungry.

Claire leaned against the doorjamb, studying me, an odd expression on her face. "Wasn't Red asking you about Rosie the other day?"

I eyed her cautiously. "Yes." I bit down into a cracker.

"And you don't think it's weird?"

"Well, yeah," I said, not sure how to answer. "But this is the second time that Tad and Red seemed to have conspired together on a story. It probably just means they're friends."

"Sounds like an awfully big coincidence," Claire said. "I'm wondering if there isn't something else going on."

My pulse started pounding in my temples. "What do you mean?" I could feel beads of sweat start to break out around my hairline.

"Maybe Rosie really did see Alan. Or whoever Alan sent to investigate. Maybe there really is a connection."

It started to dawn on me that I was going to have to tread carefully here. "Maybe," I said cautiously. "But that still doesn't explain what the connection is or why they think I had anything to do with Rosie disappearing."

"Because they think you know something about this mystery New Yorker," Claire said. "If you're tied to that person, whether it's Alan or the investigator or both, maybe they think you know more than you do. And maybe they also think that person did something to Rosie."

I shifted uncomfortably on the bench that had suddenly become quite hard. "But why would someone hurt Rosie? What does she have to do with any of it?"

Claire shrugged. "Maybe she saw something she shouldn't have. Who knows?"

The cracker I was holding snapped, crumbling into a million pieces in my sweaty fist. I picked up my napkin to try and unobtrusively clean it up, but it was too late. Claire had noticed.

"Oh, do you need another cracker?"

"No, I'm fine," I said, brushing off my hand. "Probably had enough already."

"Maybe a meal would be better than just a few crackers."

"Don't worry. I'll eat a meal later, too. Fred has been keeping a close eye on me." In fact, I realized right then that I would need to thank Fred for keeping me fed when all of this was over. If I didn't work at Aunt May's, I might have wasted away.

Claire gave me a worried look. "Are you sure it's just that? Maybe you need to go to the doctor. This has been going on for a while."

"Yeah, I think you're right. I've got to check into health insurance and then make an appointment."

Claire glanced down the hall. "I better get back, but I think you really need to be careful. I'm not sure what's going on, but I don't like how they zeroed in on you. Did Jonathan see Rosie?"

My hand jerked, sloshing ginger ale out of the can. "Crap. I didn't mean to do that."

Claire picked up another napkin and handed it to me. "Having some trouble eating *and* drinking today, aren't you?"

I forced a smile. "Remember, I didn't sleep well, either. Between that and the not eating because of my stomach, well, no wonder I'm a klutz. What did you mean?"

"That night he went to The Lone Man Standing. Was Rosie working there?"

I had to think fast. What was the best way to answer that? "I'm not sure."

She gave me a curious look. "Didn't you two talk about it? After Red accosted you in the parking lot?"

"Oh, yes, you're right." I made myself laugh. "Yeah, we did. Rosie was there that night. Jonathan didn't see anything off with her, but he doesn't know her, either."

"That's so weird that Jonathan was there too, probably right before she disappeared," Claire mused. "Again, such a coincidence."

"It is weird," I agreed as I stood up. I could feel the sweat starting to run down my back. The longer this conversation went on, the more I was worried Claire was going to start connecting the dots. I had to figure out a way to stop her. "Maybe you're right," I continued. "Maybe it does have something to do with that abandoned car. Maybe she did see or overhear something. Or," another thought struck me. "Maybe it has to do with the dead cat."

"What do you mean?"

"Well, that was why Jonathan was there that night. To ask Red about the dead cat. And maybe Rosie overhead the conversation and got scared. Maybe she knew something about that cat and didn't want anyone asking her questions about it."

Claire's eyes slowly widened. "Oh, maybe that IS it. That fits all the pieces, doesn't it? She knows something about that dead cat, probably who did it and why, and she's afraid of him. Who wouldn't be? If someone could do that to a helpless animal, what would he be willing to do to a person who threatened him? So, rather than risk someone asking too many questions, she decides to just disappear for a while."

"And, maybe Red suspects something, too," I said, warming up to the story. "That's why he's asking me questions, because if he can track down whoever owns that New York rental car, he'll be able to find Rosie."

"Claire," Fred bellowed from the kitchen. "What are you doing back there, watching *The Young and the Restless*? We need you up here."

"Coming," Claire shouted back. "I have to go," she said to me.

"I'll come too," I said. "I'm feeling much better now myself."

Which was true—I was feeling better, especially now that Claire seemed to be on board with this new theory that would hopefully distract her from anything that actually resembled the truth.

But deep down, I was still nervous. I didn't at all enjoy swimming in the cesspool of lies I'd created for myself, and I was getting more and more concerned I was going to end up tripping myself up. I had come close already, way too close for comfort. And the longer it went on, the more likely I was to eventually mess it all up.

I had to figure a way out.

The Reckoning

Chapter 22

"I can't believe this. Why can't they just leave it alone? Leave us alone?" Jonathan drained his glass of wine and reached for the bottle to refill it. "What point is there to coming into Aunt May's and harassing you? What do they expect to discover?"

"I don't know," I said, playing with my tea mug as I carefully watched him.

He showed up at my door in a foul mood and immediately headed over to the wine rack. I had mistakenly thought either Tad or Red had showed up at his work, but that wasn't the case. Then, because I had brought up Tad, I had to tell him what had happened earlier. The more I talked, the darker his face got.

"He's going to do something. I can feel it," Jonathan said, swigging most of the glass and refilling it. "First, he shows up at Aunt May's, and then he sends Tad? Something is brewing. I just wish ..." he broke off, shoving his hands through his hair roughly and pacing. He was like a caged tiger stalking around my kitchen—wanting to pounce, but not being able to.

"I'll get dinner started," I said, moving to the pantry as I kept an eye on him. He needed some food in him, especially considering how fast he was drinking. I pulled out some crackers and cheese and started arranging a platter.

"I don't like you here alone," he said broodingly, staring out the window. "I don't think it's safe."

I quietly sliced the cheese into little triangles and added olives and pickles to the tray. "I have protection ..."

"A baseball bat and some pepper spray aren't much for protection," he said bitterly.

"I also have new locks," I said calmly. "And deadbolts. You've seen all the locks."

"Yeah, I have." He kept staring out the window, studying the entire backyard.

I brought the platter over to him. "Have a snack."

While keeping his eyes fixed out the window, he reached over to take a couple of crackers and cheese. "I don't think it's enough. If someone really wanted to get in, I just ... I just don't like it."

"Maybe I do need to get an alarm system installed," I began, but I was interrupted by Jonathan's pager going off. He glanced at it and swore under his breath. "I have to take this. Do you mind?"

"Of course not."

I had expected him to use the kitchen phone, but instead, he headed to the living room to use the phone in there.

I tried not to listen as I pulled out some ground beef to start browning, but I still caught enough to know he wasn't talking to anyone from work. His voice was way too curt for a customer or someone he worked with, so I suspected it was his wife.

I focused on the food—chopped up an onion to throw into the meat along with some garlic, salt, pepper, and thyme. I wasn't sure where I was going with it, but knew I could put something together using it as a base.

I heard Jonathan slam the phone down and mutter something under his breath before he returned to the kitchen.

"I'm going to have to go soon, babe," he said regretfully, topping off his wine and snagging a few more crackers. "Felicity is ... well, she's being difficult. I have to go deal with it."

"Anything I can do to help?" I wondered why I was even asking. Was I really in a position to be giving him marriage advice?

He shook his head. "No. This has been going on for a couple of days now. She called at work, too. I was hoping I could have a break from it, but ..." He paused, running his hand roughly through his hair again. "I'm just so frustrated. I don't want to leave you alone. It's not safe, but ..." his voice trailed off and he rubbed his neck. There was a strange expression in his eyes, something I had never seen before. Something dark and disturbing. Like I wasn't even looking at Jonathan anymore, but someone else. Some stranger who had kidnapped the real Jonathan when he was in the living room and replaced him.

A doppelgänger.

"Sometimes I wonder why it can't be her having these problems with Red instead of you. Or, why couldn't she have an accident? Lots of people have accidents every day. Why couldn't she? After all, if something were to happen to her, all our problems would be solved. We could be together, the kids could be here, and I could protect you."

In shock, I dropped the spatula into the pan. "What are you saying?" I asked, backing away.

He glanced at me, and just like that, his eyes cleared, and his expression turned to horror. "I'm not ... I'm sorry. I didn't mean anything. I don't even know what I'm saying."

"She's the mother of your children," I said, stepping away from him until my back hit the cupboards. My fingers were numb, my lips were numb. "How could you say that?"

"I don't know! I don't know what I was saying. I'm just frustrated and had too much to drink. I didn't eat much for lunch. I would never want anything to happen to Felicity. I don't. I just ..." He took a few steps closer to me, his hands limp at his side, his eyes beseeching. "I just wish I could leave her and be with you."

He looked like a wounded little boy ... a little boy who only wanted love and kept running into rejection after rejection. Despite myself, my heart melted, and I found myself going to him to give him a hug. "I know," I said, the words gritty in my mouth, like sand. "I feel it, too. But you're doing the right thing in staying with her. You're keeping your promise that she doesn't have to go back to her abusive family."

He hugged me. "I knew you'd understand. That's why I love you."

I squeezed him back, mouthing the words. "I love you, too."

He held me a little longer before releasing me with a sad smile. "I better go. Call you later?"

I nodded, watching him as he picked up his keys and left. A moment later, I heard the front door slam.

I was alone. And terrified.

What had I done?

The Reckoning

Chapter 23

"Poor Rosie," Chester said, shaking his head.

My hand jerked, spilling the coffee I was pouring in Chester's cup. Coffee sloshed onto the counter. "Whoops," I said, grabbing a rag to wipe it up.

Chester didn't notice. He was engrossed in reading the newspaper in front of him. "Still no sign of her."

"Rosie?" I asked, keeping my voice as neutral as possible.

Chester glanced up. "Yeah. It's such a shame. She was so loyal to Red. I wonder what happened." He picked up his cup to take a sip.

"What do the police think?"

Chester shrugged. "It doesn't say. Just that she appears to have up and left. Her car is gone and her purse. Although according to the paper, it doesn't look like she packed anything. She apparently didn't tell anyone she was planning to leave, either. Was working her shift normally, left like any other day, and never came back. I think ..." He paused, shook his head violently, and busied himself putting his cup down and folding the newspaper.

My heart started to pound in my chest. "You think what?"

He shook his head again. "I was speaking out of turn. I shouldn't have said anything."

"What? Maybe Redemption sent her away?"

I was half joking, but Chester's horrified look immediately sobered me up. "What?"

"You don't understand," he said, lowering his voice. "There's a lot of bad people out there. Red is into some shady things. I don't think it's illegal, at least too illegal. Although the prostitution rumors ... I don't know. Rosie had been linked to those in the past, but that was years ago. It couldn't possibly have anything to do with what's going on today."

"You think Rosie was a prostitute?" I hadn't expected this at all, and was disgusted with myself at the tiny feeling of relief that shot through me. If people thought Rosie was mixed up in prostitution, they would be even less likely to view her disappearance as suspicious.

I hated myself for thinking it. Rosie's life mattered, no matter what.

I found myself marveling again at how it all seemed to be working out so well for Jonathan. What a perfect victim Rosie was for him ... someone who apparently no one but the disreputable Red would ever look for.

Chester shook his head quickly. "No, no, no. I don't think that's what was going on. Although, I suppose anything was possible, but no. I think Rosie's days of turning tricks are long gone. But ..." he bit his lip, glancing around the mostly empty restaurant before leaning closer to me. "Remember when I told you about how he was so obsessed with 1887 and '88?"

I nodded.

"It's kind of been a thing of his, figuring out what happened to all those adults. I know he's done a ton of research, but there's still so many questions. Lately, I've been hearing rumors that he might be trying other things."

"Like what?"

"Like, oh I don't know, séances or something like that. Occult stuff." Chester glanced furtively around the restaurant and quickly crossed himself, which took me aback. I hadn't pegged him as religious. "I was having a bad feeling about him a while back. That's why I stopped going out there. But I guess it's just gotten worse. So, I wonder if Rosie might have saw something, or heard something she shouldn't have, and ran off. Or, maybe something happened to her."

Another unexpected alternative. Jonathan was shockingly lucky.

Although ... *was* it luck? Or had he heard some of these rumors as well?

I pushed that thought out of my head. Rosie was an accident. He had assured me it was an accident. Jonathan didn't have it in him to be a murderer. It was just an accident. All the rest was just ... luck.

"You think Red ..." I started to say, but Chester shook his head again.

"No, no. I don't think Red would harm a hair on Rosie's head. She's been with him for years and years. No, I was thinking maybe one of those bad actors he has hanging around did something." Chester straightened up and made a big show out of putting the paper away. I got the feeling he was done with our conversation. "Mark my words—Red is playing with fire out there. One of these days, he's going to get burned. I would stay far away."

"I will," I said. One of my customers was waving at me from a table across the room and I nodded, letting him know I would be right over. "Thanks, Chester."

Chester picked up his coffee cup. "Don't mention it."

I moved around the dining room on autopilot, automatically taking orders, refilling drinks, and cleaning tables while mulling over what Chester said.

If the rumors around town were right about Rosie being involved with prostitution and Red skirting the law and dabbling in things he shouldn't be, the chances of anything coming back to Jonathan and me were pretty slim. In fact, it was possible that even if Red were to tell anyone he suspected Jonathan and me, it wouldn't matter. Everyone already thought he was guilty.

That thought should have given me peace, even if it was mixed with guilt.

But instead, that vague cloud of anxiety that never really left me anymore got a little stronger, a little more focused.

Since Jonathan had said what he did about Felicity, I kept trying to convince myself it meant nothing. He was clearly upset with Felicity; he had been upset with her when he got to my house. I heard enough to know they had a fight on the phone. People say things they don't mean all the time when they're angry. Plus, he'd had too much to drink and not enough to eat. They were just words. They didn't mean anything.

Still, another voice inside me argued. *It's not like he said he hated Felicity, or that she was being a bitch. He talked about* killing *her. Killing her! Threatening to kill your spouse, the mother of your children, is NOT normal.*

He couldn't have meant it, I mentally responded back. *He isn't a murderer.*

He killed two people.

He didn't mean to. They were both accidents.

He talked about Felicity having an accident.

Oh God.

My blood ran cold. I pressed my hand against my stomach, feeling it twist up inside me, willing myself not to be sick.

He couldn't have meant it. It was just talk.

Just talk.

Despite my inner arguments, what I was seeing was a sweet and attentive Jonathan in front of me. And not just to me, but to Felicity, as well. He had just told me about the "family game night" they'd had the night before. They ordered a pizza and played Sorry and Chutes and Ladders.

See, I told myself. *I'm being silly. Everything's fine. We're putting this ugly moment in our lives behind us and moving forward.*

The little bell above the door jingled merrily. Out of habit, I glanced over to see who it was and watched Jesse stride in.

My face relaxed into a smile, a true smile, the first one in what seemed like weeks. "Jesse! Great to see you. Are you here for lunch?" I moved closer so I could lower my voice. "It's just me and Liz today."

He shook his head, his smile forced. "Actually, I'm here to see you." Now that I was closer, I could see the strain around his eyes and the exhaustion in his face. He also had a wadded-up copy of a newspaper in his hand.

"Sure," I said, wondering what on earth he wanted to talk to me about. "Do you want to sit down or ...?"

He glanced around the diner, as if seeing how many people were there. "I was kind of hoping you could take a break and maybe we could chat for a few minutes outside? It won't take long." He gave me a self-conscious grin. "I promise."

"Uh ..." I wiped my hands on my apron and looked around for Liz, who was taking an order.

"I can come back," he said quickly. "Or wait for you. I can get a Coke and maybe a sandwich."

"Give me a sec," I said, and went over to Liz. He had my curiosity piqued, although I was a little worried, as well. Was it about Claire? I had been so consumed with my own train wreck of a life, I hadn't followed up on what was going on with her. I really hoped Jesse wasn't about to break Claire's heart.

Liz glanced up at me and raised an eyebrow as she headed to the kitchen to put in her order.

"Do you mind? Jesse just needs a few minutes to talk to me."

She blew a lungful of air out as her eyes searched the restaurant. It was near the end of our lunch rush and about half full. "Don't be gone too long," she said. "I can't cover it all."

"I won't," I said, and hurried over to Jesse. "Okay, we have about five minutes," I told him.

Jesse pushed open the door, blasting us with a wave of hot, humid air, and led me around to the back, near the dumpsters. It was already uncomfortably hot, and the smell of baking asphalt combined with the faint fumes of old grease and rotting food made my stomach want to retch. "Sorry to bother you at work," he said, not looking at me. He methodically plucked at the newspaper in his fist.

I folded my arms across my chest. "Not a problem. But I can't leave her very long."

He nodded, pulling open that day's paper. The worry I had felt for Claire shifted into trepidation about where this was going. "I saw this today," he said, holding up the crumbled paper enough so I could see the headline.

My heart sank.

Still No Leads On Missing Waitress.

"Do you know anything about this?" he asked.

My mind was racing, trying to remember everything I had told Claire. "Not really," I said cautiously. "It's a shame Rosie is still missing."

"I think Jonathan was there at The Lone Man Standing that night," he said.

I slowly nodded. "Jonathan had seen Rosie the night he was there, that's true." Where was he going with this?

"Did you know he was supposed to call me to go with him that night?"

"Yes, I was the one who wanted him to," I said. "That was the night I found the dead cat on my doorstep. Jonathan thought, well he still thinks, it was Red who left it there, and he wanted answers."

Jesse crumbled the paper back up, making a ball in his hand. He still wasn't meeting my eyes. "I guess I just need to come out and say it. Do you know what's going on with Jonathan?"

My eyes widened, and I instinctively took a step back away from Jesse. This was not what I had expected. "What do you mean?"

"He's not the same," he said. "Something has changed with him." Suddenly, the words started pouring out of him like a dam had broken, and everything he had held tightly inside came roaring out. "He's not fun anymore. I mean, I know he always had a serious side, but he doesn't laugh or smile at all. There's this constant anxiety going on. And this rage. All this anger under the surface. It was never there before. I don't understand what happened.

"I know ... I know you two are ... well, anyway. At first, I thought you were good for him. His marriage was never very good. I tried to talk him out of marrying her, but he didn't listen. And at first, with you, he was really happy. He was so happy. But now, in the past few weeks, something has shifted, and he won't tell me what, except I think it has something to do with The Lone Man Standing. He's obsessed with it. And then this happens." He shook his fist with the newspaper.

"I don't know what to think. But something is going on, something dark, and I'm just trying to figure out what it is."

I could feel my nerves fraying the more he talked. How was I supposed to handle this? *Ask questions,* a voice inside me said.

Stay on the offensive. Admit nothing. *"You don't think Jonathan had anything to do with Rosie, do you?"* I asked.

Jesse balked. "No, of course not. That's not what I'm saying."

"Then what *are* you saying?"

"Just that ... maybe Jonathan saw something that night. Something to do with Rosie. Maybe he even knows what happened to her, but he doesn't want it to come out that he was there at the bar that night because of ... because of you."

"If he saw something, he didn't say anything to me," I said slowly, but the wheels were racing in my head. Could this be another way to lead Jesse and Claire away from the truth? I thought about what Chester told me earlier—was it possible to make something up that sounded totally plausible? There were still problems with it. Both Jesse and Claire would likely insist that Jonathan go to the cops, and I was pretty sure he wouldn't agree to that.

Still. It may have promise.

"He's struggling with something," Jesse said, licking his lips. "Look, I'm not trying to say anything bad about him. Jonathan is my best friend. We've been friends all our lives. And he's always had a streak of darkness inside him, probably because of what that bastard Frank did to him and his mother when we were kids. But, it's never really been ... I don't know, that pronounced? That obvious? It's like it's come to the surface or something."

Listening to Jesse was making me more and more uncomfortable. I remembered all of Claire's warning about Jonathan, as well. And, as much as I didn't want to think about it, my mind flashed back to what I saw in his eyes the other night ... that terrible shadow, almost like a blankness, like something had possessed Jonathan in the few moments while he was in the living room talking to his wife.

Lots of people have accidents every day.

I shivered despite the heat, and hugged myself even tighter. "What do you want me to do about it?"

"Maybe you can talk to him," Jesse said. "I know he trusts you. He won't talk to me, but maybe if you ask him, he'll open up to you. Tell you what he knows, or if he did see something that night. Because whatever happened to him, it's eating him up inside. You have to try and get him to talk about it or something. Because if he doesn't, I don't know what's going to happen, but I don't think it's going to be good."

"I'll talk to him," I said.

Jesse looked relieved. "Thanks, Charlie."

I gave him a quick nod. "I better get back." I turned to go, wanting to get as far away from the cloying stench of decaying food and unsettling emotions triggered by Jesse's words as possible. My clothes were already damp and sweaty. If I stayed any longer, I would stink of garbage, too.

"Oh, Charlie," he called out. I half-turned. "Really, thanks for listening. I hope it wasn't too awkward me coming here? I wasn't trying to assume anything, but ... well, he won't talk to me. I've tried, but he just brushes me off. You were my last hope." He flashed his trademark crooked grin at me.

I forced a smile back. "I'm glad you came to me," I said. "In fact, if you're ever worried about Jonathan, definitely come talk to me. I want to help, especially since I think a lot of this stems from me." Also, if he came to me first, I would have a shot at controlling the conversation.

"Oh, don't think that," he said, the grin disappearing as his expression turned to shock. "That wasn't where I was going. You shouldn't blame yourself. I meant it when I told you I haven't ever seen Jonathan so happy. You two are perfect together. I only hope you can work it all out one day."

"So do I," I said. A hopeless feeling rose up inside me, and I quickly turned away so Jesse wouldn't see it reflected on my face.

Chapter 24

A noise woke me.

The bedroom was dark; not even the moon shone through the window.

At first, I wondered if it was Midnight, maybe snoring or purring in his sleep, but when I turned my head, I saw Jonathan was sleeping next to me, his face smooth and peaceful.

He shouldn't have fallen asleep, I thought. *He never falls asleep here. He always goes home. I should wake him.*

Instead, I found myself watching him, following his chest moving up and down, his breathing deep and even.

I had almost forgotten about the noise, had almost drifted off to sleep myself, when I heard it again.

It sounded almost like a cry. A child's cry.

Why would a child be crying in the house?

I pushed myself out of bed and started to move across the floor to the door and into the hallway. I felt almost like I was floating as I glided silently through the house, trying to figure out what the noise was and where it had come from.

That's when I noticed the light.

There was a strange orange-and-red light coming from the room at the top of the staircase. Even though the door was shut, I could see the light leaking out from the sides and below.

Was that where the cries were coming from?

I floated toward the door, my hand out to turn the knob. I needed to find the poor child who was clearly in a lot of distress.

Whatever you do, don't pay attention to the crying.

My hand jerked back, as if the door were hot and the heat would burn me. Who had said that to me? I was trying to remember, but it was all muddled in my brain, and I couldn't sort it out. It couldn't have been anyone good. Who would tell me to ignore a crying child? No one with good intentions. I needed to go in and comfort her.

Still, I hesitated, floating in front of the door, feeling a deep sense of foreboding.

Be careful with that room.

Another voice. Different from the first, and I couldn't place it, either. Nothing was making sense. It was as if my brain was a jumbled-up box of memories, nothing fitting together properly.

Surely, no one would really mean for me to ignore the room if there was a crying child in it. It was probably a "Be careful with that room unless there's someone who needs you in there" type of warning.

Or, maybe the child was crying because she needed help. The room wasn't childproof ... maybe she was in danger. Maybe that was why I was supposed to be careful with that room; because it wasn't fit for a child.

Suddenly, I was filled with fear for whoever was crying and desperate to help her before it was too late. I reached out to open the door. It sprang open at my touch.

The first thing I noticed was the light. It was a strange, reddish-orange glow that filled the room. It seemed familiar, somehow. What was it from? My mind was so mixed up. It was hard to think.

Then I saw a girl crouched in the middle of the floor. Her blonde hair was long and ragged, and her face was smudged with something dark, dirt maybe. She wore what looked like some sort of nightgown that was at one point white, but now, was grey.

"Were you crying?" I asked.

She glanced up at me, her eyes red and swollen. Her head barely moved in a slight nod.

"What's wrong?"

Her chin quivered. "I'm scared."

Her voice was so low, it was difficult to hear. I floated closer. "Scared? What are you scared of?"

"That I'll have to go back into the dark place."

"What dark place?"

She fixed her eyes on the closet.

The closet? I studied it. The door was open a crack making it impossible to peer inside.

"Are you talking about the closet? Did someone lock you in there?"

She shifted her eyes back to me, pausing for a minute as if to think, before barely nodding again.

I was suddenly full of anger for this poor child. What had been done to her? "Who locked you in the closet?" I demanded.

She seemed to shrink back from me, and I immediately tried to soften my tone. "I'm not going to hurt you," I said, lowering my tone. "I just want to know what happened to you."

She thought for a second, as if trying to figure out if she could trust me or not, before making a decision. "They did."

"Who?"

Her face seemed to shimmer, almost like the skin was a mask covering something underneath, and in that moment, I saw rage and hate. Her lips were pulled back, exposing teeth that resembled fangs, her cheeks were sunken, her eyes hot pools of darkness. "All of them," she hissed. The reddish-orange light slanted across her face, making her look almost demonic.

I quickly drew back, instantly regretting opening the door. But then her face shifted again, returning to the sweet, sad face of the child. It happened so fast, I thought I must have imagined it. This angelic, endearing child couldn't possibly be a monster in disguise.

There was a question I wanted to ask her. It hovered, flitting around in my brain, dissolving the moment I got close to it. I shook my head, trying to clear my thoughts, but it was still a jumbled mess.

The girl simply sat there, watching me intently, her eyes laser-focused on mine. "What is your name?" I asked.

"Lily," she said shyly.

"Lily. What a beautiful name," I said.

She smiled. Such an innocent smile.

"Why are you here? Where are your parents?"

Her smile disappeared. "They're gone."

"Where did they go?"

She shrugged. "They couldn't protect me."

"Protect you from what?"

Her expression turned to fear. "The dark."

"What dark?"

Her eyes continued to study me. So solemn for such a little girl. "Will you protect me?"

I was about to say "yes." I wanted to. The word hovered on the tip of my tongue. *Just say it. Yes.*

But then, from far away, I heard it again. That voice that was somehow so familiar and so strange.

Whatever you do, don't pay attention to the crying.

"Protect you from what?" I asked.

Her face fell. She looked disappointed. But there was something else. Something behind her eyes. A shadow that flickered. "From the dark," she said impatiently. "Will you protect me?"

Whatever you do, don't pay attention to the crying.

I jerked back. It felt like I had been slapped. I shook my head. "What would I have to do?"

"What needs to be done," she said. There was a hollowness to her voice.

I could feel a sense of dread rising in my chest. "What is that?"

Her eyes were boring into mine. I couldn't look away. I was drowning in them. The color was such a bright, unnatural blue. Maybe because of the streaks of red and the puffiness from crying.

Her lips, such a perfect rosebud, parted. Her mouth opened. All I could see was teeth and darkness.

Then the words came.

The reckoning is coming.

I woke with a gasp.

I was in bed. The bedroom was dark. Not even the moon shone through the window.

What woke me? Was it a sound?

I strained my ears. Was it ... a child crying?

No, that was my dream. I was sure of it. I could remember it all—the child, her face streaked with dirt, the reddish-orange room. She said something to me, something important, but it was slipping away, reduced to tattered scraps that melted away the moment I tried to focus on them.

But something *had* woken me. I turned my head to see if it was Midnight, but the bed was empty. The covers were pulled back and there was a hollow dip in the pillow, as if someone had been sleeping next to me but had gotten up.

Who was sleeping next to me? Was it Jonathan?

It came back to me in a rush. My last image of Jonathan was him lying next to me, his breathing deepening. I remembered thinking I should wake him, tell him it was time to go home, but then I must have fallen asleep myself.

He must have woken up, realized what happened and snuck out, trying not to wake me.

That was probably what woke me up. Hearing him leave.

I turned on my side, reaching out to touch the indentation. It was still warm. He must have just left.

I trailed my fingers across the sheets, replaying the night before. Jonathan had come over late. I hadn't been expecting him, and I had spent most of the evening fretting about what Jesse had told me. Was this something to be concerned about? Should I tell Jonathan?

The question had surprised me. Why wouldn't I tell Jonathan? Of course I should.

Even though the answer felt like a no-brainer, I still hesitated. There was something about Jesse's manner, and even though he didn't ask me to keep it from Jonathan, I had a strong sense he wanted me to.

But who cared what Jesse wanted? Jesse didn't know what really happened. And Jonathan needed to know the truth. He needed to realize that he was alienating his friends.

We were supposed to act normal. That was the agreement. Act normal and everything blows over.

And Jonathan wasn't acting normal.

I knew it. Jesse knew it.

Something was wrong. Deeply wrong. Would telling Jonathan make it worse or better?

I was still wrestling with the question when Jonathan showed up at my door.

Before I could do more than greet him, I was in his arms, and he was kissing me deeply. A few weeks ago, I would have eagerly kissed him back as I pawed at his clothes, but instead, the smoke in his hair and taste of beer on his tongue held me back.

Had he been in a bar? Which bar?

Jesse's words floated though my head. *He's obsessed with The Lone Man Standing.* When he first said it, I didn't think much about it. I figured that was from before, when Rosie was still alive and waitressing. But now, with my mouth tasting of beer, I wasn't so sure.

He sensed my reluctance and pulled back. "What's wrong?"

"We need to talk."

He must have heard something in my voice, because he dropped his arms and took a step back. "Are you okay? What's happened?"

"I'm fine," I said. "Do you want to sit down?"

His eyes widened. I could see how bloodshot they were. How much had he been drinking?

"That bad? What's going on?"

"It's not bad, or that bad. It's Jesse."

He looked confused. "Jesse? What about him?"

"Did you see him tonight?"

"No. Why would I?"

"Were you in a bar?"

"What does that have to do with Jesse?" He was starting to get angry. I could see the tension radiating from his neck.

"He came by to see me today."

"He what?"

His expression would have been comical if everything didn't feel so strange and serious. It was somewhere between bewilderment and jealousy. "Why did he want to see you? Did he hit on you?"

I ignored that. "He wanted to talk about you."

"Me?" Jonathan looked shocked. "What about me?"

"He's worried about you. Says you're not the same as you used to be."

Jonathan looked stunned. He ran a hand through his hair as he started to pace around the room. "Why would he say that?"

"Oh, I don't know. Maybe because you *aren't* the same?"

"He's the one who changed, not me," he said, his voice sharp with anger. "He's the one who keeps talking about leaving. We tried that. We came back. I don't understand why he can't just settle down and be happy here. Redemption has everything we need."

Something wasn't sitting right. I didn't like where the conversation was going. "What do you mean, 'Redemption has everything we need?'"

"What do you think? We have what we need. Everything is good. Why does he always want to leave?"

"Maybe because he wants to be an actor and there aren't a lot of opportunities here for him?"

Jonathan rolled his eyes. "Please. He's getting too old to make it. If he was serious, he would have made it work when we left years ago. But he's not. So he should stop all that nonsense."

I was starting to get upset on Jesse's behalf, but I also didn't want to get sucked into an argument about him. Not only did I not have all the details, but it wasn't really the point. "I think you should talk to him."

"Why? It's not going to change anything."

"He's worried about you. Don't you get it?"

"He's got nothing to worry about." Jonathan's voice had an edge to it, a warning not to push him. His eyes were flat and cold, like that wall had gone up again. It occurred to me how isolated I was, and how I wasn't even sure if anyone knew Jonathan was there.

Stop that, I told myself. *This is Jonathan. He's not going to hurt you.*

"He said you were obsessed with The Lone Man Standing," I said.

Jonathan spun around. "Damn right I am. And you know why! Red is a problem."

"Were you there tonight?"

Jonathan had the grace to look a little sheepish as he let his hands fall loosely to his side. "Someone has to keep an eye on him."

I wanted to throttle him. "After what happened, you went back?"

"No one knows what happened," he argued. "Other than you and me. And that doesn't change what Red could do."

"Red hasn't done anything though," I said. "At least not recently."

"Maybe it's because he knows we're watching him," he said darkly. "Who knows what he'd be doing if he thought he could get away with it."

"How often are you at The Lone Man Standing?"

"Not a lot," he said, but he didn't meet my eyes. "Enough."

"What is 'enough'?"

"Just enough." He came toward me to take me in his arms. "Babe, you know I'm just keeping you safe."

I pulled away. "But I don't think it's safe for *you*. Especially after what happened to Rosie."

"There's nothing to be worried about," he said impatiently, pulling me back in his arms. "I told you. No one knows anything. It's probably safer for me to be there than not. After all, if people really thought I was guilty, would they think I would be hanging out there? No, that would be the last place I would go."

Maybe, I thought, as Jonathan began to nuzzle my neck. But maybe Jesse was right. Maybe Jonathan was obsessed with The Lone Man Standing.

But why?

"Relax," Jonathan murmured. "You're so tense."

"I'm worried about you."

"Nothing to worry about. I've got this under control. You have to trust me."

Trust me. Could I trust him? After everything that happened? Did I have a choice?

"Promise me you'll talk to Jesse," I said.

He mumbled something I couldn't make out.

"Promise me," I said. "You two are too good of friends to leave this hanging, especially since he's leaving."

Jonathan sighed. "If it will make you happy, I promise. Okay?"

"Okay," I agreed.

Even though I wasn't in the mood, Jonathan was persistent, and eventually, I relaxed into it.

Thinking back on that conversation as I inhaled Jonathan's scent from the warm sheets next to me, I wondered again about this possible "obsession" with The Lone Man Standing. Was it really only because he was protecting me, like he said?

Or was there something else going on?

As my eyes better adjusted to the dark, I realized something wasn't right. There were lumps on the floor that shouldn't be there. What were they?

I sat up, crawling across the bed to get a better look.

They were clothes. But not mine. I recognized a pair of jeans, a man's shirt.

They were Jonathan's.

But ... why would Jonathan have left without his clothes? What was he wearing?

From below, I heard the faint creak of the floorboards, reacting to a footstep.

Was Jonathan still here? Why hadn't he gotten dressed and gone home?

I swung my legs around and got out of bed. I reached for the short robe that was hanging on the hook at the back of the door and was about to go downstairs when my eyes fell on the bat, propped up in the closet.

Should I take it? What if something had happened to him? Maybe Jonathan heard something downstairs and had gone to investigate and ...

With trembling fingers, I reached for the bat, the wood cool and solid under my touch. It wouldn't hurt to take it with me, just in case there was a problem. It was always good to be prepared.

Quietly, I slipped out of the room and headed down the hall, pausing at the top of the stairs. The house was dark and quiet. There were no sounds below. Was that a good thing or a bad thing? I couldn't decide.

As I stood there stewing, trying to decide if I should go down or not, my eyes fell on the door to the room right next to the stairs. Something about it made me feel unsettled. Like it wasn't empty at all, but there was someone, or something, in it. Watching. Waiting.

Be careful with that room.

I shivered and turned my attention to the stairs. One issue at a time, I told myself, and started creeping down the steps.

The living room was empty. I paused at the bottom of the steps, my eyes straining in the dark, but there was no one there. I wondered if it would make sense to turn a light on, but that would eliminate any element of surprise. No, it was better to be as invisible and silent as possible.

I continued my creeping, heading into the kitchen, which also appeared to be empty. I went down the hallway to see if there was anything in the laundry room, but everything appeared normal. Doors and windows were locked, and nothing seemed out of place.

I started back toward the kitchen, wondering if maybe Jonathan wasn't here after all. Maybe he had a change of clothes in the car or took something out of the closet, which I wouldn't have noticed in the dark. Why he would do that and not pick up the clothes from the floor, I had no idea.

What if something else was going on? The hairs prickled at the back of my neck, and I started to feel apprehensive. What if Jonathan was here, standing in the dark, his hands covered with blood, his eyes wild, like the night Rosie ...

No! Jonathan wasn't a murderer. He wasn't. It was all an accident. Besides, he hadn't left the house. He had simply fallen asleep.

Lots of people have accidents every day. Why couldn't it be her?

I squeezed my eyes shut, willing those thoughts away. I was not going to go there. There was a perfectly reasonable explanation for all of this. A perfectly normal, sane explanation that would be the same for other perfectly normal, sane people across the country.

I took a deep breath and continued my search.

The dining room appeared to be empty as well, the massive table crouched in the middle of the floor like some sort of hunched demon in the dark. I let go of the bat with one hand to press my fingertips to my temple. I had to get my head on straight. After this, I was going to turn on every single light in the house and make a cup of tea.

I moved to the family room, not really expecting to find anyone, but there he was.

He was standing motionless in the center of the room. He was naked, other than a pair of boxers, and facing away from me. I would recognize those broad shoulders and well-defined back anywhere.

I was so shocked, I nearly dropped the bat. "Jonathan," I said, my voice not much louder than a whisper. "You scared me. What are you doing?"

He didn't answer ... just stood there with his back to me like a statue as he stared at something on the far wall. I stood tiptoe, trying to peer over his shoulder and see what he was looking at, but for the life of me, I couldn't figure out what he was seeing. To my eyes, it was the same as always—an empty fireplace flanked by two bookshelves crowded with a variety of mostly dogeared books.

"Jonathan," I said louder. "Did you hear me? What are you doing?"

He still didn't move.

I put my hand out to turn the overhead light on, but something stopped me. I took a few steps closer. "Jonathan? Are you alright?"

He didn't react. I was starting to get scared. What if something was wrong? Was it possible he was having a stroke or a heart attack? No, he would probably be on the floor, not standing up. Could it be something else? I vaguely remembered learning about epilepsy when we were in school. There was a type of a seizure that caused people to freeze up, just like that. Surely, though, he would have mentioned having epilepsy. Was that what was going on?

"Jonathan," I said, softening my voice. "Can you hear me?"

"I can't stop it," he said.

I blinked. His voice sounded clear and normal. "What can't you stop?"

"There's something ... I can't control it. Not anymore."

"Jonathan, what are you talking about? And why won't you face me?"

"I don't want you to see."

"See what?" Exasperated, I decided if he wasn't going to turn around, I would go to him. I moved closer, carefully examining the wall again to make sure someone or something wasn't crouched in the shadows that Jonathan was talking to. I didn't want my back to anything like that. But there was nothing. The fireplace was empty, although it needed a good cleaning, and there wasn't anything in the corners.

"Jonathan," I began, turning to face him, but stopped short. His eyes were blank, and his face was slack, as if he were sleeping.

Of course. I could have slapped myself on the side of the head. He was sleepwalking, and apparently sleeptalking. No wonder he didn't make any sense.

I was reaching over to wake him, but stopped myself. Wasn't waking a sleepwalker bad? Like, causing a heart attack, bad?

Maybe the best thing would be to lead him back to bed, let him sleep a little longer, and then wake him up.

I gently touched his arm. "Let's get you back to bed, shall we?"

"I can't stop it," he said again.

"I know," I said.

He turned his head. "No, you don't."

I jerked, quickly searching his face to see if he had woken up, but it still had that same slack-jawed look. "I don't?"

"We did something, Charlie," he said. His voice sounded almost anguished, and I dropped my hand from his arm. "We unlocked a door and let something out, and now it's inside me. And I can't control it. I can't stop it. I can't do anything except watch it destroy everything I love."

"You're dreaming," I said, but my mouth had gotten so dry, I could barely push the words out. I could almost taste fear on my tongue. "This is a nightmare."

"The nightmare is when I'm awake," he said. "When *its* awake."

I tried to lick my lips. My mouth tasted of old pennies. "What is *it*?"

He was silent for a moment. I wasn't sure if he heard me. After all, he was asleep. He was having a bad dream, and I was having a conversation with a sleepwalker.

But then he answered me.

"Death."

And he collapsed.

The Reckoning

Chapter 25

I let out a short, hysterical scream as I ran toward him. "Jonathan!"

I had watched his eyes roll up in the back of his head before he fell to the ground. It was like his legs just gave out on him.

"Oh God," I moaned, falling to the floor next to him, trying to cradle his head. "Talk to me, Jonathan."

Was he dead? Did I accidentally wake him up and that caused a heart attack? Should I call 9-1-1? What would I tell the paramedics?

Or his wife?

Well, if he needed to be hospitalized, so be it. We would deal with the fallout later.

"I'm going to call for an ambulance," I said. "I'll be right back."

Jonathan's eyelids fluttered. "Charlie?"

"Yes, yes, it's me. Oh, thank God." Relief flooded me, making me almost giddy. "Are you okay? Are you hurt? Maybe I better call an ambulance anyway."

"No," he said quickly, raising a hand to rub his head. "No, don't do that. Just ... give me a minute. What happened?"

"You were sleepwalking," I said.

He frowned. "Sleepwalking? I don't sleepwalk. And wait." He struggled to sit up. "Ow, my head. Why are you here?"

"I live here," I said.

"But," he glanced around the room, a bewildered expression on his face. "Aren't I home?"

"You're in my home," I said. "You fell asleep. Do you remember?"

He rubbed his head. "I did? What time is it? I have to get home." He tried to get up, but I pushed him back down.

"In a minute. I don't want you driving when you're so disoriented. And I want to make sure you're okay."

"I'm fine. My head hurts, but I'm fine. Why does my head hurt?"

"Your head hurts because you hit it when you collapsed."

He stared at me. "I collapsed?"

"Let me get you some ice," I said, getting to my feet. "Don't move." I wagged my finger in front of him. For a moment, I thought he was going to argue with me, but then he slumped back down.

"Fine," he said. "Hurry up."

"At this point, another half hour or hour isn't going to make much difference," I said over my shoulder as I left.

I wasn't too worried he would try and sneak out. At the very least, he would need to make his way upstairs for his clothes, which didn't seem likely. I dug out a dish cloth to fill with ice and turned on the kettle to make tea.

I went back to the family room, where Jonathan had adjusted himself to lean against the couch. "Here," I said, handing him the ice. "I'm making tea. We can have a cup and then get you ready to leave."

He nodded, seemingly resigned, and I went back into the kitchen to prepare our drinks.

I made a point of listening carefully for footsteps on the stairs, but Jonathan stayed put. I went back to him with two steaming mugs of tea, handed him one, and then sat on the floor across from him.

"Are you sure you're okay?" I asked.

He nodded and winced. "Really, it's just my head."

I eyed him over the cup. "You know you might have a concussion. You should probably get it checked out."

"I'll be fine." He took a sip. "So, what happened?"

"I guess we both fell asleep," I said. "When I woke up ..." I paused. Why *did* I wake up? It felt like something had happened. I had faint recollections of reddish-orange light and ... crying. But who would be crying? I didn't think Jonathan had been. "Anyway," I gave myself a quick shake, getting myself refocused. "When I woke up, you were gone. I thought maybe you left, but then I heard something down here and saw your clothes on the floor ..."

Jonathan flashed a self-conscious smile. "Yeah, I noticed."

"So, I went looking for you and found you here."

"Huh." Jonathan gazed around the room. "What was I doing?"

"You were standing in the middle of the room," I said.

"That's it?"

"Well, you were talking, too." I realized I was feeling reluctant to recount the story, but why? Clearly, he had been having a bad dream.

He looked surprised. "What did I say?"

"Nothing much," I said lightly, trying to brush it off. "Finish your tea, and we'll see if you're good enough to drive."

He put his mug down. "No, really. What did I say?"

"I think it was just nonsense, really," I said. "It's not important."

"Now you really have me curious," he said. "What did I say? Did I confess to having a crush on another woman?"

It was clear he was joking, but that didn't stop a dart of jealously from shooting through me. "Who do you have a crush on?"

"No one," he said, laughing. "I mean, of course I find other women attractive. I'm not dead," he said, laughing even harder at my outraged expression. "Charlie, you have got to know you're the only woman I have ever loved. But, seriously. What's going on? Why won't you tell me?"

I stared down into my tea, adjusting my mug between my hands. "It's just ... it was just weird, is all. You were talking about how you couldn't stop something. You couldn't control it. That we unlocked something." I laughed, but it was forced. "I told you it was nonsense."

His laughter died down. "Unlock something? What did we unlock?"

We unlocked a door and let something out, and now it's inside me.

I licked my dry lips, feeling more and more uncomfortable. "You were asleep. How do I know? Obviously, you were dreaming about something, but who knows what it was if you don't remember."

He smiled slightly, but it didn't reach his eyes. "Was what we unlocked what I couldn't control?"

My eyes widened. *I can't control it. I can't stop it. I can't do anything except watch it destroy everything I love.*

He saw my expression and his eyes narrowed. "What? You're remembering something. What is it?"

What was going on? "I was wondering if *you* remembered something."

"Why?"

"Because that is what you implied." I leaned forward. "What were you dreaming about? Can you tell me?"

He didn't answer, but I could see something shift in his eyes—like a window that had just been shuttered. "I can't remember," he said, but his eyes didn't meet mine. Somehow, I knew he was lying.

"Then why do you care so much about what you said?"

"Because I've never sleepwalked in my life," he said. "I want details, to try and understand why I was doing it."

"I don't think what you said is going to make much difference," I said. "I thought sleepwalking had to do with other medical conditions, or maybe stress."

"Maybe you're right." He took a swig of tea. "I'm feeling fine. I think I can make it home."

"You sure?"

"Yeah."

I studied him as he got to his feet. He still wouldn't look me in the eyes, but there was something ... off, with him. Like it wasn't really Jonathan.

Nonsense, I scolded myself. I was letting my imagination run away from me. Who else would it be?

We unlocked a door and let something out, and now it's inside me.

He was sleepwalking. Was I really going to use what he said then as proof of him not being Jonathan?

A picture flashed in my head of Jonathan, after he talked to Felicity in the living room. How something changed. Like he had been ... replaced.

Why couldn't she have an accident? Lots of people have accidents every day. Why couldn't it be her?

He was just angry. They were having a fight. People say things they don't mean all the time when they fight.

The picture in my head changed to Jesse, standing in the alley behind the diner, one hand clutching the newspaper. *In the past few weeks, something has shifted, and he won't tell me what, except I think it has something to do with The Lone Man Standing. He's obsessed with it.*

No! I had to stop this. I shook my head, trying to clear my thoughts.

"Are you okay?"

Jonathan was looking at me strangely.

"I'm fine. I'm more worried about you," I said. "I wasn't sure if you were really okay to drive."

His expression softened. "I'm fine. Really. I just need to get my clothes and go. That was probably why I was sleepwalking. I knew I shouldn't be here." He laughed.

I forced a laugh as well. "Maybe that was it."

I collected our tea mugs as he went upstairs, but inside, it was all I could do not to scream at him. *Stop! There is something fundamentally wrong going on here. We have to talk about it.*

But I didn't. I let him go.

Home.

To Felicity.

Who had no idea of the darkness was lurking within him.

Why couldn't she have an accident?

Oh, God.

The Reckoning

Chapter 26

"So, how can I help you, Ms. Jackson?"

The criminal defense attorney sat back in his office chair and folded his hands across his flat stomach. He looked a bit like a Ken doll with his blonde hair and very tan face. I wasn't expecting someone so young; he didn't look much older than me.

I still couldn't believe I was there.

Was I really going to do this? Tell a lawyer what we'd done? How did I even get there?

At first, I didn't know what to do. I spent hours pacing—and thinking—after Jonathan left. I desperately wanted to talk to someone, but who? Anyone I told would be just as liable as I was.

I tried to tell myself to forget it. Jonathan was sleepwalking, and that was it. Everything else was my imagination. He wouldn't hurt Felicity. He had just been frustrated.

But I didn't believe it. No matter how often I repeated it, I couldn't shake the sick feeling in my gut that something was terribly wrong.

After a day of walking around in a helpless, confused fog, unable to decide on any course of action other than mechanically moving through the hours, it started to dawn on me that maybe the situation was just too big for me. Maybe I needed to call the authorities and turn us both in.

Maybe, if Jonathan was in custody, maybe that would stop whatever it was that was coming.

Maybe that was how it all had to end. Both of us in jail, paying for our crimes.

It felt fitting, at least for me. I had a lot to answer for. I was the one who started the whole disaster. I needed to be punished. The idea of prison scared me, but there was also relief. Finally, I would be back on the right path.

Once I made my decision, I asked Sue if she could cover me, as I wasn't feeling well. Now that I knew what I needed to do, I didn't want to wait another second.

I went home, wanting to be in the privacy of my home when I called. I pulled out the phone book, found the nonemergency number for the police, and dialed.

"Redemption police department. May I help you?"

I swallowed hard, clearing my throat. "I'd like to report a crime."

"Are you in danger?"

"No, no. Nothing like that." My hands were shaking so hard, I could barely hold the receiver.

"What is the crime?"

I opened my mouth to say "murder," but paused.

What exactly was I going to tell the police? My married lover and I killed my ex fiancé, except he was already declared dead by the New York police?

That my married lover told me he killed Rosie?

There wasn't even an open case on Rosie. Everyone thought she had simply left Redemption.

What if they asked me for proof?

What if Jonathan denied it?

What would I do then?

"Shoplifting," I said.

"One moment," she said. During the pause to transfer the call, I hung up.

I needed a plan. Even more, I needed to talk this through with someone, someone who actually understood the justice system and could best guide me on what I should do.

After some digging, I found a criminal defense attorney in Milwaukee who just happened to have an opening the next day. I made the appointment under a fake name, and then called Sue to tell her I was getting worse and would need the next day off, as well.

The most difficult part was calling Jonathan.

His voice was warm and caring. "Oh, babe. Do you need anything? Some chicken soup? Should I come over?"

I squeezed my eyes closed, guilt for what I was about to do flooding through me and leaving a bitter taste in my mouth. "No, I don't want you to catch anything. I'll be fine. I'm sure I just need some rest."

"Are you sure? I don't mind stopping by."

"I'm sure. I've got some soup here I'll heat up with some tea, and I'll go to bed early."

"Okay, if you're sure." His voice was regretful. "I wish I could be there to take care of you."

My throat was dry. "That's sweet, but I would feel horrible if you got sick."

"Call me if you need anything. Or if anything happens."

"I promise."

My head was pounding, and my hands were slick with sweat by the time I hung up. I wasn't exactly lying when I said I wasn't feeling well.

"Ms. Jackson?"

The attorney's name was Eric Thompson. A nice, normal name. It was predominantly displayed on his diplomas. He went to school at Northwestern Law School. A nice, normal school.

I wondered again how I ended up in this crazy nightmare. I so wished I was living a nice, normal life, too.

The nice, normal attorney watched me patiently, his expression calm and compassionate. He probably wouldn't be shocked by my story. I couldn't be the first murderer he'd represent.

"Could I get you some water? Coffee?"

I shook my head. What I needed to do was start talking before my hour ran out.

"I ... I have a question," I started.

"I'm listening."

I opened my mouth and realized I couldn't do it. I couldn't tell him the truth. It felt too reckless, too dangerous. Even though I paid him and was technically a client, I couldn't risk it.

But I still needed help. I desperately needed to talk this through with someone.

What could I do?

As I studied the attorney, who sat patiently waiting for me to continue, inspiration struck me.

"It's a hypothetical situation really," I said.

He cocked his head. "Hypothetical?"

I nodded eagerly. "Hypothetical. I ... well, it doesn't matter why." I couldn't think of a good reason, so I decided to skip that part. "So, hypothetically, what if someone told you she had information about a murder? How would you suggest she report it to the police?"

His eyebrows shot up, but otherwise, his face remained neutral. "Well, you could just pick up the phone and report the crime. If there is a tip line set up, you could even do it anonymously."

"There's no tip line."

"Well, then you would have to call the detective in charge. If you want to do it anonymously ..."

"There's no detective in charge."

He blinked. "Maybe you need to tell me a little bit more about this hypothetical case."

"Hypothetically, a ... a boyfriend tells his girlfriend he killed someone. But everyone thinks the person he killed is simply missing. So, what does the girlfriend do? How does she report it?"

Eric steepled his fingers together. "Did the girlfriend see anything?"

"No."

"Did anyone else? Any other witnesses?"

"No."

"Does the girlfriend know where the body is?"

"No."

"How about any proof? The murder weapon or maybe some bloody clothes ..."

"No. Nothing like that."

"Is the girlfriend sure this person is dead?"

"Yes."

Eric cocked his head and studied me. "How can the girlfriend be so sure?"

I licked my lips again. Maybe I should have accepted that water after all. "Because she ... she helped move the car."

"Is the girlfriend sure that it was her car?"

I hadn't thought about that. "Um ... well, the girlfriend never saw her car before, but that's what her boyfriend told her."

"Ah." Eric gave me a pitying look. "Well, if the girlfriend doesn't have any proof, it becomes a "he said, she said" scenario. It's even possible that an argument could be made there was no murder at all, and the boyfriend made it up. Is there anyone who can corroborate that this other person is even dead? Or any part of the girlfriend's story?"

I swallowed, my heart slowly sinking down into my chest. It was as bad as I thought. "No, nothing."

"Is there any reason why the boyfriend would have killed this other person? Did the boyfriend have a history with this other person? Perhaps they fought, or maybe this other person wronged the boyfriend somehow?"

"No, nothing ... nothing obvious. There was a reason, but ... but nothing anyone would know." Did I dare tell him about Alan? Even hypothetically? Would it even matter? If it was a stretch to pin Rosie on Jonathan, how big of a leap would it be for Alan? I would first have to prove Alan had survived the accident, and then, that Jonathan killed him. And I had no proof of either.

Eric reached over, picked up a pen, and started tapping it on the desk. "So, without a body, it's going to be very difficult to convict anyone of murder. You really need a body. Otherwise, it's way too easy for a good defense attorney, like me," he flashed me a cocky grin, "to argue that there was no crime committed."

Even though I had been expecting that, I still felt deflated. "What if the girlfriend testifies against the boyfriend? Tells the jury what she knows?"

Eric shrugged. "It's still 'he said, she said.' Especially if the girlfriend has no other proof. But, even if there was proof, it would still be an uphill battle. Not very many cases are successfully prosecuted when there's no body."

"So, it sounds like what you're saying is that it makes no sense for the girlfriend to go to the cops with what she knows?"

Eric was watching me carefully. "Is the girlfriend being abused?"

I shook my head quickly. "No, no. Nothing like the that."

"What is it like?"

I was momentarily caught off guard. What could I say? The girlfriend was afraid something dark had possessed the boyfriend? That she was afraid he might kill his wife?

Eric searched my face. "Is the girlfriend afraid of the boyfriend?"

I had every intention of saying "no." *Of course not. Silly. The boyfriend would never hurt the girlfriend.*

"Yes," I said, my voice barely a whisper.

Eric's expression looked grim. "As a member of the court, my professional advice would be for the girlfriend to go to the authorities, tell them everything she knows, and do what she can to help with the investigation. However ..." he paused, as if trying to decide what to say next. "Since this is a hypothetical situation, I would be very concerned about the girlfriend's safety. I would wish the girlfriend ... would do what she could to remove herself from that situation and get herself somewhere safe. Far away from the boyfriend. And then, once she's safe, to let the authorities know." He stopped tapping his pen and leaned forward. "The truth of the matter is, based on what I've been told, this hypothetical case is very weak. The chances of the boyfriend getting a successful conviction are slim. And once the girlfriend goes to the authorities, she makes herself a target. The best-case scenario is the investigation turns something up, even if it's not specific to the case, so the boyfriend will go to jail. But, it may take time to make a case. And there's no guarantee the boyfriend will be in custody while the authorities investigate."

"What if ..." My voice failed, and I had to start again. "What if the girlfriend is afraid someone else might be in danger?"

Eric went very still. "Why does the girlfriend think that?"

"Because of something the boyfriend said."

"Did he threaten someone?"

Why couldn't she have an accident?

"No. Yes. Sort of."

"What would this hypothetical threat be?"

I rubbed my sweaty hands against my skirt. My head was also sweaty and itchy under the wig of thick black hair I had on. I wished I could take it off. "It was ... wondering why something couldn't happen to her. Why she couldn't have an accident. Accidents happen every day ... why couldn't she have one?"

"Did he say anything else? Like he didn't mean it, or he was just joking or upset?"

I hung my head. "Yes, he said that, as well."

"So, to be clear, the cops aren't going to arrest anyone for saying that. But they would definitely ask a few questions. It also might not be a bad idea for the girlfriend to let the person know what the boyfriend said. Does she know the person? Would she be able to safely alert him or her?"

Tell Felicity? I felt myself grow hot and cold at the thought. *Tell my married lover's wife her husband wants her dead?*

But even as I recoiled at the thought, deep down, I knew what I had to do.

What choice did I have? Eric had made it pretty clear the cops weren't going to be much help.

If I was going to end this nightmare, I was going to need to start taking matters into my own hands.

"I appreciate your help," I said, gathering my purse and rising. "It has been very educational."

Eric rose as well, reaching across his desk to offer his hand. His handshake was firm, and his hand was warm and comforting.

I expected him to release his grip after a moment, but he held on, making a point of looking deeply into my eyes. His eyes were a light shade of blue, reminding me of the sky the morning after a storm. "If the girlfriend needs more guidance, let her know she can reach out."

"I will, thank you."

He smiled slightly and squeezed my hand gently. "Be careful," he said.

I nodded.

He let go and I turned to walk out the door. I could feel his eyes on me as I left, and my skin still felt warm where he had touched it.

Chapter 27

I pulled up to the curb, turned off the car, and sat there staring at the house while listening to the tick of the engine as it cooled down.

It looked like any other house on the block. A small, split-level ranch with beige siding. Toys were scattered across the front yard—a couple of balls, a water gun, a bike. The lawn was straggly and overgrown, and clearly in need of a little TLC.

I wondered if that was Jonathan's job to mow the grass, and if it was, what other household chores he had been neglecting the last couple of months.

I glanced at the clock. It was nearly four, later than I had thought. If I was going to do this, I needed to do it now. Jonathan would be off work soon. Trying to explain my presence would be difficult.

Especially since I was supposed to be home sick.

I rubbed my sweaty hands against my skirt. It was now or never. I couldn't keep sitting there like a fool.

And, quite honestly, I knew if I didn't do it right then, I might lose my nerve completely.

I opened the car door and got out, rubbing my hands on my skirt one more time before starting up the driveway.

The neighborhood was quiet, other than the excited shrieks of a group of kids playing the next street over. Really, this was the perfect moment to do what I needed to do. If any adults were home, their attention was likely on making dinner for their families, and the rest were probably at work.

If I wanted to talk to Felicity unnoticed, this was the time.

I rang the doorbell.

Tiny footsteps raced across the floor before the door opened, and I was face-to-face with a miniature Jonathan, all dark hair and huge eyes, a hunk of hair falling into one of his eyes.

He shoved it away, regarding me solemnly. "Who are you?"

"I'm here to see your mother," I said. "Is she home?"

"Who is it, Darrel?" A woman's voice called out from somewhere deeper in the house.

"A lady," he said, his eyes never leaving mine. "She wants to talk to you."

Footsteps, then the door opened a little wider.

Felicity.

She looked exhausted. Black, puffy circles stained her pale-blue eyes, and her blonde hair was pulled back in halfhearted ponytail. She wore a shapeless pink-and-yellow flowered housecoat that was stained with something purple. Maybe grape juice. Or wine.

She stared at me silently for a moment. "Darrel, go back inside and watch your sister."

"But, mom ..."

"Go inside and watch your sister. I need to talk to this lady."

Darrel sighed, a big huffing sigh like he was put out, and ran back in. Felicity stepped outside, closing the door behind her. "What do you want?"

"Felicity, I know we've never met, but my name is ..."

"I know who you are," she interrupted, her voice hard. "I asked you what you want."

I bit my lip. This wasn't going well. Nothing like what I had imagined. On the other hand, what did I expect?

"I need to tell you something about Jonathan."

"What, that he's screwing you?" She barked a hard laugh that had no humor in it at all. "You think that's news to me? To anyone in this godforsaken town?" She gestured with both arms.

"I'm sorry," I said. "I never meant to hurt you."

"Right," she said disgustedly. "What precisely did you think would happen when you started the affair?"

A line of sweat trickled down my back. I was acutely aware of each second that ticked by. "Look, that's actually not what I came to talk to you about," I said. "It's something else."

She folded her arms across her chest. "Make it fast. I have to make dinner for my family." She shot me a pointed look as she emphasized the word "family."

I wanted to apologize again, but also knew I had to keep the conversation moving. Every cell in my body was screaming at me to hurry. "All I wanted to do is tell you to be careful."

Her eyes widened. "*Careful?* You want me to be *careful?*"

I bobbed my head up and down. "Yeah, just, you know, watch your back and keep an eye on things. Make sure everyone stays safe."

Her eyes narrowed into slits. "You have some nerve," she hissed. "You really think you can come over here and *threaten* me? Come to my home and threaten me and my family?" Her voice was getting louder.

"No!" I said, holding my hands up with the palms out, desperately trying to calm her down. This was really, really NOT going well. On my drive back from Milwaukee, I had played it over and over in my head, hoping a simple warning to be careful would work. If she wanted clarification, I was going to talk about the dead cat on my doorstep and say I just wanted to make sure she was safe, too.

What I hadn't completely worked out was what would happen if she told Jonathan. I figured I could say something about a bad dream ... that I wanted to make sure she and the kids were okay.

It was weak. Really weak. He would likely be upset with me, ask me why I didn't just tell him and leave her out of it. I had no good answer for that.

My hope was she wouldn't say anything.

It was a far-from-perfect plan, but I didn't know what else to do. I knew I had to warn her. I would never be able to live with myself if something happened to her. But how could I tell her the truth without somehow bringing Rosie and Alan into it?

"I'm not trying to threaten you," I said pleadingly, keeping my voice low and hoping it would encourage her to do the same. "I'm trying to warn you."

"Of what? You going to make me have some sort of 'accident,' so you can have my husband to yourself?"

I flinched. I didn't mean to, but it was too close to home.

She blanched. "Oh my God. You are a monster. An absolute monster. Does Jonathan know how evil you really are? Get off my property before I call the police." She made a move toward her door.

"No, wait," I stepped forward, trying to stop her. "Please, just …"

She whirled around, fire in her eyes. "If you take one more step toward me, God help me, I will …"

"It's not me. It's Jonathan." The words spilled out of me before I could stop them.

She looked incredulous. "Oh, that's rich. Trying to blame my husband for your insanity? Jonathan would never hurt me. He would never hurt a fly."

"That's not true," I said, but then I clamped my lips down, nearly biting my tongue. *Watch yourself, Charlie.* "Look, something happened to him," I said, my voice low and urgent. "He's not the same man he was even a few weeks ago. There's something … some darkness, in him."

"That's a load of bull."

"And," I pressed on, not letting her interrupt. "Last week, when you paged him, and he called you back? You guys were having some sort of fight. He was …" I swallowed hard. "He was at my house. After he got off the phone, he said to me, 'Lots of people have accidents every day. Why couldn't she have one? Then we could …'" I swallowed hard again and dropped my voice to a whisper. "'We could be together.' And he wouldn't have to break his promise to you."

"You lie," Felicity said, her voice strangled. Her face had turned pale in the late afternoon sun. "He would never hurt me."

"That's probably true of the old Jonathan," I said. "But, I don't know anymore. I wasn't going to tell you, but you need to know. Look, I hope he was just blowing off steam and didn't mean it, but I couldn't stand it if something were to happen to you and I never said anything."

Felicity raised a hand and clutched the fabric near her neck. "I think you should go now." The anger had drained from her voice, making her sound empty.

I nodded and started to back away, trying not to think about the enormity of what I had just done. There was no making up a dream about this. If she told Jonathan ... well, I didn't even want to think about that.

I started to turn around as I got to the edge of the step, but she called out to me. "Charlie." The sound of my name on her lips sounded odd and unnatural. I looked at her.

Standing there, one hand on the doorknob, the other clutching the housedress at her neck, she looked old. Like she had aged twenty years since stepping onto the porch. "If what you say is true, how can you still be with him? Why haven't you left him?"

I gave her a sad smile. "It's complicated," I said.

She studied me for a long moment, chewing her lip. "Jonathan has been acting strange," she said. "He's been visiting my brother. Did you know about that?"

For a moment, I didn't know what she was talking about, but then I remembered. The lye. Jonathan said he was getting lye from his brother-in-law.

Did she know?

My blood turned to ice even as beads of sweat dripped down the sides of my face.

DID she know? How much did she know?

Then, an even more horrifying thought struck me.

Was that the real reason Jonathan wanted her to have an accident?

The bile rose up in my throat, and it was all I could do to keep from being sick right there in Jonathan's front yard.

Say something. A little voice inside me started screaming.

Say something. Lie. She can't know.

I opened my mouth to force something out, but nothing came. What could I even say?

If you don't say something, you could get her killed.

That voice broke through my paralysis. I lifted my chin and looked her directly in the eyes.

"I don't know anything about that," I said, my voice quiet but with an edge of steel. "And neither should you."

She cocked her head, studying me. I kept my gaze steady, hoping to God she was getting my message.

"I see," she said after a moment. "I appreciate you stopping by." She yanked open the door and gave me a final, hard, cold stare. "Don't ever do it again." She stepped through the doorway and slammed the door shut.

Chapter 28

I barely made it home and into the bathroom before I vomited out the contents of my stomach. I couldn't stop retching, even when there was nothing left but bile.

What just happened? What had I done?

My face was on fire, and my head felt like it was going to explode. I had to think—to figure out a plan—but my mind swam, and nothing made sense.

The phone started to ring, but the noise was distant and far away, as if the phone itself was buried deep within the house. I lay on my side, my burning cheeks pressed against the cool linoleum floor, and listened to the echo of the ringing.

Jonathan.

I bolted upright, stumbling to my feet, my limbs weak and shaky. What if it was him? I had to answer.

I staggered through the house, snatching the phone off the living room cradle as I collapsed onto the floor next to it. "Hello?"

"Charlie! Oh thank God it's you. I've been worried sick."

I closed my eyes. Jonathan's voice was concerned and caring, but was that all? Was it my imagination, or was there something else there, too? Something faintly accusatory.

"Yeah, it's been a rough day," I said.

"Where have you been? I've been calling and calling."

"Sleeping mostly," I said. "I turned the ringer off."

There was a pause. "You didn't go anywhere?"

Uh oh. It sounded like a trap. I had to think fast, even though my mind was already racing. "To the doctor," I said. "Well, I tried. I couldn't get in."

"You couldn't get in?"

"Well, they thought they could work me in, but they couldn't."

"Are you going to try again?"

"Yeah, if I'm still feeling this badly," I said. "Hopefully, I'll start to get better."

"Hopefully. Especially since the big party is this weekend."

Oh that's right. Lou's Labor Day weekend party. I had almost forgotten about it. "Yeah, I better rest up so I can come. I would hate to miss it my first year."

"Yeah, you can't do that," he said half-jokingly. "Lou might cancel the party.'

"Ha."

"But seriously, I feel terrible that you're suffering," he continued. "I stopped by earlier. I wanted to bring some soup and see how you were doing, but your car wasn't there."

"That must have been when I was at the doctor," I said, praying he wasn't going to ask me for a time. My stomach twisted and I bent over, trying to keep myself from retching. "I have to go," I said.

"Do you want me to stop by? I still have that soup."

My stomach cramped again, and I winced. "You'd better not. I don't want you to catch whatever this is. I'll call you later."

"Okay. Love you."

"Love you too," I gasped before hanging up the phone and lurching back to the bathroom.

It was a false alarm. Nothing came up as I sat next to the toilet. I could feel the heat radiating off my hot skin.

What was I going to do? Was there any way I could fix this mess?

The questions swirled through my head, making me nauseous. Luckily, I seemed to be done throwing up. Small mercies.

Even though there was no reason for me to continue sitting on the bathroom floor next to the toilet, I couldn't bring myself to move. My limbs were thick and heavy, and my head pounded.

I had no idea how to fix everything that was happening. None. Nada. Zip.

Suddenly, my skin prickled at the back of my neck. Someone was watching me. I whipped my head around, convinced Jonathan had somehow snuck in and was behind me, his eyes full of accusations, dangling my discarded wig by one finger.

Why do you need a wig, Charlie? Where did you go today?
But it wasn't Jonathan. It was Midnight.

He was sitting with his tail curled around his feet, his jade-colored eyes staring intently at me.

Get up, he seemed to be saying. *Get off the bathroom floor. You can't do anything when you're curled up next to the toilet. Get up.*

I dragged myself to my feet.

Better. Now clean yourself up.

Numbly, I moved over to the sink, rinsing out my mouth and splashing cool water on my face. I looked at myself in the mirror, water dripping from my chin. I looked ... ghastly. My skin was waxy, my eyes bloodshot. At least I was on my feet, though. That was a start.

You look like hell. Get some food into you. Feed me too while you're at it.

I took a moment to wipe off the toilet before heading into the kitchen. Midnight silently padded after me. The thought of food made me want to be sick all over again, but I knew I had to eat. Under Midnight's watchful gaze, I filled up the kettle for tea, put a couple of slices of bread in the toaster, and topped Midnight's bowl off with cat food before placing it on the floor. Midnight didn't move, instead fixing me with an expectant look.

"Fine," I said. I pulled out another pot, opened up a can of chicken and vegetable soup, and started heating it on the stove. Midnight trotted over to his food dish, as if he approved.

Honestly? This was what I was reduced to? Allowing my cat to 'tell' me what to do? I might be in worse shape than I thought.

On the other hand, at least I wasn't sitting on the bathroom floor anymore. That was definitely an improvement.

I started pulling dishes out of the cupboard as I tried to get my thoughts in order. First off, did Felicity believe me? Would she keep an eye on Jonathan? Would she tell Jonathan? Ugh, that caused a fresh wave of anxiety to course through me. Well, there was nothing I could do about it now. I couldn't very well ask Jonathan about it. I was just going to have to hope she kept her mouth shut. And if she didn't, I'd have to deal with it then.

Second, going to the cops was off the table. I was going to have to figure out a way to stop it on my own.

But how?

Over and over, pictures of Jonathan flashed through my mind, his eyes shuttering, something dark and terrible peering out at me from the depths.

We unlocked a door and let something out, and now it's inside me. I can't control it. I can't stop it. I can't do anything except watch it destroy everything I love.

What did that even mean?

Most likely, it meant Jonathan was starting to lose his mind. My skin prickled with cold goosebumps at the thought, and I busied myself getting the tea ready. The stress over the killings could make anyone lose it. Especially Rosie's. Alan's could be more easily explained away. He was in my house, threatening to kill me. Jonathan was protecting me.

Rosie? Not so much.

So, if Jonathan was losing his mind, what could I do? Convince him to seek therapy? Get him committed?

And what would happen if I got him to talk to someone and he confessed to the killings? Would we both go to jail?

Again, I considered the reality that going to jail was exactly what *should* happen to us. It wasn't like either of us were innocent. And maybe, just maybe, Jonathan would snap out of it.

Maybe the 'door' we unlocked was really his guilt over what he did. Maybe that was what was slowly eating him up inside, causing him to go mad. If that were the case, perhaps being punished for his crimes was exactly what needed to happen.

That explanation made the most sense. The smart play would be to figure out a way to get Jonathan help.

But, as much as my mind tried to rationalize it, deep down, it didn't feel right.

Something else was going on. Something deeper and darker than Jonathan experiencing some sort of mental breakdown.

I finished plating my food and carried it to the table, concentrating only on Jonathan clearly losing his mind.

Because the only other explanation was possession.

Jonathan, possessed.

Of course, that was silly. Nobody believed in possession in the real world. Not really. And what exactly would be possessing him? A demon? The devil?

A scene from the movie *The Exorcist* floated through my head. The daughter tied to the bed, objects being thrown around the room. That was nothing like what was going on with Jonathan. Of course, that was a movie. But, if he were possessed by some demonic entity, wouldn't there be more obvious clues? Something more than the sense of something else peering out of Jonathan's eyes?

The more I thought about it, the more I realized I needed to do some research.

Then again, even if he was possessed, then what? Do I call in a priest to do an exorcism? How would that even work?

I nibbled on my toast, rubbing my forehead. This felt like an even more hopeless situation than the therapy. Jonathan really wasn't acting that crazy or that possessed.

But he had killed two people.

One in self-defense. The other could also be called self-defense, in that he was trying to protect our secret.

What about what he said about Felicity?

He was angry. They had a fight. It could be as simple as that.

And what he said when he was sleepwalking?

He was having a bad dream.

I let out a long sigh. Really, none of this added up to Jonathan turning into the next serial killer. I had no good evidence he would kill anyone else or go on a crazy murderous rampage or deface a church in a demonic fit.

Truly, what was likely going on was the relatively normal and expected reaction to what we did. Two people were dead. Yes, both were killed in self-defense, but still. Neither of us were murderers, so of course strange things were bound to happen as we processed what we did.

Quite honestly, I was the one who was putting both of us in danger with my actions today.

The best thing I could do was keep my head down and stay quiet ... to put the day behind me and hope Felicity and that lawyer I had seen would both forget what I said, as well. Jonathan would be fine. I would be fine.

I straightened my shoulders and picked up my spoon. What I needed to do was focus on eating my meal, then maybe on taking a bath and getting a good night's sleep. Then, the next day, I could go to work and get back to my life, instead of putting a target on my back with my erratic behavior.

I firmly squashed the little voice inside me that wanted to argue, that wanted to say, "No, this is NOT normal, none of it is."

Jonathan never should have been outside that bar in the first place. It was like he was just asking to get caught.

Or, even worse, that he was trying to lure someone out there precisely so he could kill her.

Nonsense. All nonsense. Jonathan had a rough time after Alan died, and he did something foolish. Just like I did something foolish. Two foolish things, in fact.

He was not crazy. He was not possessed. He was fine. I was fine.

Everything was going to be fine.

Chapter 29

"Charlie! So glad you could make it." Bill gave me a big smile as he welcomed me inside his air-conditioned two-story colonial home. He looked cool and collected in a pressed yellow polo shirt and khaki shorts. The house was comfortable, a welcome respite from the heat of the late afternoon sun.

"Thanks for inviting me," I said, handing him a bottle of wine.

"Oh, you didn't have to bring anything," he said, gesturing to the hallway behind him. "Everyone's in the back. Just go through the sliding doors in the kitchen."

I followed the sound of music and laughter into the large fenced-in patio backyard that was already crammed with people. I paused, one hand at the door handle, already feeling a little intimidated.

"Don't be shy," Bill said behind me, making me jump a little. "Go on."

"Oh, it's just ... more people than I expected," I said.

Bill laughed. "You'll fit right in. Claire is out there, and so is Lou. They'll be happy to introduce you. We'll be firing up the grill in a half hour or so. Beer and wine coolers are in the red coolers and soda is in the blue. We also have wine, vodka, rum, gin, ah ..." he turned his head, squinting at the kitchen counter.

"That's okay," I said, sliding open the door. "Soda sounds good. I can grab one." While I was feeling better, I still battled queasiness, and the last thing I wanted was alcohol. I stepped back outside in the warm, humid air.

As I headed over to the cooler, I spotted Claire across the yard. She waved and started picking her way toward me.

"How are you doing?" she asked as I scooped up a Diet Coke.

"Better," I said, popping the top. "I think I just needed a few days to rest. I've been on the go since I moved here, really."

"Yeah, you've had a lot to deal with," she said. I wanted to ask her if she was okay. Her eyes were ringed with deep black circles and her skin was pasty. She wore a sleeveless sundress covered with blue-and-brown flowers that was too big for her, making it hang shapelessly and awkwardly on her small frame. I wondered if she was getting any more sleep. Instead, I asked her if Doug was around.

"He's asleep. Working tonight," she said briefly.

"Working? On a holiday weekend? That sucks."

"Charlie, so glad you're here," Lou interrupted before Claire could respond. Lou's voice was cool, much less friendly than her words. "I heard you've been sick. Is that the lot you've been dealing with?"

"Basically," I said. "The move, the breakup … I think it all just finally caught up with me. How's the pregnancy going?"

"Oh, you know. It's going." She pressed her 7-Up can to her neck. "It is *so* hot." Her face was bright red and her pink tee shirt sporting the words "Baby on Board" in white letters was stained with sweat. She had piled her thick blonde hair on top of her head, but a few tendrils had spilled down and were sticking to her cheeks and neck. Even her white shorts looked like they had wilted in the heat, in direct contrast with her crisp and put-together husband.

"It's definitely humid," I agreed.

She switched the soda can to her other hand and pressed it to that side of her face. "I wish we could be inside, but no. Too many people. I knew this would be a mistake." She rolled her eyes, then glanced at the cans of soda Claire and I held. "What is this? You're both drinking soda? What's wrong with you? You think for one minute I'd be drinking soda if I wasn't pregnant?"

"My stomach still isn't quite right," I said. "I thought I'd start with soda and see how I felt later."

"I'm just pacing myself," Claire said.

Lou muttered something that sounded like "waste of a good party," but something caught her eye, and she shifted her gaze. "Jonathan is finally here."

My stomach flipped over as I turned to face him. I hadn't seen him in a few days, since before I went to see his wife. I wasn't sure what I should expect.

He was fishing a beer out of the cooler. He wore a red and white baseball shirt with light-brown cargo shorts. His dark hair was getting long in the back, curling around his neck. He needed a haircut. There was something so endearing about that too-long dark hair and the wrinkle in his nose as he studied the beer selection that made my heart speed up in my chest. In that moment, I remembered why I had started the ill-advised relationship in the first place.

He made his selection, popped the top, saw us, and waved as he headed over.

"Where are Felicity and the kids?" Lou asked, craning her neck to look around. "Still in the house?"

I hadn't anticipated Felicity coming. My chest was suddenly too tight, and I could feel my heart start to pound. I wondered if I should leave.

Jonathan took a long swallow of beer before answering. "Darrel has a bit of a cold, so she thought it would be better if she stayed home with the kids."

I felt myself relax while trying not to make it too obvious.

"Oh, that's too bad," Lou said. "We haven't seen much of her at all this summer."

"Yeah, she was disappointed she couldn't make it."

"Well, hopefully Darrel isn't too sick."

"No, he should be fine. Kids are so resilient."

Lou nodded, her eyes searching the crowd. "I don't suppose you saw my brother anywhere?"

Jonathan shook his head. Lou let out an exasperated sigh.

"I could just ..." Lou started to say but was interrupted.

"Lou," screeched a short, plump woman with short brown hair and way-too-tight shorts. "This is how I find out you're pregnant? With a shirt?"

"Hi Molly," Lou said resignedly as Molly bustled over to give her a hug. She briefly greeted Claire before continuing to exclaim over Lou.

I took a couple of steps back, giving Molly and Lou some space. Jonathan moved back as well as he gave me a sideways glance over his beer. His thoughts were as plain as if he had spoken them—he wanted to talk to me, but wasn't sure if it was the right time or place.

Claire gently touched my arm. "Let me introduce you around." I went with her gratefully.

She took me around the yard, and I met most of the people. Everyone had heard of me, the woman who was now living in the Witch House. Some eyed me with open suspicion while others were gleeful at the prospect at getting a look inside a real haunted house.

"It's not as exciting as you'd think," I told one big, rawboned woman named Trish. She had a shock of short, bleached blonde hair and skin covered in freckles.

Her expression was of disappointment. "So you never walk into the kitchen and see all the chairs on the table?"

"That's a movie," I said. "Real-life hauntings are not quite that dramatic."

Trish definitely looked dejected.

A couple of women had heard I was getting back into the tea business and wanted to order some. "Nancy told me you were picking up where Helen left off," a tiny, birdlike woman named Jill said. Her wheat-colored hair was as fine as a dandelion gone to seed.

"I'm still getting settled," I said. I had completely neglected my fledging business with everything that had happened. "But I can call you when I'm ready for new orders."

"Yes, definitely. Let me give you my number." She pawed through her oversized purse, while at the same time yelling at one of her kids to stop tormenting his sister. She located a crumpled receipt and a broken pencil and jotted down her name and number.

"Here." She pressed it into my hand just as a commotion near the house broke out.

Jesse had arrived.

Claire's face turned ashen. "Oh no," she whispered and hurried across the yard. I followed behind, weaving in and out of the crowd.

"Lou, what do you want from me?" Jesse raised his hands in defeat. He looked uncharacteristically messy, wearing an old, faded Packers tee shirt, jean shorts, and a Brewer ball cap. His face was scruffy, and there was a tiredness around his eyes.

Lou, on the other hand, had turned so red in the face, I was a little worried she was going to have a heat stroke. "You always do this," she snapped.

"Should I go? Would that be better?"

"Do what you want. You always do anyway."

"Hey, hey," Bill interrupted, putting a hand on his wife's arm. "Jesse, we're glad you could make it. Lou, you look like you got a little too much sun. Do you want to lay down and take a break?"

Lou snatched her arm away. "I don't need to be babied. I need my family," she yelled and burst into tears.

"Lou," Bill said trying to comfort her, but she shook his arm off and headed toward the back of the yard.

Bill looked helplessly at Jesse, who was shifting awkwardly from one foot to the other. "Hey, it's just the hormones. You know how she gets."

"Yeah," Jesse said, scuffing his toe against the back deck. "I know my sister."

"Help yourself to a beer. They're in the red cooler," Bill said over his shoulder as he hurried over to Lou, who was standing under a tree surrounded by a knot of women.

Jesse looked over to her, a sad expression on his face. "I should go."

"Jesse, no. You should stay," Claire said, running up the steps to grab his arm. "Give her a chance to cool down."

Jesse shook his head. "This was a mistake." He untangled himself from Claire and headed back into the house, Claire on his heels.

"Well, that was quite the show," a low voice said in my ear. Jonathan. He was so close I could smell him, that familiar scent of woodsy soap mixed with his particular scent of maleness. My skin prickled with electric shocks.

I didn't turnaround. "We probably shouldn't be talking."

He laughed softly. "It's a party, Charlie. Of course we should be talking."

"You know what I mean."

"No one is looking at us anyway," Jonathan said. "They're all talking about Jesse and Lou."

"Still," I said. I wanted to ask him more about Felicity, but I was a little afraid to bring her up. I didn't think she said anything, but I wasn't sure. He had acted normally the past few days, calling me the way he always did. I didn't hear anything in his voice that suggested he knew I had betrayed him.

Even so, every nerve in my body was humming.

It had to be done, I reminded myself. *I had no choice.*

So, why did I feel like such a traitor?

"How did Darrel get sick?"

He shrugged. "Who knows? Kids are always picking stuff up. He'll be fine. Felicity thought he would be too fussy being here." He didn't look at me, and I had the odd sense he was lying to me.

But why? Had Felicity said something to him after all?

"Fine, I'll talk to him." Lou brushed past us with Bill hovering by her side.

"He's your brother," I heard Bill answer as she marched into the house.

A warning bell started to chime in my head. Claire was in the house with Jesse.

I glanced at Jonathan, who had the same worry in his eyes, and we both started running to the house.

We could hear Lou screaming before we opened up the door. "How could you?" she shrieked. "You're married, for God's sake."

"Lou, it's not what you think," Claire tried to interject, but Lou didn't stop. "How could you do this to Doug? To me?"

"This has nothing to do with you," Jesse retorted. "This is between Claire and me."

"*You're* my brother and *you're* supposed to be my best friend."

We followed the voices until we found them in the den at the back of the house—Lou, Bill, Claire, and Jesse.

"Lou, this isn't the time," Bill was trying to say, but Lou shrugged him off.

"Oh, stuff it," she said. "My brother is not only leaving, but is also having an affair with my best friend. Everyone is going to know."

"Lou, just stop it," Jesse said.

She whirled back on Jesse. "Stop what? You know how I feel about this. You deliberately went behind my back and did it anyway, even though you're both committing adultery."

"Did it ever occur to you that the only reason it became adultery is because of you?" Jesse snapped.

"Oh, that's rich. Blaming me ..."

"Yeah, it's your fault," he said, taking a step toward his sister. "If you hadn't been so hellbent against us being together, then we could have had a real relationship after high school and seen where it would have gone. Instead, because we were trying to not to hurt your feelings, we ignored ours, and now look at us."

"That's ridiculous," Lou said. "You're both ridiculous. This is lust, nothing more. And you would have broken up and ..."

"Oh, stop it," Jesse said. "I'm sick of it. I'm sick of always choosing you over me. And I'm done. You're my sister, not my wife. It's time I start living my life instead of trying to make you happy."

Lou stomped her foot like a child. "How dare you? You don't do anything I want."

"I'm here, aren't I?"

"You're leaving next week!"

"And I should have left years ago," he said. "I came back for you. I didn't date Claire, for you. Well, I'm done. Goodbye, Lou." He turned around and strode down the hallway.

"Fine. Be that way. I guess I don't have a brother, then."

"I guess you don't," he said, his footsteps retreating through the house. After a moment, we heard the front door slam.

Lou stood in the middle of the room, her chest heaving in and out. Her face was still dangerously red. That couldn't be good for her or the baby.

Suddenly, she whirled toward me. "This is all your fault," she snarled.

I was taken aback. "Me?"

"Both of you," she said, wagging her finger at Jonathan and me. "If you two hadn't been flaunting your affair, Claire and Jesse probably wouldn't have felt like they could do the same."

Claire's jaw dropped. "Lou! That is completely uncalled for." Her expression was horrified. "Jesse and I are adults. We can make up our own minds. It has nothing to do with Charlie and Jonathan."

"Then why were you two able to control yourselves before? Why is it only when Charlie shows up that everything goes so wrong?" Lou was almost crying, she was so upset. She whirled on me. "Maybe this is all YOUR fault. If you hadn't come, none of this would have happened."

Claire and Bill both spoke at the same time.

"Charlie had nothing to do with this," Claire said.

"Lou, that's enough," Bill said. "This isn't Charlie's fault. Your brother has been talking about leaving for forever and, well," he furrowed his brow as if deciding the wisdom of what he was going to say next, before he blurted out. "Claire and Jesse have been flirting forever, as well. I know this has been difficult for you, but you have to get ahold of yourself."

"Easy for you to say," Lou spat. "You're the reason why I'm in this condition." She gestured to her tee shirt and swelling belly beneath. "You know I never wanted to get pregnant, and yet you pushed and pushed ..."

Bill grabbed Lou by the arm and started leading her out of the room. "Now is the not the time," he said. "I think you need a break. Why don't you go lie down?"

"I don't need to lie down. I need to not be pregnant anymore," Lou's voice floated back toward us. "I need my brother not to be leaving. I need ..." Bill steered her around a corner and her voice faded.

Claire, Jonathan, and I looked at each other. Claire's eyes were round. "I should ... I think I should," she swallowed hard. Her skin was pale, but she had two spots of red high on her cheekbones. "I should go," she said. "Yes, I better go."

"I should go too," I said.

"Yeah, I think we all should," Jonathan added.

Claire was already moving past us and down the hallway. "I'm going to try and catch up to Jesse," she said over her shoulder. "Make sure he's okay. I'll see you later."

"Yeah, see you," I said to Claire's retreating back.

"Maybe you should check on Jesse, as well," I said in a low voice.

Jonathan shook his head. "Claire's got it."

"Did you talk to him yet?"

"We should go," Jonathan said lightly, putting his hand on the middle of my back and escorting me out. "Before Lou comes back and yells at us some more."

"Jonathan," I hissed. "You promised you'd talk to him."

"And I will," Jonathan said as he steered me to the front door. "But now is not the time."

"When will the time come?" I demanded, still keeping my voice low. "He's leaving soon."

"Exactly. So what difference does it make if I talk to him?"

I couldn't believe what I was hearing. I glanced at his face. His expression was flat, no sign of any emotion at all, and his eyes were blank, like polished stones.

What was going on with him?

I waited until we were outside the house, with the front door carefully shut behind us, before I responded. "I don't understand you. He's your best friend."

"Was my best friend," Jonathan corrected. "Remember, he's leaving now."

"Which is why it's even more important to mend fences before he goes."

"I said I'd talk to him, and I will," Jonathan said impatiently. "Now, can we drop it?"

Nothing felt right. I had no idea who this man was in front of me, and I was suddenly very afraid the real Jonathan, the one I fell in love with, was gone forever. "Did I tell you Jesse thought you might have something to do with Rosie?" I was desperate. There had to be something I could say that could break through that unemotional and aloof veneer.

Jonathan went very still. "What did you say?" His tone held a warning.

My blood seemed to freeze in my veins. Oh no. Did I just put a target on Jesse's back? "That was probably a bit of an exaggeration," I said quickly. "He didn't actually say you had anything to do with Rosie." I tried to start walking away, but he grabbed my arm.

"Then what are you talking about?"

"I ... ah," I licked my dry lips. I definitely shouldn't have brought it up. "He was carrying the newspaper article about Rosie disappearing, and he was going on about your obsession with The Lone Man Standing ..." My voice trailed off as I could practically see the rage leaking out of the cracks in his otherwise indifferent expression.

"You should have told me sooner," he said, his voice sharp and clipped.

"I did! I told you he thought you were obsessed with The Lone Man Standing."

His eyes narrowed. "You didn't tell me all of it." His fingers were digging in my soft flesh, and I let out a yell.

"Jonathan, you're hurting me."

"You didn't answer my question." His eyes glinted. "Why didn't you tell me he was talking about Rosie?"

"Because you were all over me, okay," I said. "I was trying to talk to you, but you had other things on your mind. I kept trying to tell you there was a problem, that you needed to talk to Jesse, and you kept pushing me off, telling me it wasn't a big deal because he was leaving."

Jonathan didn't answer. He just stood there, as if processing what I said. Then, his expression softened. "You're right, you did try and tell me." He loosened his grip on arm, rubbing it gently. "I should have listened."

"Look, I don't think he really believes you had anything to do with Rosie," I said. "I did ask him outright if that's what he was trying to say, and he looked shocked and said, "absolutely not." But, he's your friend. You two should make up before he leaves."

"You're right, we should definitely talk," Jonathan said. "I was being a jerk. I'm going to reach out."

There was something wrong. Something off with his expression. I couldn't put my finger on it, but even though he had a solemn, almost repentant look on his face, it didn't feel authentic. More like a mask he had slipped on.

A mask covering up that darkness that was hiding inside.

"We should go with him," I said, the words out before I could fully think through whether it was a good idea or not.

He gave me a shocked look. "What?"

"We should go with him," I repeated, warming up to the idea. Maybe getting him away from Redemption was what needed to happen, and then it would be clear what was wrong with him. "We could take a trip. Go to New York. He could look for theater opportunities there, and you and I could see the sights. It would be fun."

His mouth twisted. "Don't be absurd, Charlie. I have responsibilities. You have responsibilities. We can't just leave."

"Not forever," I said. "Only a few weeks. Like a vacation. Wouldn't that be fun, going on vacation with me?"

He had such a dark, angry look on his face that I found myself taking a step back. But then, his expression cleared, and he smiled at me. "I would love nothing more than to take a vacation with you. Let's see about planning one, as soon as possible. And, maybe that would make sense, to meet up with Jesse. I'll talk to him, work things out, and then maybe once he's settled, we can go see him."

"Okay," I said, although it really wasn't. There was something off about the entire situation. But what could I do? I'd asked him to talk to Jesse and he'd agreed. Case closed.

He started to lean over to give me a kiss, then glanced behind him at the house. "Oops, probably shouldn't do that." He smiled, but his eyes were hooded, reminding me of a snake.

"Better safe than sorry," I said neutrally. "Let me know how it goes with Jesse."

"You know I will."

I headed to my car, absentmindedly rubbing my arm where it started feeling sore. When I looked down, I saw four perfectly round bruises, right where Jonathan's fingers had dug into my skin.

Chapter 30

The storm woke me.

Since the party, it had felt like we were all in some sort of holding pattern—almost like a pregnant pause, during which things were brewing, but not quite ready to burst. Even the weather felt like it was holding its breath as the dark clouds slowly built up and the air turned thick and humid.

Maybe I was overreacting, I told myself. *Maybe I had been reading too much into everything and really, it was all going to be okay. Jonathan would talk to Jesse, work it out, and all would be well.*

Maybe.

Jonathan had been busier than normal, both with work and family obligations, so I hadn't had much contact with him other than a brief call, but he had assured me he was going to find the time to speak with Jesse before he left. I still had an uncomfortable, nagging sensation about it, but I tried to tell myself it would work itself out. Jonathan and Jesse had been friends since childhood. They would talk about it, and everything would be fine.

I just had to keep telling myself that.

I had fallen into an uneasy, twitchy sleep with dreams I could only vaguely remember—like those of a child crying. Of course, there was no child in my house, so why in the world would I dream of one?

The thunder woke me, crashing across the bedroom as lightning ripped across the sky. I sat straight up in bed, hearing the pounding of the rain on the roof. It was really coming down. It felt almost like a release—the relief of letting go.

I laid in bed listening to the pouring rain. I wondered if I should check the house to make sure I didn't leave any windows open and maybe make myself some tea when I saw the headlights cut across the yard and heard the low purr of a motor. A car, turning onto my street.

My stomach turned over uneasily. What would a car be doing on my street this time of night?

Maybe the driver was lost and looking to turn around. It was easy to lose your way, especially in the dark and driving rain.

I stayed in bed and watched, waiting for the sound of the car turning around, to see the headlights shift across the room. I was practically holding my breath, straining my ears for the sound.

But of course, it didn't come.

And I knew it wouldn't. I knew it was Jonathan's car.

But why hadn't I heard anything else? The sound of a door opening or footsteps on the floor?

Finally, I crept out of bed, threw my robe on, and headed downstairs. Maybe it wasn't Jonathan after all.

I snapped on the outdoor lights and peered out the front window. Even though the rain was sheeting on the glass and the night seemed darker than normal, it certainly looked like Jonathan's car parked on the side of the road.

But, if his car was out there, where was he?

Maybe something was wrong. Maybe he was hurt or had a heart attack and couldn't leave the car. Oh God. It felt like a huge fist was squeezing my chest, and I was having trouble breathing.

I hurried to the front door, my fingers so numb, I could barely unlock it. I flung it open, ready to dash through the rain.

But there he was. Standing motionless on the porch. Soaking wet.

I screamed. I couldn't help it.

"Jonathan," I gasped, clutching my thin night shirt. "You scared me. Why are you standing out here?"

His hair was plastered to his skull. Water dripped off of his tee shirt and jeans and pooled on the wooden slats. He didn't answer, just stared straight ahead.

I took a step closer. "Jonathan? Are you okay?" Why wasn't he talking? My mind flashed back to the night he was sleepwalking. Did he drive all the way over in his sleep? "Jonathan, answer me," I said, my voice louder than I intended, the distinct tremble still underneath.

His mouth worked, but no sound came out.

"What? What are you saying?" I moved closer.

He was mumbling something, but I could barely understand him, especially with how loud the rain was.

"*I had to do it.*"

I was shivering, standing on the porch with my bare feet and the cold rain blowing against me. "Jonathan," I said, forcing myself to speak softly, to not panic. I had to get him to tell me what was going on. I reached over to touch his hand. It was ice cold. "Come inside," I said. "Let me make you some tea."

His eyes shifted to mine. For a moment, I couldn't move. I couldn't breathe. They were so full of anguish.

Oh God, what did he do?

"I didn't mean to do it, Charlie," he said.

I was so cold. So cold. I wasn't sure if I would ever be warm again. My fingers and lips were numb

But I had to keep going. I had no choice.

"What didn't you mean to do?" My voice was barely above a whisper. I wasn't sure if he could even hear me over the storm.

For an answer, he held out his palms. At the same moment, lightening flashed through the night, illuminating the porch and his hands.

They were red. With blood.

"I killed him," he said. "Charlie, I killed him. I killed Jesse."

The Reckoning

Chapter 31

Jesse is dead.

I couldn't even process what Jonathan was saying. I just stared stupidly at him as he kept muttering the same thing over and over ...

"It's not my fault. I had no choice. I didn't mean to do it."

When it finally sunk in–*Jesse is dead!*–I collapsed on the stoop, my legs unable to keep me upright, and I started to moan.

Jesse is dead.

I have no idea how long I sat there, wailing and keening, while Jonathan stood in the doorway, trembling and repeating himself, but at some point, a voice broke through my thoughts.

Get it together. This isn't helping. You need to find out what happened.

It sounded like Midnight talking to me, but I thought Midnight was still upstairs. So he couldn't be talking to me. Of course, he couldn't be talking to me anyway. He was a cat. And why was I worried about where Midnight was anyway. Jesse was dead.

Get up. Right now.

I buried my face in my hands. What did it matter anymore? Jesse was dead, and it might as well be my fault.

There's going to be a lot more that's your fault if you don't pull yourself together. The voice hissed. *Get up. Now.*

I grasped the side of the door and dragged myself to my feet.

Now, get Jonathan into the kitchen, dry him off and warm him up. Then you can find out what exactly is going on.

I took a deep breath, squared my shoulders, and began to coax Jonathan into the house. He was docile, allowing me to lead him into the kitchen, sit him in a chair, and dry him off.

I made the tea, adding a heap of sugar to both cups to help with the shock, and set the mugs on the table in front of us. My own hands were shaking, and I sloshed tea onto the table.

I didn't care.

Jesse was dead.

May God have mercy on us.

I gently pushed the mug toward him. "Jonathan, you must take a drink." He was rocking back and forth, still mumbling to himself, paying no attention to the tea. I picked up his hands, pressing the mug into them, and guided it to his mouth. Tea dripped down his chin, but eventually, I got him to swallow most of it.

"Jonathan, you have to tell me what happened," I said quietly, once he was visibly starting to calm down. His rocking slowed, and his trembling stopped. "Why would you kill ..." I swallowed hard, telling myself I couldn't cry, not now, I had to deal with Jonathan first. "Why would you kill Jesse?"

"I had to protect us," he said. "I didn't want to. But I had no choice, I had to ..."

"I understand ... you were protecting us," I interrupted. He was getting agitated again. I reached out to touch his hand, remembered the blood, shuddered, and put my hand on his arm. "But what happened? Why would you think he was a danger to us?"

He took a deep, shaky breath. "He showed up at The Lone Man Standing and ..."

I held up my hand. "Wait. What? Weren't you two meeting somewhere? I thought you said you were going to call him?"

"I did. We talked yesterday. Or maybe it was the day before yesterday? I can't keep track."

"Hold on. Slow down. I'm not following. Are you saying you met up before you saw him at The Lone Man Standing?"

He nodded. "I went over to his house. He was packing. All that fighting between him and Lou was really getting to him, and he was in a bad mood. Anyway, it wasn't a ... a great conversation. We ... well, we argued. He said I'm a different person—that he didn't know who I was anymore. I told him he was the one who had changed. I mean, he was the one leaving. Anyway, it wasn't going well. Then the phone rang, and he told me he was too busy to deal with me and I needed to leave.

"So I did. I thought that was the end of it. He was supposed to leave yesterday. I figured ... I figured it was fine. I mean, it wasn't fine, but once he was settled wherever he was going, I could talk to him then. Some time would pass, and I figured he'd make up with Lou and be more reasonable. Or, maybe we could do what you suggested and plan a trip to see him.

"But then he showed up at The Lone Man Standing tonight, and it all went horribly, horribly wrong."

I pressed my fingers against my temples, fighting to get all my warring thoughts in order. "So you didn't invite Jesse to meet you at The Lone Man Standing?"

"No! Why would I do that? He already thought I was obsessed with the place."

"But ... you ARE kind of acting obsessed. Why were you even there? I thought you and I agreed you were done with that place."

He looked at me in surprise. "No, we never talked about that. I told you; I had to keep an eye on Red. I had to make sure he knew he was being watched, so he would leave you alone."

"Okay, but ..." I felt like I was stuck in one of those mirror mazes, where all you can see is your reflection while you hit dead ends. You could find yourself going around and around in a circle if you weren't careful. "So how did Jesse even know you were there?"

"Well, clearly, he took a guess." Jonathan frowned into his tea. I wondered if he was wishing Jesse had guessed wrong.

"What happened next?" I felt like I was pulling teeth to get every detail out of him. "You were sitting at a table and ..."

He didn't reply, just kept staring into his tea. I was starting to wonder if he had even heard me and was going to repeat the question when he finally answered. "I was in the bathroom when he came in. I saw him sitting at an empty table. He was searching the bar, looking for me. I ducked out the back."

I was astonished. "You ... you ducked out the back? Why on earth would you do that?"

"Because I didn't want to have an argument in the bar," he said, his voice terse. "Do you think I wanted Red to overhear that one of my oldest friends thinks I'm obsessed with The Lone Man Standing? No, I wasn't about to have that discussion."

"But ... but maybe he wanted to bury the hatchet. You could have at least gone up to him to see what he wanted. And if he wanted to continue fighting, you could have stopped it then."

He was shaking his head. "No, no, I couldn't risk it."

"So, what did you do?"

"I went around back and drove around the block, then circled back to wait by his car."

"Why would you do that?"

"Because if he came out, I wanted him to think I was gone ... that he had missed me."

"But ... but you were waiting for him."

"Yeah, I wanted to see what he wanted."

There was a pit of horror growing inside me, like a black hole of despair. "Then why would it matter if your car was in the parking lot?" He couldn't be saying what I thought he was saying, right?

This wasn't a *planned* killing.

It couldn't be. There had to be a different explanation.

Jonathan's eyes narrowed. "I told you, I didn't want him to see my car and get spooked. I figured if he did, he'd go back inside and start asking questions."

His answer was weak, but I had to keep pushing. I had to know what happened. "So, then what?"

"Well, it started to rain," he said. "So, I got into his car to wait for him."

"His car was unlocked?"

"No, but I knew where he kept the spare key."

"So, you were ... inside his car? Waiting for him? And he saw you and just got in?"

A faint flush crept up Jonathan's face. For the first time, I thought his expression turned hesitant, uncertain. "I don't ... I don't quite remember. Except I think I hid."

"You *think*?"

"It's all a blur," he cried out, suddenly as agitated as he was when I found him on the porch. "I can't ... I can't remember. It was like something else was in control. And that something else ... well, we didn't want to scare him. So we hid. Ducked down. And then after Jesse got in, we sat up. He was startled, but we just wanted to talk. We were trying to explain about the rain and waiting for him and not wanting to talk in the bar, but he wouldn't listen. He wouldn't listen. And ..." He stared at his tea, biting his lip. "We killed him."

I couldn't move. I couldn't breathe. I was frozen in horror. It had swallowed me whole, like a giant oozing slime. I had never been so terrified in my life. Not even the night Alan had showed up in my living room or the night in New York when he pushed me down the stairs could compete with the fear that had taken over my body. It was like a living, breathing thing.

I couldn't ask the question that was dancing on my tongue. I didn't want to know the answer. I didn't want to hear any part of it. Yet I had to ask. I was *compelled* to ask.

Through lips that were dry and cracked, I forced the words out. "Who is 'we'?"

Jonathan jerked up. "What?" It was almost like he had forgotten I was there. He was so lost in his own world, he didn't even realize I was sitting right across from him.

I licked my lips and tried again. "Who is 'we'?"

He looked genuinely confused. "What are you talking about?"

"You said 'we.' 'We' killed him. Who is 'we'?"

Jonathan shook his head. "There was no 'we.' I killed him. I didn't mean to, but he started talking about Rosie. He kept asking, 'Where is she? Did you do something to her?' I didn't want to kill him, but he just wouldn't shut up about it."

His manner was completely different. There was no grief, just disappointment. No agitation, just calm. It was almost like a mask had snapped over his face.

It was as if something inside him had taken control.

And that something was lying about what had happened.

He studied me. His eyes were like flat, polished stones that almost glittered under the bright kitchen light. I suddenly had the distinct feeling I was being watched. Some *thing* was peering out at me from behind Jonathan's eyes.

And I knew, somehow, that my life depended on how I responded.

It felt like rats were scurrying inside my chest, clawing from the inside. Drops of sweat sprang up on my forehead, yet I was also cold ... so very cold.

"I wish he hadn't forced you to make that choice," I said. My voice was surprisingly steady.

The movement was barely visible, it was so slight, but he seemed to relax. "All he had to do was believe me," he said. "He shouldn't have pushed so hard."

"No, he shouldn't have." I swallowed. "What did you do next?" I asked softly.

"I moved the body to my car, and I hid his car." He glanced up at the window. "Oh look, the rain stopped. I better go take care of the body."

My jaw dropped. "What? Where's Jesse now?"

His expression was sheepish. "In the car. It was raining too hard earlier."

Jesse's body was in Jonathan's car? I could feel the bile rising in my throat, and I fought to push it down. "Is that safe?"

Jonathan stood up. "That's why I better take care of it now. I'll come back and shower after. You've got clothes for me here, right?"

"Yes," I said faintly.

"And coffee? Maybe some breakfast?"

He killed his best friend, someone he had known all his life, and he was asking about breakfast? "I think I can whip something up," I said, purposefully ignoring the terror welling up inside me.

He smiled briefly at me. "We're a good team, aren't we?"

I swallowed hard. *Please don't let me throw up.* "We are. Did you need help with the car?"

"No, I've got it." He frowned briefly. "I didn't like the airport parking lot. I've got a better way."

He started to walk toward the front door, and I trailed after him. "What is it?"

He opened the door, pausing to give me a quick kiss on the cheek. He smelled of beer and vomit. I wondered if he had thrown up after he killed Jesse.

And I wondered who was controlling him now.

"Don't you worry about it," he said. "I'll take care of all of it. Just need your help with some of the cleaning."

"You can count on me," I said.

He smiled an empty smile, one that didn't reach his eyes, and walked out the door.

I watched him from the window as he sauntered to his car, got in, and drove away. I could almost imagine him whistling.

I barely made it to the downstairs bathroom before I threw up again.

The Reckoning

Chapter 32

I had just thrown an egg, cheese, and bacon casserole in the oven when the phone rang.

I jumped, banging my head against the top of the stove.

I wasn't expecting a call. What I had been waiting for was the sound of the car, the click of the door unlocking, and the heavy footsteps of whoever it was residing in Jonathan.

It was too early for the phone to ring. I rubbed my head and glanced at the clock.

It could be Jonathan. I knew I'd better answer it. And quickly.

"Charlie?" It was Claire, and she sounded panicked. "Did I wake you?"

"No, I've been awake for a while," I said, then closed my mouth. Maybe I shouldn't have said that. Would it be weird to be awake so early? I couldn't tell. I was so numb, so disconnected from humanity, I had no idea what was normal anymore.

And I *had* to be normal. If there was any chance of getting through what was happening alive, I had to be as normal as possible.

If Claire thought my answer was strange, she showed no signs of it. "I don't know where he is."

A shiver of fear ran through my body. "Where who is?"

"Jesse."

I closed my eyes. So soon? How could this be happening so soon? "What do you mean?" *Stay calm. How would a normal person respond? Maybe say as little as possible.*

"He didn't show up last night."

My eyes flew open. "He was supposed to meet you last night?"

"Yes! We were ... were going to leave together."

"What?"

"I know, I know, I'm sorry." It took me a second to realize Claire had mistook the horror in my voice for shock that she hadn't told me. "I didn't tell anyone, not just you."

"But ... what ..."

"I'm pregnant," she blurted out.

I felt my knees buckle and I collapsed onto to the floor. "You're what?"

"Pregnant." She sounded like she was crying. "I just found out for sure."

"Is it ..."

"I don't know," she sobbed. "It could be either Doug's or Jesse's. I don't know."

"Did Jesse know? Or Doug?" As soon as the words were out of my mouth, I bit my tongue. I shouldn't have said it in the past tense. Too late now.

Luckily, Claire was too upset to notice. "I haven't told anyone. I was going to wait to tell him."

"Wait a minute." I was having trouble processing the conversation, much less trying to figure out a 'normal' response. "I haven't had my coffee yet. So, are you saying you were planning to leave with Jesse without telling him you're pregnant, and you don't know who the father is?"

"It's not ... well, yes, but it sounds worse than it is."

"Did you tell Doug?"

"I didn't tell anyone. Just you."

"No, not about the pregnancy. I mean that you were leaving him."

Claire sucked in her breath. "I was going to," she said in a small voice. "But then I chickened out. I left him a letter."

"You ... left him a letter? A 'Dear John' letter?"

"It's not like that."

"No," I rubbed my forehead. Considering the situation I was embroiled in, this was nothing. "I'm not trying to judge. I'm just ... wow, it's a lot to hit me with."

"I know, I know. I just didn't know who to call. Jesse never showed up. I don't know what to do."

"So, you were supposed to meet Jesse somewhere?"

"I was supposed to meet him outside of town," Claire said, her voice miserable. "At ... well, it doesn't matter now. The only things I was taking from my marriage were my clothes, my books, a few things from my mother and grandmother, and the car. I was leaving the rest to Doug, including the house. But my car didn't start." She let out a harsh laugh. "Can you believe it? All the shops were closed. I thought about calling Jonathan, but ... well. I figured Jesse would come here, or at least call. But he never called! He never showed! He just ... vanished."

"Did you try calling him?"

"Yes, but his apartment number was already disconnected."

"Do you know where he was supposed to go last night? Maybe you could retrace his footsteps?" I tried to keep my voice even keeled, while inside I prayed ... *please don't let her know, please don't let her know.*

"That's the problem," she ground out. "I don't KNOW where he went. He just said he had to go deal with something."

"So, what did you do?"

"What could I do?" Her voice was bitter. "I hung around here, pacing the halls, waiting for the phone to ring or Jesse to show until the time Doug would be home. Then, before Doug got here, I hid my suitcases and the letter and got into bed and pretended to be asleep. It was ... " her voice caught, and she started crying again. "It was the worst. Lying there while Doug just fell into bed, completely ignorant of what I was going to do." She was crying so hard, it was difficult to understand her. "Doug is always there for me. Always. And here I am chasing a dream who ditches me the moment he can."

"Where are you now?" My heart hurt for Claire, and I wanted so badly to tell her the truth. But I knew I couldn't. Not ever.

"I'm ..." She sucked in her breath, trying to get her crying under control. "I'm at a phone booth, downtown. I took Doug's car. I had to ... I wanted to look for Jesse. Just to be sure. I drove around, checking all the places I could think of where he might be. I even called the hospital. But there's just no sign of him. I don't understand."

"Look, I'm sure he'll turn up eventually," I said, hating myself even as I said it. But that was what a normal person would say, and I had to act normal. "Maybe whatever he had to deal with last night just took longer than he thought. Maybe he decided to go ahead and get settled somewhere and surprise you. Until you actually hear from him, try not to panic."

"I know you're right," she said, her voice full of tears. "My head knows you're right, anyhow. I shouldn't be assuming the worst. But, Charlie, I just ..." she sucked in her breath. "I just have such an awful feeling that something horrible happened. At first, I was angry. I was sure he had stood me up yet again. I couldn't figure out who I was angrier at—him for leaving without saying goodbye, or myself for falling for it. But then, as the night wore on, I just started to get this bad feeling that something else had happened. I don't know what, but I think it's bad. At this point, I just want to hear from him. That's it. I just want to know he's okay. You know? Even if he changed his mind and decided to leave without me, I at least need to know he's okay."

I could feel the bile rising in my throat, even though my stomach was empty. The pain in Claire's voice was heartbreaking. I squeezed my eyes shut and concentrated on breathing. "Not knowing is the worst," I said. "Believe me, I get it. But, look, if he had changed his mind and just left, it could be a while before he reaches out. It's more likely that Lou will hear from him first."

"That's true," she said, her voice sounding a little steadier.

"There's probably a million other explanations for what happened, but until Jesse reaches out to someone, we won't know. So, maybe what would be best is to go home and try and relax. Have something to eat. Maybe take a shower. And just see what happens. Okay?"

"You're right," she said, sounding much calmer. "I should go home."

"He might even be trying to reach you now," I said.

"He might."

The hopeful note that had crept into her voice made me hate myself all over again. "Also, don't forget, you're pregnant. Your hormones are out of whack. Keep that in mind, too."

"You're so right. Oh my God, I am so glad I called you," Claire said. "I knew you'd make me feel better. I'm going to go home now."

We said goodbye, and the moment I hung up, I ran to the bathroom. But other than hot bile, my stomach was empty.

How could I have lied like that to Claire? What kind of monster was I turning into?

My head hanging over the toilet, I was filled with such shame, such loathing for the person I was becoming, I almost couldn't stand it.

I didn't deserve to live. Maybe I should just end it now and do the world a favor.

What about Jonathan?

There was that voice again. I looked around and saw Midnight sitting in the doorway, watching me. His tail flicked.

"What about Jonathan?" My voice was loud in the stillness. A part of me wondered if I wasn't surely going mad, having a conversation with a cat.

You're going to let him get away with it? With everything he's done?

"I'll write a letter," I said. "My confession. I'll send it to the police."

Hmm. And you think that will work? He'll be arrested and found guilty based on a letter? Without any bodies? Without any evidence?

"The police can find evidence," I said. "That's what they'll do. Investigate. They'll find what they need to put him away."

If you say so.

"I do say so," I said crossly, but even as I said it, I knew it wasn't what I really believed. Not deep down.

If you're not here, what do you think is going to happen to Felicity? Or even worse ...

"Claire," I whispered. In my head, I replayed our conversation. *I have an awful feeling something terrible happened.*

What happens if Claire decided to start poking around? And I wasn't there to protect her?

You know what happens.

I pressed the heels of my hands against my eyes, willing the voice to stop. I didn't want to hear it.

But I knew I didn't have a choice.

"What do I do?" I asked, my voice broken.

The answer came without hesitation.

Get up. Clean yourself up.

I dragged myself to my feet and went to the sink to wash my face, rinse off my mouth, and comb my hair. I avoided looking at myself in the mirror. I couldn't bear to look into my eyes.

Make the coffee. Take the casserole out of the oven before it burns.

I headed to the kitchen, getting the casserole out just in time and starting the coffee. Midnight quietly padded behind me. I mechanically fed him.

Whatever you do, don't let Jonathan sense anything amiss.

I paused. In my mind's eye, Jonathan stared at me from the kitchen table, his hair still wet from the rain, his shirt plastered to his skin. And whatever was hiding behind his eyes carefully watching me.

He'll kill you, you know.

I looked down to see Midnight staring at me, his jade-green eyes unblinking.

The moment he thinks you're a threat, he won't hesitate.

"I know," I whispered back.

Chapter 33

I had just put a batch of muffins in the oven when I heard the front door open.

"That smells wonderful."

I turned, a smile on my face. Jonathan stood there, his clothes covered with mud. "I just put the muffins in. Why don't you take a shower and give me your clothes to wash? I already laid out a fresh outfit for you on the bed."

He glanced down at them. "Yeah, they're a muddy mess, aren't they? At least the rain washed out the blood." He started stripping down.

I kept a smile fixed on my face as I collected his clothes. Why would he make a point of telling me the blood was gone? Was it a warning in case I was thinking of saving them as evidence?

"Get yourself some coffee. I'm sure you're freezing," I said, and immediately headed to the washing machine. I made a big show of putting the clothes in, adding soap, and turning it on.

"I'll catch that shower first," he called back, still standing in the doorway where he could see me. "Be right down."

I nodded and went back to the kitchen. I listened to his footsteps climb the stairs, and a few minutes later, the shower starting.

I bustled around the kitchen, washing up, as I listened to the shower run. It seemed to be running for an inordinate amount of time. The timer dinged, and I pulled the muffins out of the oven.

Still, the shower ran.

Did he still even have hot water? I listened to the rumbling of the washing machine and decided I should check on him.

Fixing him a cup of coffee, I climbed the steps and headed to my bedroom. The bathroom door was closed.

I knocked. "Jonathan?" I called out. "Can I come in? I brought you some coffee."

Silence.

I knocked again, louder, in case he couldn't hear me over the noise of the water. "You okay in there?"

Silence.

The skin on my arms began prickling, and I wrenched open the door, allowing a flood of steam to pour out.

"Jonathan, did you hear me?" The air was moist and warm and enveloped me like a wet blanket. It felt like I was walking into a sauna. Still calling out to him, I went over to the shower and pulled back the curtain, and promptly let out a shriek.

He was curled up in the corner of the bathtub, the water striking his head and arms. I fell to my knees, dropping the coffee mug onto the floor. "Jonathan, are you okay? Can you hear me? Did you fall?"

I reached out to touch him. His skin was cold and clammy, closer to a frog than warm-blooded human. He was shivering uncontrollably, even though the shower water was lukewarm.

"Jonathan, what happened?" I asked over and over. "Are you hurt? Should I call an ambulance?"

His lips started moving, but no sound came out. I moved my ear closer.

"... can't stop ... no control ..."

"Can't stop? Can't stop what?" I asked.

The words were halting. "I've ... lost ... control ... I can't ... stop it."

I felt like I had been doused with ice water. It was just like the night I found him sleepwalking. What in God's name was happening to him? "What are you talking about?" I begged. "What can I do?"

"Help ... me ..."

My heart cracked open. "How?"

"You ... must ... stop ... it."

My mouth dropped open and I stared at him in shock. "What? Me? What can I do?"

His lips were turning blue and his body shook uncontrollably, but he still managed to move his head, so he could look me directly in the eyes. And for a moment, I saw him. I saw Jonathan, peering out from the depths. Terrified and grief-stricken, but definitely Jonathan. "Charlie," he said, clearly struggling to form the words. "You ... are ... my ... only ... hope."

Suddenly, his eyes rolled up in his head and his body jerked in convulsions. I let out another scream, trying to cushion his head so he wouldn't slam it against the side of the tub. Did I dare run for the phone to call an ambulance?

What do I do?

A second later, his body stilled. He relaxed for a moment, his chest moving up and down, before opening his eyes. "What the ...? Charlie, what are you doing in here? And why am I in a cold shower?"

I realized the water had turned freezing and quickly moved to turn it off. "How are you feeling? Are you okay?"

Jonathan had a confused expression. "Yes, I'm fine. Why am I in the tub? What's going on?"

I pulled a towel off the rack and handed it to him as I helped him up. "You were ..." I froze as warning bells began blaring in my head. *You are my only hope.* In that moment, I knew, with a deep sense of certainty, that the worst thing I could possibly do was tell him the truth.

"You fell," I continued. "At least, that's what I think happened."

His expression looked more bewildered as he stepped out of the tub. "I fell? I don't remember that. And why is there coffee all over the floor?"

I looked down to see the light-blue bathroom rug stained and soaked, and the mug tipped over on its side next to the tub. I picked it up. Somehow, it wasn't broken. But holding it gave me an idea. "I was bringing you coffee when I heard the noise. Like a thump. So I came in here and found you at the bottom of the tub. You were unconscious. I don't know what happened. It took a little bit to wake you. I must have dropped the coffee when I saw you."

He shivered. "Why was the water so cold?"

I shrugged. "I guess it just ran out. I wasn't paying attention to the water. I was trying to help you. I didn't want to call an ambulance, but I would have if you hadn't woken up."

His eyes widened. "No! Don't do that."

"I didn't," I reassured him. "But I was worried. I was in here with you, trying to wake you up."

He wrapped the towel around his narrow hips. "How long was I out?"

"Long enough for the water to turn cold," I said.

He ran a hand roughly through his hair. I noticed the stubble on his chin and how tired he looked. "Let me get you another cup of coffee while you finish getting ready," I said. "Don't worry about the mess, I'll get it later."

"I appreciate that." He smiled at me, but there was no warmth in it—just flat and cold. His eyes were shuttered, as if a blank shade had been pulled down over them to hide whatever was behind them from view.

"Remember, I have clothes laid out on the bed and breakfast waiting," I said as I started to walk out of the bathroom. "You're going to need your strength to get through today."

I was closing the door behind me when he called my name. I pushed it back open. "Yes?"

He was staring at me with those blank eyes, and it was all I could do not to shiver. "I know it must have been a shock, but I'm pleased you've risen to the challenge."

I could feel the bile rising in my throat and forced it down as I stretched my lips into a smile. "Of course. You know you can count on me."

Was there a glimmer of a warning behind his eyes? "I'm gratified to hear you say that. I'm trusting that will always be the case."

My smile stayed fixed in place. "Why wouldn't it?"

He shrugged. "I don't see why it wouldn't. Of course, that's up to you." He gave me a small smile. "We make a good team, don't we?"

My fingers trembled against the doorknob and my knees threatened to buckle. "We do. I better head downstairs and see about breakfast." Slowly, carefully, I closed the door with a soft click.

I stood there for a moment, breathing a few deep breaths, willing my body not to betray me. I couldn't afford to show even the tiniest amount of weakness. After I gathered myself as best I could, I straightened my shoulders and headed back downstairs.

The Reckoning

Chapter 34

I was in the middle of cleaning the kitchen when the phone rang.

Jonathan had already left, and I had forced as much food down my throat as I could stand. My stomach was gurgling unhappily, but so far, everything had stayed down. I made myself another cup of tea as I numbly and mechanically began the clean-up process.

I didn't particularly want to answer the phone. What if it was Aunt May's needing me to come in? There was no way I could work.

On the other hand, what if it was Claire? Or Jonathan?

I huffed out a loud sigh and reluctantly picked up the receiver.

"Charlie, it's me, Lou."

For a moment, my brain couldn't process a response. My emotions warred through my body: guilt, shame, grief, not to mention suspicion. Lou had never called me before. Why now? Did she know something?

"Lou. How are you doing?"

"I'm okay," she said. "Not as exhausted as I normally am. The morning sickness seems to be getting better as well, so that's a relief."

"Well, that's good," I said, playing with the phone cord as my own stomach twisted unpleasantly. I hoped I wasn't destined to regret eating breakfast.

"I was wondering," Lou's voice was hesitant. "Have you heard from Jesse?"

I closed my eyes as a fresh wave of guilt and grief washed over me. "No," I said, trying to keep my voice neutral and normal. "But then I'm not sure why he would call me." I forced a little laugh.

"Do you think ... do you think Jonathan has heard from him?"

"I'm not really sure. Did you ask him?"

"I tried," she said, her voice fretful. "I left him a message at work for him to call me back."

"Is there a reason you're asking us?"

"It's just ... I haven't heard from him."

Steady, Charlie. "Wasn't he leaving town?" Did I sound normal? I thought maybe my voice was squeaking.

"He was," Lou answered, her voice serious. If she heard anything off in my tone, she gave no indication of it. "He left yesterday."

"Yesterday? And you're trying to track him down today?"

"I know it seems like a short time," she said. "But Jesse always calls me when he's traveling. He checks in every day."

"The day isn't over yet," I said. "In fact, it's barely started."

"He didn't call yesterday, though," she said. "I was sure he would have called me last night or early this morning to give me an update, but he didn't."

"Forgive me, as it's not my business, but aren't you two still fighting? Or did you make up?"

She sucked in her breath, sounding like she was trying not to cry. "He called me before. The first time he left. I didn't want him to go, and he called me then."

"Look, there might be a million reasons why he hasn't called yet," I said. "And who knows, maybe he did try, and no one answered."

"No, I was home all day."

"Did you go outside for a few minutes? Or take a shower?"

She paused. "I did take a shower. I also walked Jillian to the bus stop."

"Okay then. It's a little early to be getting worked up. He hasn't been gone even a day."

"Yes, but ... there's something wrong. Something happened to him. I know it."

I squeezed my eyes shut, feeling like I was going to lose my mind if I had to keep doing this. "Is it possible you're feeling like that because you're pregnant, and your hormones are out of whack?"

Another long pause. "That's what Bill told me," she said in a small voice.

Oh, thank God. "Okay, so maybe you just need to relax. Take a warm bath. You can even bring the phone into the bathroom in case it rings."

"You're right," Lou said, her voice stronger. "It's just my hormones. I just need to relax."

"Yes, that's exactly right."

I listened to her pump herself up that it was all in her head for a few more minutes before I was finally able to get her off the phone.

The minute I hung up, I found myself on the floor. My knees were weak and shaky. Actually, my entire body was trembling.

How could I keep this up? Lying to everyone? There was no one, absolutely no one, I could be honest with.

I was going to crack. I knew it. And that would be the end of me. The only question would be how many people I took down with me.

The tears gushed out of me. Big, wracking, deep sobs. I cried for Jesse, for Lou, for Claire, for Rosie. Even Alan. But, most of all, I cried for Jonathan.

What kind of monster had he turned into?

You are my only hope.

What did that even mean? What could I do?

I sobbed until there were no tears left. My head pounded, and I felt drained of every drop of fluid in my body. I was just a pile of dry skin and bones, a shell of who I once was. There was nothing left of me. Nothing left at all.

***

The child was crying again.

Except, there was no child in my house.

So, what was that sound?

I picked my head up off the kitchen floor to better listen. Could it be Midnight meowing or an animal outside?

No, it was definitely a child crying. And it seemed to be coming from upstairs.

Slowly, I dragged myself up off the hard floor, feeling stiff and uncomfortable, and made my way up the stairs.

It appeared to be coming from the room at the top of the stairs. Why would there be a child there?

Whatever you do, don't pay attention to the crying.

I cocked my head. Where did that come from? Why wouldn't I pay attention to the crying? How could I not? Didn't I need to do something about it? I tried to focus, but there was so much buzzing in my head, it was like a hoard of flies swarming.

The door was shut tightly. I put my hand on the knob to open it.

Be careful of that room.

I jerked my hand back. The buzzing seemed to grow louder. I tried to remember who had told me that, but the images seemed to break off, spinning away as they dissolved into nothingness.

The crying grew louder. I opened the door.

The room was dark. I blinked several times, waiting for my eyes to adjust. All I could see were shapeless shadows that I assumed were the bed, dresser, and desk. The room looked empty.

"Hello," I said into the stillness. "Is someone in here?"

I took a couple of steps into the room, wanting to make sure no one was there before I continued to investigate. The darkness seemed to swallow me up, like I was stepping into the maw of a monster.

"It's time."

The voice was low, almost like a hiss.

"What?"

"It's time."

I searched the room. "Where are you?"

A shadow seemed to detach itself from the corner. "It's time."

I squinted at the shadow, trying to make out the features, but I couldn't see anything. "Time for what?"

"To do what needs to be done."

"I don't understand."

The shadow took a step forward. "You know what you need to do."

My skin prickled with goosebumps. "I don't know what you're talking about."

"You do."

"No!" I put my hands over my ears, shaking my head violently, trying to squeeze the voice out, but it was no use. I heard every word.

"He's out of control. You have no choice. You have to stop him."

"No, no, no!"

"You must."

"He's not," I gasped. My face and hands were damp, as if I were crying again. "He can control it. He's in control. He is! There's no reason for all of this to continue."

The shadow seemed to advance. "And what are you going to do when he thinks someone else knows something? And someone else? And someone else?"

My stomach started heaving, and I fell to my knees. "No," I gasped, doubled over. "No. He'll stop."

The shadow stepped next to me. It seemed to bend over, coming closer. "You know he won't stop. He'll keep going and going, until one day ... it's your turn."

"No! You're wrong!"

The voice hissed. "There's only one way this ends. Only one way you protect yourself, your friends, and the house. You must stop him."

"No!" I shrieked. My voice turned into a scream that tore apart the shadow, and the room collapsed into a black hole.

Another scream jolted through me, and I opened my eyes. I was awkwardly curled up on the kitchen floor, a line of drool running down my chin.

I blinked stupidly. What the ...

A bell chimed through the house. Except, it wasn't just any bell. It was the doorbell. Someone was at the door. That must have been what I heard. I must have fallen asleep on the kitchen floor and the doorbell woke me up.

I clumsily scrambled to my feet. My right shoulder ached, and my neck had a kink in it. I stumbled to the door, wiping the drool off my chin and wincing as I rubbed my shoulder.

I was so fuzzy, so incoherent, I didn't think to look through the peephole. Instead, I unlocked the door and flung it open.

"What the hell happened to you?"

It was Felicity.

Chapter 35

I blinked at her stupidly. "Felicity?"

She narrowed her eyes, studying me closely. "Are you okay? Are you sick? Did I wake you?"

I stared down at myself. I was still wearing the shorts and tee shirt I wore to bed with my untied robe thrown over them. "I'm ... ah ... I'm okay."

She didn't look convinced. "Well, all right. Do you have a minute? I'd like to talk to you."

I ran my hand through my hair, trying to smooth it out. My eyes felt swollen and hot. The last thing I wanted to do was talk to Jonathan's wife, but I shrugged and took a few steps backward, leaving the door open.

She gingerly walked through the entry way, her eyes darting all over the place as if she expected to find Jonathan hiding in the corner. "He's not here," I said.

"I wouldn't be here if I thought he was," she said, and shut the door behind her. Her straight blonde hair was loose around her face, and she appeared to have quite a bit of makeup on. She also seemed overdressed for the weather in a pale-blue long-sleeved shirt that was buttoned all the way to the neck along with a pair of white slacks. Her movements were stiff, almost unnatural.

"Would you like something to drink? Tea? Coffee?"

She shook her head. "I won't be long." Underneath her thick makeup, her face was quite pale, and her ice-blue eyes were bloodshot. She squared her shoulders and faced me. "You need to do something."

"About what?"

"Jonathan."

I frowned. "Are you asking me to break it off with him? Because if you are ..."

She took a step forward, her eyes sparking with rage. "You did this to him," she hissed.

I took a step back, a little unnerved by her reaction. "I did what?"

"Stop playing dumb. You know what I'm talking about."

My hand crept up my chest as my blood went cold. Did she know about Jesse?

Or ... my visit to her flashed through my head, and my mouth dropped open. "Did he do something to you?"

Something flashed in her eyes ... something I couldn't quite recognize. "That's not important."

I took a step forward. "What did he do?"

She stared at me, her earlier bravado evaporating. "It was nothing," she muttered, her eyes shifting so she was no longer looking at me.

"Tell me!"

She hesitated, and for a moment, I thought she wasn't going to respond. Then, she slowly raised her arms to her neck and began to unbutton her shirt. She pulled it back, exposing an ugly black and purple ring around her neck. I instinctively recoiled.

"Did Jonathan do that?" I whispered.

"What do you think?" She retorted, buttoning the shirt up again.

I didn't know how to respond. Despite knowing this might happen, despite hearing Jonathan casually toss it out as a possibility, I was still having trouble believing what my eyes were telling me. I felt ill.

"This is your fault, you know," she said, finishing the buttons. "You have to stop this."

I couldn't tear my eyes from her neck. The swollen bruises on the delicate white flesh. *This was his wife. The mother of his children. How could he do that to her?* "You give me too much credit," I said dully. "I can't stop anything."

She stepped forward. "You can." Her eyes gleamed with some emotion I couldn't quite put my finger on. Was it anger? Jealously? A combination? I couldn't immediately decide, yet seeing it was making me feel distinctly uncomfortable. "But you need courage. Do you have any? Or are you weak and pathetic ... just a slut ruled by your base emotions?"

I winced, but figured I deserved it. "I guess it depends on what I would need to do."

She moved closer, so close I could smell her perfume. "Stop. Him."

I opened my mouth to ask how, but then it hit me—the awful, terrifying choice she was asking me to make. My eyes widened in horror as I violently shook my head. "No. No. No. I can't do that."

"You must," she hissed. Her eyes were unnaturally bright. Was it madness I saw in their depths? "He's not going to stop."

"But what you're asking me to do ..."

"You did this to yourself. You put yourself, and me, in this position. You have no choice."

"I could call the police ..."

She laughed, a harsh sound. "And tell them what? Do you have any proof? Any evidence?"

"Your neck ..."

"Isn't enough," she answered flatly. "It's his word against mine. And what do you think is going to happen the moment he finds out I went to the cops? What do you think happens to my children?"

"But, I can't." I pleaded. "There must be another way."

The smell of her perfume was so strong, it was starting to make me sick. Her eyes narrowed. "There is no other way. You must see that."

That was the worst part of it. I *did* see that.

The cops couldn't help. I had nothing to give to them.

And, if Jonathan could kill Jesse, who else would he kill? Would anything stop him?

Still, my brain kept scrambling for an answer. "What if you leave? Run away?"

She took a step back. "I should have known," she snapped. "No spine at all. Just a stupid whore who doesn't care what happens to anyone else."

"That's not true," I said. "I do care ..."

"Then prove it," she ground out. "Do something about it."

"I'm trying," I almost shouted. "You could leave. You could go away."

"I can't!" She shouted back. "Do you really think he'd let me go? That he wouldn't figure out what I know? And what about my kids? He still has a legal right to see them."

I grew very cold. "And what *do* you know, Felicity?"

Her fists clenched. "I know enough to be terrified of him. As should you be, if you were smart. Do you really think he's going to stop with me? What do you think happens when he gets tired of you? Which he will. Don't kid yourself."

My stomach lurched uncomfortably, and I pressed my fingers into my belly. She was right. It was only a matter of time before he got around to me. And while I maybe deserved the same fate as poor Jesse and Rosie, what about other people? What about Lou? What if she asked too many questions? Or Claire? Or, really, anyone?

The real question was how many more innocent lives could I live with on my conscience, knowing I could have done something and chose not to?

"What would I do?" I asked, my voice barely audible.

Felicity briefly closed her eyes, a hint of relief passing over her face. "He trusts you. At least, at the moment. He'll let his guard down. Then, you could strike. He wouldn't see it coming."

My body shuddered with revulsion. "When?"

"Tonight."

She must have seen the horror on my face, because she quickly continued. "The sooner the better. You must see that. Every day, you run the risk of him figuring it out. Not to mention you don't know what he'll do in the meantime."

Oh God. I definitely was going to be sick. "But I don't even know if he's planning on coming over."

"He'll come," she said swiftly. "I'm going to call him and tell him one of Darrel's friends is having a party and I was asked to help chaperone, so he's on his own for dinner."

My head was spinning. This was all happening way too fast. "But what do I do ... after?"

"Leave that to me," she said. "Call me when it's done, and I'll take care of the rest."

"Maybe I should just call the cops," I fretted. "Confess everything. I could ..."

Before I knew what was happening, Felicity had charged over and grabbed my arm. "You will do no such thing," she hissed, digging her nails into my arm. "Do you honestly think the cops will be able to do anything? He'll get off on a technicality. Mark my words. And then what? My children will have to grow up not only in fear for their life, because you know he'll come after us, but with their daddy's reputation in ruins."

"What are you going to tell them? He just ran off?"

"You just leave my children up to me," she said, squeezing her hand even tighter. "People disappear all the time in Redemption. We have no idea what happened to them."

"Let go of me," I said, wrenching my arm out of her grasp. I stared at the deep gouges. "Look what you did. How do I explain this?"

She gave me a look. "Welcome to my world. You'll figure it out. Are we clear?"

I really didn't want to agree. There had to be another way. This couldn't be the answer.

Yet even as I ran all my objections through my mind, I knew Felicity was right. It's what had to be done.

The cops couldn't do anything. And, even if they did try to stop him, chances were slim they'd succeed. So much had worked out for him. Alan had already been declared dead, legally. Rosie was not only the perfect victim, but had basically presented herself to him. Apparently, it was just as easy with Jesse. Why would I think bringing the cops in would change anything? Why would I think that whatever it was living inside Jonathan would *allow* the cops to interfere in any way?

This had all been too easy for Jonathan. Everything kept working out for him. Murder shouldn't be so easy.

It couldn't just be luck. No one was this lucky.

Something else was behind it. That had to be what was going on.

Even worse, it was getting more and more bold. Killing Jesse was proof of that.

The image of Jonathan as he pleaded with me in the shower flashed in my mind.

You must stop it. You're my only hope.

It was my fault. I started everything that had happened. I brought Alan into our lives.

It was up to me to end it.

I owed it to Jonathan. The real Jonathan. The one trapped in a living nightmare. If I truly loved him, I had to do it.

I took a deep breath and squared my shoulders, even as my heart broke inside. "Clear."

She straightened up, giving me a slight nod. "Remember to call me when it's done."

I couldn't even answer. I just stared at her, watching as she walked over to the door, opened it, and stepped through. She was about to close it when she paused and glanced at me. "Oh, and Charlie? Word to the wise. Whatever you choose, make sure it does the job. The first time. Because you won't have a second chance." With that, she left, closing the door behind her with a soft click.

Chapter 36

"Dinner smells wonderful," Jonathan said, coming into the kitchen.

I threw him a quick smile over my shoulder as I pulled the mushrooms stuffed with cheese and sausage out of the oven.

It had been a surreal day. The moment I had made the decision to do what I was going to do, it was as if my emotions dried up. I had become cold and calculating, focused only on what needed to be done. "Should be ready soon. Did you want to get washed up? I have fresh clothes laid out for you on the bed. I'll pour the wine."

Jonathan leaned over to kiss me on the cheek as I started plating the mushrooms. "You spoil me," he said.

"Why wouldn't I?" I asked, putting the platter down and reaching for the bottle of wine and an opener. "Go on before you get grease stains all over everything."

He picked up a mushroom, blowing on it to cool it before popping it into his mouth. "Yes ma'am." He was almost out the door when he paused. "What did you do with my clothes from this morning?"

I concentrated on opening the wine. "Already washed and put away. I hung them in the closet."

He grinned. "You really *do* spoil me."

I glanced at him from under my eyelashes. "Hurry up. You don't want dinner getting cold."

I listened to him climb the stairs as I poured our drinks.

By the time he returned, the candles were lit and the steaks grilling. "This is amazing," he said, looking around. "Candles, fresh flowers. What's the occasion?"

I handed him his wine. "It started with the flowers," I said. "As everyone keeps reminding me, winter is coming. So I thought it would make sense to bring them in, so we can enjoy them before they freeze. Once I arranged them, I thought it would be nice to have a romantic dinner this evening, too. So here we are."

He sipped his wine and fingered one of the flower bouquets I had arranged in a basket. "These baskets are a cool idea."

"Aren't they?" I answered, pushing the tray of mushrooms toward him. "I saw it in a magazine. Thought it would be fun to try."

"It is," he said, his eyes shifting toward me. I had taken great pains with my appearance, dressing in a black mini skirt, a white, lacy, long-sleeved peasant-style blouse (to hide the marks Felicity left on my arm), and black boots. I had to cinch the mini skirt with an oversized black belt as it was a little too loose. I really needed to start eating normally.

"Definitely worth trying," he said, his eyes hungry as he reached for me. "Maybe dinner can wait?" he whispered into my neck as his fingers trailed down my spine. I turned my face away, trying to keep him from seeing the battle between revulsion and grief raging inside me over what he had become.

"After I spent all this time in the kitchen?" My voice was playful. "Besides, I've got another surprise for after dinner."

His eyebrows went up. "Oh, really?"

"Mm hm. And the anticipation is just going to make it that much better."

I slipped out of his grasp and he let out a groan. "You're killing me Charlie, but I have to admit ..." he popped another mushroom in his mouth. "The steaks do smell fabulous."

"And who wants to eat overcooked steaks?" I moved back to the kitchen to plate the food. The twice-baked potatoes and sautéed asparagus were already done, and the salad was on the table. "Have a seat," I said.

He dug into the salad as I brought the rest of the meal to him. "You really outdid yourself."

"Thanks." I helped myself to salad as I watched him. "How was your day?"

He shrugged. "Fine, for the most part. There was an accident up by the lake. A couple of teenagers were messing around and not paying attention to their driving. No one was hurt, but both cars required towing." He shook his head. "Kids."

"Well, I'm glad no one was hurt."

"Yeah, so am I. Kind of a miracle, actually. One of the cars will probably end up being totaled."

I played with my salad. "Lou called me," I said casually.

Jonathan stopped chewing and stared at me. His dark hair was still damp and curled against his chin. He had even taken the time to shave, I noticed, and the dark-blue polo shirt I laid out for him made him look even hotter than normal. It had always been one of my favorites.

I wished with everything in me that I could turn the clock back to the night Alan broke in and call the police rather than Jonathan. If only I had done that.

If only.

I met Jonathan's penetrating gaze. "What did she want?" he asked.

"What do you think?"

He paused before shaking his head and turning his attention toward his food.

"Claire called, too," I said.

He sighed, loudly, and looked at me again. "Why are you bringing this up now? I thought you wanted to have a nice night."

"I do. But this isn't going away. We need to talk about it."

"What do we need to talk about?"

I speared a tomato. "I need to know why."

His expression was puzzled. "I already told you why. Because he was asking about Rosie."

I shook my head. "There has to be more to it. Jesse was leaving. What would it matter even if he did suspect? It's not like he had any proof."

Jonathan eyed me as he cut his steak. "Again, why are you bringing this up? What does it matter? What's done is done."

I carefully laid my fork down and folded my hands. "Because of what I just said. Claire and Lou. And Bill, and people at Aunt May's, and everyone else. This isn't going away. Jesse isn't Rosie. His disappearance is going to lead to rumors and gossip and everything else. And if I don't know the full story, the true story, I can't support you."

He picked up his wine glass. "That doesn't even make sense."

"Are we partners?" I raised my voice slightly.

"Of course."

"Then why aren't you treating me like one?"

He paused, his glass to his lips. "I don't understand."

"If you believe we're in this together, if we're true partners, I need to know the truth. Because if I don't know the truth, how can I do my best to make sure no one else makes the same mistake Jesse did?" My voice was getting louder, even though I was trying to rein myself in. But it was too late. The pain and grief over Jesse's death rushed through me.

"I messed up with Jesse," I confessed with tears in my eyes.

He put his wine glass down. "What? No, you didn't."

I picked up my napkin, holding it against the corner of my eyes, willing myself not to cry. "I must have," I said. "He came to me. With that newspaper article. I thought I dissuaded him. I thought I had put his suspicions to rest. I thought I had taken care of it. But I clearly didn't, because you just said that his being suspicious is why you had to ... you had to kill him. So how will I know what to do in the future if anyone else comes to me, if I don't know the truth now?"

Jonathan's mouth was open slightly. "But, but, that's just not true," he stuttered. "You had nothing to do with it."

"How do I know that?"

"Because I'm telling you."

I took a deep breath and met his eyes. "Do you trust me?"

I knew it was a gamble, and I saw his eyes widen in surprise. I could see the shadow inside him, the beast inside him, recoil. The beast *didn't* trust me, and I knew it.

What I didn't know was whether the beast was willing to admit it yet.

"Of course," he said. "You know I do."

"Then, trust me with this," I said. "Trust me with the truth."

Jonathan dropped his gaze to his plate. He started cutting his meat into smaller pieces. I waited, practically holding my breath.

He kept cutting his steak into smaller and smaller pieces, his eyes set firmly on what he was doing. I was just about to despair that he wouldn't say anything at all when the words finally came.

"Jesse told me I changed. He told me there was a darkness inside me. That he was worried about me ... worried that I was letting the darkness take control. He said it was always there, even when we were children, but he was afraid I was losing control.

"But that's what he didn't understand. I AM in control. In more control than I ever have been in my entire life. No one controls me. It's me who is in charge. Me who is in control. *Me.*

"My entire life, I have been at the mercy of other people. Frank. Felicity. Even my mother. All this time, I've felt like I was being tossed around, responding to things that were happening to me. Never have I been in the position of making things happen.

"Well, that's all changed now. Finally, I *am* the one making things happen. I have the control. I have the power. And that's what I was trying to make Jesse understand."

He stopped talking as he looked off into the distance, his eyes unfocused. I held myself completely still, barely breathing, afraid if I did anything at all, it would break the spell he was under and the words would stop. "He just wouldn't see. No matter what I said, he just refused to understand.

"I would have let him go. I had every intention of letting him go. He could have run off with Claire and lived happily ever after. But no. Instead, he shows up at The Lone Man Standing. And that was when I knew I had to kill him. Because he was never going to stop. He was going to keep harping on this. He would definitely tell Lou and Bill. God knows who else. He would share his suspicions with all of them.

"And it would never stop. All these people would be watching me, asking me questions, poking around, getting more and more suspicious. It would never end.

"The only way I could see of getting in front of it was by killing him."

He turned his face, finally meeting my gaze. His eyes looked anguished. "Do you see now? What choice did I have? What else could I have done?"

I felt like I was completely paralyzed. Every muscle in my body was frozen solid. I wasn't sure if I would even be able to answer. But I had to. I had no choice.

I forced my very dry lips to part. "There was nothing else you could do." My voice sounded rusty, like I hadn't spoken in years. "You had to do it."

"See! You understand. I had no choice."

"No choice at all," I said.

He slugged back a mouthful of wine before getting up to fetch the bottle. "You know," he said, as he topped off his glass. "I think you're right. This was a good conversation to have. Because now you know what I'm up against. What we need to be watchful of." He held up the bottle, gesturing to ask if I would like more. I gave my head a quick shake. He shrugged as he took a long drink. Pouring the rest of the bottle into his glass, he said, "Especially Claire and Lou. Bill, not so much. He's pretty practical. But Claire and Lou will need ... proper guidance. Are you up for that?" He returned to his seat, giving me an earnest look.

I forced myself to smile. "Of course."

He smiled back, his face and manner completely relaxed, and started eating with renewed appetite. "It's going to be amazing," he said. "Just you wait and see. We make such a good team. There will be no stopping us."

"Nothing will stop us," I echoed.

He forked up another bite of steak and studied my plate. "You haven't eaten much."

"Yeah, my stomach has been acting up again," I said, scooping up some potato and eating it. "I'll be fine."

He looked concerned. "Maybe you need to see a doctor."

"Yeah, I'm going to make an appointment," I said, making a bigger show of eating, even though my stomach wanted to revolt.

"Do that," he said. "We need you healthy. Lots going on."

"Yep, I know it. I'll be ready."

I picked up my wine, watching him carefully over the rim of the glass. He still looked normal except for a couple of beads of sweat near his hairline. He reached for his wine glass. "Wonderful meal," he said. "What's for dessert?" He gave me a wicked smile.

"Homemade cherry pie," I said. "To start."

He sighed, rubbing his belly. "My favorite. You're so good to me."

"Let me cut you a piece," I said, pushing back to stand up. My legs felt wobbly and stiff, but suddenly, I couldn't bear to sit at the table any longer.

"But you haven't finished your meal," he protested.

"I will," I said, my movements feeling jerky and uncoordinated as I went into the kitchen. "But there's no reason why you can't have a piece while I finish."

"Got another bottle of wine?"

"Of course," I said. "I'll bring it in a moment." I sliced the pie and put it on the plate, along with ice cream, and carried it and the bottle of wine to the kitchen table.

"Thanks, but I'm thinking I need to wait on the dessert," Jonathan said as I placed the dessert in front of him. He was sweating profusely, and his face was flushed.

"Are you feeling okay?" His hands were trembling slightly, and I noticed his pupils were dilated.

"Something just hit," he said. "I wonder if I caught that stomach bug that's been making you so sick."

"Maybe," I said, reaching over to feel his head. His skin was clammy. A thin line of drool trailed down his chin. "Maybe you should lay down."

"That's a good idea," he said, lurching to his feet. Almost immediately, he collapsed, shaking all over.

I fell to my knees next to him. "Jonathan, are you okay?"

His body was starting to convulse. "Call ... ambulance"

I stroked his face. "It won't help," I said, fighting the anguish as my heart broke into a million pieces.

It had to be done, I kept repeating to myself. *You had no choice it had to be done.* "There's no antidote for hemlock poisoning."

His eyes widened. "You ... *you* ... did this?"

"I'm so sorry," I whispered. "I had no choice. Someone had to stop you."

He lunged at me. It was clumsy, as he was losing control of his muscles, but the force of it knocked me backward. He garbled something, trying to speak, flailing out for me, but I just kept backing up to stay out of reach of his arms.

His eyes were terrifying. I could see the beast peering out at me, so full of rage and hate, it stopped my breath. The expression "If looks could kill" floated through my head. I had never understood it before that exact moment.

Then, in the next breath, the beast was gone. Jonathan was there, looking out at me, his eyes wide and scared. Still, I could see something that looked like relief, too.

"Jonathan?" I crawled over to him, stroking his cheek, his forehead. Water dripped on my hands and I couldn't figure out where it was coming from until I realized it was tears streaming down my face. "I'm so sorry," I gasped. "I'm so, so very sorry."

His lips moved. He was trying to say something. I bent my ear closer. His voice was so low, I could barely make out the words.

"Thank ... you ..."

His eyes closed, and his body seized up into the final throes of death.

I stayed with him until he took his final breath, watching him die. I stayed with him even after, stroking his face, his hair, his neck. I don't know how long I stayed there on the floor beside him.

I know it was long after I heard the click of the tape recorder as it reached the end of the recording. I had hidden it in one of the flower baskets, so I could record his confession for Lou and Claire. It was long after the two tapered candles sputtered and burned out, no longer reflecting the empty poisoned bottle of wine on the table that I had added the hemlock to after I poured both of us a glass while he was upstairs, cleaning up in anticipation of a romantic night.

Long after my tears had dried up and I could no longer cry, I stayed.

Long after his body grew cold and there was no longer anything anyone could do, I stayed.

It was only when the kitchen began to fill with the grey silvery light of dawn that I staggered to my feet, my limbs no longer working, and rushed to the bathroom to vomit. Over and over again.

The Reckoning

Chapter 37

Now you've done it.

I was so sore. Every part of my body hurt. I didn't want to move. I didn't want to breathe. I especially didn't want to talk to anyone.

We need to talk.

I squeezed my eyes shut. If I didn't respond, whatever was bothering me would go away.

I'm not leaving, so you might as well look at me.

The voice was slightly amused. I sighed loudly and rolled over. "What do you want?"

The black cat was sitting there. Except it didn't look quite right. It was way too thin, and its fur was matted. *We don't have much time.*

"Fine," I closed my eyes. "You can leave now. No one is stopping you."

Charlie. The voice was urgent. *You made things worse. Without Jonathan as a host, there's no telling what it will do.*

I opened my eyes. "I don't understand."

What you call the "beast." It's free now. And now, it's up to you to contain it.

I slowly pulled myself to a seated position. "What are you talking about? I killed it."

You didn't kill anything. You released it. And now you have to contain it.

"But that's what I thought I was supposed to do," I said, my frustration rising. "I thought I was supposed to do whatever it took."

I told you not to listen to the crying.

I stared at the cat in bewilderment. "What crying? What are you talking about?"

Never mind. Look, there's not much time. You need to make sure the body is protected. Use jade.

"Jade?"

The Reckoning

Bury the body with jade. It's not ideal, but it's the best we can do for now. Then ... the cat paused, moved closer to my face, its jade-colored eyes staring into mine. *You must burn it down.*

I blinked. "Burn *what* down?"

Where it all started.

"Where *what* started?"

The evil. Where it came to Redemption. You must destroy it. That's the only way to buy us enough time.

"I don't understand."

You will. The voice seemed to fade as the cat started to back away. *You will.*

"Wait," I called out, stumbling to my feet. "Come back. I don't understand."

The cat looked back at me, opened its mouth, and let out a high-pitched shriek.

I opened my eyes. For a moment, I couldn't figure out where I was. I was lying on something cold and hard, surrounded by odd, giant pieces of furniture.

The phone was ringing. That must have been the shrieking I heard that I thought had come from the cat. Slowly, stiffly, I dragged myself to my feet. I was in the bathroom. The downstairs bathroom. I must have fallen asleep at some point in the middle of the night. I stared at myself in the mirror. My face was pale, and my makeup smeared. I still wore the same outfit as I had on the night before, but my blouse was stained and wrinkled. No matter. I had every intention of throwing it away.

The phone was still ringing. I didn't want to answer it. Somehow, I knew the moment I did, the "warm and fuzzy" bubble I was in would pop, and I didn't want that to happen.

But it wouldn't stop. It kept going and going and going.

Finally, I left the bathroom and answered the extension in the living room.

"Charlie? Finally. What's going on? Why haven't you been answering the phone?"

I didn't recognize the voice. "Who are you?"

There was a pause. "It's Felicity."

Felicity. The pieces began clicking together in my head, and it all came roaring back to me.

What had I done?

I dropped the phone as a wave of grief and despair flowed through me.

"Charlie!" I could barely hear Felicity's voice from the dangling receiver. "Charlie! What's going on?"

I closed my eyes, took a deep breath, and picked up the receiver. "I'm here," I said.

"What happened?"

"It's done."

There was a long pause. "You did it?"

"Yes."

"Why didn't you call me? I told you to call me the moment you did it."

My voice was expressionless. "You really want to do this now?"

A pause. "I guess not. Where is he?"

I flicked my eyes toward the kitchen. "Lying on my floor."

Another pause. "What about his car?"

"Probably still where he parked it last night."

"Which is?"

"On the street, most likely."

She huffed out a loud sigh. "This is why I wanted you to call me the moment you did it. All right. Stay there. Do you have to go to work today?"

I thought about it. Did I? I couldn't remember. "No."

"Okay. So, move the body somewhere where no one will smell it. Maybe a freezer? Do you have one big enough?"

"A freezer? What are you talking about? He wouldn't fit in a freezer."

"I meant a chest freezer. Do you have something like that?"

Something niggled at me. In the basement. "I think so."

"You *think*? You don't know?"

"I think I have something that will work," I said impatiently.

"Okay. Do that. I'll take care of the car right now."

"But, then what? I'm going to put the body somewhere and ..."

"I'll take care of it," she said harshly. "I need a little time though. So, move the body somewhere where you can store it a few days. I'll be in touch." There was a click as she hung up.

I stared at the receiver for a few minutes, wondering how on earth I had managed to mess up my life to such an extent that my dead lover was lying on my kitchen floor and his wife was helping me cover it up. It wasn't until I heard the angry beeping from the phone being off the hook that I roused myself to hang it up.

There were things I needed to do, no matter how unpleasant.

***

"Can I help you?"

The man standing on my doorstep seemed familiar, although I couldn't place where I had seen him. Had he come into the restaurant at some point? He was wearing worn jeans and a red-and-blue plaid shirt over a white tee shirt, and a backwards baseball cap over his straight blonde hair. "Are you Charlie?"

"Yes."

"I'm Felix." He waited expectantly for a moment, as if his name should mean something to me. When I continued to stare at him blankly, he added "Felicity's brother."

"Oh." Of course. Now that he'd said it, I could see the resemblance. "Felicity and Felix, huh?"

A ghost of a smile touched his lips. "What can I say? My mother liked matching sets."

I wondered what else was matching, but decided it was none of my business. "Do you want to come in?"

He stepped into the house, carefully wiping his shoes on the mat. "Want some coffee? I just made a pot."

"Sure. I hope this isn't too early," he said, following me into the kitchen. " I wanted to stop by before work."

"I was up," I said, gesturing for him to sit down while I went to fetch him some coffee. "I'm not sleeping a lot these days."

It had been three nights since my last dinner with Jonathan, and two days since Felicity called. Since then, I had discovered there *was* a chest freezer in the basement. After a lot of struggle, sweat, and tears, I finally was able to drag Jonathan down the stairs and get him into the freezer.

Of all the horrible, awful tasks I had found myself doing since moving to Redemption, that one was the worst.

Afterward, I threw myself into cleaning, scrubbing the kitchen multiple times before moving onto the rest of the house, including the room at the top of the stairs.

The room where the whole nightmare began.

It was time to end it.

I joined Felix at the table with the coffee and a basket of homemade blueberry and bran muffins. I had been forcing myself to eat more, including a decent breakfast. I had even made myself a cheese and mushroom omelet to go along with the muffins, and managed to finish it all. I didn't even throw up afterward, although the day was young.

Baby steps.

"So, what can I do for you?" I asked, although I could guess why he had come.

Felix helped himself to a muffin. "It's probably more like what I can do for you," he said.

I stared into my own cup of coffee. While I still preferred tea, since that night, I had found myself craving coffee more. "Felicity sent you." It wasn't a question.

He nodded. "That she did."

I glanced at him over my cup. "How much do you know?"

He made a face. "Felicity didn't move Jonathan's car on her own."

I hadn't seen her take care of it. At some point, I had gone outside, and the car was gone.

Just like that.

He carefully broke the muffin apart and reached for the butter, his movements slow and deliberate. "Where is he?"

I still couldn't look at him. "In the basement."

He raised his eyebrows. "Just in the basement?"

"In a freezer."

He nodded and took a bite. "That's good. I was thinking the basement would be the best place to put him."

I gave him a sharp look. "The basement? I had assumed we would bury him."

"Bury him? Where?"

"In the backyard." I gestured with my head. "I thought I could plant a nice tree or bush over him."

He gave me a strange look. "You dragged him downstairs planning to bring him back up?"

When he said it like that, I realized how silly it sounded. "At the time, I hadn't thought it through," I said. "I was in a shock. Maybe I'm still in shock. Felicity told me to do it, and, well, I couldn't bear looking at him anymore so ..." I sighed. "Maybe you can help me bring him back up."

He didn't respond for a minute, focusing instead on eating. Everything Felix did was careful and deliberate, from the way he talked to the way he buttered his muffin. "I think burying him in the backyard is a bad idea," he said. "You can't hide a hole that big, even if you plant something over it. People talk. And if it isn't deep enough, you may end up having a problem with animals."

He had a point. "So, what do you suggest?"

He swallowed a bite and took a drink of coffee. "Let's check out your basement and see about our options."

I led him downstairs. He didn't say anything as he walked around examining the dirt floor, the walls, the ceiling. We both avoided the chest freezer.

Finally, he turned to me. "What do you think about a cement floor?"

I shrugged. "Probably better than the dirt, I would imagine."

He nodded. "Yep." He looked around again. "A cement floor would be perfect."

It took me a moment to realize what he was suggesting, and when it sunk in, I blanched. "You're not suggesting ..."

"Yes," he said, cutting me off. "It's the perfect alternative. No one is going to find him under a cement floor."

I wanted to refuse. I wanted to insist on my garden idea. Surely, we could make that work.

But, deep down, I knew he was right. Burying him in the basement would be easier for me to keep an eye on things. It would be easier to keep other people away. I could add the jade, and no one would be the wiser.

No question burying him in the basement would be easier all around.

It was also exactly what I deserved—being forced to live in a house with the body of my dead lover in the basement. If I wasn't going to jail for my crimes, this would be punishment enough.

"Okay," I said. "What do I need to do? Although I will warn you, I know nothing about cement or basements."

"You don't need to do anything," he assured me. "I'll take care of it all. You've done enough, protecting my sister and saving my nephew."

I cocked my head. "Saving your nephew?"

He sighed. "Jonathan is—was—a bad influence on Darrel. Felicity told me how Darrel was starting to act up, showing more, well, difficult behaviors."

I frowned. "She didn't tell me that."

"Yeah, well, she wouldn't. She's pretty protective of her children. Now, believe me, I don't approve at all of what you were doing, but I still appreciate your help."

The conversation was so odd. It felt like he was thanking me for giving Darrel extra tutoring. I wondered what exactly Felicity had told her brother. "I appreciate your help with ... well, you know."

He inclined his head.

The moment stretched out, growing more awkward as we stared at each other. I finally broke the stillness. "Did you need to see anything else, or do you want to go back up?"

"I've seen enough," he said.

I led the way back into the kitchen, where he reached down to pop the last bite of muffin into his mouth. "I better head off to work, but thank you for the coffee and muffin."

"You're welcome," I said. "Sure you don't want anything more?"

"No, I'm good."

I followed him as he made his way to the door. "So, just so I have some idea, when do you expect to start?"

He paused, his hand on the front door. "Not right away," he said. "Felicity thought we should wait a bit, maybe a couple of weeks. Let the initial interest in the case die down. After everyone starts to realize Jonathan really is gone for good, then I'll come back, and we'll get it taken care of."

"Felicity seems to have thought this through quite a bit," I said.

He nodded. "My sister is a planner. Always was. You have a good day. I'll be in touch."

"You too," I said, watching him as he headed toward his pickup truck.

I had to wonder ...

What else did Felicity plan?

Chapter 38

Red gave me the side eye as I made myself comfortable at the bar. He tossed his dirty rag over this shoulder and sauntered over to me. "Your lover isn't here."

"Don't know who you're referring to," I said lightly. "But I'd love a Diet Coke."

"Only have Pepsi."

"Fine." *Figures,* I thought.

Red reached behind him and pulled a can out of a refrigerator, popped the top, and slid it over to me. "Want a glass?"

I picked it up. "Not necessary."

Red watched me as I took a sip. He looked even more unkempt, if that was possible. His beard needed to be trimmed and his Ozzy Osbourne tee shirt sported two holes along with a stretched-out neck. "Can I get you something else? A shot of whisky, perhaps?"

"I'm good," I said, putting the can back down and trying not to wrinkle my nose. The bar was as disheveled as it was the first time I was there, but I had forgotten about the smell of mildew, mold, old cigarette smoke, and sour beer. "I do have a question, though. If you have a moment."

Red raised a furry red eyebrow. "Oh?" He plopped two meaty arms on the bar. I could see the edges of a tattoo on his right bicep. "What might that be?"

"You mentioned your interest in the Witch House because of its history. I was wondering if you could tell me more about it."

His eyes narrowed slightly. "Didn't Helen tell you?"

"So, that's what you were talking about? Helen's mother killing herself and her maid there?"

"Ever wonder why it was that particular house?"

"Because that's the house Martha was living in?"

He shot me a disgusted look before pushing himself off the bar. "Mock all you want. I know the truth."

"I'm not trying to mock. I was under the impression Martha had some mental health issues. That was why she did what she did."

Red start wiping down the bar. "Maybe she did, maybe she didn't, but that certainly wasn't the reason."

"So, what was it?"

"Need a whisky and a Miller Lite," a waitress called out, her voice bright and cheery, not fitting at all with The Lone Man Standing environment. It was impossible to tell how old she was as she was all blonde hair and makeup.

Red pulled out a shot glass. "Did you know there used to be a shed where the Witch House was built?"

"No."

"Yeah, they had to tear it down."

The waitress put the beer and the whisky shot on her round black tray and whisked it away.

"Okay," I said. "Was there a significance to the shed?"

He paused for a long moment, wiping the counter a few times. "No one knows why the adults disappeared in 1888. But one thing seems clear. It was all linked to that shed."

Now he had my attention. "How so?"

He shot me an unreadable look. "No one knows."

"Well, then how do you know it's even a thing?" I was starting to feel impatient. "Maybe it's just another unfounded rumor."

"Maybe," he agreed. "Or maybe it just needs the right owner."

A cold draft seemed to trail down my spine. "What do you mean?"

"I mean," he paused, polishing a glass before looking around. "This bar is also linked to whatever happened back then. So, maybe with the same owner ..." he shrugged. "Who knows what would happen?"

Who knows what would happen?

I thought about Jonathan's obsession with the bar, and Red's obsession with my house.

Could there be a connection?

The evil. Where it came to Redemption. You must destroy it. That's the only way to buy us enough time.

I was cold all over.

The gas cans in my car. I had filled them at a gas station in another town earlier that day, paying cash. I didn't have a plan for using them. I was just ... hedging my bets.

But in that moment, I knew.

It had to be done.

I had to do *whatever* needed to be done.

Maybe not right then. Maybe I would wait a couple of days and come back after the bar had closed, in the darkness and silence of the night, to douse it with gasoline before lighting a match. I would park a few blocks down, in the park that would be deserted at night.

No one would know.

I could almost see the flames as they roared. The wood was old. Soaked in gasoline, it would go quickly. Even without the gas, it would burn hot and fast because of the alcohol.

And then, maybe, just maybe, I could put this entire nightmare behind me. Once and for all.

I put a couple of dollars on the bar and slid off the stool.

Red glanced up at me. "You going? It's pretty early."

I glanced at my watch. "Yeah, I've got an early shift at Aunt May's. You know what it's like."

He picked up the money. "Thanks for coming in. And let me know if you're ever in the market. I'm still interested."

"I will," I said as I slid off my barstool.

"You!"

The voice was loud and clearly drunk. I assumed it wasn't meant for me. After all, who did I know at a place like The Lone Man Standing? I continued on my way toward the door.

"You!" The voice shouted again. "I'm talking to you!"

My hand at the doorknob, I turned to see what the commotion was about.

An older unkempt man was staggering toward me. His grey hair was dirty and matted, and his plaid shirt and old jeans was filthy and full of holes. "It's *your* fault."

I glanced around, trying to see if he was talking to someone else. "Are you talking to me?"

"Who do you think?" The old man yelled, his words slurring together. His eyes were filmy, and his teeth were yellow.

"I don't know you, sir," I said.

"Hey, Frank, we talked about this," Red said, coming out from behind the bar.

Frank! Of course. How could I have forgotten?

"You did something to Johnny," he snarled. "I know you did."

"Do you mean Jonathan?"

"You know who I'm talking about," he said, as Red grabbed his arm.

"C'mon Frank, let's let the lady go."

Frank shook him off. "Where's Johnny?" he yelled.

"How on earth would I know?" I asked. "Have you called his house? Asked his wife?"

"What would *she* know?" He snorted in disgust. "Something has happened to Johnny. I know it." He pounded his chest. "I can feel it. In here. I can feel it."

"Maybe Jonathan just doesn't want to talk to you," I said. "Have you considered that?"

Frank's eyes went wide. He screamed something incoherent as he lunged awkwardly toward me. Red grabbed his arm again, which may have been the only thing that kept him on his feet. "Frank, that's enough."

Frank jerked away again, stumbling and almost falling. "What does she know? What do *you* know?"

"I know you were a lousy stepfather," I said. "Everyone in Redemption knows that."

"Frank," Red said loudly as Frank flailed helplessly at me, sputtering and spitting. "Let's walk away. Okay? Let's take a walk."

Frank whirled on Red. "Why are you taking her side? Why doesn't anyone believe me? Something happened to Johnny, and she ..." he straightened up, still weaving on his feet, and pointed at me, "is involved."

"I know, I know," Red said soothingly, throwing me an unreadable look over his shoulder. "Let's walk it off, okay?"

Frank eyed Red suspiciously. "Do you believe me?"

"Of course," Red said. "C'mon. Let's walk."

Frank paused in consideration, and then allowed Red to lead him away, still muttering to himself.

I studied Frank, noticing how skinny he was, how the sharp bones of his elbows poked out from his sleeves. He truly was pathetic. No wonder Jonathan had so much disgust for him. Maybe Frank should have shown some of that compassion and caring while Jonathan was still alive. Maybe things would have been different. Maybe he was as much to blame for what ultimately happened as I was. If he hadn't been such an abusive son of a bitch, who may very well have killed Jonathan's mother, none of this would have happened.

I left the bar without another backward glance. Good riddance to the lot of them.

The Reckoning

Chapter 39

"So nice to see you, Tad," I said smoothly, my hand poised above my order pad. "What can I get for you today?"

Tad glanced up at me, pushing his glasses up. I noticed he had a copy of the *Redemption Times* at his elbow. "Tuna salad sandwich. What's the soup?"

"Tomato and mushroom."

"A cup of that as well. And a Diet Coke."

I wrote it down and went to fetch his drink. When I brought it back, he had the paper spread out in front of him. "Have you heard?" he asked, tapping the picture.

I flicked my eyes toward the image of a charred bar. "Oh, yes. Too bad about the Lone Star bar."

"The Lone Man Standing," he corrected.

"Right." I turned to leave but Tad kept talking.

"Do you have any idea what happened?"

I paused. "Why would I?"

He gave me a bashful smile. "Oh. I heard you were there."

I smiled back. "I prefer Tipsy Cow. Much cleaner," I said over my shoulder as I walked away.

Tad tried again when I brought his food. "It's strange that Jesse Vanders and Jonathan Decker have both disappeared, too. Don't you think?"

"I really don't know, but my understanding is that Jesse has been talking about leaving for years."

His eyes gleamed behind his thick glasses. "But don't you think it's ... strange? Both of them disappearing a few months after you arrive?"

"I don't know what one has to do with other. Can I bring you anything else?"

"Look at it from our standpoint," Tad continued, slowly and deliberating unfolding a napkin. "You arrive. You buy the Witch House, which, quite frankly is a stunner. No one thought Helen would ever sell. Then, a very short time later, Rosie disappears,

Jesse disappears, and Jonathan disappears. THEN, the bar that Rosie worked at, and Jonathan spent a lot of time at, burned down. Don't you think it's all a little ... coincidental?"

I shrugged. "Never really thought about it. Can I bring you anything else?"

"There's just a lot of questions that I think you could answer," Tad said. "Maybe I could buy you a cup of coffee or a drink after work?"

"I'm busy," I said lightly.

"How about tomorrow?"

"I really don't think I can help."

"You know, no one has seen Red since the night of the fire," Tad said. The light seemed to bounce off his glasses. "That's odd, too, isn't it?"

"If you say so," I said. "I really don't know him at all."

"But you were there," he pressed. "You were just there. Earlier this week."

"I told you, not really my hangout. I'm not sure why you think I was there."

He pressed his lips together in a thin line. "I have my sources."

I bit back a laugh. His "sources." Right. I wondered if Frank was one of his "sources."

"Well, your sources are mistaken. If I can't bring you anything else," I tore off the ticket and placed it on the table, "I'll let you enjoy your lunch."

I walked away, leaving him with his mouth hanging slightly open.

I wasn't sure what happened to Red. The night I burned down The Lone Man Standing, I was sure I had seen him leave. The bar had certainly seemed empty when I doused it with gasoline and lit the match.

But why Red hadn't come forward, why he wasn't out there screaming about his bar having burned down, I didn't know. I had been very careful that night, assuming I might be questioned at some point. After all, I had practically accused the man of leaving a dead cat on my doorstep. But none of that happened. Red was nowhere to be found, and according to the gossip around town, it was likely his shady past had finally caught up with him.

And I suppose in a weird way, it had.

"Charlie!"

I turned and saw Nancy standing next to the counter, beaming at me.

"Oh, hey," I said, wiping my hands on my apron and returning her smile. It was easy to do—Nancy had such an infectious nature. It was probably part of what made her such a good hotel owner. "Can I get you something?"

She clucked her tongue and wagged her finger at me. "Yes, you can bring me some more tea."

Tea! With everything that had happened, I had completely forgotten about my tea business. "Oh! Did you like it?"

"Like it?" She put a hand on her hip. "Charlie, I only left you like twenty voice messages. Didn't you listen to any of them?"

I winced. Something else that had fallen through the cracks. "Well, I ..."

She waved her hands. "Never mind. I hate those machines myself. Wouldn't have one anywhere near me, but I need it for the business. Your tea was amazing. It actually made my arthritis better."

I blinked. "It did?"

"Yes! I shared some with my friend Sally. Oh, she's in so much pain, and it helped her as well. When can we get more?"

"I, um ... next week?" I hoped I had the ingredients. I would have to check.

She clapped her hands. "I'm going to hold you to it. Next week! And, let me know how many customers you can handle. I have a lot of friends you could help."

"Okay, then," I said faintly, as I watched her bustle away, stopping to chat with a couple of women sitting in a booth.

Tad was still sitting at his table, finishing his lunch. I watched him for a bit, wondering if this was going to be the new normal—him stopping by every few months to eat lunch and pester me with questions.

He wasn't the only one. I was already getting my share of dirty looks and requests for table swaps when people realized I was going to be the one serving them.

Not everyone, of course. There were plenty of patrons who were still happy to see me, like Nancy.

But, as an employee, I couldn't control who I waited on and who I didn't. I was at the mercy of whoever walked in.

Did I really want to keep doing that to myself? Force myself to endure snide remarks and hostile looks?

Or did I want to make tea for people who were delighted to work with me?

When I thought of it like that, it really wasn't much of a decision.

I pushed open the door to the kitchen to give my notice.

* * *

I ran into Felicity in the grocery store parking lot.

We passed one another as I was heading in and she, out, while attempting to balance pushing a stroller, carrying a bag, and keeping track of her young son.

We both paused and stood awkwardly behind a bright-red convertible. "How are you doing?" she asked, not meeting my gaze. She didn't have any makeup on her puffy face, and the black circles under her eyes were significant.

"I'm okay," I said. "Every day is a little easier." Which was true, although I still woke up screaming more nights than not, sure I could hear Jonathan coming up the stairs for me. "Felix has been wonderful."

She brightened. "Oh, that's good. Is it done?"

I shook my head. "He just got started. I appreciate you sending him over."

"Of course," she said, her voice a little sharp. "I told you I'd take care of it, and I did."

Okay, then. "How are you?"

"We're good," she said, her eyes sliding toward Darrel, who was starting to fuss. She slapped his hands. "What did I say about that?" She glanced back at me. "We're moving."

That was a surprise. "You are?"

"Yes. With Jonathan gone, there's no reason for us to stay."

"Well, I can see that, but don't you think it's a little ... fast? After all, Jonathan hasn't been gone that long. People might, you know, talk."

Her face twisted into something ugly. "Let them," she snapped. "Everyone knows he's a cheater. Good riddance." Her smile turned cruel. "He left you too, after all. Cheated on both of us."

I felt like she slapped me. Was that what she had been saying to everyone, making us both look like fools?

Although, on second thought, I certainly had been acting foolish. I probably deserved it.

"I guess he did," I said.

"Yes," she said firmly. "That's exactly what he did."

"So, where are you moving?"

She stopped smiling. "To my parents. At least initially. Just long enough to get my feet under me. But I won't be staying long. Just long enough to figure out what I'm going to do."

"Of course."

"It's not permanent," she said again. "Just temporary."

"I'm sure it is."

Darrel fussed again, and Felicity glared at him. The whole exchange was making me uneasy. I remembered the deep fingermarks she had left in my arm.

But no. I pushed that thought away. It's one thing to hurt the woman who your husband was cheating with. It was quite another to hurt your own children.

She was probably just stressed and exhausted. And who wouldn't be in her position?

"I probably should get going," I said. "I've got a lot of shopping to do."

She looked a little relieved. "Yes, I have a lot to do, as well. You wouldn't believe my to-do list just to get out of here by next week."

We said goodbye, and I was about to walk past her when she called me back. "I meant to tell you. I'm sorry about your cat. Hopefully, things have settled down enough that you can get another one."

I turned and gave her a funny look. "My cat? What are you talking about?"

She looked the tiniest bit flustered. "Your cat. You know, found dead on your porch." Her voice trailed off as I stared at her with my mouth hanging open.

"How did you know?"

Now, she was definitely flustered. "Well, Jonathan told me. Of course."

I took a step closer. "You and Jonathan talked about me? And my *cat*?"

"Well, ah," her one hand fluttered nervously. "Maybe I heard it around town."

"And you think it was my cat?"

She looked perplexed. "Wasn't it?"

"No. It was some other black cat."

Her eyes went wide, and in that moment, I saw it. I sucked in my breath. "*You* did it?" I strained to keep my voice low, but I was practically vibrating with anger. "You killed a cat?"

She angled her head away from me. "It wasn't like that."

I took a step closer to her. "Then what was it like?"

Her head snapped up, and she bared her teeth at me. "You were sleeping with my husband, *that's* what it was like. Are you really so surprised to find out that I want you to leave?"

I was horrified. "But you killed an innocent animal! There was no reason to do that."

"There was every reason," she hissed. "I had to find some way to stop you. You have no idea what it was like. The looks people were giving me. How they felt sorry for me. Or were laughing at me. Or thought I was pathetic. Everyone thought I was weak. I had to stop it somehow."

"But ..." a terrible thought occurred to me. "Did Jonathan even try and strangle you?"

She smoothed out the front of her shirt. "Of course he did."

"What was the story behind it? Were you two fighting or what? And why did he stop?"

"What does it matter now? He's gone, right? Let's forget about it and move on."

"Move on?" I squeaked. "Felicity! I believed you. I ..."

She gave me an angry look before grabbing my arm to jerk me closer. "Look," she breathed in my ear. Her breath smelled of sour milk and hard-boiled eggs—her skin, like unwashed hair and old bed sheets. "After you left that day, I found something. We have a step stool in our kitchen. I went to stand on it like I always do, and I fell off. When I checked it, there were two screws loose. Two! It was exactly what you said. Don't you see? He was trying to make it look like an accident. I wasn't lying. He *wanted* me to have an accident."

I stared into her bloodshot ice-blue eyes. They were wild, crazy even. Did I believe her? I didn't know what I believed anymore. The only thing I was sure of was that I had to let it go. Focusing on whether or not Felicity had been lying to me ... had manipulated me ...

That would lead to madness.

I had to hold onto Jonathan's last words.

Thank you.

Still, the doubt crept in.

Maybe I should have saved him another way. Maybe this was all wrong. Maybe I *had* made things worse.

Maybe.

But the one thing I could hang onto, that I knew without a shadow of a doubt, was that Jonathan was finally at peace.

"Fine," I said, shaking her off. I couldn't decide who my rising anger was directed toward—her or myself.

"You have to believe me," she insisted, stepping closer.

"I believe you," I said, taking a step back. "Although I don't know why it matters. Nothing can change it now."

She opened her mouth as if to protest more, then checked herself. "No, that's very true." She took a deep breath, straightened her shoulders, and lifted her chin. "Goodbye Charlie."

"Goodbye."

We stared at each other for a moment longer before she nodded slightly, as if dismissing me, and bent over the stroller. "Get in the car, Darrel," she said.

"Bye Darrel," I said.

Darrel paused, glancing at me over his shoulder. The expression on his face was filled with so much hate, so much rage, I found myself backing up.

If looks could kill ...

I was suddenly very certain that would not be the last time I saw that boy.

And that was not a good thing.

I turned without another word and headed into the store.

Chapter 40

I was working in the garden when Officer Murphy showed up.

"Apologies Ma'am," he said after he got my attention. "I rang the bell, but no one answered."

No one answered because I was back here, I thought. I considered asking if it was common practice for cops to just walk around a property when no one answers the doorbell but decided it didn't make sense to be antagonistic.

"No worries," I said, straightening up. I took off my floppy broad-brimmed hat to wipe my brow. The unseasonably warm fall hadn't let up yet. "Can I get you something to drink? I have some lemonade."

"No, thank you," he said.

I nodded, pulling off my gardening gloves and walking over to the little table holding my own glass. "What brings you out here?"

"Just a couple of questions," he said. "Shouldn't take too long, and then you can get back to your garden."

"I was overdue for a break anyway," I said, gesturing to the two metal chairs.

We both took a seat. "So, how can I help you?" I asked, trying to unobtrusively adjust the waistband of my jeans. I had been gaining weight despite a daily habit of throwing up first thing every morning, typically immediately following one of my Jonathan dreams. It was good I was gaining weight, as I had been getting too thin. But the weight appeared to be concentrated in my midsection, which was odd, but with everything that had happened this summer, was it a surprise my body might respond differently?

I noticed Officer Murphy was taking a few minutes to adjust his clothing now that he was sitting, smoothing his uniform over his substantial paunch. "Are you aware that both Jesse Vanders and Jonathan Decker have gone missing?"

I sat back myself. "I wasn't aware they were missing per se, but yes, I knew they both left Redemption."

Officer Murphy's eyebrows went up. "Left?"

I took a swallow of the lemonade. The ice had melted, and it was watery and a little warm, but at least it was wet. "Well, yeah," I said. "From my understanding, Jesse wanted to leave Redemption. He wanted to be an actor. He had said on multiple occasions he was leaving after Lou's Labor Day party. And, as far as I can tell, that's precisely what he did. Why? Is that not true?"

Officer Murphy cocked his head. "And Jonathan?"

I shrugged. "I don't know what happened to him. He was here, and then he was gone. Didn't even say goodbye." I put my glass down a little bit harder than I intended, and it made a "thunk."

"Yeah, that's what Felicity says as well."

"Well, she should know. She's his wife."

"That she is." Officer Murphy watched me closely. "Some folks seem to think you had a ... close relationship with Jonathan."

"Apparently not close enough to say goodbye," I said drily.

"Has he reached out? Tried to make contact?"

"Not a word," I said.

"You don't think that's odd?"

"Does it matter what I think?" I countered. "We weren't married. We had no official relationship. If he decided he wanted to cut ties, there's not a lot I can do about it."

Officer Murphy made a grunt of what sounded like sympathy. "So, back to Jesse. Have you heard from him?"

I looked at him in surprise. "Why would I hear from Jesse? We weren't close."

"Do you know if Jonathan had heard from him?"

"I have no idea," I said. "Why? Do you think they left together?"

"Possible," he said. "We're exploring a lot of angles."

"Well, if I hear from either of them, I'll let you know," I said.

"I appreciate that," he said. He hoisted himself out of his seat. I stood as well.

"Oh," he said. "Before I forget. You heard what happened with The Lone Man Standing?"

"I did. Such a shame." I shook my head. "It burned down, right?"

"Right. Yeah, it certainly has a, well, checkered past. So, it's not entirely a surprise it burned down. Especially with Red disappearing. I wanted to check in with you ... did you ever get any more threatening messages?"

The sun went behind the clouds, and the breeze that brushed over my bare skin was cool enough to form goosebumps. I folded my arms across my chest. "No, nothing else."

"Well, that's a relief. I know you thought Red was behind it."

"Yeah, Jonathan especially," I said.

"So, you wouldn't know anything about the fire, would you? Or what happened to Red?"

I cocked my head. "You just said it wasn't a surprise it burned down. So why are you asking me about it?"

He shot me a bashful grin. "Just covering all the bases. We had a report that you were at The Lone Man Standing a few days before the fire, and you caused quite the uproar."

"Ah yes, you must be talking about Frank," I said. "He wasn't very happy to see me."

Officer Murphy adjusted his belt. "Mind telling me what it was about?"

His voice was casual, like he was just making conversation, but I wasn't fooled. "Sure," I said. "Frank has got it in his head that I had something to do with Jonathan's disappearance."

"Mmm hmm. I had heard something about that. Do you know why he thinks that?"

"Not really. He was mostly just yelling at me. I couldn't really make sense of it."

"Yeah, he certainly has had his mind pickled by alcohol," Officer Murphy agreed. "Although, it's not surprising he thinks that, is it? You came here a few months ago, and suddenly, a lot of people have gone missing."

"I don't see how one has anything to do with the other. My understanding is that Jesse has been talking about leaving forever, and as for Jonathan, that's between him and his wife."

"You forgot Rosie. And Red."

I spread my hands helplessly. "I really didn't know either of them well enough to have an opinion. I met Rosie once and Red just a few times."

"Of course." He smiled, but it was perfunctory and didn't quite reach his eyes. "I'll be on my way."

He had only taken a few steps across the lawn when he turned back. "Oh. I just have one more thing. Why were you in The Lone Man Standing, anyway?"

I smiled sweetly. "Am I a suspect?"

He held his hands up. "Oh, no. Of course not. I'm just curious. It doesn't really seem like your, well, cup of tea, shall we say?"

"You're right … it's not. I was there because I wanted to talk to Red about my house. He did want to buy it, and I wanted to know why, as well as whether or not he was behind the cat that was left on my porch. I thought getting to the bottom as to why he was trying to scare me away would help."

"And did you?"

"I think we came to an understanding," I said. "Although, with him now missing, I'm not sure if it matters."

"Probably not," Officer Murphy said. He studied me for a moment before touching his hand to his hat. "I'll leave you to your gardening."

* * *

I was just finishing up when Lou showed up.

"Hey," I said cheerily, straightening up and wiping the sweat from my eyes. "Perfect timing. I was just about done. Do you want some fresh lemonade? Give me a second to clean up, and we can sit back here and enjoy it."

"I'm not staying," Lou said, her voice curt. I took a closer look at her. She looked exhausted, and her hair was a greasy, stringy mess. I wondered when the last time was that she had a decent night's sleep or shower. Even her clothes were wrinkled and stained, like she had just plucked them off the floor and put them on again.

"Are you okay?" I asked, trying to take her arm. "Let's sit down."

"Don't touch me," she snapped, jerking away.

The venom in her voice brought me up short. "Okay," I said quietly, putting my hands up, palms facing out. "What can I do for you?"

"I want to know where Jesse is."

I gave her a surprised look. "I don't know where he is."

"I don't believe that." Her voice was flat.

"Well, it's true," I said. "Why would you think I would?"

"Because it's all your fault."

"My fault?"

"Yes!" Her voice became more agitated. "Everything was fine until you came here. Now, it's all fallen apart. Jesse," she swallowed. "You did something to Jesse. I know you did. He wouldn't have left otherwise."

"Lou," I said soothingly, trying to pacify her. "You knew Jesse was going to leave. He'd been talking about it all his life. It was his dream."

"I knew no such thing," she yelled. "All I know is before you got here, everything was fine. He was here, safe. There was no talk about him leaving. It was only after you got here that everything changed." She took a step closer to me, her eyes narrowing. "It's not just Jesse, you know," she said. "It's Jonathan, too. Where is he?"

"I understand you're upset, but me moving here is just a coincidence," I said. "Jesse was going to leave regardless of what I did or didn't do. I know you know this. This had nothing to do with me."

Lou took another step closer. "Where. Are. They?"

"I don't know," I snapped, my patience frayed. "Don't you get it? Jonathan left me, too! I don't know what happened. All I know is they're both gone." I stared straight into Lou's eyes.

"He left me, too," I said again more quietly, but the grief and rage were still there. There was no question Jonathan, the real Jonathan, had left me. And every day, I grieved him.

Lou's eyes glittered. I couldn't tell if it was from anger or unshed tears. "This is all your fault," she said, but much of the anger had drained out, making her sound hollow and sad. "I'll never forgive you for this."

I thought about the cassette tape, tucked away in a drawer. My intention had been one day to play it to her. I would edit it, of course, telling her Jonathan had disappeared after that confession.

But, looking at her now, seeing the hatred in her eyes, I wondered if that day would ever come.

"That's your right, of course," I said calmly, although I couldn't stop a fresh wave of sadness from rising up inside me. I had so hoped it wouldn't come to this. "But I hope you'll change your mind someday. I know you're hurting. I am, too. And if you do change your mind, I'll be here for you, Lou."

Lou studied me for a long moment. "My name is Louise," she said flatly. "Don't ever call me 'Lou' again."

I dipped my chin. "Okay, Louise."

She gave me one final last look before turning on her heel and stalking out of the backyard.

I watched her go, my chest sore and aching. I wondered how many heartbreaks I could stand before my heart would just give out.

***

I was sitting on my porch swing, having lost my interest in gardening after my confrontation with Lou—I mean *Louise*—when Claire walked up.

My heart sank. Oh, no. Not her, too. I didn't think I could handle another incident.

She paused at the bottom of the driveway. "Want some company?"

"Sure," I called back. I held up my glass half full of lemonade. "Want some?"

"I'd love a glass," she said. Her face was red, and I could see the sweat beading on her cheeks as she slowly made her way up the driveway. She wore a loose blue and white checkered sundress that looked pretty dreadful on her, and her hair was pulled back in a messy and tangled ponytail.

I got up and went into the kitchen to pour her a glass and refill my own. By the time I made it back to the porch, she was sitting on the swing. I handed her a glass and sat down next to her.

"This is perfect. Hits the spot." She drank deeply, fanning herself with one hand.

"Do you want to go in? It might be cooler," I said.

She shook her head. "No, this is nice."

We sat for a few minutes in silence, listening to the creak of the swing as we rocked it. I watched the tall pine trees swaying on the side of the property and wondered if this was all worth it.

"I've been thinking," Claire said.

I turned my head slightly. "Oh?"

"I keep thinking about that abandoned car."

My stomach twisted into a giant knot, but I was careful to keep my face smooth and expressionless as I waited for her to continue.

"The more I think about it, the more I wonder if it has something to do with Jonathan going missing. Maybe even Jesse."

My mouth was dry. I took a drink of lemonade, but I still didn't trust myself to speak.

"And the fire at The Lone Man Standing. That's peculiar, as well. Not to mention Red disappearing." She sighed and took a drink before shifting on her seat to face me. "Jonathan was protecting you, wasn't he? That's what happened to him."

I was so surprised, I wasn't sure how to respond. I didn't expect her to come to that conclusion. I had been bracing for an accusation or something. I opened my mouth to say something, although I still wasn't sure what, but burst into tears instead.

It all hit me at once.

Alan. Rosie. Jesse. Jonathan.

And Claire was right, in a way.

This had all started because Jonathan *was* trying to protect me.

Claire gathered me in her arms, holding me as I sobbed, rocking me back and forth. She didn't say anything, just let me cry it all out.

"We'll get through this," she whispered, stroking my hair as my tears dissolved into hiccups. "I'm here if you ever want to talk about it, but I get it if you don't."

"I miss him," I said, my voice cracking. I couldn't breathe. I felt like my chest was being squeezed by a giant hand. Nothing would ever be okay again.

She kept stroking my hair. "I know."

Finally, I sat up. "Thanks," I said sheepishly, blowing my nose in the napkins I had brought out for the drinks. It wasn't enough, but Claire pulled a packet of tissues from her purse and handed them to me. "It's been a rough day. Lou, I mean, Louise, stopped by, as well."

Claire sighed. "If it makes you feel any better, she's furious with me as well. But she'll get over it. Once the baby comes and her hormones have settled down, she'll be fine."

I thought about our last encounter, the hate in Louise's eyes, and had my doubts. "Speaking of pregnancy, how are you doing?"

She flashed a shy smile and rubbed her hand over her belly. "I'm doing better. I'm eating more, which is good. Doug is excited."

"You told him?"

She nodded, her cheeks flushed. "He always wanted to be a father. It will be fine. He'll be a wonderful father to little Daphne."

I clapped my hands. "Oh, you're having a little girl! Congratulations."

"Well, it's not official. I just have a feeling. And I've always loved the name Daphne. Hopefully, Doug loves it, as well."

"It's a beautiful name," I said.

She smiled. "I heard you're quitting Aunt May's?"

"Yeah, I'm focusing on my tea business," I said.

She nodded. "I'm quitting, too," she said.

For the second time, she surprised me. "Really?"

"Yeah. I never really needed to work. Doug makes enough, but I liked being around people." She was silent as I thought about how often Jesse would stop in for lunch, and wondered if that was the real reason why she worked as a waitress for so long. She gave her head a quick shake as she roused herself. "Well, things are different now. I have a lot to do before little Daphne gets here, so it's time."

"Makes sense."

She reached over to squeeze my leg. "And, since neither of us are working at Aunt May's, we can spend a lot more time together."

"I'd like that."

We were quiet for a few moments. In the silence, I could hear the birds chirping and the sound of a car driving down the road.

"It won't be easy, you know," she said.

"I know."

"There will be people who believe the gossip and rumors," she continued. "And there are some insane things being said. Lou, I mean Louise, is crazy right now, between grief for Jesse and her pregnancy hormones. And Frank. Oh God, he's a mess." She rolled her eyes. "First, he claims he had cancer. Then, he was either misdiagnosed or miraculously healed, and now he's gone full conspiracy theory about Jonathan. Like anyone will take him seriously after how dreadful he was to Jonathan growing up."

"Frank doesn't have cancer?"

She shook her head. "Apparently not. And depending on what day you catch him, sometimes it's the incompetent doctor's fault, and sometimes it's a miracle. So, who knows? But most people won't take him seriously. Louise is a little different, but even she sounds crazy right now. It should work out fine. I'm just warning you. There might be some rough patches."

"I appreciate it," I said. "I'll be prepared."

Claire glanced at me, a question in her eyes. "You ARE staying, right?"

I thought about the basement floor, which was done now. My garden. How Annabelle was still barely talking to me. I thought about everything that had happened and how much I had to atone for. I thought about the future and decisions I would have to make.

I had set a lot of things in motion, and I owed it to everyone to see them through.

"Definitely," I said. "Redemption is my home. I'm staying."

A Note From Michele

There are more secrets to be revealed, starting with Book 6: *The Girl Who Wasn't There*.

While attending a funeral, a woman claims her daughter was kidnapped.

Except … it appears she doesn't have a daughter after all.

Grab your copy right here:

https://MPWNovels.com/r/breckgirlwide

****

You can also check out exclusive bonus content for *The Reckoning*, including a deleted scene. Here's the link or QR code:

https://MPWNovels.com/r/reckoning-bonus

The bonus content reveals hints, clues, and sneak peeks you won't get just by reading the books, so you'll definitely want to take a look. You're going to discover a side of Redemption that is only available here.

***

If you enjoyed *The Reckoning*, it would be wonderful if you would take a few minutes to leave a review and rating on Goodreads:

goodreads.com/book/show/56377685-the-reckoning

or Bookbub:

bookbub.com/books/the-reckoning-a-gripping-psychological-thriller-secrets-of-redemption-book-5-by-michele-pariza-wacek

(Feel free to follow me on any of those platforms as well.) I thank you and other readers will thank you (as your reviews will help other readers find my books.)

All my series are interrelated and interconnected. Along with my psychological thrillers, I also have a cozy mystery series that takes place in the 1990s and stars Aunt Charlie. (It's called the Charlie Kingsley Mysteries series.)

You can learn more about Redemption and my other series at MPWNovels.com. You'll also discover a lot of other fun stuff such as giveaways, puzzles, recipes and more.

For now, turn the page for a sneak peek at *The Girl Who Wasn't There*.

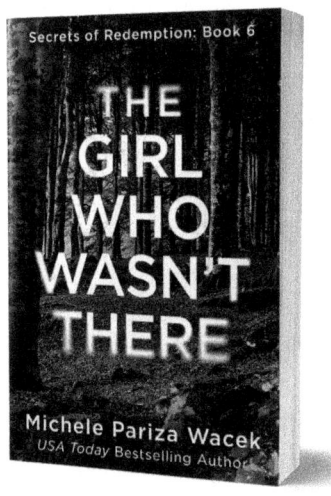

The Girl Who Wasn't There
Chapter 1

"I can't believe it." Mia dropped her phone on the butcher block kitchen table with a clatter, a stunned look on her face. "Penny Schroeder is dead."

"Oh, that's too bad," I said. Admittedly, I was only half-listening as I stood behind the counter, measuring dried lavender for the custom tea blends I was making. It had been a productive, peaceful day—I'd caught up on all my orders and was now getting ahead.

The afternoon sun slanted through the side window, and Oscar, my black cat, soaked it up as he slept on a chair beneath it. The kitchen smelled like potpourri and coffee, as Mia had just made a fresh pot. Ever since she'd decided to return to school to become a lawyer while continuing to work part-time as a waitress at Aunt May's Diner, her coffee consumption had gone way up. I was surprised she was able to sleep at all with all the caffeine coursing through her veins. Although now that I thought about it, she had also been drinking a lot more wine in the evenings, as well ... probably to counterbalance the coffee. "Who is Penny Schroeder?"

Mia ran a hand through her straight, dark hair, which was cut in a chin-length bob. Half-Japanese from her father's side, she was petite with a narrow face and high cheekbones. Like me, she was in her early thirties, but since returning to school, she appeared significantly older. "I always forget you haven't lived here very long," she answered.

"Nope. Barely a year," I reminded her.

I had moved to Redemption, Wisconsin, from New York, with my husband at the time and 16-year-old stepdaughter Chrissy. My Aunt Charlie had died, leaving me the big, rambling old farmhouse I currently resided in along with Chrissy and Mia, who had moved in to save money while she went to school. She paid for the utilities in lieu of rent, and we split the grocery bill.

The house, along with being well over 100 years old, was also haunted. Not so much by Aunt Charlie, although I did suspect she was one of the ghosts, but by former occupants "Mad Martha" and Nellie. Back in the early 1900s, Martha's husband built the house for his blushing bride, but sometime after the birth of their second child, Martha lost her mind and ended up killing her maid Nellie and then herself. No one was sure why Martha did it, but rumor had it that Nellie and Martha's husband were having an affair. Ever since, the townspeople were convinced that Mad Martha, and probably Nellie, were haunting my house.

My house wasn't the only haunted place in Redemption, either. In fact, the entire town had the same reputation, ever since all the adults disappeared in the winter of 1888, leaving only the children behind. No one knows what happened to the adults; the children all swore they knew nothing about it. When they went to bed, the adults were there, but when they woke up, they were gone.

To this day, I wasn't sure how much I believed the story. I had a sneaking suspicion the kids knew more than they'd let on. But alas, since none of them were still around to question, I suspected the truth was also dead and buried.

"Penny Schroeder is, I mean *was*, a fixture in Redemption," Mia said. "Her family has lived here since the 1800s, and her great-great-grandparents—maybe it was her great-grandparents ... I can't remember—were two of the adults who disappeared."

I paused, a sprig of lavender in my hand. "Seriously? I didn't realize there were people here who could trace their lineage back that far. That's actually really cool."

Mia didn't respond, as she seemed to have stopped paying any attention to me. Instead, she pressed her hands to her cheeks and slumped over in her chair. "Man, I can't believe she's gone."

I put down the lavender and walked around the counter to sit next to her as she stared down at the table. "I'm so sorry. Were you two close?"

Mia didn't respond, and I put a hand on her knee. I expected to see tears, but her eyes were dry. "I can leave if you need some time alone."

She still didn't say anything, but just as I was about to get up to give her some space, she released her breath in a heavy whoosh and shook her head. "No. Stay. It would help to talk. I'm just ... I'm in shock, I think."

"I can imagine," I said, rubbing her knee gently. "Getting a text like that would definitely be shocking."

She scrubbed at her face. "That's part of it, sure. But mostly ... I guess I just thought I'd have more time with her."

"So her death wasn't ... expected?" I wasn't sure how to phrase it delicately.

"Not exactly. It's just ..." she sighed again and dropped her hands in her lap. Her skin was bright red where her fingers had dug into her face. "The last time I saw her, we had a terrible fight."

"Oh no," I sympathized. "That's really rough."

"Yeah," she said, her voice wooden. "It was really bad. I've known Penny nearly my entire life. She was like a second mother to me. But in past couple of years, she ... wasn't herself."

"That's too bad. Was she sick?"

"Well, yes. But there's more." Mia blew the air out of her cheeks. "She was always busy ... always doing something. She constantly volunteered while working full time as a teacher AND maintaining a massive garden in the summer. So, several years back, when her health started to decline, she had no choice but to stop doing so much. She put a good face on, but it was clear it upset her to not be as involved as she was used to. She started getting worse, and I suspect it became a vicious cycle—as she stopped being active, she became depressed, which made her health decline even further, causing her to stop doing even more stuff. Regardless, it was clear she wasn't doing well physically, which would have been bad enough. But then she started to deteriorate mentally, and it was just ..." She paused and shook her head again.

"That's when you argued?"

"Yeah." Her head was bowed, and her voice was so quiet, I had to lean forward to hear her. "It was awful. She was saying all these crazy things. Just ... really nutty stuff. All sorts of conspiracy theories and other insanity. And she kept getting worse. There was no talking sense into her or convincing her otherwise, and if you tried, she would accuse you of being a part of it."

"Oh, Mia," I said, feeling my heart break for her. "I'm so sorry. Was that why you had the fight?"

Mia dipped her head in acknowledgment. "In retrospect, I think she was having a particularly bad day when it happened. She was convinced someone was sneaking into her house at night and poisoning her food. She reduced her meals to items that came out of a can. The only exception was coffee, which she carried around with her constantly. She even slept with it at night, so it couldn't be contaminated. Since she wasn't eating much, she was losing an incredible amount of weight. One day, I decided to bring her a bunch of groceries—some canned food, yes, but I also brought things like meat and cheese and bread.

She told me not to leave the perishables, as she wouldn't be able to store it all in her bedroom at night. I tried to convince her that she was safe ... that no one was trying to poison her. And she just blew up at me. Threw me out of the house and told me to never come back." Mia paused to blink rapidly, and I noticed her eyes glistening. "So, I didn't. That was the last time I saw her."

"It wasn't your fault," I tried to reassure her. "When someone is that paranoid, there's not much you can do."

"I get that. Logically, I know you're right, but emotionally?" She pressed her hand to her chest, over her heart. "I feel like I should have done more. I should have gone back sooner or tried to get her help. Something. But ..." she raised her shoulders helplessly. "I didn't. I didn't want to upset her any more than I already had. Plus, I had heard through the grapevine that people were keeping an eye on her and making sure she was eating and whatnot, so I thought it best to give her space. She had a doctor who was working to get her stabilized on the right meds, too. I honestly figured it was just a matter of time before she would be better, and I could go see her. But then it was one thing after another. I met you and decided to go back to school ... I've been trying so hard to balance everything, and ... I guess I ran out of time."

She looked so miserable, I leaned forward to give her an awkward hug. "Do you want anything? More coffee? Tea, or wine? I think we might have ice cream, as well."

"Maybe a glass of wine," Mia said.

I immediately got up and fetched a bottle of white from the fridge along with two glasses. "Did Penny have any other family?"

"No. Her husband died years ago, and she never remarried." Mia mashed her lips together in a flat line and stared off into space. I sensed there was more to the story, but she wasn't ready to share. I turned all my attention to opening and pouring the wine. When I handed Mia her glass, she immediately gulped down half of it without looking at me. I left the bottle on the table and returned to the kitchen and my custom tea blends. I figured if she wanted to keep talking, she would, but I didn't want her to feel pressured.

The house was quiet as I worked and Mia sipped wine. The only sounds that broke the silence were the ticking of the grandfather clock and Midnight's quiet snores, so when we heard the front door opening and closing, it seemed louder than normal. Both of us jumped, and what was left of Mia's wine sloshed in her glass.

"Becca? You here?" Daniel's voice floated in from the living room.

"In the kitchen," I called out.

A moment later, Daniel appeared in the doorway, still wearing his Redemption Police Department uniform. His blonde hair was messy, like he had been running his hands through it, and his dark-blue eyes looked exhausted. He leaned forward to give me a quick kiss, his eyebrows raising when he saw the wine. "You two are starting early."

"There was a death," I explained.

His expression immediately shifted to shock. "Oh no. Who?"

"Penny Schroeder," Mia said, taking another sip.

"What?" Daniel looked stricken. "Oh, I'm so sorry to hear that. She was one of my favorite teachers."

"Mine too," Mia replied. She was still staring off into space, her glass almost empty.

Daniel watched her for a moment, his expression torn. He obviously wanted to say something but didn't quite know what. I came to his rescue, lightly touching his hand. "Would you like something to eat or drink?"

He turned to me, raking his hand through his hair again. "Absolutely ... but unfortunately, I can't stay. I just stopped by to tell you I have to cancel our date tonight."

"Oh, bummer," I said, feeling deflated. We had plans to go to Mario's, my favorite restaurant in town.

"I know," he said. "I normally would have texted, but I was close by and was hoping I could at least see you for a minute."

"What's going on?"

Daniel sighed. "Oh, it's that case I've been telling you about."

"The gangs?" I asked.

That got Mia's attention. She swiveled around in her seat to face us. "Gangs? What gangs?"

"That's what we're trying to figure out," Daniel said. "It seems at least one, maybe two, have moved into Redemption, but we haven't narrowed down which ones they are yet."

"But it's been years since we've had any gang activity," Mia said.

Daniel nodded. "Exactly. Well over 20, actually, but it appears to be starting up again."

"That's scary," Mia said. "Is it drugs?"

"Drugs and theft, mostly, along with a little graffiti and vandalism. Thankfully, there's been nothing violent, so far, but we know how fast that can change."

"Has there been a break in the case? Is that why you have to work?" I asked.

Daniel's expression darkened. "I wish. There's been another break-in."

I raised my eyebrows. "Another one?"

"Fifth this week alone." Daniel shook his head.

"Wow," Mia breathed.

"Yeah, 'wow' is right. Anyway, it's all hands on deck, at least in the short-term, to try to get ahead of it." His phone buzzed then, and he pulled it out of his pocket to look at it. "Oh, I gotta deal with this. Call you?"

"Of course," I said as he leaned over to give me another kiss, this one a little longer than the first.

"I promise to make it up to you," he said. The look in his eyes sent a shudder up my spine.

"You better," I teased.

"Oh, please," Mia said, her voice sounding more like herself. "Get a room."

Daniel laughed as he headed out of the kitchen. "Bye, Mia."

Mia waved at him as she drained the rest of her wine.

I went back to making my tea as Mia swiveled around to refill her glass. She eyed me as she poured. "Have you guys talked about which one of you is going to sell your house?"

"Why would either of us sell our house?" I asked.

"Well, unless you're planning a pretty unorthodox marriage, one of you is going to have to," Mia answered.

"Two marriages are more than enough for me," I said lightly. Mia gave me a look. "Uh huh."

"It's true," I said. "Besides, I have Chrissy to think about. And you. Is that why you're asking? Are you worried I'm going to kick you out?"

"Just don't want any surprises," Mia said, setting the bottle back down.

"Trust me, you have nothing to worry about," I reassured her.

Want to keep reading? Grab your copy of **The Girl Who Wasn't There** here:
https://MPWNovels.com/r/breckgirlwide

More Secrets of Redemption series:
It Began With a Lie (Book 1)
This Happened to Jessica (Book 2)
The Evil That Was Done (Book 3)
The Summoning (Book 4)
The Reckoning (Book 5)
The Girl Who Wasn't There (Book 6)
The Room at the Top of the Stairs (Book 7)
The Search (Book 8)
The Secret Diary of Helen Blackstone (novella)

Charlie Kingsley Mysteries:
A Grave Error (a prequel novella)
Ice Cold Murder (Book 2)
Murder Next Door (Book 3)
Murder Among Friends (Book 4)
The Murder of Sleepy Hollow (Book 5)
Red Hot Murder (Book 6)
A Cornucopia of Murder (Book 7)
A Wedding to Murder For (novella)
Loch Ness Murder (novella)

Standalone books:
Today I'll See Her (novella)
The Taking
The Third Nanny
Mirror Image
The Stolen Twin

Access your free exclusive bonus scenes from *The Reckoning* right here:
https://MPWNovels.com/r/reckoning-bonus

The Reckoning

Acknowledgements

It's a team effort to birth a book, and I'd like to take a moment to thank everyone who helped, especially my wonderful editor, Megan Yakovich, who is always so patient with me, Rea Carr for her expert proofing support, and my husband Paul, for his love and support during this sometimes-painful birthing process.

Any mistakes are mine and mine alone.

The Reckoning

About Michele

A USA Today Bestselling, award-winning author, Michele taught herself to read at 3 years old because she wanted to write stories so badly. It took some time (and some detours) but she does spend much of her time writing stories now. Mystery stories, to be exact. They're clean and twisty, and range from psychological thrillers to cozies, with a dash of romance and supernatural thrown into the mix. If that wasn't enough, she posts lots of fun things on her blog, including short stories, puzzles, recipes and more, at MPWNovels.com.

Michele grew up in Wisconsin, (hence why all her books take place there), and still visits regularly, but she herself escaped the cold and now lives in the mountains of Prescott, Arizona with her husband and southern squirrel hunter Cassie.

When she's not writing, she's usually reading, hanging out with her dog, or watching the Food Network and imagining she's an awesome cook. (Spoiler alert, she's not. Luckily for the whole family, Mr. PW is in charge of the cooking.)

The Reckoning

www.ingramcontent.com/pod-product-compliance
Lightning Source LLC
LaVergne TN
LVHW010253260326
834688LV00044B/1258